1.50

Enjoy!
Lamar Fine
Mary Agnes Fine

Yesterday's Gone

Lamar Fine

&

Mary Agnes Fine

Fine Publishing Company
245 Garretts Chapel Road
Chickamauga, GA. 30707

Copyright © 1996 by Lamar Fine & Mary Agnes Fine

All rights reserved. No part of this book may be reproduced or transmitted in any form or by any means, electronic or mechanical, including photocopying, recording, or by any information storage and retrieval system, without the written permission of the Authors.

YESTERDAY'S GONE

A Novel By
Lamar Fine & Mary Agnes Fine

ISBN 0-9671552-0-7

Printed in the United State of America

Yesterday's Gone is a work of fiction. Names, characters, places, and incidents either are the product of the authors' imagination or are used fictitiously. Any resemblance to actual events, locales, organizations, or persons, living or dead, is entirely coincidental and beyond the intent of the authors and publisher.

For Further Information, Please Contact:
Lamar Fine or Mary Agnes Fine
245 Garretts Chapel Road
Chickamauga, GA 30707
Tel. (706) 375-2062
E-mail: Lamarfine@aol.com
Web Site: http://members@aol.com/lamarfine/index.html

To the two special men in my life... my husband, W. C., who allowed me to follow my dreams... and my son, my business partner and my co-writer, Lamar, who was one of those dreams.

And to the host of people who have touched my life in so many wonderful ways. Yesterday's Gone is for you.

Mary Agnes

To my two best friends in the world, my Dad & Mom, W. C. & Mary Agnes Fine, who have been there for me, worked, sacrificed, and done whatever it took to give me the opportunities I've had in life.

And In Memory of my grandparents, Jack & Mary Lamar... Although they are no longer with me, their love and influence lives on... They were the inspiration for the names of our two principle characters, as well as my own.

Lamar

*All the yesterdays of our lives
are but stepping stones
to all the tomorrows.*

Mary Agnes Fine

Yesterday's Gone

CHAPTER 1

AUGUST 20, 1971

The late afternoon sun gave way to twilight as Mary tied the ribbon around the old hatbox and placed it on the upper shelf of the closet. Most of her things had already been taken to the new apartment. And while the things that remained, including the contents of the hatbox, were without value to anyone else, she was not ready to discard them. In time she would, but not now.

Her legs were numb from sitting so long in the same position poring through the contents of the box. There was a dried-up corsage from her senior prom, gardenias of course, a Perfect Attendance certificate from seventh grade, some old movie stubs, an old Chattanooga Lookouts Baseball program, a stupid little plastic ring from a box of *Cracker Jacks*, and countless other items, each with its own story. As she handled them one by one, she remembered the time and the place and the story. She was moving on to a new life, and perhaps this was her way of saying goodbye to the past, a past that like all pasts was part good, part not so good, but certainly worthy of remembering. And for the better part of the afternoon she had allowed herself to remember.

She would sleep one more night in this room she had occupied all of her life. The room held many memories. It was here she had laughed, and here she had cried. It was here she had lain awake nights dreaming dreams and making plans for the future. Now the future was here. All of her dreams were about to come true. Tomorrow wasn't just any day. Tomorrow was her wedding day! The nostalgia that had filled her afternoon vanished and was quickly replaced with thoughts of tomorrow and their wedding and the untold happiness they would share.

Henry Howard sat on the front porch, his mind also on tomorrow, his feelings mixed. He was happy for Mary, but he was sad for him and Kate. They would be losing their only daughter, maybe not losing her, but things would be different. He lit his pipe and stared out into the darkness.

"Hi Daddy," Mary said, as she came to sit beside him in the swing. He placed an arm around her shoulder and for awhile they sat in silence, lost in their own thoughts.

Mary looked about her at her surroundings. They were all so comfortably familiar. The swing had hung in the same place all her life. The planters at the top of the steps still held the same red geraniums. By the sidewalk the petunias bloomed in shades of red, purple and pink, as they had as far back as she could remember. While some people found 'sameness' boring, to Mary it was comfortable and dependable.

Henry wondered where the years had gone. It seemed only yesterday that she had taken her first steps.

"Is everything ready for your big day?"

"I think so... Where's Mama?"

"She went to the church to make sure everything is in order."

Suddenly Mary felt the brush of soft fur, and then one quiet "Meow." It was Mandy. Mandy and Henry had worked out a system. She meowed... He uncrossed his legs... And she jumped into his lap, and after circling a time or two, with another soft "Meow", curled up and went to sleep.

Although Mandy liked Mary and Katherine, she showed a slight preference for Henry. Strange, because he hadn't really wanted the cat in the beginning, and had consented only to make Mary happy. But it hadn't taken the little yellow tabby long to win him over.

Mary remembered the day Mandy was born. It was the last day of school of her fourth-grade year. She had been home only a short while when she heard someone pounding frantically on the front door. As she hurried to open the door, she saw it was Jack. Whatever could have happened? They had walked home from school together only a few minutes before, and now he stood at her door with a look of sheer panic on his face.

"What's wrong?" she asked.

"Is your daddy here? It's Sarah! She needs help."

"What's wrong?" she repeated. "Did she get hit by a car?"

"No, she's about to have her kittens, and I don't know what to do." It was obvious he had no time for small talk.

Moments later the three of them went down the street to Jack's house to see about Sarah.

"Mr. Howard, I hope you can help her. I didn't know what to do. She's acting real strange."

"She'll be all right, Jack. Giving birth takes time. Get her a box and something soft to lie on, and we'll make her a bed, and then we'll just have to let nature take its course."

Jack hurried to follow Mr. Howard's instructions. Sarah was crying out in pain. She would lie down for a moment, and then get up and begin to pace about. Mary started to cry, thinking surely Sarah was going to die.

"Don't cry, Mary. Your dad will take care of her... These things just take time." Jack repeated Henry's assurance. Jack Roberts believed Henry Howard could fix anything... from mending a broken bicycle to re-stringing a catcher's mitt, and he was sure he was doing the right thing for Sarah.

Mary wasn't quite as sure. She had never seen anything give birth, and had no idea how much pain was involved in the process.

But in time nature did indeed 'take its course' and four tiny baby kittens made their entry into the world and were soon squirming around their mother, trying to find a place to nurse.

Mary breathed a sigh of relief. She was only ten years old and had witnessed a miracle... the miracle of birth.

Jack smiled down at Sarah and her new family with the pride of a new father.

"My mama probably won't let me keep all of them," he sighed. "Would you take one, Mr. Howard?" His warm brown eyes looked intensely at Mary's father, imploring him to provide a home for one of Sarah's offspring.

"We'll see," Henry replied, avoiding the question for the moment, yet knowing full well it would come up again.

"Right now they need to be with their mama."

On their way home, Mary asked, "Daddy, please could we have one? I don't think Mama would mind."

And six weeks later Jack personally delivered the fluffy orange kitten wrapped in a bath towel, and loudly protesting the whole situation. As he placed the furry bundle in Mary's arms, he proudly proclaimed that her name was "Mandy"... And "Mandy" she had remained.

In the distance a flash of lightning lit up the August sky, followed by the faint rumble of thunder. The gentle breeze, which had cooled the air earlier, now grew stronger. Mandy stirred in Henry's lap sensing the approach of a storm.

"Do you think it will rain tomorrow?" Mary asked, as she had so many times when she had special plans and there was threat of rain.

"I doubt it. It's probably nothing more than an evening thunder shower."

"I hope it doesn't. You know the old saying about rain on your wedding day."

"What's that?"

"They say that for every drop of rain that falls on her wedding day, the bride will shed a tear. Haven't you ever heard that?"

"Oh, Mary, honey, that's just another old wives' tale. Happiness is not the result of a twist of fate. It comes from loving each other, and working together and growing closer as the years go by. Take your mother and me, for instance. We've had good times, and we've had hard times, but we never stopped loving each other. I want you to be just as happy as we've been. Marriage is like everything else in life that's worthwhile. You have to work at it. If you do your part and that fellow of yours does his, you'll be fine. And he 'better' do his part or he'll have me to reckon with."

Mary smiled at the fiercely protective nature of her daddy. She was still his little girl... Nothing would ever change that. No man would ever do her wrong and get away with it, not if Henry Howard knew about it.

She laid her head on the shoulder of this man who had loved and protected her all of her life, knowing full well he would continue to do so as long as he had a breath in his body.

"Daddy, I don't think you have to worry about that. Garrett loves me very much."

Katherine Howard's car pulled into the driveway as the rain began to fall, and the three of them went inside, each keenly aware that this would be their last night together in this house to which Kate and Henry had first brought their newborn daughter twenty-two years ago.

Mary and her dad had talked a lot this past week, and as she tried to get to sleep, she found herself thinking of one of their conversations. They had taken some of her belongings to the new apartment, and on their way home had stopped for ice cream. Over a milkshake, Henry told Mary about the money her grandmother had left.

"It's not a lot, but it was her life's savings." He paused as he drew the last of the milkshake up through the straw. "She said she saved it for a rainy day. It was a little over $10,000 when she died, and your mother and I have never spent a penny of it. We've just let the interest accumulate. Your mother insisted that I set the account up in your name and mine. She said it was Mama's money, and we shouldn't waste in on unnecessary things. Kate felt that since it was Mama's money, it should be yours some day."

"But you would have used it if you had needed it? You didn't deny yourselves of things you needed just to save it for me?"

"Sure, we would have used it if we had needed it, but we've been fortunate. We haven't had many rainy days. I hope it will be the same with you, but when you need it, it's there, and it's yours. I know you young people make more money in a month now than your Mom and I made in a whole year when we were starting out. And while $10,000 may not seem like a lot to you, it was a lot to your Grandma.

Although her dad had not asked her to, Mary would not tell Garrett about the money. It was her grandmother's money, saved from years of frugal living and personal sacrifice. It had been passed on to her parents, and they also had made sacrifices to leave the money intact. While her daddy had made a pretty good living at the railroad, they had lived modestly, and she knew there had been times when they could have used the money. Although he said there hadn't been many rainy days, she knew better. She remembered a time when he was laid off from his job, and both the car and washing machine broke down. They walked to the grocery store and to church, and her mother washed their clothes at Aunt Clara's. She also remembered another time when her mother made slipcovers for the sofa when it really needed to be upholstered or replaced. The money had been there all along. All they had to do was write a check. Yet they had not touched it.

That night Mary made a vow to herself. She would never use the money, or allow it to be used, unless it was absolutely necessary. Then one day she would pass her Grandmother's legacy on to her own children.

The rain, which had fallen during the night, was gone by morning and the day dawned bright and sunny. A gentle breeze stirred the air, and Mother Nature seemed to be cooperating fully to make the day perfect for the wedding of Mary Ann Howard and Joseph Garrett Davenport.

Katherine Howard looked at her beautiful young daughter and found it hard to believe that it had been twenty-five years since she packed away her wedding gown, hoping one day she would have a daughter who would wear it on her wedding day. Now that day had come.

When Mary was only a week old, the doctor told Kate and Henry that it was not advisable for Kate to have other children.

For a moment she had been solemn. They had hoped for at least one more child, but the delivery had been extremely difficult, and she knew Dr. Brooks was right. Then she looked at the beautiful little girl she held and said, "Then I suppose I'll just have to give all my love to this one." And that she had done.

Now as she looked at Mary, so radiant in the gown, which she had so carefully preserved from her own wedding day, she knew she could not have asked for a more special gift from God. All the trouble Mary had ever caused was the difficulty of her birth, and that was by no means her fault. Over the years she had brought only joy and happiness into their lives, and as she fastened the strand of pearls around her daughter's neck, she hoped the years would bring to Mary an equal amount of joy and happiness.

There was a soft knock on the door, and they both knew who it was.

"Can I come in?"

Kate let him in and excused herself to finish getting ready. She knew Henry needed some private time with Mary to say those things that fathers say to their daughters on their wedding day.

Mary reached out and hugged her dad.

"Daddy, I love you."

"I love you too." And as he looked at her he thought how much she looked like her mother.

"I'm not too good with words," he began, "but there are a few things I want to say."

Mary took her father's hand and waited to hear what those 'things' were.

"You know I love you very much, and if you ever need anything... money, advice or just someone to talk to... I hope you'll let me know. I'm still your Daddy and the fact that you're all grown up and about to be married doesn't change things between you and me. I'll always be there when you need me."

"You always have, Daddy."

Mary reached for a tissue and smiled at him through misty eyes, and they both knew they had said what needed to be said, and anything that had not been said was completely understood.

First Presbyterian Church was filled with family and friends as Mary and Garrett stood before the ornate circular altar and repeated their vows. Garrett Davenport's eyes were fixed on his beautiful young bride with a look of total adoration. He had thought Mary was beautiful from the first time he had seen her, but today she was more than beautiful. She was gorgeous. There was a look of eager anticipation on her face. She was about to become his bride "to love and to cherish until death do us part."

Now he felt complete. While he had already achieved substantial success in his professional career, he knew he had only begun, and with Mary to share his life, the future seemed bright and filled with promise.

Suddenly he was aware that the minister had paused, and Mary was smiling up at him, and from somewhere he remembered the words he had almost missed...

"You may kiss your bride..."

And Garrett held Mary tenderly and kissed her before God and all who had come to share their special day.

As the huge plane left Lovell Field on its way to Miami and the Bahamas, Mary settled back into her seat. She was dressed in a pale pink suit that enhanced her dark eyes and auburn hair, and she felt safe and secure with the handsome young man seated next to her. Life for her too had just begun.

Sensing her thoughts were of him, Garrett turned and whispered softly, "Are you as happy as you look, my love?"

Once more the mist covered her eyes, as it had done off and on all day.

"More than I've ever been in my life." Her voice quivered as she looked into his eyes, and yearned for him to hold her and make love to her. They were husband and wife... forever... until death do us part.

"I know. So am I." There was a pause before he continued. "How does it feel to be Mrs. Garrett Davenport?"

"Wonderful."

No further words were necessary. They smiled into each other's eyes as the plane left Chattanooga far behind, and Mr. and Mrs. J. Garrett Davenport were lifted high into the clouds of their new life together.

CHAPTER 2

AUGUST 21, 1971

COLUMBUS, GEORGIA

There was not a cloud in the sky. Only the muggy sweltering South Georgia heat hung low over Golden Park, home of the Columbus Astros, the Class AA minor league team of the Houston Astros. The Saturday afternoon crowd was small, but the faithful few who had braved the heat were seeing one heck of a ballgame.

The Savannah Southerners, Class AA affiliate of the Memphis Jazz, were engaged in a nerve wracking pitcher's duel with the Columbus Astros. Savannah led 1 to 0 going into the bottom of the ninth. And through eight innings of play the Savannah pitcher had not allowed a hit or a base runner. He needed only three more outs for the victory and the highly coveted no-hitter.

Jack Roberts slammed the white powdery rosin bag down onto the bright red Georgia clay, stepped up onto the mound and looked in at his catcher for a sign. His uniform, drenched with sweat from two hours and forty minutes of pitching his heart out in this South Georgia version of nature's oven, hung limply on his tall frame. It was late August and the dog days of summer were wielding their influence.

The once white uniform was now dirty and stained from eight innings of wiping perspiration. Beads of sweat dripped from the bill of his cap, as he leaned forward and shook off the catcher's signal. The catcher had called for the curve, but Jack wanted to blow his fastball by the hitter, just as he had all afternoon.

He went into his windup, rocked and fired. The batter swung hard, but connected only with the thick Columbus air. The umpire bellowed "Stee-rike Three!" and the batter turned and walked slowly back to the dugout.

The next batter was Columbus shortstop, Jim Slayton, the weakest hitter on the Astros team. The stocky catcher smiled a cocky grin and thought to himself, "We've got 'em now! This guy can't hit his way out of a wet paper bag!"

As the Savannah catcher looked at his pitcher, he realized something was wrong! Jack wasn't on the mound. Instead he stood behind it and appeared to have suddenly lost his composure and confidence. The six-foot, 185-pound pitcher who had dominated the opposing team all afternoon, setting them down one after the other as if they were a group of little leaguers, now seemed nervous and distracted. He was fidgeting, first with his hat, then with the rosin bag, and then with his hat again. He glanced at the stadium clock. It was 4:08. But what did that matter? He was only two outs away from pitching a perfect game. The time of day should be the last thing on his mind.

Seeing Jack's nervousness, the catcher called time and jogged out to the mound.

"What in the devil's wrong, Jack? Is the heat getting to you?"

"I'm okay," Jack muttered, still staring aimlessly down at the ground.

"Well, then let's finish this bunch off and get out of this heat."

Then he grinned through the wire catcher's mask and said, "If Hell's any hotter than Columbus, I'm sure gonna' have to change my ways." With that the catcher turned and headed back to the plate.

Jack took a deep breath and slowly walked back up on the mound, toed the rubber and nodded in agreement to the catcher's signal for the curve ball. After one more deep breath, he wound and fired. But this time the pitch got away, and hit the batter square on the hip. There went the perfect game, and on a pitch to a guy who could barely hit the ball past second base.

The batter glared at Jack as he jogged down to first. He knew he hadn't thrown at him intentionally. When a pitcher throws at a batter intentionally, he throws a fast ball at his head, not a slow curve at his hip. Besides, with the command of his pitches and the success that Jack had today, he didn't need to throw at anybody.

The hit batsman brought the Savannah manager out of the dugout. He quickly made his way to the mound, and his words of wisdom were much like those of the catcher.

"What the Hell are you trying to do? Give this thing away? You know as well as I do, Memphis is looking for pitching. And they're particularly interested in you. So let's get this guy out, and go home!"

With that the manager reassuringly patted Jack on the butt and turned toward the dugout, without waiting for a reply.

Again Jack pulled his cap off and wiped the sweat from his brow, then swatted at a covey of gnats flying around his face, and readied himself to pitch to Big Matt Hicks, the Southern League home run leader.

Jack got his signal, checked the runner at first, and once again glanced at the clock in left field. Then he took a deep breath and delivered. It was a fastball, belt-high in the strike zone. Hicks swung and connected and drove the ball deep toward left field. Jack turned and watched in disbelief as the ball sailed over the left field wall and into the bleachers.

It was over! The no-hitter was gone! The game was lost! In two pitches Jack Roberts had lost it all.

His whole body was numb, as he stood there on the mound staring at nothing in particular, as Hicks circled the bases. Jack's teammates were already leaving the field. Hicks leaped into the air and almost bounced on home plate, as he was swarmed by the entire Columbus team, as they celebrated the sweet come-from-behind victory.

Once more Jack glanced at the stadium clock... 4:17... He slammed his fist into his glove, cursed quietly to himself, and hung his head as he slowly made his way to the dugout. There was nothing he could do now. It was over... It was all over!

CHAPTER 3

Garrett emerged from the pool, his body glistening from a vigorous swim, and came to join Mary on the deck. The sun and earlier dip in the pool had made her drowsy, and Garrett watched her as she dozed. The sky blue Catalina swimsuit molded her figure in just the right places, and as he looked at her supple, young body, his passion for her mounted.

She was so beautiful, so sensual, that it was an exercise in self-control to keep his hands off her. Their sex life was everything he had hoped it would be. Mary was warm and willing and completely responsive. She was uninhibited when it came to making love, and it was obvious she wanted him as much as he wanted her. She was not like some women he had known who merely wanted to play games. She loved him and gave herself freely to him. She had never refused him, even when he awakened her in the middle of the night. She would ease into his arms, press her body against his and without complaint, yield herself completely to him. Later when he apologized for disturbing her sleep, she would say, "Don't apologize for wanting me. I want you to want me."

The *Princess Maria* was in port for the day, and most of the passengers had gone ashore for a day of sightseeing and shopping, but Mary and Garrett had preferred to stay aboard the ship. There were only two more days remaining on the cruise, and they jealously guarded the time they had left. Instead of going to the island, they had chosen to spend the day swimming and basking in the sun, and relishing the joy of this special time in their life. There were plenty of shops on the ship where they could pick up souvenirs, and they would do that tomorrow. This day belonged to them.

The drink steward approached with a tray of cold exotic concoctions, and Garrett ordered a Mai Tai. Mary heard their conversation and opened her eyes.

"Welcome back to the world." Garrett smiled down at her. "You told me you didn't take naps."

She smiled back. "Only on my honeymoon."

He handed her his drink and she took a sip, wrinkling her nose as she swallowed.

"Would you like one?"

"No, I just needed a sip to cool off."

With a mischievous grin, Garrett turned to Mary and said, "I needed this to break the spell."

His statement puzzled her.

"What are you talking about?"

"The spell of looking at you. One look at your body, and a few private thoughts, and my hormones are out of control... It's all your fault. You shouldn't be so damn seductive."

Mary blushed as she reached again for Garrett's drink. Her husband was flirting with her, and she loved it. She picked up her tote and got up from her seat.

"Let's go to the cabin, and you can take a cold shower while I finish my nap."

Garrett placed his arm around her slender waist and possessively pulled her close.

"To hell with the cold shower, and to hell with your nap. I've got other plans for you."

They were the lone occupants of the elevator, and as it made its descent they engaged in a long breathtaking kiss. A few moments later both swimsuits dropped to the floor just inside the cabin door, and they were on the bed, exploring, touching and pressing their bodies together in a wild sense of urgency. The look on Garrett's face told Mary he had not been kidding with his earlier remarks. He was consumed with passion for her, and she responded with the same yearning and desire... waiting and wanting to be taken by this man whom she loved completely.

Their lips parted for a moment and he smiled into her eyes, and held her close. "And I thought you were a very proper Southern lady."

She sighed as he held her close. "I was before I met you. It seems you've taken the proper Southern lady and made a wanton hussy out of her."

"You like it though, don't you?" He challenged, aware that she was just as out of control as he.

"Yes, I like everything you do to me."

And once more they gave themselves to each other in complete gratification of their unrestrained passion. And while the sightseers walked the streets and visited the straw markets and shell shops on the island, Mary and Garrett lay in the cool of their cabin lost in their love for each other.

Tomorrow it would be ending. The thought saddened her as she dressed for dinner. She had chosen a dress she was sure Garrett would like. It was pale yellow chiffon with a sweetheart neckline and cape sleeves. The color enhanced her golden tan, and her reflection in the mirror told her she would likely get her share of attention from the other passengers, but tonight she yearned only for the attention of one person.

"Wow!" Garrett exclaimed as he beheld his new bride.

"Where have you been hiding that dress? It's gorgeous. You look like a beautiful yellow rose."

She was thrilled by his reaction. She had hoped he would like it. She had spent far too much for the dress, but it was his favorite color. She had saved it for their last night on the ship, as she wanted the end of the honeymoon to be as perfect as the beginning. The cost seemed unimportant when she saw the look on Garrett's face. He fairly beamed as he continued to look at her. She felt lovely and loved as she smiled up at the handsome blonde man who had chosen her to be his wife. How lucky she was to have someone so wonderful to share her life!

The dinner was elegant, and as they waited for the dancing to begin, Mary was aware of the admiring glances of those around them. The band was very good, and Garrett held her close and they danced as if they were the only ones on the floor.

After what seemed like hours of dancing and flowing together in each other's arms, they withdrew from the crowded ballroom and went upstairs to be alone. She accepted the glass of champagne he offered, and they strolled along the promenade deck. The sky was clear and a million or so stars twinkled above.

"Aren't they beautiful, darling?"

"I think they like your dress."

"Oh, Garrett, it's only a dress." She was almost embarrassed. She had never seen him so taken with anything.

"Promise me you'll wear it to our fall office party. I want those guys to see what I've got waiting when I come home at night."

For a long time they stood in silence staring out to sea, and thinking how wonderful their honeymoon had been. Finally Garrett broke the silence.

"Let's get some more champagne and sit on the deck for awhile."

They had danced for a long time and Mary was tired, and sitting sounded wonderful.

"I'd like that, except I think I'll pass on the champagne. I'm not much of a drinker, you know."

"Neither am I, but this is our last night, and I'm feeling a little tense. I suppose it's the realization that the honeymoon is almost over and soon we'll have to get back to the real world."

He also passed up the champagne, and they sat and held hands in the moonlight.

Mary looked out over the waves and then turned to her husband. "Do you realize we scarcely know anyone on this cruise? We've been so caught up in ourselves that we haven't bothered to get to know anyone else."

"Who cares! It's not their honeymoon. It's ours. I wouldn't have given up a moment of our time together to meet the Queen of England!"

"How about the Chairman of the Board of Anderson-Walton?" Mary asked coyly.

"I have met him... We're not exactly on a first name basis, but we will be... Wait and see!"

Mary started to laugh, and then realized he was dead serious. While he had not mentioned his job all week, she had sensed a little restlessness the last couple of days, as if he were ready to get back to work. Not that he wasn't attentive to her, or for that matter, perfectly willing to spend his every waking hour taking his pleasure from her, but when they had taken an intermission from their lovemaking, she thought she had noticed an anxiousness to get on with the rest of his life.

The cool ocean breeze breathed its blessing upon them as they sat on the deck and talked of their future. Garrett was dreaming aloud.

"I've got it all planned, Mary. The investment business is definitely the place to be. A lot of people have big money to invest and are looking for the best yields they can get. The potential is unlimited for someone who is willing to work hard. I like the business, and I'm willing to work and do whatever it takes to be successful. Anderson-Walton is a first class organization. They're very selective in their hiring. They look for intelligent, career-minded professionals with charisma. The fact that Anderson-Walton believes in you enough to hire you gives you some pretty classy credentials."

"In other words, you're saying that an Anderson-Walton business card opens a lot of doors?"

She had not been aware Anderson-Walton was so prestigious.

"Exactly! Anderson-Walton hires the best and then trains them to be even better. They don't keep you forever paying your dues. The promotions come quickly if you can produce, and if you can't, they don't fool around with you."

"That's kind of scary, isn't it? Sounds like they don't have a lot of compassion for the little guy who's having trouble getting started."

"There are no little guys with Anderson-Walton. They hire the cream of the crop, and they expect big things. I knew when I applied for the job what would be expected. It's like this... They feel that if you've got anything on the ball, you won't be a slow starter. I've seen four move up the ladder since I've been with the company. Two are now in the Atlanta office, one is in Birmingham, and the woman is in Boston."

"Do they hire many women?"

"In the past they hired very few, but now they're beginning to hire more. They have to exercise more caution in hiring women and be certain they are career-minded professionals who are willing to put their

job and financial goals ahead of family. They must be willing to move wherever the company needs them on fairly short notice. Twenty years ago there were not many women who were willing to do this, but times have changed."

"Does this mean we'll have to move a lot, too?" An uneasiness filled Mary's voice.

"I hope not. Probably in another year I'll get a chance to transfer to the Atlanta office. Think you can handle that?"

"Sure, I love Atlanta. But suppose you continue to 'move up the ladder'... after Atlanta, what then?"

Atlanta she could handle, but she wasn't sure about moving clear across the country away from her parents. Suddenly she realized how little she knew about Garrett. She had assumed he would continue working in Chattanooga, and she would keep her job at Hamill, Headrick and Martin, and in time they would buy a house in the suburbs and have a couple of kids. By that time hopefully Garrett would be making good money and she could give up her job and devote herself to being a full time wife and mother.

"After Atlanta, if I'm super executive stuff, then maybe New York or Boston."

He saw a look on her face that indicated she wasn't so sure about New York or Boston.

"Don't worry, honey. A lot of the guys work out of Atlanta for years. They travel a lot, but they buy homes and settle their families there. And while they're not there all of the time, it's still home base."

He realized she was overwhelmed by all this.

"Don't worry. Everything's going to be fine." He smiled reassuringly. "Now how about that glass of champagne? I'm not going to get you drunk, baby. You don't have to worry about that. I don't ever plan on being an alcoholic. I've seen too many careers go down the tube because of booze, but tonight is the grand finale to the loveliest honeymoon I've ever had. Let's drink a toast before we call it a day."

She was smiling. "Okay. One more glass of champagne and one more dance."

Suddenly all her concerns about the future were gone. They linked arms, and touched their glasses together.

"To us... together... 'til the end of time."

She touched her glass to his and continued the toast. "To love everlasting."

They sipped their champagne and stood side by side on the deck, oblivious to everything but each other. Then he gently took her in his arms, and they glided together to the music below, and Mary wished the dance would never end. As they smiled at each other, they both sensed they had moved from the bride and groom stage to the deeper, more wonderful relationship of husband and wife.

As Mary hung the yellow dress in the closet, she looked at it with a sense of longing. Would wearing it again ever produce the same euphoria it had tonight? It had been such a beautiful evening, and she didn't want it to end, but all good things must, and even honeymoons can't last forever. But theirs was not over yet. They still had the rest of the night, and it would be rich and warm and loving, and sleep would not matter... not tonight. As she crawled into bed, Garrett pulled her close, and the ship listed and swayed, as if in perfect harmony with their lovemaking. They clung to each other, and claimed each other, and pledged their love. When his mouth was not hot upon hers, she was reaching out to him in an invitation to kiss me, take me, love me again. He was upon her and entering her, and she felt again and again the wondrous feeling of yielding one's self completely to another person. Finally toward dawn, their passions satisfied, they fell asleep with Mary resting comfortably against the curve of Garrett's strong body, as the ship moved closer to shore.

CHAPTER 4

Mary closed her book and looked out at the freshly mowed lawn and the red geraniums blooming profusely in spite of the hot August days. She had meant to study all afternoon, but it was no use. She was too excited.

As she thought about the first year of her marriage, many of the events seemed to flash before her eyes like moving pictures on a screen.

The year had passed quickly, and so much had happened. Three months after their wedding, Garrett had been transferred to Atlanta. While they had not expected it to happen so soon, Garrett was delighted. It was a big promotion, and he was pleased that his performance had not gone unnoticed.

Business was great in the investment field, and Anderson-Walton was one of the biggest and most respected brokerage firms in the country. Garrett was already making good money, and the opportunities for advancement were unlimited.

In November they had moved into a small apartment in the Buckhead section of Atlanta, and Mary had set about selecting draperies and bedspreads and making everything look nice. Sometimes she could not believe how good things were going for them. They had decided that she would wait until after Christmas to look for a job. She enjoyed staying home and keeping house and preparing supper for Garrett, and admittedly she could very easily get used to being 'just a housewife'.

On weekends they slept late, made love, and ate a leisurely breakfast. Then they drove around the city, looking at houses and dreaming of the time when they would own one of their own.

Being married was wonderful. Mary had never expected it to be like this. She was prepared for the sacrifice and financial struggle that most young couples encounter during the early years, but Garrett had an excellent income, and even without her working, they had no financial problems and were saving money for a house.

The company provided Garrett a car, and Mary had sold her old Ford, and now drove the Olds 98 that Garrett owned when they got married. He had specially ordered the car, and it was equipped with every option available. It was the nicest car she had ever seen, and she loved driving it.

Sometimes she felt almost guilty having so much so soon, especially when she went home for a visit. Many of her friends from high school were struggling to make it on low paying jobs, some with children to provide for as well. Life had been very good to her.

They had decided against having children for awhile.

"I don't want our lovemaking to be inhibited, but we don't need an unwanted pregnancy. So, we have to be prudent," Garrett had said.

She was not ready for a baby either and was glad he was assuming responsibility in the matter. They were young and passionate, and they enjoyed the wonderful intimacy of each other. Often when he came home in the evening, he would take her in his arms and pull her close.

"Baby I couldn't wait to get home to you. I want you so much... Can supper wait?"

And feeling the same desire for him, she would set the food in the oven, and they would escape to their bedroom and make love until their passion was consumed and they lay damp and warm in each other's arms.

She treasured these intimate times with her husband. She knew there would come a time when the demands of life would not allow them to give themselves to each other with such reckless abandon, whenever and wherever they chose. Garrett was a masterful lover, and she felt weak and wanton in his arms, and never grew tired of his demands. It was a wonderful feeling to be desired so intensely and to respond with the same eagerness.

On the 22nd Mary went to Chattanooga to spend the holidays with her parents, and Garrett came up on Christmas Eve. It was nice to be home with her folks. Her mother cooked all of Mary's favorite things, and after dinner they decorated the tree, while munching on Christmas cookies and sipping hot chocolate. The cookies and hot chocolate were as much a part of the tree decorating as the tinsel and garland and the time worn angel that Mary had always begged her mother not to replace.

"It wouldn't be right to get a new one. We've had her all her life," Mary said each time the subject was brought up.

Mary's Dad read the paper and smoked his pipe while his two girls laughed and decorated the tree, a detail he was happy to leave to them.

It had been a happy time, but when it was time to leave Chattanooga and return to Atlanta, Mary was glad to be going home. She had loved being with her parents, but her home was somewhere else now. She moved closer to Garrett and took his hand in hers and felt warm and very content.

He smiled at her and softly said, "Are you happy?"

And when she turned to answer, there were tears in her eyes. She squeezed his hand tighter.

"I've never been so happy in my entire life."

They drove the rest of the way home in blissful silence wrapped in the warmth of the love they felt for each other.

On the following weekend, Garrett's parents came for their holiday visit. They were laden with gifts, and it was like a second Christmas. Mary had decorated a small white tree and put up wreaths before they went to Chattanooga, so everything looked festive. Garrett's mother complimented Mary on the great job she had done decorating the apartment.

Mary had looked forward to cooking a nice holiday meal for them, but they insisted she not go to all the bother.

"Don't worry about it." Garrett reassured her. "Dad likes to do things his way, and he insists on taking us out. They rarely eat at home anyway."

They went to the club, and the meal was delicious and extremely elegant. Emily Davenport was very nice, but it was evident that Garrett's dad made the decisions. However, Mrs. Davenport seemed content with the way things were, and they appeared quite compatible.

Mary couldn't help wondering if Mrs. Davenport was really satisfied with doing everything her husband's way, but if it worked for them, which apparently it did, then it shouldn't bother her. Actually, they were very nice people, and they seemed to be fond of her.

"Have you kids been looking at houses yet?" Garrett's dad asked the day before their visit was scheduled to end.

"That's how we spend our weekends," Garrett replied. "We've had a ball chasing the 'For Sale' signs. There are some beautiful homes around Atlanta."

"Have you seen any you like?" Mr. Davenport inquired.

"We've seen several, but we can't afford a house yet. We just look."

"Sounds like fun. Why don't we all go look?" Garrett's dad was already getting his jacket. "Come on girls. We're going house hunting."

Mary laughed. She liked Joe Davenport's spirit. He was aggressive and enthusiastic. He, too, was in the investment business, and according to Garrett, had done quite well over the years, and now mainly managed his own portfolio of stocks and bonds, although he still went to the office every day when he was in town. But mostly he and Emily did whatever they chose, whenever they chose, whether it was house hunting on a Saturday afternoon in Atlanta or flying to New York to see a Broadway show or trout fishing in a mountain stream in the foothills of North Carolina.

They drove through the neighborhoods where Garrett and Mary had looked at houses, but Garrett saved their favorite for last. It seemed that wherever else they looked, they always came back to this house. It was Southern Colonial with tall white columns and a large yard, which had been beautifully kept by the previous owner. The huge magnolia trees contributed to its imposing appearance and made it look very 'old South'. Mary had loved it from the first time she saw it, but she knew they could not afford it. It was Garrett, however, who was utterly captivated by the place. They had been here a dozen times or more, and each time, he would linger in the winding driveway and say, "This is beautiful. I wish we could buy it... One of these days we'll drive by and the 'For Sale' sign will be gone."

"I suppose so, but that's okay. Then we'll start looking for another one, and we'll find one we like even better."

It was the same every time they came. She wished he wouldn't come back every week. He was just torturing himself as it was bound to sell before they could afford to buy. And besides, she wasn't sure she was ready to give up the apartment. It was nice and cozy and a breeze to look after.

When they arrived, the realtor was about to leave. She had just finished showing the house to someone else and was locking up.

"Could we see it?" Mr. Davenport asked.

"Sure, I need to meet some people at three, but I've got a little while."

Garrett and Mary had seen it before, and they had been just as impressed with the inside as they had with the outside. And so were Mr. and Mrs. Davenport.

Mr. Davenport followed the realtor from room to room, asking a number of questions, and then a look at his watch told him they needed to clear out, so she could make her other appointment.

"May I have your card, please?" He asked.

They shook hands.

"Please let me know if I can help you further, or if you would like to look at it again. I hope I haven't rushed you. I'll be glad to show it again. Just give me a call."

"It's a nice house," Joe Davenport said as they took one last look and drove away.

The Davenports left the following day to return to St. Louis. It had been an enjoyable visit, but it was nice to once more have the place to themselves. It was snowing in Atlanta when Mr. and Mrs. Davenport left, but it would not amount to much. Atlanta was too far south to get much accumulation.

The following week Garrett was scheduled to go to Birmingham for a couple of days. It would be the first time he had been away since they had gotten married. She knew he would have to do some traveling when he got the promotion, but hopefully, it would only be for a day or two now and then.

On Sunday afternoon after he finished packing his bag, Garrett said, "I've got something to ask you, Honey... How would you like to go back to school?"

"Go back to school! I need to go to work. Sure, I would like to go to school, but we agreed that I would look for a job after the first of the year. Remember?"

"I know, but I really think you need to finish your education. The house can wait. We'll get around to that later."

Mary could not imagine what had prompted this. She had her associate's degree and had hoped someday to finish college, but now was not the time. More than going back to school, she needed to get a job and go to work. While Garrett was making good money, and they had saved some, it was earmarked for the down payment on a house, and with two incomes they could buy a house sooner.

"There must be some reason you mentioned it. Are your parents disappointed that I'm not a college graduate? Does that somehow make me not good enough for you?"

Mary had never been angry with Garrett before, but there was something about this whole thing she didn't like, and she insisted on knowing why he had suddenly decided that she needed to go back to school.

"My parents love you and they're not disappointed that you haven't finished college. They had nothing to do with this. It was my idea completely. I just think you need to get your degree. You've got two years behind you. Why not go ahead and finish before we have kids?"

But it was more than that. Mary could tell. It was as if Garrett had a vested interest in her finishing college. Then it hit her. It wasn't Garrett's parents... It was Garrett and the damn Anderson-Walton image.

"Is there a pre-written rule that Anderson-Walton wives be college graduates? Because if there is, you should have thought of that before." Mary was angry, and she could not contain her fury.

"Honey, the only prerequisite for Anderson-Walton wives is that they be pretty, and you certainly fit that bill."

He took her in his arms and tried to hold her close, but she was rigid and unwilling to be humored. He had made her feel inferior, and in her whole life no one had ever done that... And now he was trying to appease her.

Garrett continued to hold her and stroke her hair.

"I love you so much, baby. I didn't mean to upset you. I just thought you would like to finish college, and now seemed like the proper time. If you don't want to, it's okay. I'm not going to love you any less."

Mary was crying, but at least she was allowing Garrett to draw her close. Finally she got control of her voice. "Honey, I'm sorry. I didn't mean to overreact. It's just that sometimes I don't feel in the same league with those women. They're so stuffy and pompous. They play bridge and golf, and go to the country club every other day, and sip martinis and talk about their days at *Vassar* and *Smith*. I don't fit into their lifestyle. And suddenly I felt as if you were ashamed of me because I'm not like them."

Garrett held her for a long time and let her cry. He realized he had hurt her. He hadn't meant to, but it was expected that Anderson-Walton wives be college graduates. Why in the hell it made any difference he didn't know. It was just the way of the crazy world... "Image"... They call it... But that's just the way it is, and there's nothing you can do about it.

Then they made love, long and tender and lovingly, and Garrett assured her over and over again that he loved her, which was what she needed to hear. Finally, they wound up laughing about the whole incident.

With an impish grin, Mary asked. "If Anderson-Walton wives are supposed to be pretty, what happened to Madeline?"

Mary was not the type to be catty, but they needed something to lighten the mood.

"I'm afraid Madeline slipped through somehow."

Now they were both laughing. Madeline was not pretty, but she was probably the nicest of all the Anderson-Walton wives, and Mary liked her very much. In fact, Madeline was the only one she felt completely comfortable being around.

This was one of the few misunderstandings they had encountered, and as time went by, Mary was sure she had taken the whole thing wrong. She really wanted to finish college, and Garrett was right. It was better to do it before they had children.

It was challenging to be back in school, and she was determined to do well. She had always been a good student, and although she had wondered if she might have trouble learning to study again, she was soon back in the groove.

A couple of weeks after Joe and Emily Davenport returned home, their letter came, and with it a check for $25,000... the down payment on the house. Mary could not believe it.

"We can't let them do that, Garrett," she protested. "It's too much money."

Garrett was still reading the letter. "Dad said you wouldn't want to accept the check. Apparently he understands you pretty well."

He continued to read, this time aloud...

"Emily and I want to do this for you. It's part of your inheritance, and we want to be able to see you enjoy it. I've talked with Mrs. Baldwin, the realtor, and she knows arrangements are being made for the down payment. She has agreed to hold the house for ten days. You should contact her immediately to complete the purchase."

Two weeks later they vacated the apartment and moved into the house which a few months earlier had been only a dream. Now it was theirs.

Mary would never forget the look on Garrett's face after they unloaded the last of their belongings. He stood in the middle of the parlor, surrounded by stacks of cardboard boxes filled with things yet to be put in their rightful places.

"I can't believe it's actually ours. Honey, tell me I'm not dreaming."

And for the first time Mary thought she saw a tear in Garrett's eye. He had loved this place from the first time he laid eyes on it, and was simply overcome by the joy of knowing it was really theirs.

Garrett was travelling some, but it was not too bad. Usually, it was for no more than a couple of days at a time, and no farther away than Birmingham, and some weeks he didn't have to be away at all.

Mary missed him when he was gone, but she used the time to study. She quickly learned that absence indeed 'makes the heart grow fonder', and found herself filled with eagerness and yearning on the day he was scheduled to return.

Even when they had been apart for only a couple of days, these times of re-uniting were wonderful. They clung to each other, filled with the wonder of once more holding and being held, and consumed with burning desire for each other. The coming together was almost worth the being apart.

This was how she felt now as she looked forward to the weekend. Garrett had reserved a condominium in Gatlinburg for a combination vacation and first anniversary celebration.

Her school schedule had interfered with their plans for an earlier vacation, but now they would have four glorious days in the mountains.

She dreamed of what it would be like. Garrett said the condo had a fireplace with gas logs. If it grew cool at night, as it usually does in the mountains, they would light the fire, sip wine by the flickering firelight and listen to soft music. Then they would spend the rest of the night making love.

During the day they would stroll through the enchanting little shops, stop for tacos for lunch, and go back to their condo and stretch out on the king-size bed to rest, but they would not rest. They would make love, and then they would take a nap. Afterward, they would sit on the deck or stroll through the grounds down by the duck pond. Then they would dress for a relaxed dinner in one of the town's elegant restaurants. Later they would dance to soft music as Garrett held her close. It would be like a second honeymoon, only better.

She was too excited to study. Garrett had been in Birmingham all week and should be back in the office anytime. The ringing of the telephone interrupted her reverie and drew her back to the present. That would be Garrett, and as she hurried to answer, she felt a sudden weakness in the pit of her stomach from the anticipation of hearing her husband's voice and knowing that soon they would be together.

CHAPTER 5

As a kid Jack Roberts loved baseball. Every afternoon he would wait patiently for his dad to come home from work and hit him some ground balls or play catch. He made such a cute sight -- the little boy in the gray flannel baseball jersey that his mom had found at a church yard sale. It was his most prized possession, even though it had long since seen its better days. The collar was frayed, the material had worn thin and there was a big patch just below the number on the back, but Jack didn't see those things. He would run around in the back yard chasing pop-ups, which he often threw too high or too far away to be able to catch before they hit the ground, but that never dampened his spirit. Then he and his dog, Ajax, would take off after the ball before it rolled down the hill and into the drainpipe.

The ball didn't even look like a real baseball. Real baseballs are white, but not this one. It was covered with grass stain and mud from the times Jack and Ajax had not been able to recover it before it reached the drainage ditch.

John Roberts was a good man. He worked very hard and often long hours, but he always made time to play with his young son and to give him that special time a little boy needs that can only come from his father.

Although he often got into trouble for wandering too far from home without his mother's permission, he would roam through the neighborhood looking for someone to get up a game. Usually he could find a few kids who would play long enough to get their bat, but then they would get bored and quit, or remember they had something else to do before Jack got his turn to hit. But he didn't care. He just wanted to play, and if he didn't get to bat, at least he got to pitch.

One night when Jack was only seven, his dad came home early and couldn't find him anywhere. His mom said he had been out back with Ajax only a little while ago, but he wasn't there now. John and Virginia combed the neighborhood looking for their little boy, but they couldn't find him anywhere. Finally one lady said she had seen him on his bike with his baseball glove hung over the handlebars and 'that dog' right behind him, but that had been at least an hour ago, and neither he nor the dog were anywhere to be found.

Darkness was fast approaching, and John and Virginia were beginning to worry. Jack had never just disappeared like this. They had walked for almost an hour with no sign of their young son, and were at their wit's end, when they heard the sound of children playing. John ran ahead to the top of the next hill and stood smiling as his wife caught up. He then pointed to a group of kids playing on a makeshift ball field on a vacant lot where an old building had been torn down. There was Jack in the center of the diamond with Ajax at his side. It wasn't hard to pick him out, as he was the only little white boy in the group. Jack, who even at that age, never seemed to meet a stranger, obviously had no problem with this. In fact it didn't appear that he even noticed. He just wanted to play ball. To him the other kids weren't black, they were just kids playing ball, and that's all that mattered.

Although Jack got a pretty good 'talking to' when he got home, John couldn't bring himself to punish his little boy. That day his seven-year old son had put into practice a lesson that a lot of grownups still needed to learn.

When he couldn't find anyone else to play with, he would bounce a rubber ball off the side of the chimney, except to Jack it was not a chimney in his back yard. It was Yankee Stadium and the seventh game of the World Series. His team was leading one to nothing and he was pitching in the bottom of the ninth. First he faced Mantle, then Maris, then Berra, and he struck them all out, and the crowd went wild.

Jack never missed a year of Little League. He made sure his dad took him down to sign up on the first Saturday of registration. While Little League sign-ups lasted for four Saturdays, he didn't want to take a chance that they might "get too many kids or something." Jack wasn't any more talented than the other kids, but he had more heart than any kid out there. Every year he would play his heart out and then after the last game of the season, he would wait with the other kids on the front row of the bleachers as the all-stars were announced. He always worked so hard to make it and a couple of years he really deserved to make the team, but his name was never called. It always seemed to be the coaches' sons or the councilmen's sons or this year, Frankie Taylor. Frankie didn't even like baseball. He only played because his dad made him, but that didn't matter. He had made the team, and once again Jack had not... but there was no denying that the all-star team looked good in the new uniforms that Frankie's dad, who owned the local carpet store, had bought the week before.

The same thing happened when Jack tried out for the high school team. He made it to the final cut before being let go. Once again Frankie Taylor made the team. This time it was a new pitching machine the high school needed.

It was a tough lesson, especially at such a young age, but one that everyone has to learn sooner or later... Life is not always fair.

Jack never gave up on baseball. He loved it too much. It was a part of him, of who he was, not just something he did for fun. He played in the city leagues during the summer, but he never again tried out for the high school team. He didn't make a big deal about it, but inside the scars ran deep. He told himself, "If they don't need me, then I sure don't need them." And although he never spoke it aloud, he swore to himself that one day he would show them.

Two years after graduation, Jack got his chance. He had continued to play summer ball, and at this level only the more serious players remained. The "Frankie Taylor's" of the world had left baseball, and their fathers were now attempting to wield their influence in other areas.

Jack worked as an apprentice in a local printing shop and had gotten quite good at his trade in a relatively short time, but come summer he donned the cap and spikes and headed back to the ball field. Most of Jack's teammates were college players home for the summer, who played summer league to keep their skills sharp. Jack had never had much formal coaching and had picked up most of what he knew from watching other players and the major leaguers on *NBC's Game of the Week*. But he was not bashful, and he didn't mind asking questions. He talked to the other players and picked their brains for any scrap of information or strategy that he might learn, especially the pitchers.

He was a pretty good pitcher in his own right. He had worked hard to strengthen himself and to hone his skills, but he had never had the opportunity to work with anyone who could teach him the proper mechanics of pitching. Jack was a thrower, a good one, but he knew there was a big difference between being a thrower and being a pitcher. A thrower, no matter how good he was, would never play professional baseball. To make the majors he had to become a pitcher.

In the summer of '69 Jack Roberts became a pitcher.

For the last several years the summer league team had been coached by one of the retired guys in town. Fred was a nice guy, but he wasn't much of a coach. Mainly he made out the lineup, and the team coached itself. But in '69, the local community college coach asked Fred if he could help with the team. Fred welcomed the help Coach Mathis offered, and it didn't take long for Carl Mathis to recognize Jack's talent. When he discovered Jack's openness to instruction, the two were almost inseparable, and for the first time ever, Jack's abilities were being recognized, and a coach was taking a real interest in him. In one summer Carl Mathis taught Jack more baseball than he had learned in all his years of playing ball, and by the end of that summer, Jack was no longer just a thrower. He was a pitcher, and in Coach Mathis' words, "A damn good one."

The following spring Jack pitched for Coach Mathis at Chattanooga Tech, and the following June when Major League baseball's newest expansion team, the *Memphis Jazz*, held a tryout camp in Chattanooga, Jack was ready.

Ten days later he signed his first professional baseball contract and was on his way to Savannah to play for the *Southerners*.

CHAPTER 6

As the huge Delta 707 touched down on the runway at Logan International Airport, Mary felt as though her stomach was suddenly catapulted into her throat. The flight had been smooth, but as the plane started its descent she began to feel queasy, and by the time the plane landed, everything seemed to be spinning around her. She sat very still for a few moments unsure if she should try to get up. Finally, she unfastened her seat belt and slowly got to her feet.

"Are you okay?" the flight attendant asked, as she noticed how pale Mary was.

"I think so. The landing bothered me a little... I've never had a problem with flying before. I'm probably just tired from a lot of late night studying."

"Let me help you." The attractive young flight attendant took Mary's arm and assisted her down the exit ramp. "Is Boston your destination or will you be connecting with another flight?"

"This is it. My husband is meeting me."

"Do you see him anywhere?" The attendant was still holding Mary's arm, unsure if she should leave her unattended.

"No, but he'll be here. He's a stockbroker and he's probably tied up with a client. I'm sure he won't be long."

"I'll be glad to get someone to stay with you until your husband arrives."

"No, I'm fine. Thank you."

Mary scanned the lobby once more, but saw no sign of Garrett. She was almost glad he was late. It would give her a chance to go to the ladies room and freshen up a bit. As she applied blush to her cheeks and ran a brush through her hair, she felt almost normal again. She wouldn't mention it to Garrett. This probably happened to a lot of people. She was fine now. One final glance in the mirror told her she looked okay, and that there were no telltale signs of the incident.

She returned to the lobby and found Garrett anxiously looking for her. When their eyes met, warm smiles broke across their faces as they hurried to embrace each other.

It had been a month since their Gatlinburg trip, and Garrett had spent most of that time in Boston. Monday morning he would be going to

Chicago for a seminar, and rather than come home, he had suggested that Mary fly to Boston for the weekend.

She hated it when he was away from home for so long, but she tried not to complain. She had known when they moved to Atlanta that the promotion would involve some travelling, although she had not expected it to be so much.

As they made their way hand in hand to the baggage section, Mary was aware of how much she had missed him. The time in the mountains of Tennessee had been everything she had dreamed it would be, but they had seen so little of each other since.

She gazed out the window of the rental car at the city where her husband spent so much of his time. It was strange and foreign to her, yet for Garrett it had become a second home. The day was gray and foggy, and there was an unceasing drizzle, which only added to the dreariness and made it look like nighttime, though it was only four o'clock.

"We're having dinner with Scott and Linda Cannon. You'll like them. Scott is General Manager of the Boston Division. The company brought him up from Dallas. They were originally from California, but they're 'damn Yankees' now."

Garrett realized that Mary was very quiet.

"Are you okay? You're quieter than usual... Is something wrong?"

"I'm fine," Mary smiled, "I'm just happy to be with you again. It seems like forever since I've seen you." She moved closer to Garrett and continued. "Honey, I don't mean to complain. I know you have a good job and travelling is part of it. I accept that, at least most of the time, but I miss you so much and I get so lonely when you're away."

"I know, Baby. I miss you too. I don't like it anymore than you do, but it's an extraordinary opportunity. Try to understand that."

Then he went on to repeat the story she had heard before.

"There's a lot of money being invested in this part of the country, and that's why Anderson-Walton is concentrating their efforts in New England. We've hired twenty-five new sales reps over the last six months, in addition to those that have transferred from other offices. These aren't rookies either. They have proven track records. Most of them we've stolen from our competitors."

His voice softened, as he took Mary's hand into his own. "It isn't easy being away from you either, but I'm a part of something big, and it's very exciting. Incidentally, I just got another salary increase and my bonus for this quarter should be pretty handsome."

Mary tried to smile. She knew Garrett loved his job, and the income was certainly nice, and she understood that right now this was the place he had to be. But deep down inside she yearned for the day when they could once again have a normal marriage, and Garrett could work a regular nine to five schedule and come home to her every night. That's what she really wanted.

As they entered the lobby of the ritzy Carlton Hotel, Mary looked about her. Everything was elegant and plush, and she was sure their suite would be equally luxurious. Yet, all the amenities failed to impress her. Maybe it was the result of her sick spell earlier in the day, but, try as she might, she could not get excited about the things Garrett found so important.

She wished they didn't have to go to dinner with the Cannons. She would rather spend the time with her husband. Lately, they did well to have two weekends a month together and she didn't want to waste the precious little time they had with someone she didn't even know.

She understood that socializing was important to Garrett's career, and the Cannons were probably very nice people, and they would have a pleasant time together. However, she hoped the evening would end early.

She wished her mood would go away. Hopefully, the sun would shine tomorrow. Rainy days always made her blue. But this was no time to be blue. She was with her husband, and that was what mattered most of all.

As Garrett turned the lock on the hotel door, he took Mary in his arms, and held her close, and suddenly nothing else mattered. They were together and alone, and it didn't matter whether they were in Boston or Atlanta or Gatlinburg.

The moodiness she had felt earlier vanished. They weren't going to dinner until eight o'clock, and for a few priceless hours, it was just the two of them. The rain and the fog no longer seemed ominous, but rather formed a comfortable barrier insulating them from the rest of the world, and for now they belonged only to each other.

CHAPTER 7

FEBRUARY 5, 1973

It was the most exciting day of his life, as he pulled his 1966 Volkswagon van off of Interstate 95 and headed east to West Palm Beach. About a mile and a half down the road he saw the huge state highway sign, and pulled off to the side of the road to take it all in.

WEST PALM BEACH, FLORIDA
SPRING TRAINING HOME OF THE MEMPHIS JAZZ

"The Memphis Jazz!" Jack thought. "That's me!"
The date was February 5th, and this was Jack's first major league spring training. Pitchers and catchers were to report on February 12th, two weeks earlier than the position players. He realized he was a week early, but he couldn't wait any longer. He had lifted weights and worked out all winter, and was in as good physical condition as he could be.
Finally he told his mom, "I've waited as long as I can. I'm going to drive on down. Maybe some of the other guys will be there too."
The Jazz spring training complex was beautiful. Jack gazed at the well-groomed green outfields and the immaculately manicured infields. He had never seen anything like it. Then he saw the padlocks. Everything was locked up tight as a drum. Apparently no one else had showed up. The other players and coaches were still at home with their families and would report on the dates they were supposed to, and due to visa problems and contract negotiations, some of the players would not arrive then.
Jack couldn't understand this, but when the other players chose to arrive was not important. What was important was he was here. He had finally made it to the majors.
He had been placed on the team's forty-man spring roster and invited to camp as a major leaguer. It didn't mean that he had made the team... far from it, in fact. Before the actual season began that roster would be reduced to twenty-five players and those who did not make the team would be either sent back to the minor league or released. Nevertheless, he was here and he would work as hard as he could to make the team. If

he didn't make it this spring, then he would go back to the minors and work that much harder to make it back.

He walked around the complex, taking everything in. Like a farm boy who had come to the big city for the first time, he was awe struck by the magnitude of everything.

Finally, he found one person, an old black man, who appeared to be in his seventies. He was slightly stooped from what Jack assumed to be the effects of many years of hard work. He wore a felt hat like the kind bankers and lawyers wore years ago, only like Jack's yard sale baseball jersey, Mr. Bradshaw's hat had seen its better days.

The old man was putting away a rake and locking up a tool shed. Jack walked over to him and introduced himself.

After staring at Jack with a disbelieving expression, the old man started to smile. "Boy, you mean to tell me you a big league ball player?" The old man then laughed out loud.

"Yes sir. Well, I pitched at Knoxville last year, but the Jazz invited me to spring training."

The grounds keeper was still less than impressed, and finally said, "Son, you either lyin' or you a damn fool... Coming down here a week early. They ain't nothing going on yet."

Jack knew he wasn't lying, but from the predicament his enthusiasm had gotten him into, he couldn't put up much of an argument about the latter statement.

He couldn't help but grin.

"Well sir, I guess you're right. I probably am just a damn fool."

After about fifteen minutes of trying to convince Mr. Bradshaw who he was, the old grounds keeper finally agreed to unlock the gate and let him run in the outfield each day until the team arrived the following week, but he was not as willing to grant Jack's other request.

He had not realized when he left Chattanooga, that the motel accommodations the team management had made started on February 12th, and not on February 5th. So he had nowhere to sleep and very little money to rent a place.

He tried to talk the old black man into letting him sleep in the clubhouse, but Mr. Bradshaw refused.

"Boy, you know I can't do that. I'd lose my job if they find out I'm letting somebody stay in here, some vagrant from off the street... I know you say you a ballplayer, but I don't know. I never seen no ball player show up a week before spring training." Mr. Bradshaw looked at Jack as if he still didn't know whether to believe him or not, and then continued. "I tell you what... you a good kid. You dumb as Hell, but you a good kid! My couch is lumpy, but you welcome to it."

So for the first week of his first major league spring training, Jack spent the nights on the old black man's living room couch. But he didn't mind.

Mr. Bradshaw's grandkids lived with him, along with three old hounds who looked like they had been around almost as long as Mr. Bradshaw. The kids loved having Jack stay with them. They would hurry home from school every afternoon, and play 'catch' and 'hot box' with Jack until it grew too dark to see. Then they would go inside the old rundown house and sit down to some of the best eating Jack had ever tasted, especially Mr. Bradshaw's cornbread.

It was a thrill for Jack. He would go out each morning, do his running and work on his conditioning and his exercises as if the whole team were there, but it was kind of nice they were not, as he had the whole complex to himself. He didn't have the distraction of the other players, although he looked forward to having the other guys around -- the camaraderie, the kidding, the practical jokes, and the learning and working together to become the best team they could be.

A week later when the rest of the team reported, Jack moved into the dorm-style apartments with the other players, but he still spent as much time as he could with Mr. Bradshaw's grandkids, and managed to get them free tickets to a couple of games.

He worked hard that spring, harder than he had ever worked in his life, but it wasn't quite enough, and with one week to go before the season started, he got the news that he was being sent back to Knoxville. The beer-bellied manager shook Jack's hand as he cleaned out his locker.

"Son, don't worry. You keep pitching like you've been and you'll be back... maybe sooner than you think."

Jack shook the manager's hand and thanked him for the opportunity, but regardless of his words, his face could not hide the disappointment he was feeling inside. It was the same feeling he had in Little League when he sat on the front row of the bleachers waiting for his name to be called for the all-star team.

Jack Roberts was not a quitter. He had lost before and he would probably lose again, but each loss had made him tougher, and that's what this one would do. He went back to Knoxville and pitched his heart out, and in late June he got the call. It came on a Monday night only minutes before the *Knoxville Owls* were to take the field.

"You're pitching up here on Thursday," the gravel toned manager said.

Jack couldn't believe it.

"Can you be here by game time Wednesday night?"

"Yes sir! I'll be there tomorrow!"

"That's not necessary. Just be at the stadium by around four."

Jack had plenty of time to get to Memphis. He could take a day off, or even go home for a day and still be in Memphis by Wednesday afternoon, but he didn't want a day off. After all these years, he had finally made it to the majors. He was now a member of the *Memphis Jazz*, and all he wanted was to get there and get into that uniform.

He drove straight through to Memphis. It was about two a.m. when he got into town. Naturally, the stadium was closed and because of his eagerness to get there, he once again had no place to sleep. He pulled his van into the stadium parking lot and bedded down for the night. Sometime around 3:30 he was awakened by a rather large Memphis policeman tapping on his window with a flashlight.

Jack told the officer and his partner the story and how he was a member of the *Memphis Jazz*, but neither cop had ever heard of him. Finally, the officers took him downtown to the police station, and in the middle of the night called the *Jazz* manager to verify Roberts' story.

Although the temperamental coach substantiated Jack's story, he wasn't happy about being awakened in the middle of the night because this damn rookie couldn't wait.

It wasn't exactly the kind of start Jack had dreamed of, but he was here. And that was all that mattered.

Although the skipper frowned and cursed on the outside, inside he smiled at the vigor and enthusiasm the young kid had shown, and he thought to himself, "That's the kind of guy I want out there when the game's on the line."

Jack had a good year for the *Jazz* in '73. He finished the season with a record of 8 wins and 2 losses and an Earned Run Average of 2.34, not bad for a team that finished last in the National League in pitching with a team ERA of 4.95.

His statistics had been good enough to earn him a regular spot in the *Jazz* pitching rotation and second place in the Rookie of the Year balloting.

And Jack had kept his silent promise to himself... He had showed them... but he wasn't doing it for that. He was playing for the same reason he always had. He loved baseball.

CHAPTER 8

In the wee hours of the morning of May 7th, 1973, Joseph Garrett Davenport, III made his entry into the world. It had been a prolonged and difficult delivery, and the last thing Mary remembered was hearing the doctor say, "We're going to have to sedate her and give her some help. She can't handle anymore."

Then sometime later she heard someone calling her name. With great effort she slowly opened her eyes, and the nurse was saying, "Mrs. Davenport, you have a fine baby boy."

She tried to look at him when the nurse held him up for her to see, but her eyes kept closing. She felt groggy and disoriented, and she wasn't sure if she was still in the delivery room or if she had been taken to a room.

The same voice was speaking again. "Just rest now. You've put in a hard day's work for this little fellow. Tomorrow you'll feel better and the two of you can get acquainted."

She was glad it was a boy. Garrett would be pleased. But mostly she was glad it was over. She knew now why they called it labor. Totally exhausted, she closed her eyes and slept.

It was morning now, and the little baby she had worked so hard to bring into the world lay in her arms. She had just given him his first bottle, and as she fingered the tiny hands and feet, she thought about the miracle of birth, which had produced this beautiful little child. He was healthy and without blemish, and he was hers to love and to cherish and to watch over and protect. She drew him close and whispered a prayer of gratitude for this precious gift. He sighed softly as he slept contentedly, much like the almost inaudible purr of a young kitten. Mary smiled down on her son, realizing that at this very moment a special bond was being formed... the bond between mother and child that would last a lifetime.

The nurse had come into the room and was adjusting the blinds to let in some light. She was in her thirty-fifth year at Piedmont General, and although she had worked all over the hospital, the maternity section was her favorite. Birth, if the mother and child did okay, and usually they did, was such a happy occasion.

She approached Mary's bed and asked, "Your first?"

"Yes," Mary replied, and grimaced as she tried to change positions, "and the way I feel right now, my last."

"Oh, honey, you'll feel much better in a day or two. I promise! Sometimes the first one can be awfully hard to bring into the world." She could tell from looking at Mary that the delivery had not been an easy one. "But this little guy is going to be worth all the trouble he put you through."

"He already is."

"The doctor will be in later to check on you. Let us know if you need anything."

Mary looked at her watch. It was 9:30. Their baby was eight hours old, and his daddy hadn't even seen him. On the dresser sat a vase of yellow roses, which had arrived a few hours earlier.

Her mother had placed the roses on the dresser and handed Mary the card. She was surprised when Mary didn't read the card, but instead laid it unopened on the table beside her bed.

"They're from Garrett! He should be here! Sometimes it seems I'm the farthest thing from his mind."

"Honey, I know you're disappointed that he isn't here, but he'll be here soon. He called a little while ago and said that he's waiting at the airport for his flight to be cleared. The Boston flights have been delayed because of the fog."

During the past several months there had been other yellow roses with other sentimental messages when Garrett was supposed to be home for the weekend and at the last minute found he needed to 'stay over'. Lately, it seemed he spent more time in Boston than at home.

There had been an opening in management in the Atlanta office when Frank Fine decided to take early retirement. Shirley Mihalic, whose husband, Steve, also worked for Anderson-Walton, told her Garrett had been offered the job.

Mary was surprised to hear this. Surely Garrett would have mentioned it to her... unless he didn't want her to know about the offer. She could not believe he would pass up the opportunity to work in Atlanta and be at home with her, especially with their first child on the way. Maybe he intended to surprise her with the news. That had to be it. For several weeks she didn't let on that she had heard about the promotion and waited instead for Garrett to tell her, but he never did. Finally after a lot of worry and confusion, she confronted him with what she had heard. He was surprised she knew about Frank's retirement and appeared almost trapped by her inquiry.

"Yes, I was offered the job, but the timing wasn't right... Right now I need to be where I am... Trust me, honey... I can move up faster doing what I'm doing now. There will be another opening before long that will be far better than Frank's job. I'm sorry I didn't tell you. I should have, but I knew you would pressure me to take the job, and I knew it wasn't the right move for me."

Mary was angry.

"You could have at least discussed it with me. I don't like hearing these things through the rumor mill and having to pretend I knew all about it when I didn't know a darned thing."

The next weekend Garrett had come home on Thursday instead of his usual Friday schedule, and they had slept late and he had taken her out for breakfast. On Saturday they had spent the day roaming through antique stores and had driven to Jonesboro for dinner at a restaurant Mary especially liked. Mary knew she was being courted and appeased, but at least he was home, and they were spending time together.

Garrett finally arrived at the hospital late in the afternoon, some thirty hours after she had gone into labor. He beamed with pride at the sight of his firstborn. The child was unmistakably his father's son. There was nothing about him that even remotely resembled Mary. He was fair with blue eyes and the little bit of hair he had was definitely blonde. He looked exactly like Garrett's baby pictures.

"Honey, I'm so sorry you had to do this all by yourself. I was in Worcester at a sales conference, and Jan didn't reach me until after midnight. I should have come home last weekend and waited things out. Are you okay? You look a little tired. Was it hard for you, Baby?"

Garrett seemed sincere as he bent over Mary and gently stroked her forehead.

Mary had mixed feelings. She had been angry that he wasn't here, but now she was glad that he was.

"Yes, I'm okay, and yes, I am a little tired... And yes, it was hard, harder than I ever dreamed having a baby would be. I couldn't have him on my own." She began to cry. "I tried so long and so hard, but he just wouldn't come. I wanted to be awake when he was born, but I couldn't make it. They had to sedate me. I can barely remember someone saying that it was a boy. Then I went back to sleep, and I didn't really get to see him until this morning." She paused to look at their newborn son, the tears still in her eyes. "Isn't he beautiful?"

The baby made a weird little sound and sleepily opened his eyes. Garrett bent closer to get a better look at him.

"Jody, this is your father."

A few minutes later the nurse came to take Jody back to the nursery, and Mary and Garrett were alone.

"Can you ever forgive me for not being here? You shouldn't have had to go through this without me. We were both present at his conception, and I should have been with you for his birth. I am truly sorry."

Mary could not say anything to console Garrett in his remorse. He would have to bear that on his own. He was right. She should not have had to go through this without him at least pacing the halls. She wanted him there. Damn it! She needed him there! But he was not, and there was nothing either of them could do about that now.

At least he was finally here, and they had a fine, healthy son. They were no longer just husband and wife. Now the three of them were family.

Garrett sat by Mary's bed and held her hand, and once more she dozed. It seemed she would never get rested again. Once she roused and squeezed his hand, as if to make sure he was still there. She was glad it was today, and not yesterday, and that her husband was by her side. And down the hall their little one was sleeping the peaceful sleep of the very young.

CHAPTER 9

MARCH 29, 1974

Spring training is more than just endless days of grown men playing a boy's game in the warm Florida sunshine. It is a proving ground for the players, an opportunity to show that they are good enough and deserve to be in the major leagues. Jack knew he had proven himself well. Not only had he pitched well for the *Jazz* after being called up mid-season the previous year, but he had also had an excellent spring training.

There are no politics at this level of the game. Baseball is a business... a big business. And the players who make the team are the ones management feel can get the job done.

Seven very talented pitchers were competing for the five starting spots in the *Jazz* pitching rotation. Five of the pitchers would make the team. The other two would not. It was as simple as that. There had been many times throughout Jack's career when he had worried about being one of those who got cut, but this time he was confident he would not be one of them.

As spring training was drawing to a close, *Memphis Jazz* manager, Buck Foster, named Jack Roberts as his opening day pitcher. This was quite an honor, especially since this was only Jack's second season in the majors. Being named the opening day starter usually meant that you were considered the ace of the pitching staff. Buck Foster met with Jack before the announcement and told him they were counting on him.

"You're young and aggressive, and you're a damn good pitcher. We think you've got a great future in baseball. This is a good organization. They treat their people right, and if you have another year like you had last year, you'll be offered a long term contract with a very nice pay package."

Jack had not expected this. His first season with the *Jazz* had been a good one, but he never anticipated being given this much responsibility so soon.

He waited for Buck to continue, but when the robust manager got to his feet and extended his hand, Jack knew he had said all he intended to say.

There was a vote of confidence in the firm handshake of the seasoned manager.

"Thank you Mr. Foster. I'll do my best."

"That's all I ask, and 'Buck' will be fine."

When the meeting was over, Jack found the nearest phone. He wanted to tell his mom the good news. As he dialed the phone, he thought about his dad. How proud he would have been. Jack remembered calling him so many times after a game to celebrate a victory or discuss a loss. John Roberts was a gentle man who always knew just what to say. He never got too high or too low, and was always there to encourage and help him through the bad times. John Roberts also knew baseball and often helped Jack work out problems in his delivery.

He wished his dad was here to share the news, but he wasn't. Two years ago John had come home from work and sat down to supper. A few minutes later, he slumped over in his chair, the victim of a massive heart attack. Jack was playing minor league ball in Knoxville at the time, and rushed back to Chattanooga as soon as he got the word. In less than three hours he was at the hospital, but it was too late. His dad was gone.

At times likes these he really missed his dad. His father had not lived long enough to see him make it to the majors... And Jack regretted that most of all.

Virginia Roberts was delighted to hear the good news.

"I'll be there. Just get me a good seat. No, get two. Helen will want to come, too."

"Great!" Jack replied. Then there was a long pause.

Jack's mother knew what he was thinking even before he spoke.

"Mom, I would give anything if Dad could see me pitch this game." His voice broke and he could say no more.

"Jack, maybe he will. Just because he's not here doesn't mean he's not watching you."

"Yeah, maybe he will... And I'm going to do my damn best for him."

And for once Virginia Roberts didn't say anything to her son about his swearing.

*   *   *   *   *

APRIL 7, 1974

His head tossed feverishly on the pillow as he tried in vain to clear his mind and gain control of his thoughts. His tongue was thick from the morphine they had given him to ease the pain. He was vaguely aware of his surroundings. There were people who came and went from time to time, but mostly it was very quiet. His dark hair was moist from the constant thrashing about as he tried to shake the effect of the drugs.

Sleep, when it came, was only short fitful naps. And there were the dreams... over and over the dreams. Or were they dreams? They seemed so real.

It was the night of the high school prom, and he was there with a beautiful girl. She had dark brown hair and was wearing a yellow formal, and as they danced, she smiled up at him. But he couldn't remember her name... Over and over again he tried, but he couldn't remember... Then they were no longer at the dance. They were on a ball field, and he was pitching to her. She still wore the yellow formal, but she was not wearing a batting helmet. And he was afraid he would hit her. She was so pretty. They shouldn't be on the ball field. They should go back to the dance, except he didn't know how to get there, and he couldn't remember where he had left his car.

Finally he aroused himself enough to realize it was only a dream. He tried to open his eyes, but his eyelids were too heavy. Someone offered him a drink of water. The water was good and momentarily relieved the parched feeling in his throat. It was the lady in the blue pants suit. She was always there. Sometimes she sat in the big chair in the corner, and other times he would awaken to find her sitting beside his bed. But who was she? And what was she doing here?... And what was he doing here? He shouldn't be here. He should be at the dance with the girl in the yellow formal... But now she was gone. He mumbled something inaudible, and he heard the lady in blue say quietly, "Just try to rest. You'll feel better tomorrow."

Once more he drifted off to sleep, and once more he dreamed. He was a child running through the meadow. He tripped over a log and scraped his knee. It was bleeding and he was frightened. He managed to lift his head off the pillow and cried out, "Mama".

The lady in blue was immediately at his side trying to comfort him, but she did not bandage his knee. Instead, she placed a cold wash cloth over his forehead, and said, "It's okay. You just had a bad dream."

Whoever she was, she was kind, and he was glad she was there.

Finally, he dozed again, and this time he slept quietly and without dreaming. When he awakened, he still felt the confusion of his tortured brain, but it was not as bad as it had been before. Slowly he looked around the room and after awhile, he knew, or thought he knew, where he was. He was in a hospital. But why? Something must have happened to him, but he wasn't sure what. Then a nurse entered the room. She checked his I.V. and took his temperature and blood pressure, and then smiled down at him.

"Mr. Roberts, how do you feel?"

"I feel... kind of crazy... like my mind doesn't work right."

"I'm sure you do. You've had a lot of medication, but we'll begin to cut back tomorrow, and you'll start to clear up... We don't want you to hurt though. You can have another injection if you need it."

"I don't want another shot. I just want my head on straight."

A tear dropped involuntarily from his eye, as he wondered if she would give him the shot anyway. He felt as if he had no control over what was happening to him.

"You don't have to take the shot if you don't want it. That's up to you. But if you start hurting, let me know."

"Thanks," he mumbled.

He watched her leave the room and tried to get comfortable. God, he didn't want to hurt, but he didn't want another shot either. The medicine was blowing his mind. Everything was a blur.

As he turned on his left side, someone said, "Do you need anything before you settle in for the night?" It was the lady in blue. She was again standing by his bed.

"A drink of water, please. I'm so thirsty."

With extreme effort he opened his eyes and watched as she bent the straw and gently placed it in his mouth. He drew on the straw and drank the cool refreshing water she offered and stared intently at her as she held the cup. Finally, the faintest smile appeared as he struggled to keep his eyes open, and whispered the word, "Mom".

She was the lady in blue. She had been there all along, and he hadn't even known who she was.

"I'm glad you're here, Mom... I love you."

"I love you too."

Once more she watched his eyes close. The medicine was still taking its toll, but he needed the rest. Out of a need to do something for him, she turned off the lamp and adjusted the blinds to allow the soft amber glow from the streetlights to filter through. Then she settled into her chair and took comfort in the knowledge that tonight Jack knew she was here.

*   *   *   *   *

For the first time in several days he was able to discern between reality and the illusions that had haunted his dreams. He glanced at his watch on the nightstand. It was Monday, April 8th. Where had Saturday and Sunday gone? He remembered being brought to the hospital after the game on Friday, but that was the last thing he remembered, that and the worried expression in his Mom's eyes as she walked along beside the stretcher.

A large container of white mums sat on the bedside stand, along with an even larger arrangement of cut flowers, which he would later learn were from the ball club. His thoughts were quickly interrupted by the pain in his right shoulder. It felt as if his arm was on fire, and as he reached to rub it, he saw it was wrapped in yards of gauze and was held firmly in place by a jacket-type sling.

Across the room his mother was dozing in the chair where she had kept vigil throughout his ordeal. He could tell she was worn out, and he was certain she hadn't left his side since the surgery.

After awhile an aide brought in a lunch tray. Apparently he had slept through breakfast. The clear liquids and *Jell-O* didn't look very appetizing, but he tried to eat. He realized he needed his strength.

Later in the afternoon, the doctor who had performed the surgery came by to check on him. He ordered a new dressing put on the incision and told him he had prescribed pain pills if he needed them.

"They're not as hallucinating as the shots, so they shouldn't give you any problem, although they may make you a little drowsy. Just tell the nurse when you need them. We don't want you to be uncomfortable."

He would not take the pills unless he absolutely had to. He had already lost two days, which he had almost no recollection of, and he didn't want to lose anymore.

As the doctor made notes on his chart, Jack asked, "Will I be able to pitch again?"

"It's a little early to say, but with therapy and some hard work on your part, I don't see any reason why you shouldn't be as good as new."

"This year?" Jack had never been known for his patience.

Dr. Burnham smiled at Jack's eagerness and looked at the young man, so full of life, who had been struck down so quickly.

"Mr. Roberts, I don't want to give you false hope. You're a pitcher and I'm sure you understand the severity of a torn rotator cuff. I specialize in this kind of surgery and I've treated a lot of them. It's true, careers have been ended by this type injury, but yours is not that bad. The tear was not very long, and the surgery should take care of it. Right now it just needs time to heal."

Dr. Burnham could still see the question of 'when' on his patient's face.

"If you're looking for an exact date you'll be back on the mound, I can't give you that, but in all honesty, I don't think it will be this year."

The doctor saw the disappointment in Jack's eyes. He had seen a lot of young athletes who would have given their eyeteeth to get as good a report. Jack would pitch again. They never would. Nevertheless, he understood human nature and the frustration of a young man who, no doubt, had worked very hard to make it, only to be delayed by a freak injury.

Later in the day Jack asked for the pain pill which he had sworn earlier he would not take. One could only stand so much pain. Many thoughts ran through his head as he lay back on the pillow. He was frightened and uncertain. The doctor had said everything was going to be okay, but doctors aren't always right, and the doctor didn't know how bad it hurt.

Finally, the medication began to take effect and he slept, but it was not a peaceful sleep. He tossed and turned and the crazy dreams returned. Nothing seemed to fit or make sense. And just before he awoke, he dreamed what he feared most... In spite of all the doctor's reassuring words, the shoulder had not healed, and he would never pitch again.

He awoke screaming. As he sat upright in bed, his mother rushed to his side and held him close, as she had when he was a small boy and had a nightmare. And Jack realized it was only a dream... a very bad one.

Virginia sat quietly by his bed until he drifted off to sleep. He slept through most of the evening and when he awoke around ten o'clock, he felt better.

Virginia smiled down at him.

"Guess what?... Hank Aaron just hit number 715."

"Well, how about that? I'm proud for him. He's certainly paid his dues."

Jack was disappointed that he had missed it. It was probably the most historic moment in baseball history. Hank Aaron had just hit his 715th career homerun and broken Babe Ruth's all-time record.

He and his mother watched the rest of the Braves - Dodgers game, and waited eagerly for the post game interviews. One of the sportswriters asked Aaron how he felt when he realized the ball had cleared the fence, and he had broken Ruth's record.

Aaron replied, "It's over!... I'm just glad it's over."

"It's over!"... The words provoked a strange reaction in Jack... Was it also over for him?... Of course not. Why was he even thinking such a thought? The doctor said he would pitch again, and in time he would be 'as good as new'.

CHAPTER 10

The summer of 1974 was a period in Jack Roberts' life he would never forget... The newspapers were filled with accounts of Watergate. John Denver was singing *Take Me Home Country Roads*. And Jack had come home to Chattanooga to recover from his shoulder injury.

Virginia was glad he had decided to come home to recuperate, and so was Jack. There was no reason to stay in Memphis. His ball playing was over for the year.

The doctors said if everything went well, he should be able to pitch again, probably by next spring. However, all had not gone well, and after four weeks of daily physical therapy, it had been necessary to operate again.

Jack's mother spoke to the doctor immediately after the surgery.

"Everything went fine, Mrs. Roberts. He'll be in recovery for about an hour, and then they'll bring him to his room. We'll keep him overnight, and he should be ready to go home tomorrow. Next week we'll start the physical therapy again, and see how it goes... Do you have any questions?"

"Will he have full use of his arm?"

"I think so. It's going to take time and a lot of effort on his part. The physical therapy hurts like hell, but without it, he'll wind up a cripple. If he'll hang in there and not let up on the therapy, I think he'll be fine, but it's going to take time and a lot of patience. It was a bad injury. There's no denying that."

"Will he be able to play baseball again?"

"We'll have to wait and see. Sometimes these things do better than we anticipate. Pitching puts an unnatural strain on even a healthy arm. With therapy, Jack's arm should fully recover, but whether it will be able to bear that degree of pressure only time will tell."

Dr. Thompson looked at the attractive lady who stood before him. She was no fool. She understood that what he was really saying was 'probably not'. "It's tough being a parent, isn't it?... My daughter is going through a divorce. She's thirty-five years old, and I still wish I could take her on my knee and assure her that everything is going to be all right, but I know it won't be. I guess you never stop wanting to make everything all right for them."

As the doctor started to leave, Virginia extended her hand. "Thank you Dr. Thompson... for everything."

* * * * *

Jack grew weary of the daily therapy, but he kept at it. It seemed everything in his life was on hold, and he hated it. Patience was not one of his virtues. He was twenty-four years old, and he wasn't sick. He just had a shoulder that wouldn't work and that hurt like hell. The inactivity was driving him crazy. He tried jogging to keep in shape. He thought he could hold his shoulder stationary in the sling while he ran, but he quickly found that didn't work. Mostly he spent his time listening to the radio, playing his eight-tracks and reading the sports pages. Simon and Garfunkel, the Eagles and Olivia Newton-John filled in the background while he read the box scores. He would come home from the therapy sessions physically spent, and the music seemed to produce a soothing effect to both body and soul. After he got rid of the sling, he tried picking the guitar. He hadn't fooled with it since high school when he played with a rock group. He would strum for a little while, and then the pain would commence, and he would be forced to stop.

Everything hurt. He couldn't even move his fingers without feeling the pulling in his shoulder.

It was a slow and painful process, but he was gradually improving, and maybe in a couple of months he could put all this behind him and get on with his life.

One evening while Virginia was preparing supper, she heard Jack singing as he picked. He had played for several weeks, but he had not sung.

"Hey, that sounds pretty good," she said, as she set the table. "Maybe, you missed your calling."

The song was *Desperado* and his voice was mellow and strong.

He smiled as he laid the guitar aside. "That's a good song."

While they ate, he put a couple of tapes in the player and they listened first to the *Eagles'* version and then to the Johnny Rodriquez rendition.

"Which do you like best?"

Virginia considered the question, and with a mischievous grin replied, "I think I like yours best."

Again Jack smiled. "I think you're prejudiced."

"Could be, but you really sounded good."

As Virginia cleared away the dishes, she could hear Jack playing and singing on the patio. Lately he had been so frustrated and depressed. She was glad to see he finally had found something he enjoyed doing.

* * * * *

Kay's Kastle was the corner ice cream store. Almost every community had one, and the familiar red and yellow sign was particularly inviting on a hot summer day or on any day, for that matter, to an ice cream lover.

A feeling of nostalgia swept over Jack as he approached the store. It was the place he had come as a kid to get a chocolate ice cream cone. In his high school years it was the place everybody went after the game or came just to hangout. And it was the place he and Jeff Edwards had come to check out the girls. Jeff was a natural when it came to flirting, while Jack was a little shy, but before long Jack was getting his share of the attention.

"Damn!" Jeff would say. "You don't even try and the girls fall all over you."

Although Jack had tried 'playing the field', it just wasn't his style. He only had eyes for one girl. He began dating Mary Howard as soon as her parents would allow it. The two of them had been best friends since grade school, and their 'special' relationship seemed a natural progression of something that began a long time ago. It wasn't long until he knew he loved her, and it was obvious she felt the same about him, and they both knew that someday they would get married.

To everyone's surprise, Jeff was no longer the local flirt, but devoted all his attention to Karen Jefferson. It was their senior year, and they were doing some heavy fooling around. Everyone wondered if they would finish the year without Karen getting pregnant. Somehow they managed to graduate, and a few weeks later were married.

Jack knew he would never be content to spend his life working in a grocery store like Jeff. His dream was to play professional baseball. He was no Nolan Ryan, but he was pretty good, and if he continued to work hard and got a few breaks, he believed he had a chance. There was one thing for sure... He had to give it a shot.

Mary would wait until he got things worked out... He knew she would... Over and over she had told him he was the only man she would ever love.

And she had waited for awhile. But marriage seemed more important to her than to Jack. And eventually she grew tired of waiting. And eventually Garrett Davenport came along and convinced her he was her knight in shining armor.

Jack had been so sure she would wait... It wouldn't be long. He just needed a decent contract with a decent salary they could live on... But he had been wrong... 'How wrong we sometimes are when we think we've got life all figured out.'

He was about to order when he heard someone call his name, and he turned to see Susan Bennett.

"Hey, Susan! It's good to see you." And the smile on his face told her he was. "What are you doing these days?"

"I'm working at *Loveman's* this summer and hoping to get a job teaching this fall. I just finished college in June."

"How about a milk shake?"

"Sure. I'd love one."

Jeri was already scooping strawberry ice cream into the stainless steel container. It was what Susan always ordered.

"What are you doing home this time of the year?"

Apparently, she hadn't heard.

They found a table in the corner, and Jack told her the story. "So, I'm home to recover. It's not what I had planned for the summer. I had hoped to have a 10-2 record by now..." His voice trailed off as he added, "Maybe next year."

Susan wasn't sure what to say. It was a terrible thing to have happen, and she knew how much baseball meant to him.

"I'm sorry, Jack. I heard you were doing great."

Jack grinned. "Who told you that, my mom?"

"No! She doesn't have to brag on you. News gets around. We keep up with our hometown heroes."

"I don't feel like a hero, not now anyway." Again the frustration showed and he changed the subject. "Well, fill me in on everybody." Being away the last few years, he had lost touch with a lot of the people he had grown up with.

"Kathy Miller works at the library, and Barbara Jones is a nurse at Erlanger. Jeff and Karen Edwards have two boys, and Jeff works at a carpet mill in Dalton."

Jack smiled. "It's kind of odd, isn't it? Jeff was the biggest flirt around, and Karen rolled those big green eyes at all the guys, but when those two got together, it was dynamite. I don't think either of them ever looked at anyone else."

"We should all be so lucky."

He could tell from the tone of her voice and the look in her eyes that she had not been.

The conversation flowed easily between them. Jack hadn't realized how much he had missed the camaraderie of people his own age.

Finally Susan said, "I need to go. I have to do some more resumes. I think there must be at least a hundred applicants for every teaching job out there."

"Are you walking?" Jack asked.

"No, I've got my car."

Jack grinned mischievously. "Too bad. I was about to offer to walk you home. "

The thought brought back old memories and Susan started to laugh. "You did one time... remember? I was in fifth grade, and I won a blue ribbon for my science project, and you carried my nuclear reactor home for me, so it wouldn't get squashed." Suddenly she was embarrassed. He had probably long since forgotten, and it had been silly of her to mention it.

"And your mama made lemonade when we got to your house."

He had remembered! Susan no longer felt embarrassed. They were just old friends reminiscing, and it was pleasant to remember the days of their youth when all their problems now seemed very small.

"There's something else I bet you never knew... I was madly in love with you from the day you walked me home until tenth grade."

Jack looked straight into Susan's eyes, and with an easy smile asked, "What happened in tenth grade?"

"Someone else came along."

"He must have been pretty special to make you drop me like a hot potato."

Susan's eyes grew a trifle sad. "He was."

Something in the tone of her voice told Jack he shouldn't pursue the matter further. He suspected 'his replacement' was no longer a part of Susan's life, and that the remembering made her sad.

As they left the ice cream shop, Susan motioned to a '65 Mercury Comet that looked somewhat older than its years.

"Hop in, and I'll give you a lift."

The windows were rolled down, and the car had either never had air-conditioning or the air-conditioning had long since ceased to work, but this didn't bother Susan. She was, as Jack remembered, just Susan, and she didn't feel the need to be something she was not.

It seemed they got to his house in no time, and as he got out of the car, he was reluctant to say good-bye. He walked around to Susan's side of the car, and as he propped his elbows on her window, a big smile broke across his face.

"Thanks for the ride, shortstop."

Susan laughed.

"Nobody has called me that in years... I was pretty good, though, wasn't I?"

"Yeah, you were... and pretty damned cocky, too."

That year they only had eight guys for the neighborhood baseball team, and Susan said she would play, but only if she could play shortstop. But they didn't need a shortstop. Bucky Martin was their shortstop. They needed a first baseman. But Susan wouldn't play unless they let her play short. Bucky finally agreed to play first, and Susan played short.

Jack had a mental picture of the twelve-year-old girl who had completed their ball team that summer. She was short and had thick blonde curls that bounced under her cap, which she always wore turned slightly sideways. But she played her position well, probably better than Bucky, and she finished the season with the second highest batting average on the team.

"I guess those were what they call the 'good old days'... Jack, it's really good to see you. Thanks for the milk shake."

"Same here, Susan. Take care of yourself."

He started to walk away, and then turned and walked back. "I'll call you sometime... Okay?"

"Sure!"

Susan quickly scribbled her number on a *McDonalds'* napkin and handed it to him. Then she was gone, but for Jack the day seemed a little brighter.

*　　*　　*　　*　　*

On August 9th, Jack came home from therapy to find his mother standing in the living room with one hand on the vacuum cleaner and her eyes fixed intently on the television screen.

"What's going on?"

Without taking her eyes off the screen, she replied, "The president has just resigned."

As they watched the historic event unfold, he wondered how many other people across the nation had been stopped dead in their tracks by the news that Richard Nixon was vacating the highest office of the land.

The now 'former' president stood on the White House lawn with his wife Pat at his side. She was smiling bravely and attempting to hold back the tears. Beside her were their daughters, Julie and Tricia, and their husbands. Nixon had briefly addressed the American people and was now waving the familiar V for victory sign. It was a poignant moment and a sad time not only for him and his family, but also for the American people who had placed their trust in him. In a few moments the Nixons would board the waiting helicopter which would take them to the presidential plane, and for the last time they would board Air Force One, forever leaving behind the power and prestige of the Washington years.

Pat Nixon probably didn't mind leaving it all behind, for her it was no doubt a relief, but for Nixon, it was different. Men seem to find it harder to walk away from their dreams, especially when they have given up so much and worked so hard to attain them.

"It's kind of sad, isn't it?" Virginia said with a sigh, not really expecting a reply.

"Mom, the man messed up. He was the president, and he betrayed the trust of the people who put him there. I don't feel any compassion for him. It was his own fault. A lot of people have their careers ended through no fault of their own."

It was the first hint of bitterness she had seen in Jack, and she understood how he must feel. He had done nothing to cause his problem. It had been an accident... a cruel twist of fate.

Day after day he went for therapy and returned home to begin again the painful exercises designed to rehabilitate and strengthen his arm. Was it all for naught? She wondered. Would he ever be able to pitch again? But she held onto the small remnant of hope the doctor had given her, and she prayed daily that Jack would get a second chance to play the game he loved so much.

* * * * *

On August 16th, Dr. Thompson told Jack he would never play baseball again. It came as no great surprise. On that fateful night in April, he had somehow known it was the end of baseball for him. It had felt as if the shoulder had literally been torn from his body, and he seriously doubted it would ever work properly again. He had seen a few players come back after injuries such as this, but it took something off their game, and they were soon washed up. Or they tried so damn hard to throw like before that they ruined their arm and paid for their efforts with a lifetime of pain. Jack was not a fool. He wouldn't throw away the rest of his life in a futile attempt to be something he could never be.

Dr. Thompson assured him that the shoulder had mended well and would continue to grow stronger as he exercised and used it more. "It has done amazingly well, and you should be able to do just about anything you want, but in all honesty, I can't recommend that you return to pitching. It would put too much stress on the shoulder."

There was nothing more Dr. Thompson could say. At times like this, it was difficult being a doctor. He had just written finished to this young man's dream, and he sensed how much it had meant to him. Yet, as he looked into the solemn eyes of Jack Roberts, he saw something that defied defeat... He would make it. The determination was there... In a lifetime of practicing medicine, Joe Thompson had seen a lot of injuries such as this one. Oftentimes the patients wound up cripples for life. They would go home, lie on the couch in their underwear, drink beer, and live off their families, or manage to get a welfare check, and 'cop out' on life. But as the two shook hands, Dr. Thompson knew Jack Roberts was not one of these. He had more to him.

The thermometer over the bank showed 93 degrees, and the day was miserable in more ways than one. He unlocked his car and for a few minutes sat in silence, searching for something that wasn't there. Then he cranked the car and pulled out of the parking lot. He was not ready to go home. There was someone there who would hurt just as much when she heard the news. But somehow the car turned instinctively homeward... Sometimes there's just nowhere else to go.

Jack's mother listened to the report in silence. Although she had known the probability of him playing baseball again was unlikely, still she had dared to hope and had prayed daily for a miracle.

There was not a trace of tears in his eyes. Perhaps they had all been cried, or would be, at some private time in some private place, as would her own. She could not resist putting an arm around him, as she searched for something to say. He returned the embrace and for a moment, they clung to each other, each drawing strength from the other.

It was Jack who spoke first.

"I'll be all right Mom. It's just gonna' take time. I guess I wanted a miracle, and apparently that was not meant to be."

As hard as she tried, Virginia could not find the words to say to give hope to her son, and finally looking up into his eyes, she said simply, "I love you."

"I love you, too, Mom... very much."

There was nothing she could do. In time Jack would find his own way. Eventually a new door would open. It always did.

Virginia Roberts was not a bitter person. She had learned a long time ago that "it's an ill wind that blows nobody good," and out of all this something good would ultimately come, but right now that was of little consolation.

After supper Jack picked his guitar, but today he did not sing. This would be a tough weekend for him. When he was little, she could pick him up, and hold him close, and soon the pain would go away, but this time she couldn't make the pain go away. One day it would, but right now it could only be endured.

Jack played his guitar as long as he could. Finally he got into his car and backed out of the driveway, not knowing where he was going, only knowing he had to get away. Almost without direction the car turned onto Van Cleave, the street he had avoided all summer. But tonight, for some strange reason, he felt compelled to drive by Mary's old house.

It looked the same. Mr. and Mrs. Howard weren't people given to making a lot of changes. The porch swing had a fresh coat of paint, but it was the same shade of green, and the petunias were still blooming in the same planters where they had bloomed as long as he could remember.

It was like going back in time. They were happy times that he and Mary had shared in those days. He had a part-time job that didn't pay much, but they had not needed much. Being together was enough. They were young and happy, and terribly in love, as only the very young can be, and still largely unscathed by the world's cares.

Mary had it all planned... They would finish school, get married, and have two kids, a boy first and then a girl... Jack would work at something... They didn't know what... And he would come home at night to her and the kids... And they would make love, and nothing else would matter... In time he would get promotions, and they would have more money, and they would take vacations like regular people, and go out whenever they chose, and live the so called 'good life'. Until then she would be content to be Jack's wife and the mother of their children... These were her dreams.

He thought of Mary... Crazy little thing... All she ever wanted was to be his wife, and he had thrown it all away to play baseball. Now that too was gone. He had wanted more from life than Mary had. The chance had come for him to play professional baseball, the one thing he wanted more than anything else. He had worked hard at it, and he had made it, but in the process he had lost Mary... But baseball hadn't loved him back. It had given him a taste of glory, then snatched it all away.

It isn't fair, Jack thought. I tried so hard. I gave up so much. Why did it have to turn on me? And why didn't Mary wait? Why did she have to marry that damn stockbroker? It was me she loved. But he knew the answer... It was the damn baseball. He had given it all he had, but he also had given Mary all he had. Professional baseball was not a job that you come home from every night or where you have your weekends free to spend with your loved ones. He had come home every chance he could, but those chances were few and far between. He had called as often as he could, but he couldn't hold her close or look into her eyes over the phone. And all the telephone "I love you's" could not make up for not being there.

But she knew he loved her. He had told her a thousand times.

"Why didn't you wait, Mary? Why? I never stopped loving you. I still do." He found himself speaking aloud.

Tears welled up in his eyes and obscured his vision, and he pulled the car off the road and into the old cemetery at the top of the hill. And there bent over the steering wheel, he cried like a baby.

It was a place where many had wept before and many would weep again. Jack was alone except for the grounds' keeper who was cutting grass in another section of the cemetery, and the distant roar of the mower muffled his sobs.

Finally, the tears subsided and he lifted his head and looked out at the place where he had taken refuge. The tears he had shed seemed to bring cleansing to his tormented mind. It was not over. Hurt has a way of lingering, but the heartrending experience he had just been through had produced some measure of acceptance... Acceptance of two things... One, he would never play baseball again... And two, regardless of how much he loved Mary, she belonged to someone else.

He got out of his car and walked. It was a quiet peaceful place, and now more than anything else he needed peace.

After awhile he returned to the car. And although he was still in the valley of despair, today the healing had begun.

*   *   *   *   *

Monday would be Labor Day, the official end of summer. Susan had taken a position teaching public school music with the Davidson County School System and would be leaving Sunday.

He would miss her. She had been one of the few bright spots in his life during this frustrating period, and he was glad their paths had crossed. They had spent a lot of time together during the summer. Sometimes they swam or played rummy, and sometimes they just talked and listened to the stereo.

Today they had packed a picnic lunch and left early in the morning to go to Lookout Mountain. It had been years since either of them had been to *Rock City* and they laughed as they made their way through *Fat Man's Squeeze* and crossed the swinging bridge. Then they stood high atop Lookout Mountain where from a certain vantagepoint you can see seven states.

From there they went to Point Park and spread a blanket on the ground, and ate fried chicken and potato salad and drank lemonade. Susan had fixed pimento cheese sandwiches, but those would have to wait until later. They both agreed they could not eat another bite.

It was not as hot as it had been earlier in the week, and they were having a good time. Tomorrow was Saturday and Susan would be packing, so this was their last real day together.

After lunch they rode bikes and explored the mountain trails. Being with Susan was comfortable and easy. As they came down one of the ruggedly beautiful parts of the mountain, Jack again wondered about Susan and the guy she had mentioned the first day they ran into each other at *Kay's*. Obviously she had been in love with him, and he wondered what had happened to the relationship. He had thought that perhaps one day Susan might choose to talk about it, but she had not.

Sometimes when they were listening to music a particular song would seem to touch off something inside her. She would momentarily seem to lapse into another place and another time. He knew there was a story, but he wasn't sure he would ever hear it. But Susan had been his friend, and her companionship had made what otherwise would have been an almost unbearable time in his life at times very pleasant.

With their legs spent from the bicycling, they returned to the park and got cokes from the cooler.

"You want something to eat?" Susan asked.

"Yeah, I think I do."

Susan brought out the sandwiches and brownies they hadn't gotten to earlier. It was nice to rest. They had put in a pretty good day of it, and they sat quietly, lost in their separate thoughts. Finally, Jack lay back on the blanket and pulled his cap over his eyes to shut out the sun that was just starting to go down.

"I don't know about you, shortstop, but I can't handle anymore biking. Mind if we sit awhile?"

"That's fine with me. My legs feel like toothpicks. I don't think they would bear me up."

Susan stretched out on the blanket beside him and thought of her future. She was excited about her new job. She had always wanted to teach, but the job market had been so saturated with teachers, she had wondered if she would get the opportunity.

After a while Jack sat upright. Susan suspected he had been dozing.

"A penny for your thoughts." He offered.

"I was just thinking about Nashville and my new job. I hope I'm going to be what they want."

"You'll be fine, but I'll miss you."

"I'll miss you, too." She realized the whole course of Jack's life had been altered. "Do you know what you'll do?"

"Week after next I'll meet with the team management, so I can't officially make any plans until I've talked to them. They're still paying my salary, but that's about to change... I guess I could try selling vacuum cleaners." Jack smiled and then continued. "I thought I might go to Florida for a few days. Mom hasn't had a vacation in a long time. She has spent her whole summer looking after me. So I'm hoping she'll go to Panama City with me."

"She's a nice lady, Jack. I'm sure she'll go... Think of me in Nashville trying to teach a bunch of first graders to sing *My Country 'Tis of Thee* while you're basking in the Florida sun."

"Yeah, and you'll love every minute of it, and they'll love you, 'Miss Susan'," Jack teased, as he tried to sound like a little kid in elementary school.

"I hope so."

Far off in the distance an occasional streak of lightning lit up the summer sky, but it was too far away to pose any threat.

"It's beautiful out tonight," Susan remarked. "In fact, it's been a beautiful day." Her voice trailed off, almost as if she were talking to herself.

A gentle breeze had started to blow, and with the setting of the sun, the mountain air was suddenly quite cool. Susan sat with her arms locked about her.

"Did you bring a jacket?" Jack sensed she was cold.

"No, but I'm fine," she lied, as she wrapped the corner of the blanket around her legs.

"You're not fine. You're freezing! You want to go?"

"Not really. I think I could stay here forever. It's so peaceful. Let's stay awhile longer."

Neither of them had brought a jacket, as they hadn't expected to be here when the sun went down.

"I've got an idea. Why don't you put the picnic stuff away?" Jack said.

As Susan put away the picnic basket, Jack took a couple of stadium cushions from the car and covered them with a blanket. As they sat down, he pulled the blanket around them.

"How does that feel?"

"Wonderful! I was about to freeze." Susan confessed.

"I knew you were. Are you okay now?"

"Yes, I'm snug as a bug in a rug."

"That's what you look like... 'A bug in a rug'," Jack joked as he looked at the unpretentious young lady sitting next to him. She had been his friend through one of the most difficult times of his life, and he knew that wherever their respective lives might take them, there would always be a special bond between them.

For awhile they sat without talking. Finally Susan broke the silence. "Jack, how long did it take you to get over Mary?" She asked without any concern that perhaps she had no right to ask.

"I'm not sure that I ever did." Again there was a pause. "After awhile you learn to put it behind you, and you don't think about it quite as often as in the beginning. For the most part, I suppose I'm over it, but there are still things, certain reminders of the past, that hurt like hell. I don't know how long it takes to get past that."

Susan sat very still for a moment.

"I just wondered. There was someone in my life too... someone I've never quite gotten over," and then she was very quiet again.

"Want to talk about it?" He asked.

"I don't know if I can. It's something I've never been able to discuss with anyone."

He waited for Susan to continue, and when she did not, he said, "Look, Susan, if you want to talk, I'm here to listen. If you don't want to, that's okay too. I understand... believe me, I do. I probably have told you more tonight about how I felt about Mary than I've ever told anyone. It isn't easy to talk about things that open up old wounds, but sometimes it helps."

He moved closer and took her hand in his and waited. Either, she would tell him or she would not, and the decision would have to be hers.

And there on the mountaintop, Susan finally told Jack the story of her off-and-on relationship with Mike Kennedy. They had dated during high school and later when they had both gone to college at U.T.C. The problem was that Mike could never be content with just one person in his life. They had broken up a number of times, and each time Mike would come back to her and penitently declare how much he loved her and assure her that there would never be anyone but her. She had loved him so much that each time she wanted to believe that this time it would be different.

There had been one point in their relationship when everything was going well, and Mike had not cheated for a long time, and they were truly happy. Susan thought that perhaps he had sowed his wild oats and was ready to settle down. He had asked her to marry him and she had said, "Yes". He had given her a beautiful engagement ring, and they had been gloriously happy for six months. Then it happened again.

Susan had a late class and rather than wait for her, Mike went home to study for finals or at least that was what he told her. However, as she drove home later that night, she saw his car parked at Ross' Landing, and she knew he had not gone home. Suspecting that he was back to his old habits, she circled the parking lot and saw what she feared most. There he was in the back seat of his car engaged in a passionate embrace with another woman.

Susan did not concern herself with who the woman was. It didn't matter anymore. There had been so many over the years. The only thing that mattered was she was engaged to marry a man who had no idea what truth and being faithful was all about.

This had happened two years ago, and since then, each time Mike had grown tired of his current lover, he had come running back to her. He would tell her he still had the ring, which she had promptly returned after the incident at Ross' Landing, and that no one else would ever wear it. Then he would insist that he had never loved anyone but her, that he never would, and that he wanted her more than anyone else in the world.

"You know, the truth is I believe he does love me, as much as he's capable of loving anyone, but he could never be faithful. There would always be someone else. I know that. I don't think I can settle for that, Jack, even though there are times when I feel like I'll never stop loving him."

Her voice quivered and this time it was not from the cold. Jack put an arm around her and wished he could have a round or two with this jerk who had hurt Susan so much. He knew Mike's type. Their egos kept them constantly seeking new conquests, while at the same time assuring the one who really loves them that their latest fling didn't mean a thing. They won't just walk away and leave. They torture and torment with their false promises. Jack didn't even know the guy, but he hated him.

"How long has it been since you've heard from him?"

"The day before I met you at Kay's."

"Susan, you don't deserve this. You're a person of worth. Don't let him do this to you. Get out of his life and get him out of yours. Please promise me you won't let him play with you like this anymore."

"I haven't seen him in almost a year. It hasn't been easy to say 'no', but I can't live like this. I don't plan to see him again... ever! He may love me, but he doesn't love me enough!" Then Susan hesitated and very sadly declared. "But there were some good times, and that's the part that's so hard to put behind."

It had been hard for Jack, too, and he knew that time was the only answer. He just wished he could say something that would help.

"I'm doing better, and eventually, I'll be okay. I just wondered how long it took you to get over Mary. I know you loved her very much."

Jack was silent for a moment, and then quietly said, "Yeah, I did... very much... and it does take awhile. And even then, there are times when it all returns like a mighty flood and you have to deal with it all over again... I suppose it's like losing someone in death. One day they're here and the next day they're gone."

Again he pulled her close.

"Susan, promise me you won't go back to him. You deserve better than that."

He waited for a response, but she said nothing. She only stared out into the darkness. Then he asked, "Have you gone out with anyone else?"

"Only one. His name is Phil Warren. We were in school together at Middle Tennessee. He graduated last year and works in Memphis. It isn't anything serious. We've gone to a couple of movies and once to a James Taylor concert."

"What's he like?"

Susan thought for a moment and then smiled weakly. "Compared to Mike, he's a little dull."

"And if you don't compare him to Mike?"

"Then he's probably very nice."

"Good."

They sat very still and quiet for awhile, and Jack felt Susan's tight little body begin to relax as he held her close. He felt there had been some sense of relief in the telling of her story.

Once she looked up at Jack and said simply, "Thanks, Jack... Thanks for being my friend."

"Thanks for being mine. I'm going to miss you, Susan... You know that?"

Susan nodded. "Yeah, me too."

Jack felt his throat grow dry and a strong physical yearning surged through his body. It would be easy to make love to Susan tonight. The whole setting was right... the moon, the stars, the mountaintop, even the blanket. And Susan was lonely and uncertain of what lay ahead for her, the same as he was. It would be so easy to lose themselves in the passion of the moment and their shared pain, and to assuage their physical needs with little sense of guilt. He had seen the look in Susan's eyes and suspected that she had similar feelings.

But he and Susan had been friends, and although they had shared a lot throughout the summer, they had not been lovers. There would be nothing wrong with it, if they allowed themselves to make love tonight. They were two consenting adults. But it would change their whole relationship. They could never be 'just friends' again... And sometimes 'friends' are better than 'lovers'.

*　　*　　*　　*　　*

Susan was gone... And so was the summer of '74.

Jack was unsure of what lay ahead for him, but the one thing he was certain of was that time does not stand still. He had to move forward in some direction.

Everything was ready for the trip to Panama City, and he and his mom would leave early the next day. He hoped they could locate Buddy Bowers. The last time he had heard, Buddy was playing guitar at a club in Panama City, but you never knew about Buddy. He didn't stay in one place long.

Jack and Buddy had grown up together, and Buddy was the best friend Jack ever had. They had played together in a rock group in high school, although Buddy was probably the only one in the band who had any real talent. Jack knew his mom would like to see Buddy too. She had been almost a second mom to Buddy.

Once again Jack's thoughts turned to Susan. She should be settled into her apartment by now. She had come by earlier in the day to say good-bye. Everything was packed and she was ready to leave for Nashville. When she got out of the car, he noticed she was carrying a package.

"What have you got there?" He grinned.

"It's just a little something for you for being such a good friend."

Jack could tell from the package it was an album, but when he unwrapped it, he was surprised.

"Kris Kristofferson! When did you turn country?" He laughed.

"He's not country! He's Uh... Uh... He's good. That's what he is."

Susan, like most of her generation, had grown up on rock and roll, and this guy was definitely not rock and roll. So it seemed strange that she would be into someone like Kristofferson.

Jack placed the record on the turntable, and began to read the profile on the back cover, but there was something about the singer and his lyrics that commanded his full attention, so he laid the album cover aside. He would read it later.

He listened to the album all the way through and then played it again. Susan was right. The guy was good! Real good!... And before Jack went to sleep, he knew every word to *Me and Bobbie McGee*.

And when he slept, he dreamed of a little blonde shortstop and a summer picnic high atop Lookout Mountain.

CHAPTER 11

The date was July 4th, 1976, the bicentennial of the United States of America and all across the nation people were celebrating the two-hundredth birthday of their country. Parades and speeches by local dignitaries highlighted the festivities, which would be concluded by brilliant firework displays. The celebration stretched from rural America with its high school marching bands and decorated floats to Fifth Avenue and a celebration more grand than the Annual Macy's Thanksgiving Day parade.

Atlanta also was celebrating, and while Mayor Andrew Young and soon-to-be President Jimmy Carter were heading up the ceremonies on Peachtree Street, the Anderson-Walton employees were celebrating with a lavish picnic at a private club in the suburbs.

The affair was catered in grand fashion with a traditional Fourth of July menu of barbecue, baked beans and cole slaw, and the typically American hot dogs and apple pie. Near the pool was a well-stocked bar with a professional bartender on hand. No expense had been spared to make this the perfect summer outing. Even C.E.O. George Anderson was present to meet and greet the employees and their families.

This was the one party of the year where the employees' children were included, and they were having a fabulous time, jumping in and out of the pool and plying themselves with hot dogs and homemade ice cream.

The tennis courts were open for the tennis buffs, and there was horseshoe pitching for those who opted for something slower paced. A lot of the adults, however, were gathered around the pool, eating and drinking, and mixing and mingling.

The casual summer clothes worn by the women were indicative of a very exclusive fashion show, and it was clear that many came to see and be seen.

Shortly after dark, there would be fireworks and a laser display, followed by dancing to the music of *Southwind*. Everything was extremely elegant, and as always, Anderson-Walton was doing things in style.

All afternoon Mary had tried to avoid Elaine Douglas, mainly because she didn't want to listen to her. Elaine thrived on scandal and always had a late-breaking story to tell. As usual, she was cornering one woman after another spreading her vicious gossip like wildfire.

A couple of times before, Mary had been placed in the position of having to listen to her dirt. What the other Anderson-Walton couples did was of no concern to her, and she didn't care to hear it.

Elaine was dressed in royal blue hot pants with an off-white satin top that barely covered her midriff, and while she was spending her time with the women now, after dark she would concentrate on the men. Alex was stupid to put up with her, but he was a little strange himself.

Mary spent most of the afternoon with Madeline. Garrett and Doug joined them when they were not talking shop with some of the other fellows. The party was nice enough, but Mary had never felt really comfortable with the Anderson-Walton crowd. They seemed to live in a different world, and it made conversation difficult beyond the usual "Hello... How are you?" point.

It would soon be time for the dancing to begin, and Mary excused herself to go to the ladies' room. As she approached the lounge, she overheard Elaine talking to Cynthia Mason.

"Cynthia, have you heard the latest about Garrett Davenport?"

Mary stopped in the hall and waited. So, now her husband was the target of Elaine's slander.

Cynthia said she had not.

"Well, you're not going to believe this." Elaine paused. "Let me get something to smoke, and I'll tell you about it."

Things were quiet for a moment while Elaine apparently lit her cigarette.

"Elaine!" Cynthia exclaimed, "are you smoking pot?"

"Sure... You want some?"

"I don't think so. I've never fooled with the stuff."

"It won't hurt you. Honest. It just gives you a nice buzz and loosens you up a bit... Come on, Cindy, take a toke."

"That last martini I had loosened me up enough... Maybe I better not."

"Cindy, would I offer it to you if I thought it would get you high? It just gives you a nice warm glow. Come on. You'll feel great, I promise you."

Cynthia did not protest further. Mary heard her cough and knew she had taken a toke of the joint.

"Now sit down and let me tell you about Garrett. He's been having an affair with a Citibank rep in Boston."

"Really? Does his wife know?"

"Do we ever? They get on their big jet airplanes and fly off to some distant city, and who knows what any of them get into or who they sleep with while they're away from home."

"You don't think Alex is sleeping around, do you?"

"I don't know and frankly, I don't give a damn, just as long as he keeps me up in the style to which I've grown accustomed. He's not doing anything that I wouldn't do if the right guy asked me."

"But anyway, getting back to Garrett. He's a good-looking devil, you know, and they say she's quite a looker herself. Her father owns a steel mill in Pittsburgh and is reportedly filthy rich."

"Is she married?"

"No, she's footloose and fancy free, and they say she has a fabulous apartment in Boston. Very convenient for Garrett, wouldn't you say?"

"I don't know how well I'd deal with it if I found out Kirk was fooling around."

"Well, keep your eyes closed and look the other way. It happens, you know. And why should you give up your nice lifestyle? Divide the spoils! That's the way I look at it. I'm not saying that Kirk would. Maybe you've got one of the good guys who takes his wedding vows seriously. Unfortunately, honey, the majority don't... How are you feeling? Are you buzzing yet?"

"I'm buzzing," Cynthia admitted. "I feel like I'm floating."

"That's it exactly, and we all need to float sometimes. Now you don't even have to worry about whether Kirk's getting it on with some sexy blonde. When you're floating, it doesn't make any difference."

"Please, Elaine, you're torturing me."

And that was exactly Elaine's game... to torture while pretending to be your friend. She was getting Cynthia high on pot, telling her lies about Garrett and some Boston hussy, and at the same time insinuating to Cynthia that her own husband was probably cheating too. How cruel and vicious Elaine was, Mary thought, as she tried not to think about what she had just overheard.

She wanted to go home immediately and have it out with Garrett. The thought of having to dance and act like everything was okay angered her, but what she had overheard was a lie, nothing more. That's all Elaine had to do, go about spreading lies and making people miserable.

And that's exactly what she had succeeded in doing... to both her and Cynthia. It had ruined Mary's day and made her totally miserable. And there was probably not the slightest truth in what she had said... But what if there was? What if Garrett was having an affair? And deep down inside her was the gnawing reminder that where there's smoke, there's usually fire.

It's just not true, Mary reasoned. He couldn't be. I would know it. I'm not that naive... Or was she?

She tried to let it go, to brush it off and forget about it, assuming it was just another one of Elaine's stories, but it would not go away. The harder she tried to forget it, the stronger it laid hold, until finally she knew she had to confront Garrett.

The next evening as they dressed to go to the club for dinner, she asked Garrett about the alleged 'other woman'.

Garrett didn't bother to turn around as he tied his tie in the dresser mirror, while surveying his image approvingly.

"Mary, it's you I love. Why would I want to fool around with someone else?"

"Well, it's making the rounds of the office rumor mill. It's the old story that the wife's the last one to know, isn't it? Garrett, I don't think it's a rumor. I believe it's true. And I shudder to think how much I've loved you and longed for you while you were off sleeping with some other woman."

She could see the muscles in his back stiffen as he slowly straightened and stared blankly into the mirror. He still avoided looking at her.

"Surely, you don't believe that?" He said, as he finally turned to face Mary. The look in his eyes reflected his guilt.

Mary dropped her head and stared blankly at the floor. How could he?

She was hurt more than she had ever been in her life. She felt cheap, cheaper than the Boston whore he had been sleeping with all this time. She had been so naive. She had missed him so much all week, and she could hardly wait to see him on Friday. She had longed for him so badly, to see him, to touch him, to feel him touch her, and to turn herself completely over to him. And all the while he was sleeping with another woman.

She hated him! And she hated Elaine Douglas. If it wasn't for her, this wouldn't be happening... But that wasn't true. It wasn't Elaine's fault. Elaine was not the one who had been unfaithful. Garrett was the one.

"God, what a fool I've been," Mary cried out and ran from the room, tears flowing down her cheeks, as Garrett followed her, still insisting it was all a mistake and he could explain if she would only listen.

But she was in no mood for listening. She had heard quite enough. She knew his game. He would take her in his arms, and hold her, and kiss her, and cajole her. He would say it was the worst mistake of his life, that it had happened only once, and that he was so ashamed. It would never happen again, and he could never love anyone but her.

Now she knew why the condoms had been in his brief case. The signals had been there all along, but she had chosen to ignore them. She closed the door to the guestroom and fell across the bed, wetting the pillow with her tears.

CHAPTER 12

SEPTEMBER 1977

Summer lingered on even though it was late September. Any day now the frost would come signaling the arrival of fall. Mary loved the autumn months, but this year she was reluctant to bid good-bye to summer.

She had graduated college in the spring and with studying behind her, she had purposed to spend the entire summer with Jody. Each day was a new adventure. They planted flowers, worked in the yard and spent endless hours in the pool. Jody had learned to swim the summer before just when it was time to close the pool, and had been certain he would 'forget how' before summer came again.

The summer had been especially beautiful with just enough rain to keep everything fresh and green, and lots of clear, sunny days. It was definitely not a summer to spend indoors, and while there were some hot, muggy days interspersed with the more pleasant ones, she and Jody still chose the beauty of the outdoors over the cool comfort of indoor living. Jody was at a wonderful age, and they had enjoyed doing so many things together these last few months.

At the close of the day, Jody would curl up in her lap, the lingering smell of bubble bath still on his body, tired from the day's activities, and eager for a bedtime story. Most of the time he was fast asleep before she finished the story. Each time she carried him to bed and reached down to brush back the damp, blonde curls from his forehead, she was keenly aware of how much she loved him. He was the fulfillment of all her fondest dreams, and as she tucked him in and placed Winnie the Pooh by his side, she understood completely the natural instinct that causes the mother lion to fight so fiercely for her young.

Garrett continued to spend most of his weeks in Boston, but he usually came home on the weekend. It had been four years since he turned down the offer to work in Atlanta. The 'better opportunity' had not materialized, and she doubted that he would have accepted it if it had. He obviously enjoyed what he was doing, and the travelling didn't bother him. He liked Boston and it wasn't hard to sense the excitement he felt on Sunday when it came time to pack his bags and head for the airport.

Although he insisted he missed her and Jody terribly and looked forward to the time when they could be together more, it was plain to see he wasn't anxious to change anything.

There was a time when she had worried about it, but now she had come to accept it almost as a way of life. The sad part was that Garrett was missing a truly wonderful time in Jody's life that he would never be able to recapture.

The weekends, however, were nice and gave them something to look forward to, and Garrett certainly provided well for them financially. She tried not to dwell on the fact that Garrett had passed up the opportunity to work in the Atlanta office, where he could be home every night, because when she did, she inevitably felt that not only had he rejected the job offer, but he had also rejected her.

As she sat on the park bench, she thought of the party Saturday. It was not something she had looked forward to, but Garrett had insisted that they needed to entertain more, and had suggested they have the crowd from the office over this weekend for an informal get together.

She never cared for office parties and couldn't help resenting the fact that the party would leave them little time to spend together as a family. However, as she had made preparations, she found she was actually looking forward to it. She hoped it would go well and everyone would have a good time.

It would be nice to have company, and it would give Garrett's co-workers a chance to see their home. He was very proud of it, and so was she. She never dreamed she would live in such a beautiful house, and almost everyone who saw it remarked that it looked like Tara in *Gone With the Wind*.

She was anxious to be a good hostess and make Garrett proud of her, and she especially hoped he would like the dress she had chosen for the occasion. It was made of pale blue eyelet with a scoop neckline, and it seemed to sort of 'go with' the house.

Her thoughts were suddenly interrupted as Jody came running up, accompanied by a little black boy he had met at the park. They were dusty and sweaty from playing on the monkey bars and pushing each other on the swings, but obviously they were having a good time.

"Mama, this is Corey. He's my friend. We've been playing on the monkey bars."

"That sounds like fun," Mary said, and turned to Jody's newfound friend. "Hi, Corey. How are you?"

"Hi. I like your son. We've been having fun. Can he come to visit me sometime at my house? I don't got nobody to play with. My daddy was a soldier, and he got killed in the war. My mama works at the hospital, and my grandma lives with us and looks after me."

Poor little guy. He no doubt had summed up his entire life history in that one brief statement. She assumed Corey's daddy had died in Vietnam, and that Corey was just one more casualty of that terrible, senseless war.

"Well, maybe he can," Mary replied, and before she could say more, the two of them were off to the swings again in a dead heat, apparently unwilling to waste anymore time in conversation.

As they scampered away, she realized how accurate Bob Dylan was when he wrote *The Time They Are A Changin'*. Men had fought and died on this very soil. The entire area had been ravaged in an effort to avoid the integration of the races; and now, a hundred years later, Jody and Corey cared not that the color of their skins was different. They were simply two little boys having a good time on a warm September afternoon at a place called Grant Park.

Mary watched the squirrels frisking in the park and thought how radically her own life had changed. Only a few years ago she was living with her parents in Chattanooga, working for a downtown law firm, and looking forward to marrying her childhood sweetheart. Then one day Garrett walked into her office, and consequently into her life, and she soon found herself and her future moving in an altogether different direction.

For five years she had lived in Atlanta. She had finished college, something she probably would not have done if she had not married Garrett. Life had not been all she had expected, but it never is, she supposed. And the best part of it all was that she had been blessed with this wonderful little boy who made every day truly special.

It was a quiet, cozy sort of afternoon. The park, which had been packed with both vacationers and locals throughout the summer, was for the most part abandoned except for a few mothers and their pre-schoolers still enjoying the beautiful September days. All those who had come to see the Cyclorama or visit the zoo while they waited to see a Braves game had returned to the normal routine of home and school, and it was evident that vacation time was largely past. For once Mary was glad she didn't have to go home and prepare supper for her husband. She and Jody could stay as late as daylight allowed and grab a pizza on the way home. She had brought along a book, intending to read while Jody played, but it was not a day for reading, and she found herself lost in her thoughts instead.

Atlanta was an exciting place to live, but Mary had never felt completely at home here. Most of her neighbors worked, and she and Garrett pretty much isolated themselves on the weekends, since it was their only time together. Then she had started to college, and later Jody had come along.

Now that Jody was older, she had started taking him to Sunday School. She regretted leaving Garrett on Sunday mornings, but she felt it was important for Jody. Usually Garrett spent this time going over his client files and organizing his schedule for the week ahead. And he didn't seem to mind that they were not there. She had met some very nice people at the church and was especially fond of Jody's teacher, Beverly Shaw.

Madeline Sexton was the only office wife she knew very well, and while Madeline was the one person in Atlanta she felt really close to, they didn't spend a lot of time together. Madeline was, in her own words, a "crazy artist" and spent hours in her studio. Lucky for her, because her husband also traveled, and she didn't have a child to spend time with.

Mary missed seeing her mother as often as she would like, but they talked often on the phone. She also missed the people she had grown up with and known all her life, but most of all she missed her daddy.

It had happened so suddenly. Her mother had called to say she had finished the bridesmaid's dresses for Judy Moore's wedding, and that she and Henry were going to Santa Rosa Beach for a few days, and wondered if she and Jody would like to go with them. Mary was so excited and had called Garrett in Boston to see what he thought of the idea.

"By all means, you should go. I just got word that I'm to be one of the instructors for a seminar in Hartford next week, so I probably won't be coming home this weekend anyway. Take lots of pictures, so I can see Jody's first impression of the ocean."

It had been a wonderful vacation. They rented the old beach house where they had stayed when Mary was a kid, and walked on the beach and played in the ocean. It was like a trip back in time, except this time Jody was the child. But it didn't make any difference. They were family once more... plus one... and everyone was having a wonderful time.

Mary's mother was tired from weeks of working on the wedding dresses, and she and Jody were usually the first in bed after a long day on the beach. Mary and her dad were by nature 'late night' people, and they sat on the porch far into the night, listening to the waves crashing on the beach and talking of days gone by.

Mary had always known she was the apple of her daddy's eye, and she felt safe and secure with him, as if no harm could ever befall her as long as he was around.

At one point he had dared to inquire about her marriage. He asked if she were happy, and if things were okay.

"Just remember, little girl, you are God's best creation, and you have a right to be happy. Don't ever let anyone convince you otherwise. As long as I'm around, I'll always take care of you, but there may come a time when you have to take care of yourself. If it does, I want you to be strong. You can do it. You've got it in you. It's just that sometimes it seems a little harder for you."

She assured him he had no reason for concern, and he changed the subject. He asked about her grandmother's legacy, and if she had used any of it to finish college. She told him it was still intact, and she would not use it unless there was a real emergency.

"Well, remember it's there for you. If you ever need it, you don't have to ask anybody. You'll know when the time is right."

Two weeks later she and Jody went to Chattanooga for the weekend. Her daddy took Jody to his first baseball game and plied him with hotdogs and cotton candy. Jody was so excited, and Mary knew this was the stuff of which memories are made.

They were loading the car for the trip back to Atlanta when it happened. Suddenly her daddy grabbed hold of the car and eased himself down on the ground. He was very pale, and Mary knew something was terribly wrong. Her mother called an ambulance, but less than twenty-four hours later Henry Howard was gone, the victim of a massive stroke, and Mary knew she had lost the best friend she would ever have.

The rumble of distant thunder reminded her it was time to go. She and Jody said good-bye to Corey and his grandmother and headed for home. And as the soft September rain fell on the car, Jody dozed on the seat beside her.

*　　*　　*　　*　　*

Mary proved to be an excellent hostess. She was friendly and gracious, and everyone appeared to be having a good time. Garrett found it hard to keep his eyes off her. From the moment he had met her, he knew she possessed a certain natural beauty, which he sometimes took for granted, but not tonight. Her blue dress seemed to make her auburn hair and brown eyes fairly glow, and in his eyes, she was the 'Belle of the Ball'.

Mary was aware of his approving glances, and she could tell he was delighted with the way the party was going. It was nice to get to know the office crowd better. Most of them were from other parts of the country, transplanted here by their jobs, and like herself, she assumed many of the wives had felt somewhat lonely when they first came to this city. Atlanta, like any large city, can be very intimidating to an outsider.

Because of their jobs, most of the couples spent a great deal of time apart, and unlike many parties where the men paired off to talk business or sports, and the women visited among themselves, this was not the case tonight. Garrett played the role of the perfect host, mixing and mingling with the group, but he frequently returned to Mary's side to tell her how great everything was going, and how much he appreciated her efforts.

She regretted they had waited so long to entertain. The house looked nice, and the refreshments were both attractive and delicious. Most importantly, everyone seemed to be having a good time. She had hoped they would feel comfortable and welcome in her home. She hated stuffy social affairs where everyone was so busy doing the proper thing that no one enjoyed the pleasure of being together.

They had planned for Jody to go to his grandmother's for the weekend, but he was so excited about 'the party' that they decided he could stay. He was well behaved and enjoyed meeting the people from his daddy's office. When it was his bedtime, Madeline insisted on putting him to bed, so Mary wouldn't have to leave her guests.

Madeline loved Jody and was delighted with the chance to do a little surrogate mothering. She and Doug had been trying to have a baby for a long time, but so far she had not been able to get pregnant. She was willing to adopt, but Doug still believed that in time they would have a child of their own.

Madeline tucked Jody in and read him a bedtime story, and as she came back to the living room, Mary could see the look of longing that lingered on Madeline's face. Maybe, God willing, this would be the night Madeline would conceive.

Like Garrett, Doug spent a lot of time on the road. He would make an excellent father, but regardless of whether or not they had a child, he had his work. Madeline, on the other hand, had nothing but her paints to occupy her time, and Mary was sure that sometimes she painted just to fill the lonely hours when Doug was away.

After dinner, the guests nibbled hors d'oeuvres, sipped their drinks, and engaged in pleasant conversation. After awhile Garrett put some albums on the stereo, dimmed the lights, and announced, "Anyone want to dance?"

Then he led Mary to the center of the room, placed his arm possessively around her slender waist, and smiled down at her. Drawing her close, he nestled his chin in her hair, and whispered in a husky voice. "God, I love you. You're the most wonderful thing that ever happened to me."

Mary looked up at the handsome blonde man who held her and thought, "Why can't it always be this good?"

The music was soft and romantic as they danced and he held her close. Others were now dancing, but she was aware only of the presence of her husband. She wished the music would never stop. She wanted to dance until, completely exhausted, she and Garrett slowly slithered to the floor and lay entangled in each other's arms forever.

The group continued to dance, stopping occasionally for hors d'oeuvres or to fix themselves a drink. The party was not at all as Mary had feared it might be. No one was drinking to excess. They were just having a good time... except for Jan.

Her date, Tom McKenzie, was in charge of computer operations for a major insurance carrier in Atlanta. Earlier in the evening his pager had sounded. There was a problem with a program, and he had to return to the office to see that the glitch 'got fixed' so normal operations could resume. It went with the territory and was one of the sacrifices that came with success.

Jan was the office manager at Anderson-Walton, and she understood full well the demands your job often makes on your personal life. Nonetheless, tonight she was not happy being the only one there without a partner. She left with Tom, but later returned in her own car.

Realizing her evening had been spoiled when Tom had to leave, Mary tried to be attentive to her, but Jan was not very receptive. She seemed to withdraw to herself, and Mary suspected she was having more to drink than she should, but she was quiet and not causing any problem.

Awhile later, Mary noticed Jan approach the refreshment table. She and Garrett chatted for a minute, and then Garrett asked her to dance. Mary was glad he was going out of his way to be nice to Jan. It was plain to see she felt like a fifth wheel.

Jan was a very striking woman. Her hair and complexion were the same as Garrett's, and as Mary watched them dance, she thought how easily they could pass for brother and sister. Everyone said Jan was an efficient administrator and could handle any problem that arose with professional expertise, but tonight it was obvious she was not handling the interruption in her personal plans very well.

Mary wondered why in her present mood, Jan had bothered to come back. She certainly didn't seem to be having fun. Once more she tried to talk to her, and this time Jan seemed more amiable.

"Please forgive me if I seemed brusque earlier. It's not my nature... I was just disappointed that Tom had to leave... This is such a lovely party, and I'm glad I decided to come back."

"I'm glad you did too," Mary replied as she smiled and touched Jan's shoulder.

"You have such a lovely home. It's nice of you to have us over. Everyone seems to be having a good time." Jan paused and it appeared that she wanted to continue their conversation, perhaps to make amends for her earlier rejection of Mary's hospitality. "Garrett is doing a great job with Anderson-Walton. I guess I don't have to tell you that. I hope you've been able to adjust to having him away from home so much."

"I don't think a woman ever adjusts to that, but I've accepted it, I suppose. We just have to try harder to make the time we do have together count."

"Yes, I suppose that's what's important."

Shortly after one o'clock, the guests began to leave. Everyone said they had a wonderful time, even Jan, and they thanked Mary and Garrett over and over for such a lovely evening. And as she said goodnight to her guests, Mary was glad she had decided to give the party after all.

* * * * *

MONDAY

Unlike the mild weather of the weekend, a cold drizzle fell upon Atlanta, and the day dawned dark and gloomy, only adding to the despair that had laid hold on Mary. She wandered aimlessly from room to room, trying to escape the dreariness of the day and the pain that pierced her heart, but it stalked her. Each room served only as a reminder of happier times, and only amplified the fact that it would never again be like it was before. Finally she settled in the den and lit the gas logs in an attempt to chase away the shadows. Her anger had subsided, and only sadness and disappointment remained.

She knew it would never change. Once a man cheats, it is rare that he stops. Garrett was no exception. In his own way, perhaps he loved her, but there would always be other women. He could not live without the thrill of the chase. He was good looking and charming, but he seemed to need constant reassurance that these attributes still worked.

There was no need to call a lawyer. She had done that last year, and he had plainly laid out her options. His words echoed in her ears.

"Mrs. Davenport, the one thing you will ultimately have to decide is whether you would be better off with him or without him. That may seem like an oversimplification, but in the end that's what it all boils down to."

"I cannot make that decision for you, nor can anyone else. You have to make it yourself... Don't act in haste. Give it time... You have a child to consider." He paused and handed her a tissue. "One thing more... Things will either get better or they will get worse. Consider everything carefully, very carefully. Be sure you are fully aware of the changes a divorce will bring about in your life. Make sure you are ready and able to deal with those changes before you decide to end your marriage."

Once again, her thoughts turned to Saturday night. It had been such a nice get-together. Everyone seemed to have a good time, and she had been anxious to entertain again.

David and Jan had been the last to leave. They would both go home to empty houses, and neither seemed inclined to 'call it an evening'. David's wife was in Savannah, and it was apparent he missed her very much. They were expecting their first child in a couple of months, and Shari had wanted to go see her mother before the doctor restricted her driving. However, she had insisted David go on to the party.

Jan was twice divorced and a career lady by choice. She had only recently met Tom, but she was quite fond of him, and his leaving early had been disappointing to her.

Mary was anxious for the two of them to make their departure. Selfishly, she wanted the rest of the evening alone with her husband. Earlier in the day she had hung the ivory colored nightgown and negligee in their bedroom closet. It was a gift from Garrett once when he had been away from home for two consecutive weekends. Perhaps it was a peace offering, but it was beautiful beyond words, and she had saved it for a special time.

Jan had insisted on helping clear away the food while David and Garrett talked about some new investments they were sure were going to be a boon both for the company and themselves.

When they were finally out the door, Mary went upstairs to check on Jody. She heard Jan's car start up and assumed David would not linger long. Garrett would be upstairs shortly, and the rest of the evening would be theirs. She arranged Jody's covers, placed a kiss on his soft forehead, and thought how richly blessed she was.

She noticed that Madeline had not completely closed the blinds and went to adjust them, so the sun would not wake Jody in the morning.

The moon was shining through the partially opened blinds, and she paused to look out. Down below on the patio she saw Garrett and Jan talking. It had not been Jan's car that she had heard leaving, but rather David's. Garrett and Jan were standing very close, and Garrett reached out and pulled her to him, and his mouth closed hungrily over her partially opened lips. Then his hands moved slowly down her back, cupping her slender hips, and pulling her body tightly against his own. It was only for a moment, and then Jan pulled away. Mary quietly opened the jalousies, wanting both to hear, and at the same time, not to hear their exchange.

"I have to go," Jan said, and moved quickly to her car.

Garrett followed her.

Her voice grew stronger. "I'm sorry. That shouldn't have happened... I hope Mary didn't see it."

But Mary had seen it.

She really didn't blame Jan. It was Garrett who had taken advantage of the situation. If it hadn't been Jan, it would have been someone else. It had happened before, and it would happen again.

As the florist van circled the driveway, Mary's thoughts returned to the present. She was rather expecting it, and she didn't bother to answer the door. The deliveryman would leave them on the patio. Later she would bring in the one dozen perfect yellow roses and place them in the parlor, where she would not have to look at them. They brought no joy. Right now, nothing did. The roses served only as a reminder of a miserable ending to what had been a lovely party.

There had been a brief, but bitter exchange when Garrett had come upstairs. She had slept in Jody's room, and Garrett had slept in the den. Their bed had not been disturbed.

On Sunday afternoon when she returned from the airport, she carefully removed the nightgown and negligee from the hanger and packed them away. She doubted she would ever wear them.

As the rain dripped from the eaves of the house, her thoughts returned to the advice of her lawyer. As much as she wanted to, she could not leave Garrett now. The lawyer was right. There was a lot to consider. She was not strong enough to make it on her own without hurting Jody in the process. She had no choice. She had to stay with Garrett for Jody's sake... at least for now.

Felix slowly uncurled himself and came to stand beside her. He had been lying on the hearth, enjoying the warmth from the gas logs. As if sensing her misery, he let out a soft meow seemingly meant to assure her that he was still her friend.

Mary lifted the orange tabby cat into her lap. It was nice to have something to share her loneliness. Felix was the grandson of the cat Jack had given her when she was ten years old. He had made the move to Atlanta with her, and even though Garrett did not care for cats, Felix had remained.

As she stroked his head, tears dropped down her cheeks and onto his fur. And the misery that was welled up inside her spilled out, and she cried deep, heart-wrenching sobs.

She wished Garrett had loved her as much as she had loved him, but with each incident a little of her love for him died. He was killing her love by degrees, and one day there would be no more.

CHAPTER 13

This was the first Sunday afternoon in four years that Garrett was not packing his bag for the evening flight to Boston. C. R. Smitherman would be in Atlanta on Thursday and had called to say he would like to finalize an investment they had been working on for quite awhile, if Garrett could arrange to see him. It involved big bucks and a handsome commission, and Garrett was happy to rearrange his week's schedule.

He would take the first three days of the week off from work and spend some time with his family. On Thursday he would meet Smitherman for lunch, hopefully clinch the deal, and on Friday fly to Boston to meet another client for a dinner engagement Saturday night. If he could close both deals, it would be a very profitable week.

Mary looked forward to having some extra time with her husband. Maybe it would be good for both of them. It had been almost a year since Garrett's indiscretion with Jan, and it seemed the distance between them had only increased. She had been angry and hurt in the beginning, but as time went on, she had tried to forgive him and had done everything she could to make things right between them once more.

However, Garrett showed little interest in making things right. He blamed her for 'making a mountain out of a molehill', and if anything, he only drew farther away. He was cold and indifferent, and improving their relationship seemed to be the last thing on his mind. At one time they had talked about divorce, at least Mary had, but Garrett refused to even discuss it. Apparently the Anderson-Walton organization didn't particularly mind adultery, provided it was discreet, but they seriously frowned on divorce. It tarnished the 'family image' they were so eager to project.

She had hoped they could take Jody to the park on Sunday afternoon. He enjoyed playing with the other children and was anxious to show his dad how high he could swing, and how proficient he had become on the monkey bars. She had planned a picnic and had prepared some of Garrett's favorites, including baked beans, a special German potato salad she had made during the early years of their marriage, and rich, gooey brownies, which Garrett used to describe as "positively sinful". There was lemonade and barbecue, and if the weather would cooperate, it would be a delightful time for the three of them to spend an unhurried afternoon in the park.

Garrett had said it was a great idea, and when Sunday arrived, it was a made-to-order day for a family outing. The weather was beautiful, and Jody could not wait to be off to the park with his mother and daddy. It was a rare treat for him.

Everything was packed into the picnic basket, and Mary and Jody were ready to go when Garrett said, "Why don't you two go on without me? I have some paperwork to do before I meet with Smitherman. I hate to miss it, but I really need to get this taken care of."

Mary would not beg him. He knew what he wanted to do, and apparently what he wanted to do was not spend a day with his family. She and Jody would go by themselves, as they were accustomed to doing. It wouldn't be the same, but maybe something could be salvaged of their plans. Once Jody got there, perhaps he would momentarily forget his disappointment as he played with the other children.

When they got home from the park, she was especially provoked to find that Garrett had spent a good part of the afternoon scheduling golfing dates for the next three days. Once again he had chosen not to be a part of her and Jody's life, and this time he didn't have 'being out of town' for an excuse. He simply didn't want to. She attempted to hide the hurt, but it was there, and Garrett knew it. However, unlike the early years of their marriage, when he had hurt her and would attempt to cajole her with roses and tender words, now he didn't seem to care.

*   *   *   *   *

C. R. Smitherman was an executive vice-president of the Boston Red Sox and was in town to scout a couple of the Braves' younger players. Smitherman normally did not do any scouting, but because he had formerly held a similar position with the Braves, he knew their organization well and seemed to be the best man for the assignment.

Garrett had made reservations at *The Imperial Ballroom*, one of Atlanta's finest restaurants. It was internationally known and was the perfect place to take someone you wished to impress.

However, when Garrett told him of his plans, Mr. Smitherman appeared a little disappointed. Garrett detected this immediately and offered, "Is there somewhere else you would prefer?"

Smitherman wrinkled his brow and breathed a frustrated sigh. "No, that will be fine. You've already made reservations." He looked out the window at the busy Atlanta traffic and added, "I was hoping we might go to *Kelly's*. A friend of mine is the featured performer there this week and I've never had the opportunity to hear him sing, but the *Imperial* will be fine. I'll catch him another time."

"That's no problem at all. Why don't we go to *Kelly's*? I would love to hear your friend sing."

Although Garrett could sometimes be a jerk, he certainly knew how to handle people. He was suave and polished and knew exactly when to give in to get what he wanted, a tactic he had used many times over the years with Mary.

"If you're sure it's not a problem, I'd really like to hear him sing."

"No sir. It's no problem at all." Garrett had scored and he knew it. "By the way, what type of music does your friend do?"

"Country!"

"Country?" Garrett replied, "That's great! I love country music."

He was lying. He couldn't stand country music, but Garrett was no fool. If Smitherman liked country music, then country music it would be.

Kelly's turned out to be a very nice place, quite different from what Garrett had expected. It was not some honky-tonk or redneck joint. On the contrary, it was a very classy place with attractive furnishings and an excellent sound system, and the meal was superb. The marinated steaks were cooked to perfection, and even Garrett was impressed by the singer. He was not one of the traditional country musicians Garrett had heard before. As a matter of fact, he didn't fit into any musical category. He had a style all his own, not really country, but not rock either.

The trip to *Kelly's* clinched the deal. Garrett knew that the way you treat the client was oftentimes more important than the product you were selling. Today's meeting evidenced that. After the performance, Smitherman introduced Garrett to his friend, and he listened as the two of them shared old memories. Garrett had noticed how poignant the lines of his songs were, and his conversation was similar. While he was cordial and easy to converse with, he didn't waste a lot of time on small talk. And in a strange sort of way, Garrett found himself impressed with this sad song singer.

* * * * *

Mary was still upset with Garrett over the trip to the park, and since Sunday they had done little more than pass in the lonely confines of the large stately mansion.

However, when Garrett came home from his lunch with Smitherman, he sought her out. He told her about his experience at *Kelly's*, and that he believed Smitherman would have signed anything after seeing his old friend. He had made the deal of a lifetime and had not needed to make the concessions he was prepared to make.

This was typical, Mary thought. Garrett would act anyway, do anything, including selling his own mother, to close a business deal. It was sickening! And that was exactly what she thought of Garrett. This man to whom she had been married for seven years, who was the father of her child, and to whom she had pledged "until death do us part", was a sickening con artist. She didn't care to be in the same house with him, much less listen to the details of his latest manipulation. And the huge commission he would make meant little to her. It was not money their marriage needed.

*   *   *   *   *

FRIDAY

Mary glanced at the books she had selected at the library and wondered if she would bother to read any of them. Normally she had trouble finding time to read, but that was certainly not her problem this weekend. Garrett was in Boston and Jody was in Chattanooga with his grandma. She had the whole weekend to herself and could read all she wanted, but she was not in the mood for reading.

She laid the books on the kitchen table and looked around for something that needed doing. Her house was in order, and it was ridiculous to start cooking, as she frequently did when she was bored or lonely. There was no one to eat it but herself.

Madeline had mentioned a new art gallery a few weeks earlier and had suggested they go there sometime. Maybe this would be a good time to visit the new gallery and later they could go to some place nice for dinner. While Mary was not an art buff, she enjoyed Madeline's company. Doug was probably out of town, and Madeline would no doubt welcome something to do. She dialed Madeline's number, but there was no answer.

She then went upstairs and reached in her closet for an overnight bag. She would pack a few things and go to Chattanooga and spend the weekend with her mother and Jody. Then she hesitated. Jody enjoyed spending time with his grandmother, and no doubt her mother had the whole weekend planned around him. If Mary showed up, she would spoil their 'special' time together, and Jody would have to share his grandmother. It probably wasn't such a good idea after all, and she put the bag back in the closet.

She remembered how nice it had been to spend the weekend with her own grandmother when she was a little girl. They would do special things together, just the two of them. Her grandmother would spoil her, and there was no one to interfere.

This was their time together, and these special times with his grandmother were memories Jody would have for the rest of his life. Mary would do nothing to spoil it for either of them.

What a wasted week, she thought, as she wandered about the yard. Nothing had gone as she had hoped or planned. She had looked forward to having Garrett at home, but they had been like strangers living in the same house. He had ignored her all week in favor of playing golf with his friends, and even when he wasn't busy pursuing his own interests, he had seemed bored with her and totally preoccupied. It was obvious that he could not wait to board the plane and get away from her. And by the time he left, she felt pretty much the same.

She never knew what to do anymore. Most fathers enjoyed doing things with their children. There had been a time when Garrett had, but lately he lived in another world, a world that included neither her nor Jody. For a while she walked around the grounds and then went in to try Madeline again. Still there was no answer. She must have gone to Birmingham for the weekend.

The walls of the house were closing in on her. She thought of going shopping and stopping somewhere for dinner. She had to do something. Selfishly, she was sorry she had let Jody go to his grandmother's. It was so lonely in the house without him.

As she drove downtown, she remembered Garrett's suggestion about going to the restaurant where he and his client had dined. He had said the entertainer was very good.

"Why don't you call Madeline and the two of you go over and have a steak, and listen to the music? You'll like it. It's a real nice place."

He had not had the time nor the inclination to take her himself, but he had suggested that she go. She just wished Madeline was home.

She almost dismissed the idea from her mind. It would be no fun to go by herself, but then nothing else was any fun either. She was in no mood to shop, although it had seemed preferable to staying home by herself. But she had to eat somewhere, and Garrett had said the food was good. Maybe it would be nice.

As she parked her car, she still wasn't sure it was a good idea for her to come here. She was a lady alone, and too often a lady alone can be taken the wrong way, especially in a dinner club. If Madeline were here with her, it would be okay. Maybe she should just leave. Instead she locked her car and walked toward the entrance. If she felt uncomfortable, she could get up and leave. It was as simple as that.

The side table where Mary was seated afforded her a good view of the dining room and the stage. It was nice in a relaxed way, not elegant like the club, but very nice. It was not crowded, but neither was it empty. There were quite a few men in business suits, several couples having an early dinner, and at least one other lady dining alone.

The lady appeared to be a lawyer. She had finished eating and was looking over some documents. It was not just the blue manuscript covers that indicated her profession. She had a certain look about her, an air of confidence and control. Mary admired her. The legal profession was still largely a man's world, but things were changing. It was not a career choice for the fainthearted, and she was sure that the attractive lady with the open briefcase, who was letting her coffee grow cold, had paid her dues. Mary had once considered such a step herself, but that was a long time ago.

The waitress placed a menu in front of her and asked, "Would you like to order now or do you need some time to look over the menu?"

"Now will be fine."

She chose the marinated sirloin with a baked potato and a garden salad. Contrary to what she had feared, she felt neither awkward nor improper dining alone. There were several men also eating by themselves, and she assumed the lady lawyer probably ate alone quite often. Mary wondered if she had a husband and children, and then decided she probably did not.

When her meal arrived, it both looked and smelled wonderful, and she realized she was quite hungry.

"What time does the music begin?" She asked the waitress.

"Actually, in about ten minutes. You'll like the musician. He's not your typical performer." The waitress paused as if searching for just the right words to describe the singer. "He's real! He makes you feel as though he's singing straight from his heart to yours... Do you like *Desperado*? He usually closes with that, and I get chill bumps every time he does it. It's so beautiful."

"It's one of my favorites."

"Is everything all right?"

"I think so," Mary smiled.

"Good, I'll check with you later."

The steak was delicious, as was everything else, and Mary was glad she had come. If the music was half as good as the food, then this place must be Atlanta's best kept secret, she thought, as she settled back in her chair and waited for the music to begin.

Suddenly she realized she didn't even know the name of the musician she was about to hear. She had not bothered to ask Garrett because when he first mentioned it, she had no intention of coming anyway.

"Ladies and gentlemen, in just a few minutes, we will present for your dining pleasure Mr. Jack Roberts. We hope you will enjoy hearing him as much as we enjoy presenting him."

Mary smiled. With a name like that, there were bound to be a lot of them. For a moment she thought about Jack. It had been so long ago. She wondered what he was doing now. She had heard about his injury and knew it must have been devastating for him. But no doubt he was still connected with baseball in some way or another.

"Can I get you desert?" the waitress asked.

"No, thank you, but I would like another cup of coffee, please."

The club was filling rapidly. Apparently a lot of people came to hear the music first and then dined afterwards. The soft strumming of a guitar quickly quietened the large crowd, and Mary's eyes turned away from the waitress and toward the stage. She stared in disbelief. All of the strength seemed to drain from her body, and a lump arose in her throat almost taking her breath away. Her pulse was beating furiously, while the rest of her body felt numb.

What was he doing here? What was she doing here?

I've got to get out of here, she thought, but she couldn't move. Her eyes were fixed upon the tall dark man on the stage. She tried to get up, but her legs would not work. She had to leave. Yet she had to stay. She had to hear him, see him, but she could not let him see her. Finally, she decided she would stay for a little while and then leave quietly, and he would never know she had been here.

As the initial shock wore off and her nervousness subsided, she began to examine the man that stood before her. While he looked much the same, the boyishness which she remembered was gone, and in its place a certain maturity which comes with the years. The expression on his face was more serious than she recalled, and he was a little thinner than when she had last seen him. The remembrance of that last encounter pained her.

She was brought back from her reverie by the song he was singing. It was Michael Martin Murphy's classic, *Wildfire*. Then he continued with Rod Stewart's *Maggie May* and Pure Prairie League's *Amy*. They were all beautiful. His voice was warm and real, and sad when the lyrics were sad. It was obvious the crowd loved him.

Once when he paused between numbers, someone called out, "Can you do *Me and Bobbie McGee*?"

Jack smiled. "Yeah, I think maybe I know that one."

She remembered the first time she had heard the song and the profound effect it had upon her. She and Madeline had spent the afternoon shopping and had come home with nothing to show for their efforts but Swiss cheese and ham and a bottle of Chablis. They were sipping wine and listening to the stereo. Their husbands were both working out of town, and they were enjoying a pleasant evening together... Then she heard it... They stopped talking and listened intently to the words. When it was finished, she asked Madeline to play it again.

Mary sat motionless as Madeline reversed the tape and played the song once more.

"Was there a Bobby McGee in your life?" Madeline asked, when the tape cut off.

Mary was slow to answer, and there was a faraway look in her eyes.
"Yes... There was."
"Were you in love with him?"
"Sort of..." Mary hedged. "Yes," again she hesitated. "Yes I was."
"What happened to him?"
"He loved something else more than me."
"Some*thing*?" She asked, emphasizing the "thing".
"He was a baseball player." Mary said it simply with no explanation, almost as if saying he was 'a baseball player' explained everything.

Madeline sat quietly, wondering about this fellow who had apparently chosen baseball over Mary, and realized she should not pursue the matter further.

Mary continued to stare intensely at nothing in particular, never moving or even raising her head until Madeline finally broke the silence.

"You're lucky... At least you had a Bobby McGee. Some people never do."

Even though her thoughts had wondered, she had not missed a word Jack was singing.

> *"And somewhere near Salinas,*
> *Lord, I let her slip away,*
> *Looking for the home I hope she finds,*
> *I'd trade all of my tomorrows*
> *for one single yesterday,*
> *Holding Bobbie's body close to mine."*

He sang it like it was written for him, and she wondered if there was a Bobby McGee in his own life. Then she realized he was probably married by now.

She still could not imagine Jack doing anything but playing baseball. But he was, and he was doing it well.

She wondered if she should wait and talk to him after the show and tell him how good he was and how much she had enjoyed his music. But her hands were already shaking just from hearing him, and she knew if she tried to talk to him, her voice would tremble as well. It would be much too emotional. This was the man she had once loved. They had grown up together and had been best friends long before they were lovers.

She would listen to another song or two and then leave. Later she would write him a note and tell him how much she had enjoyed his music and wish him well, but deep down inside, she knew she would never write such a letter. It would be one of those well-intended, yet awkward things that you mean to do, but never get around to doing. She knew that when she left *Kelly's*, she would be leaving Jack for good, just as she had seven years earlier.

As she listened to song after song, she sat mesmerized until finally she heard the familiar notes of *Desperado*. The waitress was right. She also felt the chill bumps rise as she listened to the man she had loved sing the classic *Eagles'* song. The words almost haunted her. It was as if Jack knew she was there and was singing only to her... But he wasn't. He could not see her table from where he was standing on stage, and she was sure he had no idea she was there. Maybe it was better that way.

She took one long last look at the singer whose name she had not even known when she arrived and whispered, "Good-bye, Jack." Then she hastily made her way to the door.

Desperado,
Why don't you come to your senses?
You've been out riding fences
for so long now.

You're a hard one,
But I know that you got your reasons.
These things that are pleasing you,
Can hurt you somehow.

Don't you draw the queen of diamonds, boy,
She'll beat you if she's able.
You know the queen of hearts
Is always your best bet.

Now it seems to me some fine things
Have been laid upon your table,
But you only want the ones

That you can't get.

Desperado,
Oh, you ain't getting no younger.
Your pain and your hunger,
They're driving you home.

Your freedom, oh your freedom,
Well, that's just some people talking.
Your prison is walking
through this world all alone.

Don't your feet get cold in the wintertime.
Sky won't snow and the sun won't shine.
It's hard to tell the nighttime from the day.

You're losing all your highs and lows,
Ain't it funny how the feeling goes away.

Desperado,
Why don't you come to your senses?
Come down from your fences.
Open the gate.

It may be raining,
But there's a rainbow above you.
You better let somebody love you,
Let somebody love you.

You better let somebody love you,
Before it's too late.

- DESPERADO – Written By: Glen Frey & Don Henley

* * * * *

The Braves were playing at home and there was a rock concert at the Omni, and the traffic was unreal as Mary made her way home. She liked living in Atlanta, but she had never grown accustomed to the traffic. It was a lot different from Chattanooga. As she stopped for a traffic light, she tore the cellophane from the tape she had purchased and was about to insert it in the tape player when the light changed. Up ahead she could see flashing blue lights, and she knew there had been an accident. She would wait and listen to the tape when she got home. Right now she needed to give her full attention to the road.

It was a relief to pull the car into the garage. She could not remember when the traffic had been so congested or people so impatient to get where they were going. She poured herself a cup of coffee and went to the den to listen to Jack's tape.

Several of the songs were the same ones he had done at the dinner club, but there were others he had not done, yet they were all good. She wondered why she had not heard that he was singing. Surely someone at home had told her mother, but if so, she had never mentioned it. Their lives had gone in entirely different directions after she had married Garrett, and until now their paths had not crossed.

It was all so strange, almost as if fate had willed her to go hear him. She wondered if Garrett could possibly have known that the performer he had sent her to see had once shared a special place in her life, but of course not. They had never talked about Jack. Once Garrett had asked if she had ever been in love before, and she had answered, "Only once, but that was before I met you."

He had held her close and kissed her and had not seemed interested in pursuing the subject, and it had never been mentioned again.

Finally, she removed the tape, turned off the stereo, and went upstairs to get ready for bed. But she wasn't sleepy. Her mind was filled with thoughts of yesteryear. Seeing Jack and listening to the songs he sang took her back to places and events she had long ago put behind her. The remembering was warm and pleasant, as she allowed herself the luxury of reminiscing.

Times had been simpler then and in many ways, better. She was happy then and filled with hope. Now hope seemed far away. She had tried so hard to make things good again, the way they used to be between her and Garrett, but lately she had come to doubt they ever would be.

Her life had been so wonderful back then. She was surrounded by people whose love for her was real... her mother and daddy... and Jack... He had loved her. It was just that he loved baseball more.

She wondered how he would have reacted if he had known she was there tonight. It would have been nice to speak to him, to hear his voice, and see that slow smile cross his face, but it would have made it harder, harder than it already was, to walk away.

Well past midnight Mary turned off the light and tried to sleep, but she could not let go of her thoughts. She thought of Garrett and wondered if he was sleeping. She thought of Jody and knew he was nestled fast asleep in the big bed at her mother's which had been her own bed during her growing up years, and the thought made her happy.

After awhile she got up for a drink of water, hoping somehow to break the endless cycle of her thoughts. Then she walked to the bedroom closet and from the uppermost shelf she took down the hatbox labeled *Mary's Things* and slowly untied the string and removed the lid. Right on top she spied the corsage, which she had worn to her high school prom. The yellow ribbon was still bright and crisp, but the gardenia had long since turned brown and dry. Yet, as she lovingly handled the corsage, it seemed as though she could still smell its delightful fragrance.

* * * * *

TUESDAY

She sat in the floor in front of her bedroom closet, encircled by boxes of shoes, blouses she had not worn in years, and various other items that had somehow gotten pushed to the back of the closet, and wondered how she had collected so much stuff. She had always been a tidy person and kept her house immaculate. However, her closets were another story. She hated to throw anything away. She always had. Her Mom was the same way. Katherine Howard credited it to growing up during the depression and knowing that once an item outlived its intended use, maybe it could be used later for something else. Most people out of that era grew up with the same innate philosophy. And although this was not Mary's excuse, she nevertheless inherited her Mom's tendency.

Garrett was still in Boston, and Jody's grandmother would not be bringing him home until Thursday, so she decided today would be a good day to get started on the closet. She had picked up some large cardboard boxes at the grocery store and had promised herself if it wasn't something she had worn in the last year, it would go into the box for Goodwill.

As she sorted through the clothes trying to decide what should go and what should stay, the phone rang.

"Mary, this is Madeline. Have you got a minute?"

"Sure, I'm just cleaning out closets. What are you up to?"

"I just got in from Mom's. I went to Birmingham for the weekend. Doug had to work over, and then I came back by Mom's and spent last night with her."

"I thought you might have," Mary sighed as she looked at the clutter all around her and almost wished she had never started this project.

"I got your message. Did you go to the gallery?"

Mary laughed. "Madeline, can you imagine me going to an art gallery without having you there to explain everything? I wouldn't know a Picasso from Jody's finger painting."

Madeline laughed too, realizing the truth of Mary's statement. "With some of today's modern art, I'm not sure I can always tell the difference either... So what did you do instead?"

"Oh, not much. I've had the house to myself all week and I've been enjoying the peace and quiet... I did go out to eat Friday night though."

"Really? Where did you go?"

"A place called *Kelly's*. Garrett recommended it. He took a client there last week and told me how good it was."

"Well, was it?"

"Madeline, it was wonderful. They had the best marinated steaks I've ever tasted." Then she hesitated. "And they have live music at night."

Madeline started to grin, "Mary, it sounds like you've been out 'clubbing'."

She loved to tease Mary about her old fashioned ways. She had lived in one big city after another and enjoyed giving Mary a hard time about her 'sheltered' life. She knew Mary had never been to a nightclub in her life, at least not without Garrett.

"It's not a club. It's just a restaurant... where they play music."

Madeline laughed, "I know and there's not a thing wrong with it. I am a bit surprised that you went alone though. That just doesn't seem like you."

Madeline was simply having some good-natured fun, but she was definitely right about one thing. Going to a dinner club alone was not Mary's typical style.

"So, tell me about the music. Was it good?"

"Yes, he was wonderful!"

Madeline could almost see the smile on Mary's face.

"What kind of music did he do?"

"He sang *Wildfire* and *Desperado* and *Me and Bobbie McGee*. It was so good!"

Madeline remembered the time she and Mary were listening to *Me and Bobbie McGee* and the effect it had on Mary.

"Is he still performing there?"

"I guess so. I think he's a regular there."

"Then let's go see him sometime."

Mary suddenly got very quiet.

"I don't know, Madeline. I don't know if that's such a good idea."

"Why not? You said he's great and the food is wonderful."

"Yes, I know, but after all, it is a club and we're married ladies. Now, how would that look?"

Madeline knew that was just an excuse.

"It won't look near as bad as you going by yourself."

Madeline was a person who always called a spade a spade. She could tell when someone was trying to give her the runaround, and she didn't mind letting him know he wasn't pulling anything on her. It was one of the things Mary respected most about Madeline.

Mary paused while she tried to think of another excuse not to go back to *Kelly's*, but before she could, Madeline spoke again.

"How about tonight? You're there by yourself and I know you don't cook when Garrett and Jody are away."

"Madeline, I've got too much to do. I just can't get away today."

"I thought you were cleaning out closets."

"I am and I've got boxes spread out everywhere."

"Mary, everybody knows the only time you clean closets is when you don't have anything else to do. You can do that tomorrow. I'll pick you up around five, okay?"

Mary knew Madeline was right and she would like to see Jack again. She just wasn't sure if she was ready, and she certainly wasn't ready for him to see her.

"So, around five?" Madeline repeated with an encouraging tone to her voice.

"Okay, I'll see you then."

With the contents of the closet finally sorted and her bedroom restored to normal, Mary realized she had little time left to do her hair and be ready by five. She was glad she had been busy. Otherwise, she would have had more time to think about seeing Jack again.

As she looked through her now neat closet for something to wear, her feelings were mixed. She looked forward to the evening, and yet at the same time she dreaded it. Suppose he saw her? How would he react? With Madeline along, it wouldn't be as easy to make a quick exit. As she blow-dried her hair, she was aware her hands were shaking, and she almost wished she had declined Madeline's invitation.

*　　*　　*　　*　　*

She liked the table where she had sat last Friday and was about to ask for the same one when Madeline spoke up and told the hostess they would like something "down front".

She could have died as she followed Madeline and the hostess to a small table just to the right of the stage.

Madeline was delighted with the location.

"I think we've got the best seats in the house," she said as she looked around the large dining room, which was filling quickly.

As they finished their steaks and waited for the music to begin, Madeline said, "You didn't tell me what the singer's name is."

"It's Jack Roberts."

"Jack Roberts? That sounds original. He must be from the South."

"Why do you say that?" Sometimes Mary was still taken aback by Madeline's candidness.

"Because Southerners tend to be very proud of their birth names and generally feel no need to change them or come up with some catchy substitute. Actually, I think it says a lot about knowing who you are and not trying to be something you're not."

"I suppose so," she responded, but her eyes never left the stage.

Then she heard the familiar announcement being made and Jack walked out on stage. He opened with John Denver's *Annie's Song,* and it was obvious Madeline was impressed with the mellow-toned singer whose only accompaniment was his guitar.

She turned to Mary. "I love that song."

Mary nodded, and they both sat quietly listening to the tall dark troubadour.

After he finished his third song, Mary asked, "Well? Do you like him?"

"Do I like him? I think I'm in love with him. He's about the best-looking thing I've ever seen. You never told me how great he looked. All you could talk about was his singing."

Again Mary smiled at Madeline's outpouring of compliments. "What about Doug?"

"Forget Doug. He's in Birmingham."

Mary knew Madeline was only kidding. She and Doug's marriage was as solid as they came.

There was something about Jack's music that made you hang on every word. The songs he chose were beautiful, but more than that, they spoke to you down deep inside. Madeline watched Mary and noticed how completely caught up she was in the performance. They were both into the music, but Mary was into the musician. She never took her eyes off him, and when he sang *Loving Her Was Easier Than Anything I'll Ever Do Again*, Madeline thought she saw a mist cover Mary's eyes. She had never seen Mary so enraptured.

After awhile he switched from singing other people's songs and sang several of his own. He had not done this on Friday, and Mary was surprised to learn he was writing some of his own material. It was very good. The words were sometimes tender and loving, and sometimes strong and intense.

The audience applauded loudly when he sang *Alone Again*. Loneliness was something most people could relate to, and Jack's lyrics were a poignant description of this common plight of mankind.

For a moment Mary's thoughts wandered as she tried to imagine the path he had traveled from baseball to music. No doubt it had been quite a journey. She wished she could know how it had happened, but felt certain she never would.

He was nearing the end of his performance when he saw her. Her eyes were fixed on him as they had been all evening, and she knew instantly that he had recognized her.

Madeline also saw the look he gave Mary. He never skipped a beat, but as he continued to sing, again and again his eyes returned to her.

Then there was the familiar closing number, *Desperado*. Again, a mist clouded Mary's eyes.

"He's wonderful, Mary. That's one of my favorite songs."

"Mine too," she whispered, and again her eyes were drawn to the singer like a moth to a flame.

When he left the stage to come out to speak to some friends in the audience, he motioned to Mary and said, "Please wait."

"Was he speaking to you?" Madeline asked and without waiting for an answer, continued. "You know this guy, don't you?"

Madeline had risen to leave, but quickly sat down. She was not about to leave now. She wanted to know 'the rest of the story'.

Jack shook hands and spoke with a number of people in the crowd and then approached their table.

"Hey, Mary! What are you doing here?" His voice was soft, yet solemn. Whatever the reason for her coming, it was obvious he was pleased to see her.

"Hello, Jack! We came to enjoy some good food and some great music. Jack, this is my friend, Madeline Sexton."

"Hello, Madeline."

"Hi, Jack. It was a great show!"

"Thanks."

His eyes quickly returned to Mary. "I had heard you were living in Atlanta."

"Yes, seven years now. I'm practically a native. I've almost learned to drive in this crazy town."

"That's quite an accomplishment. Maybe when I've been here seven years I can say that."

It was a lot of small talk, Madeline realized, as she tried to figure out what was between these two. Finally she blurted out, "Okay, let me guess. You two are obviously old friends, although neither of you are admitting it. You probably lived down the block from each other and went skinny dipping in the creek when you were kids, and went to your first school dance together."

Jack and Mary were both grinning as Madeline sought to learn the story by playing her little guessing game. It was strange how close she had come to the truth.

Jack continued to grin, but now his expression seemed more natural and a little less controlled. He was looking at both of them, but he directed his question to Mary.

"Has this lady been reading your diary?"

Now they were all laughing.

"Madeline, you're crazy! You and your guessing games... I've never seen this man before in my life... Honest!"

"Sure. I can tell. You're perfect strangers."

Thanks to Madeline, the tension was now broken, and while she did not know the whole story, she was sure there had been a relationship between Jack and Mary, probably a very special one, which still evoked a great deal of emotion on both their parts.

CHAPTER 14

THURSDAY

Tomorrow Garrett would be home, and Mary was busy trying to get everything in order. Garrett had a fetish for neatness and order, and she normally cleaned house on Thursday so everything would look nice when he got home. She had shopped for groceries yesterday, and bought the things she needed for their Friday night meal.

Friday was ordinarily a good night. Garrett was excited about his week's work and not yet bored with being home. Usually they went to the club for dinner on Saturday. The food was good, and though the country club atmosphere was not particularly her cup of tea, Garrett insisted it was important to mix with the 'right people'.

She barely heard the phone ringing above the buzz of the vacuum cleaner.

"Mrs. Davenport?"

"Yes." She did not recognize the voice.

"This is Kevin at the Downtown Marriott in Boston. I have a call from your husband. If you'll hold, I'll connect you."

"Thank you."

She had not heard from Garrett since he boarded the plane in Atlanta a week ago. Their last exchange had not been a pleasant one, and she wondered what this one would be like. Lately she never knew what to expect from him. Sometimes he was warm and loving. Other times he was cold and indifferent.

She listened as the phone rang and Garrett answered.

"Mary, it's good to hear your voice. I've missed you... How are you?"

Apparently he was in a pleasant mood. Maybe they would have a good weekend. She would make any concession necessary to avoid a replay of last week.

"I'm fine, Honey. I miss you too. How are things in Boston?"

"Busy! We've been working like crazy. In fact, that's why I'm calling. I need to work this weekend. We've got a new investment line that was supposed to be placed on the market in December. Now management has decided they want it out by the end of October, and I've been asked to come up with an effective marketing method for the new line. It's a great product and investors will go for it big time if it's properly presented."

There was a pause on the line as he waited for Mary's response, but she gave none.

She was disappointed that he wasn't coming home. It was no fun spending the whole week alone, looking forward to the weekend only to find she would be spending it alone too.

There was quiet on both ends of the line. Then suddenly Mary heard the sound of unconcealed laughter in the background. There was someone else in the room.

"Garrett is someone with you? It sounds like there's a party going on."

"It's nothing really. One of the account executives had a birthday and the girls in the office bought a cake. You remember Ted. He just turned thirty, and the girls are giving him a hard time about 'growing old'."

"Are you at the office?" She waited for the lie, which she knew would come.

"Yeah, I'm finishing up some proposals for a couple of clients."

Apparently he was unaware that Kevin had told her he was calling from the hotel. It would be easier to 'cover his tracks' if he didn't have to play Mr. Big Guy and have someone else place his calls. She felt like telling him she knew he was lying, but what was the use?

"Mary, are you still there?"

"Yes, I'm still here. Where else would I be? It's where I live and where I stay... alone... for the most part."

He ignored her remarks and prepared to end the conversation. "Listen, Honey. I'll be home next weekend for sure. Take care of yourself and give Jody a big hug. Love you!"

She hung up the phone and stared aimlessly at the floor. As much as she hated to admit it, this had been going on for a long time. A lot of men cheat. She knew that. But how could he stand there in his hotel room and tell her he loved her, while another woman waited for his attention? As she tried to erase from her mind the mental picture of what was going on this very moment in that hotel room, the phone rang again.

"Mary."

"Hi Mom. How are you and Jody doing?" She hoped her voice did not bear witness to her feeling of despair.

"We're fine!" Jody's shrill little voice came through the extension.

It was a joyous sound, and momentarily she felt better.

"Well, I'm not fine. I miss you. When are you going to come home and spend some time with Mommy?"

"I don't know," Jody replied, and then giggled at his answer. It was a phase he was going through, and his answer to everything seemed to be, "I don't know."

"Mary, Clara is coming for the weekend. She's keeping Gary while his parents are at a convention. She's taking him to Opryland on Saturday and wants Jody and me to go with them."

"Please, Mom... Can we, please?"

Mary could hear the excitement in Jody's voice.

Clara was Katherine's sister who lived in Raleigh, and Gary was Clara's only grandson.

"Please, Mom. I've never been to Obbryland."

While Mary had looked forward to having Jody home, she knew how much he wanted to go and her mother and Aunt Clara would have a good time with the boys.

"Okay, but Jody, you be good and do what Gramma tells you, and I'll see you next week."

"I will Mom. I love you!"

"Don't worry, Mary. He'll be fine. You know I'll take care of him. You and Garrett have a nice weekend. It looks like the weather is going to be perfect."

Mary didn't tell her that Garrett wasn't coming home. There was no need. She had kept things to herself and had not discussed her marital problems with anyone, although she was sure her mother had sensed things weren't exactly right between her and Garrett.

"You all have a good time."

"We will and I'll bring Jody home the first of the week."

As she hung up the phone, Mary almost wished she had said no. She would spend another weekend by herself, while everyone else did their thing and had fun.

As she put away the vacuum cleaner, she realized it was lunchtime, but food was the last thing on her mind. She opened a Coke and turned on the stereo. Jack's tape was still in the cassette player, and once more she listened to it.

He was a very good singer, but it was his writing that impressed her most. It was incredible what he did with words. He had never been the studious type. He didn't do a lot of reading. It interfered too much with his ball playing. In fact, she had often done his book reports in high school.

Once, however, he had done an essay completely on his own. It was entitled *Freedom*, a subject he felt strongly about. Mrs. Bolean said it was excellent and asked him to read it aloud to the class.

Jack had always been keenly in touch with his feelings. He wasn't a radical, but he knew who he was and what he believed in. And this was unmistakable in the lyrics he had written.

Mary knew baseball was Jack's first love... How well she knew it... And she knew how hard he had worked to make his dream come true only to have it ended so abruptly.

Losing baseball must have been devastating for him. It was probably the hardest thing he had ever experienced. No one could understand this better than she. But he had moved beyond it and found something he could do, rather than dwelling on the things he could not do.

Jack was a strong person and she respected that. Unfortunately, she was not.

When the cassette cut off, she removed the tape from the stereo, and for the first time noticed the insert included a phone number where he could be reached for bookings and other information.

Earlier in the week she had considered calling to say how much she had enjoyed the show, but she hadn't known how to get in touch with him, and she wasn't sure if she should.

She had never been so miserably lonely in her life. Her child was gone... Her husband was spending the weekend with another woman... And there was no one for her to even talk to. It couldn't be so terribly wrong to call Jack and chat for a few minutes.

Twice she dialed the number and hung up before the phone had time to ring, but finally on the third attempt she let it ring. She had no idea whether the number she had dialed was his home or his office. Perhaps his secretary would answer or an answering service, but on the third ring he answered.

"Hello?" He repeated.

"Jack," Mary paused. "This is Mary... Mary Howard." Why had she said that? She hadn't said 'Mary Howard' in years.

"Mary! How are you? It was good to see you the other night."

"I'm fine. It was nice to see you, too."

Suddenly she was speechless. She had called him, and now she didn't know what to say. It was very awkward.

"I really enjoyed hearing you, and your tapes are wonderful."

"I'm glad you like them." He sensed her nervousness and tried to break the tension. "Your friend, Madeline, seemed nice."

"Madeline's a bit of a character, but she is nice. I'm sure you could tell she's a Yankee," Mary laughed, "and she's not afraid to speak her mind. She kind of took me under her wing when I moved to Atlanta, and we've been good friends ever since."

"She was really taken by you," Mary continued. "In fact, she told several of her friends about you, and they're planning to get together and come hear you."

Jack laughed.

"I appreciate that, but they had better hurry. Tomorrow night's my last show at Kelly's. Monday I start a tour through the Carolina's."

She hadn't considered the possibility of his leaving. She assumed he was a regular at Kelly's. This couldn't be happening. He was slipping out of her life just as quickly as he had slipped back into it, and they hadn't even had a chance to talk.

"Mary?"

"I wasn't expecting you to be leaving so soon."

Jack sighed. "That's how this business goes. It seems I spend more time on the road than anywhere else."

"Is Chattanooga still your home?" Mary asked.

"No. I have an apartment in Atlanta. I'm not here much, but it's where I get my mail, and where I live when I'm not on the road."

She asked about his mom. She had always loved Virginia Roberts and had one time thought that someday she, too, would call her "Mom".

As the conversation continued, she was aware that this would very likely be her last opportunity to talk with Jack, and the thought saddened her. And for probably the first time in her life she acted on impulse.

"Would you like to come to dinner tomorrow night?" She couldn't believe she had asked him, and she doubted he would accept, but it would be nice just to sit awhile and talk.

"I'd love to, but I have to be at the club by six."

"That's not a problem. We can have an early supper. How would four o'clock work?"

"That's fine, if you're sure it's not too early. I'm kind of out of sync with the rest of the world."

"Four will be fine. I'll look forward to seeing you."

And then suddenly it seemed they both had run out of words.

"See you then," Mary finally managed to say and was about to hang up.

"Hey, where am I supposed to come?" Jack asked.

While she could not see him, she visualized the sly grin that had crept across his face.

"I'm sorry. I suppose you do need to know that. I live at 2150 Elmwood. Do you know where it is?"

"Elmwood!"

"Yes."

Jack was laughing... "You're not going to believe this, but we only live a couple of blocks from each other. I live on Oakdale."

"You've got to be kidding?" Mary laughed. "Then you should have no trouble finding me."

And as she sat on the sofa, a smile crept across her face. She still couldn't believe after all these years that Jack was coming to dinner, and that once again he lived only a couple of blocks away. It was like old times.

Again she smiled. She would have to go back to the grocery store. Somehow she could not picture herself serving Jack lamb chops.

* * * * *

From her kitchen window she watched him as he got out of his van and came up the sidewalk. He was wearing white slacks and a navy blue shirt, and he looked wonderful.

She had no idea how it would turn out. She should have told him that Garrett and Jody wouldn't be here, but she wasn't sure he would have come if she had. Then she heard the doorbell ring.

"Hi. Come in."

Jack returned her greeting as his eyes scanned the large beautifully designed kitchen.

"Supper's almost ready. I thought we would eat first and then visit. I know you have to get away early for your performance."

"It's okay. I have plenty of time. I'm sorry you had to rearrange your dinner hour for me. It's too early for most people."

"It was no problem. I'm glad you could make it. Sometimes Jody and I eat early when we're by ourselves... I thought we would eat in the breakfast room since there's only the two of us."

Jack did not respond, but the look on his face was response enough. It was obvious he was expecting her husband and son.

The sound of silence filled the room, and Mary realized she should have told him. She didn't know what to say, so she turned to check the rolls, which were browning in the oven, but mainly to avoid the look in his eyes.

He still had not answered her.

"Jack, I'm sorry I didn't tell you. Garrett is in Boston this weekend and Jody is spending a few days with mother. I saw no harm in asking you to dinner, especially at four o'clock in the afternoon... I'm sorry. I should have told you."

There was nothing more she could say.

Finally he spoke. "It's okay. I just thought your husband would be here. Wherever you want to eat is fine with me... Can I do something to help?"

"You can pour the tea, if you like."

She motioned first to the refrigerator and then to the room just off the kitchen where the table was attractively set for two. Maybe it would be better if he had something to do. Things certainly weren't going well so far. Everything seemed stiff and formal, and neither of them seemed to know what to say.

She had fixed roast beef and mashed potatoes and a garden salad, and although it seemed like a good idea at the time, now she wished she had fixed stuffed flounder or chicken cacciatore or the lamb chops. Even the meal seemed designed to recreate memories of times they once shared together.

She realized she had messed up royally. The last thing she had wanted to do was make Jack feel uncomfortable, and that was exactly what she had done. He was bound to believe it was all a setup. Her husband was out of town. Her child was visiting his grandmother. And she had invited him to dinner, conveniently neglecting to tell him they would be dining alone.

Jack smiled as she brought out the food. "I like your menu."

"I hoped you would. I thought perhaps you ate out a lot and you might like something a little more ordinary."

"Roast beef is never ordinary to me. You know that."

Indeed she did. Roast beef had always been one of Jack's favorites. At least the mood was lightening up a little.

She saw Jack glance at a couple of pictures on the wall. They were portraits of Jody and Garrett. Then he walked over to view them closely.

"Your husband and son, I assume... They look a great deal alike."

"Yes, Jody looks just like his dad, but his ways remind me more of my daddy."

"Then he should grow up to be a good man."

"Thank you for saying that. I think Daddy would probably say the same about you. You were always his favorite."

"No way!" Jack laughed. "I was that crazy kid who was in love with his daughter, and he was sure we were going to run away and get married before we finished school. I doubt that he thought very highly of me in those days."

Finally they were able to laugh together and it was becoming a little easier to talk. Mary brought more hot rolls and Jack refilled their tea glasses.

"Everything is delicious. You cook a lot like your mom."

"I suppose so. That's where I learned how. Eat all you want, but save room for desert. I made lemon meringue pie."

"Do you realize I have to sing after you ply me with all this food?"

They ate their desert on the deck. The earlier tension had eased and the moments of silence were no longer awkward.

It was a very nice place, Jack thought, as he viewed his surroundings. Apparently she had done all right for herself. The house must have cost a fortune, but no doubt Garrett Davenport made a lot of money. Jack was not resentful. Financial success had not come to him as quickly as it had to some, but he was doing all right, and at this point in his life there were other things that were more important to him than wealth.

As the water rippled gently in the pool, Mary knew there was nothing clandestine or wrong with having Jack to dinner. They were simply two people who had once cared a great deal about each other before their lives had taken them in different directions. The dinner was pleasant and not at all uncomfortable, and she was glad he had come.

"Do you mind if I smoke?" Jack asked.

Apparently her husband did not smoke, as there were no ashtrays in sight.

"Of course not. Let me get you an ashtray."

"You don't smoke?" Jack asked as he lit up a *Winston* and hesitatingly offered Mary one. It had been awhile since they had been together and he didn't know how much her habits had changed.

"No. Madeline and I used to have an occasional cigarette with a glass of wine, but when I got pregnant with Jody, I quit completely."

"The wine too?" Jack grinned.

"No, I still have a glass of wine from time to time, but I'm afraid that's as close as I've come to becoming worldly. Sometimes it's nice to enjoy a glass of wine with a good friend at the close of the day... Would you like some? There's a bottle in the refrigerator."

"Yes, I would, but it's not the close of the day, and I'm gonna have enough trouble singing after this big meal. I guess I better pass."

Mary wished it were the close of the day. It would be pleasant to share a glass of wine with Jack.

"Thanks for asking me to dinner. It was a wonderful meal. I don't suppose I have to tell you how much I enjoyed it."

They stood opposite each other as he prepared to leave, Jack in his navy shirt and white pants, and Mary in a navy cotton dress with a white sailor collar with navy piping and an embroidered anchor. It was strange they had chosen outfits so much alike. Her shoulder length auburn hair was caught back with a yellow band that matched the rope on the anchor. She caught a glimpse of the two of them in the full-length mirror Garrett had installed on the patio, and she thought they looked rather striking.

For a few seconds, neither of them spoke. It was time for Jack to go, but they were both reluctant to say good-bye.

Finally Jack broke the silence. "Maybe some day we'll have time for that glass of wine, but right now I've got a show to do. It was great seeing you. Thanks again for the dinner... Take care of yourself. Okay?"

"You take care too." She hesitated, then added, "Good luck, Jack."

"Thanks."

And he turned and walked quickly down the sidewalk to his van. Her eyes followed him all the way. When he reached the van, he instinctively looked back to see if she was still there.

Suddenly he turned and started walking back toward her. She walked down the steps to meet him, although she wasn't sure why he was returning.

Then he spoke. "I was wondering... Would you like to come over for the last show?"

"Yes, I would like that very much."

"Good! I'll look for you. Maybe I'll do something you haven't heard before."

As he turned to leave, she called out to him, "Jack, please be careful. The traffic is terrible on Friday."

He smiled when he heard her warning and remembered how she had always told him to drive carefully after he kissed her good-night and started to leave.

*　　*　　*　　*　　*

Jack was busy checking the sound system when Mary arrived. She quickly found a seat down front and, unlike her two previous visits, she felt very comfortable being there.

She sat almost spellbound as she listened to Jack sing. He was so good. She hoped that this time he would make it all the way. He was good enough, and he certainly deserved it. But he had been good enough at baseball too. Yet fate had not been kind to him. She realized that success in the entertainment business is often more a matter of who gets the breaks than how good you are. Nonetheless, she earnestly hoped this time it would be different, and that all the good things he deserved would come to him.

A glance at her watch reminded her that in just a few minutes the show would be ending. She wished it were only beginning. After tonight their lives would again turn in different directions. This was as it should be, but she would still miss him.

Her thoughts were interrupted by the sound of Jack's voice as he spoke to the audience.

"In my shows I frequently sing songs about home. Home is a special place. Someone once said, 'Home is where the heart is.' It's the place where we grew up, where we fell in love for the first time, and perhaps where we lost our innocence. There are those who say you can't go home again. But once in awhile there is something that takes you there, if only for a brief while, and in your mind, you're home again. And all the things you left behind are yours once more... Home for me is Chattanooga, Tennessee, and I go there as often as I can, which is not nearly enough."

Then he strummed his guitar and for a moment seemed lost in his own private reverie. Then he continued. "And sometimes when I'm lonely and feeling a little down, it seems like *I'm Five Hundred Miles Away from Home.*

And he began to sing the sad and lonely lyrics of the country classic. When he reached the chorus, many of the people were on their feet, and it was obvious they were feeling some of the same sentiments Jack had expressed, as they clapped and sang along with him:

"Lord, I'm one... Lord, I'm two... Lord, I'm three... Lord, I'm four... Lord, I'm five hundred miles away from home."

Mary rose with the others and clapped to the beat, but she could not join in the singing. A lump rose in her throat as she realized how very far she was from home and the life she had known and loved. The distance could not be measured in miles. It was more than that. It seemed like a lifetime.

Jack changed keys and moved quickly to another song about home, *Take Me Home Country Roads,* and again the audience responded with obvious approval.

"Thank you all for coming. This is my last show here for awhile, but I'll be back in a few months. *Kelly's* is a great place to play, and I look forward to seeing you all again."

And then he began to play the familiar chords of *Desperado* and Mary knew this was the finale.

* * * * *

"Do you still like waffles?" Jack asked as they were leaving the club.
"Sure."
"Good. I know the best place around. Why don't you follow me, and we'll get some coffee and a waffle and talk awhile. You don't have to go home just yet, do you?"
"No, I guess not. There's no one waiting up for me."

* * * * *

The Waffle Hut was in the Buckhead section of Atlanta and served everything from hamburgers to T-bone steaks, but their specialty was waffles.

When the waitress came to take their order, Jack said, "Maggie, we'll have a waffle later, but right now just bring us some decaf."

"Sure thing. Be right back."

Mary wondered how often he came here and with whom. It was obvious he and Maggie were not strangers.

"It takes awhile for me to unwind after a show. I'm still relatively new at this and I always wonder if I did okay or whether the audience liked the songs I chose. So I get a little uptight and I have to come down."

"You did a great job tonight! It was obvious the audience loved you... Your comments about home and the two songs... Do you always do those on closing night?"

"I've never done the first one before in my life, at least not before an audience. I took a real chance on that one. It's an old Bobby Bare song. I love the song, but I didn't know if anyone else would. It's kind of crazy, but sometimes you're up there on stage and you get an inspiration, and you just go with it. Sometimes the audience responds and sometimes, well, sometimes you fall flat on your face."

"They certainly responded tonight." Her voice grew pensive. "I guess at sometime or another, we all feel like we're five hundred miles away from home... It's a lonely and foreboding feeling. I know. I've felt it many times." Mary paused and then asked. "Was there a reason you were thinking of home tonight?"

"Yes, there was. You were the reason... You're a big part of home to me. I can't go home without being reminded that it's different, that it will never be the same. When I stood on stage tonight and thought of home, I thought of you and me... and Mom and Dad... and Jenny... and all the good things from my years of growing up. I know our lives are different now, and yours is probably a hell of a lot better than mine, but there were some good times, some really good times, that we left behind in a place that was once home for both of us."

He took a sip of his coffee and continued.

"You've probably long since put those memories behind you, and for the most part I suppose I have too, but every now and then they sweep over me and fill me with nostalgia, and I remember the way we were."

"They were good times, very good times. I haven't forgotten them, Jack. I never will. They were probably the happiest days of my life." She could say no more. She could only stare across the table deep into the eyes of the one who had been such a vital part of the special memories she would carry with her always.

They talked far into the night, as Maggie continued to refill their coffee cups. It was as if they had a lifetime of catching up to do. They talked of old times, old friends and events they had all but forgotten, but which now came back as though it were only yesterday.

As Jack shifted positions in the booth he brushed against Mary's feet and a grin came across his face.

"You still kick your shoes off in restaurants."

"It's one of life's simple pleasures to be able to kick your shoes off in a restaurant or a movie theater and slip them on when the lights are turned up, and nobody knows but you."

She had always done this. Jack thought of the time he slid his foot quietly to the side while they were engaged in something other than watching the movie, and eased Mary's shoes over under his own seat, and when the movie was over, she reached for her shoes and couldn't find them.

Finally Jack told her about his baseball injury and the terrible summer of '74 when he learned he would never play baseball again. Mary fought to keep back the tears, as she realized what a tremendous blow this had been. He had lost his dream and she was sure that for awhile, he had almost lost his way.

He told her about Susan and how her friendship had sustained him through that period in his life. He spoke often of his mother. Mary knew they had a special relationship. The Roberts family had always been a close knit family and after losing Jenny, they had drawn even closer together. Then Jack's dad died and there was only Jack and his mom. Mary had always liked Virginia Roberts. She had never interfered in Jack's life, but she had always been his strongest ally. Her home was always open to his friends, and a lot of kids in the neighborhood felt as though Jack's mom was their second mother. Mary was glad he had been in Chattanooga when the doctor's final word had come.

They talked about Mary and her life in Atlanta. Jack noticed she glowed when she talked about Jody. It was apparent that he was the best thing in her life. She told him some things about her marriage, but he felt there were other things she had left unsaid.

She was wearing a yellow pants outfit, and Jack thought that it must be true what they say about motherhood making a woman beautiful. Mary had always been pretty, but now she was radiant, although at times he could detect a hint of sadness in her eyes, and he suspected life had not dealt her the best of all possible hands.

But mainly they talked of happier times. They reminisced of their childhood and all the crazy things they had done. Mary mentioned the cat he had brought her when he was eleven. And she reminded him that he had not had the decency to even let her name her own cat, but had already named her himself.

Jack grinned, "I suppose you could have changed her name."

"Oh, no. I tried, but she wouldn't have it. She was already 'Mandy', and that was what she intended to stay. It was the only name she would answer to."

"Well, what's wrong with Mandy?" Jack defended. "I thought it was a pretty good name."

"I suppose so, but I wanted to call her Misty."

"Misty?... What sort of a name is that for a cat?"

There was a lot of silly conversation. Mary hadn't been silly in a long time, and it was nice to simply be herself and not feel the necessity to act in a particular way.

Suddenly they were aware that they were the only ones left in the restaurant, except for the cleanup crew. Even Maggie had gone.

"It looks like they're about to close the place." Mary remarked. "I think we had better go."

"I don't know. It might be fun to spend the night with you at The Waffle Hut." Jack smiled. "Have you got your shoes on yet?"

"I'm working on it," Mary replied as she groped to find them under the table.

He reached down and slipped the sandals on her feet and took her by the hand as she got up from her seat.

She was sorry to be leaving. It had been the nicest evening she had spent in a long time, and she would treasure it always. She would rehearse it again and again in her mind, so she would not forget a single detail of the time they had shared together.

Even Atlanta seemed to have finally gone to sleep as they left the restaurant. Jack took the keys from her hand and opened the car door and reminded her to lock the door once she was inside.

"I'll follow you and make sure you get home safely."

"Thanks, Jack. Thanks for one of the most wonderful evenings of my life. It has been so much fun."

Then Jack moved closer.

"I can't do this in your driveway, so I guess it's now or never."

And he reached over and softly kissed her on the lips. It was not a passionate lover's kiss, but a warm and loving expression of affection.

"Love you, Babe. Thanks for spending the evening with me."

And Mary found herself saying, "Love you too."

As they made their way through the streets of Atlanta at four o'clock in the morning, she glanced time and again in her rear view mirror and saw Jack following her. She felt secure knowing he was there... She had always felt secure with him.

CHAPTER 15

SATURDAY

Jack enjoyed what he did for a living, but occasionally it was nice to get away from it all, and that was exactly what he planned to do today. He didn't have to be in Charlotte until Monday afternoon, and he had the whole weekend to himself.

There was a place high in the mountains of Northeast Georgia where he loved to go. It was peaceful and quiet, and the perfect place to be alone with your thoughts. From time to time he had written songs there, but mostly it was a means of escape from the harried pace of everyday life.

He loved the mountains and he had looked forward to this day for a long time. He wished he could go more often, but the place was remote and out of the way, and with the demands of his work, it was hard to find the time.

Today nothing was going to stop him. He had done his laundry on Friday, and as soon as he finished packing for the tour, he would be out the door and on his way.

As he folded his last shirt, the phone rang. He almost didn't answer. It was probably someone selling siding or storm windows, and it would only delay him. Then realizing it might be a last minute change in one of the tour dates, he reluctantly lifted the receiver.

"Jack... Did I get you up?"

"No. I've been up a couple of hours." He was surprised to hear from her. "I thought you'd be sleeping in this morning."

"I wanted to call Jody before he left. Mom's taking him to Opryland today... By the way, I've got some news. Mom told me something you're not going to believe... You remember Miss Peabody, the high school librarian?"

"Penelope Peabody!" Jack answered with a chuckle. "I haven't thought of her in years. Is she still alive?"

They both grinned as they remembered the tall, prim, stone-faced high school librarian, who had kept watch over her books as though they were her most prized possession.

"Very much alive!" Mary confirmed. "Miss Peabody got married last week."

"You're kidding!"

Penelope Peabody was an old maid. She and her twin sister, who also had never married, had lived together in the house where they were born for the last seventy years. Throughout her career Miss Peabody had dedicated herself to "maintaining silence" in the high school library, and since her retirement she had served on various 'Morality Boards' and had worked tirelessly to ban everything from kissing on television to Sunday baseball.

"So, who's the lucky guy?"

"Theodore Zimmerman."

"Theodore Zimmerman!" Jack repeated. "The undertaker?"

"Yes. Can you believe it?... Rumor has it they've been seeing each other for ten years, even before Mrs. Zimmerman died... Anyway, Wednesday night, right after prayer meeting, they eloped. She left her sister a note saying they were taking a cruise."

"Wow! Who would have thought?"

Suddenly the remembrance of Miss Peabody reminded him of something else. "You remember the time in study hall when she went out in the hall to talk to Principal Summerour and I lit a firecracker?"

"I remember. She came storming back in like an army sergeant, demanding to know who did it, and when nobody confessed, she asked me who did it... I don't know why she always asked me 'Who did it?' anytime something happened."

"You were her pet. That's why!"

"I wasn't her pet! The only pet she had was Theodore Zimmerman." Mary laughed.

He had forgotten how easy it was to talk to Mary. It was almost as if they had never been apart, and although she was married to someone else and whatever they had shared in the past was long gone, the friendship and the easiness were still there. He was glad their paths had crossed once more, if only briefly, and he was glad he had not ignored the ringing of the phone. One story led to another and they talked for almost an hour.

"Jack, I'm sorry. I've kept you much too long. I'm sure you've got things to do, but I just had to tell you about Miss Peabody."

"I'm glad you called. It's nice to talk about the old days and the good times we had."

Jack paused for a moment, as if contemplating something. Then he spoke.

"Mary, you know the place in the mountains I told you about? I thought I might drive up there today. Would you like to come with me?"

As soon as he said it, he wished he had not. It was stupid. He couldn't ask a married woman to go off into the mountains with him, but that was exactly what he had done.

"But you said you went there to write. I'd only be in your way."

"I'm not going to write today. I'm going to relax. But I understand. I guess it's not the smartest idea I ever had." His voice grew suddenly pensive. "I'm sorry, I shouldn't have asked... It just seemed like fun."

Mary pondered his words. He was right. It wasn't the smartest idea for either of them, but it did seem like fun.

She didn't know what to do. She wanted to go, but what would people think? It probably wasn't right, but neither did it seem wrong. Her mind vacillated. She couldn't just take off with a man to some remote place in the mountains. She was married... but Garrett was married too, and it didn't seem to make any difference to him. Nonetheless, two wrongs don't make a right. She could not go... But she wanted to. Jack was not just any man. They were not looking for an affair... They were friends. They respected each other... They would keep things under control. Neither of them wanted to do anything to hurt the other. Of this, she was sure.

Finally, Jack spoke, "It's okay. I understand... I'd love to have you come with me, but I understand."

Mary interrupted, "I want to. I just don't know if I should... Jody had an earache last night. Mom said he was fine this morning, but you never know about those things."

"It's okay... I understand."

"Jack," Mary interrupted again. "I want to go!"

"Are you sure?" His voice was very serious.

"Yes, I'm sure. When do you want to leave?"

"As soon as we can. It takes a couple of hours to get there, so we don't need to kill a lot of time."

"Can you give me fifteen minutes?"

"Sure! I'll go by the Colonel's and pick up some fried chicken for a picnic.

"I'll be ready."

It was almost ten when he arrived at her house. She met him at the door and handed him a jug of lemonade and a tin of chocolate chip cookies.

"My contribution to the picnic."

She was dressed in jeans and a red and white striped shirt. Her hair was caught back at the nape of her neck in a matching bow, and the smile on her face mirrored her excitement about the trip to the mountains.

As they pulled out of the driveway, once more Jack observed the dignified elegance of the neighborhood where she lived. The houses were stately, and the yards were well groomed, and there were huge magnolia trees everywhere. It was definitely not the 'poor side' of town.

Before long they were out of Atlanta and headed for the mountains of northeast Georgia. It was a beautiful fall morning, and it was nice to leave the hustle and bustle of the city behind.

The winding two-lane blacktop curved gently up the rugged mountain, reminding Mary of Chattanooga and the mountains that overlooked it. It had been a long time since she had spent a day in the mountains.

The simple beauty of their surroundings defied words, and neither spoke as they drove along. The early fall foliage with its vast array of colors was gorgeous, and Mary watched as a gentle breeze pulled a golden leaf from its branch and playfully swirled it in a twisting motion to the still green meadow below.

There was a comfortable easiness between the two of them as the van plied its way up the mountain. An occasional glance and a smile conveyed their feelings far better than words could express, and Mary could not remember when she had felt such contentment.

Farther up in the mountains Jack pulled off the blacktop and onto a narrow dirt road. Turning to Mary, he said, "I've got something to show you that will take your breath away!"

Excitement showed in his eyes, and as grand as the trip had been thus far, she knew it was only the beginning. She didn't know what he "had to show her", but whatever it was, it would be wonderful, and what's more, it would be Jack.

The early morning sunlight reflected like a diamond off the drops of dew on a young maple as it stood guard alongside the narrow road, and for another half-hour they followed the dusty wagon road deeper into the mountains. Finally, Jack pulled off to the side of the road and parked in the shade of a giant oak.

He looked at Mary, his eyes still sparkling. "The rest of the way is on foot."

As they got out of the van, he pulled a blanket from behind the seat and picked up the picnic basket.

"It's beautiful, Jack... Who does this place belong to?"

"God."

"I know, but somebody owns it, don't they? We're not trespassing, are we?"

"It belongs to a friend of mine. His family lived here for generations. Now they're all gone but him. He lives in Valdosta and comes up when he can. He brought me here a few years ago and told me to come anytime I wanted."

For a few moments they stood in silence and surveyed their surroundings. Then they began their trek up the winding rocky trail to the high country. They walked for probably a mile along the seldom-used trail, stopping from time to time to partake of the view and the sounds and smells of the forest. The pungent fragrance of pines and cedars penetrated the early morning air, and songbirds fluttered in the trees high above their head. In the distance they could hear the gentle sound of water flowing over the rocks in the creek below.

Gradually the sound of the running water grew louder, and as they rounded a bend in the trail, they could see the shallow creek. Jagged rocks jutted out of the water, making numerous tiny waterfalls as the water surged over the rocks and down the rambling creek bed to the lowlands below.

Mary watched, almost in disbelief, as the frosted white foam created by the rush of the tiny waterfalls splashed and gushed its way downstream.

He saw in Mary's eyes the same wonder he felt when he had seen the creek the first time. She was captivated by the beauty and wonder around her, but in his eyes, she was the real beauty and true wonder on the mountain today. She still made his heart throb as no woman before or since ever had. He couldn't understand how they had slipped away from each other seven years earlier, anymore than he understood why their paths had once again crossed.

For a brief moment he wondered if he had been wrong to bring her here. Then she looked at him and smiled, and nothing seemed wrong. All he wanted to do was be with her, if just for today.

He longed to take her in his arms and hold her and tell her he loved her. But he knew he could not. She was not his. She belonged to someone else.

His thoughts were interrupted as suddenly she touched his arm.

"Jack... Look at that!"

She was pointing about a hundred feet up the creek to two beavers, who were busying themselves carving a log with their teeth as they worked like Trojans to build their dam.

She had never seen anything like it before.

"Oh Jack, this is so beautiful."

She slipped her arm around his waist and gazed almost spellbound at the two beavers. He pulled her closer and hugged her gently and wished they could erase all the years in between... but they could not.

Slowly he released her and took her hand in his, and they walked along the creek bank as the warm sun caressed their bodies. Once he stopped to skip a pebble across the creek, then quickly used his old baseball injury as an excuse when the rock sank as soon as it hit the water.

She laughed at his excuse and picked up her own pebble, and on the first try made the little rock skip three times across the surface of the creek. Then she teasingly flexed her muscle and gave him a hard time about how the 'weak little city woman' could out throw the 'big professional baseball pitcher'.

Jack shook his head and smiled. "Okay, Nolan Ryan, you win."

Suddenly, their laughter stopped and their eyes met, and feelings that neither had allowed themselves to feel in years overtook them. And there in the sanctity of the North Georgia mountains they reached out to each other. It was neither lust nor mere passion they had succumbed to. It was the love they had known for each other so many years ago. It had not died, but had lay dormant all these years, waiting for a moment like this to spark their feelings and rekindle the flame. The flame had not been put out, no matter how hard each had tried. He took her in his arms, and she yielded herself to his tender embrace, and they kissed, long and loving, and the feelings they had kept locked away inside for so long surfaced.

As they strolled arm in arm alongside the creek, they treasured the nearness of each other and enjoyed the rugged beauty of the mountain. They stopped high above a cliff and looked down at the valley below. Everything seemed so small and far removed. It was as if they were in another world.

"You haven't seen the best part yet."

"You mean there's more?"

"Just listen." He motioned toward a small bluff below them.

As she listened, she faintly heard the sound of falling water.

"A waterfall?" Her eyes seemed to come alive and he smiled at her enthusiasm.

"Want to see it?"

"Oh, yes!"

He took her hand and helped her down from the huge gray rock formation, and they walked along the creek and across the meadow in the direction he had pointed. A soft breeze swept down from the mountain peaks, bringing a cool sensation to her face, which was red from the sun and the physical exertion she was not accustomed to.

Eventually they came to a narrow rocky trail, which appeared to be used mainly by the wildlife that inhabited the area. The deer were probably the largest animals that used the trail, as most of the animals watered at the creek or the wet-weather springs that abounded throughout the mountain. The trail was almost grown over, and there were several places where Jack had to take a limb and beat the undergrowth down so they could go on.

The sound of the rushing water grew louder and finally the pathway became large smooth rocks, which had been held firmly in place for centuries. For awhile the rocks made walking easier, but as they approached the falls, the rocks were wet and slippery from the constant spray of water.

Up ahead the unmistakable croaking of bullfrogs could be heard, and a groundhog scurried across the trail in front of them and quickly disappeared into his hole. Mary was suddenly aware that she was far from the safety and security of her home in Atlanta, and was deep in the wilderness of a mountain she had never seen before, but she felt safe. She always had with Jack.

The air that had been hot and humid at the top of the trail was now cool and fresh, and as they made their way across a small stream, which had deviated from the main flow of the water, she saw the falls.

It was more grand than she had imagined. It was wide and forceful, and the strong current dropped almost a hundred feet to the natural reservoir below. As she stepped forward to get a better look, she slipped on one of the wet rocks. Jack grabbed her before she hit the water and pulled her up to him. As he held her tightly, he was aware of her heavy breathing and rapid heartbeat. Her breathing slowed, but still she clung to him, grateful for the feel of his strong arms around her.

Once more he kissed her, tenderly and lovingly, and she responded in the same way, and there in the mist of the rushing falls, they recaptured the love they had once known.

For awhile they sat on a large rock shaded by the cliff above them. It was cool and refreshing as the mist from the roaring falls gently sprayed above them. Except for the sounds of nature, there was a heavenly quiet all about them as they sat alone, each absorbed in their own private thoughts.

"Would you like to go wading?"

Her eyes sparkled. "Why not?" She hadn't waded in a creek since she was a little girl, and if her memory was correct, it was Jack who had talked her into it then.

They took off their shoes and socks and rolled up their pants legs. He waded in first and then extended his hand to her. "Come on in."

The cold water sent shivers up her spine and almost took her breath, but everything about this day had been breathtaking. As she moved farther out into the water, still holding his hand, her body adjusted to the coolness and she no longer shivered.

She had almost forgotten how nice it was to be with Jack. There was something about being with him that brought out the best in her. It wasn't just the way he made her feel, but the way she felt about herself when they were together.

She wanted to feel and experience all there was of this day, realizing the memories would echo in her heart forever.

The water felt wonderful, and they splashed each other and playfully taunted the other with dunking. Neither of them had laughed or had so much fun in a long time. They were being silly, but sometimes 'silly' can be nice.

All of a sudden, Jack felt something against his foot. It had been a long time since he had been barefoot in a creek, but he knew the feel, and before he could get out of the way the crawfish grabbed his toe and he lost his balance and fell backwards into the cold water.

Mary couldn't help but laugh, and as she reached down to help him up, he playfully pulled her down into the water with him. They were drenched to the skin, but they didn't care. They were happy and a little cool water and a few wet clothes didn't matter.

An hour or so later, they were back at the top of the mountain. Their clothes were still wet and the warm sunshine felt good against their bodies. It had been an incredible day, and they felt an innate sense of contentment as they made their way back to the meadow, where their picnic awaited them.

She had changed... He knew that. But today it was as though time had stood still, and they had never been apart. And no matter what the future held, they would always cherish this day.

Jack spread the blanket on the ground next to the creek, and then wrapped it around Mary's wet shoulders as she shivered from the dampness. Then he leaned close and kissed her, and there in the middle of all this beauty, he pulled her close and held her tightly and passionately. She looked hungrily into his eyes and then slowly eased herself back onto the blanket and pulled him down upon her... And there high in the mountains, on a grassy knoll with the warm sun shining down upon their bodies, they made love.

They touched and held each other... They kissed... They laughed... but most of all they loved... and not just each other's body, but each other... Heart to heart! Soul to soul!

The afternoon lapsed endlessly on. Neither of them had any concept of time or how long they had been there. Time did not matter. It was as if they were the only two people in the world.

Suddenly, there was a noisy clatter behind them and Jack quickly pulled the blanket over them, afraid someone had discovered their lovemaking. As they looked around, they saw the intruders had no interest in them or what they were doing, but were preoccupied with their own doings.

As their hearts raced from the shock of these intruders who had so rudely interrupted their lovemaking, they slowly began to laugh. The clamoring noise was being made by three raccoons, who had found the picnic basket and were helping themselves to Jack and Mary's lunch.

Their laughter startled the little black and gray critters, but when they saw the humans meant them no harm, they went back to finishing their lunch.

"Oh Jack, look at them go."

One was busying himself with a biscuit, while the second was holding a drumstick between his paws and gnawing away at it, and the third little raccoon, who had been climbing around on the top of the picnic basket, suddenly lost his balance and fell in.

"The little thieves even wore their masks," Jack grinned, referring to the dark coloring around the raccoons' eyes, as they watched the little animals devour the remains of their lunch.

Finally the little rascals finished their meal and moved on to see what other mischief they could get into.

Afraid someone else might come upon them, they found their clothes and dressed. Then they lay back on the blanket and watched the puffy white clouds drift slowly across the blue sky. All about them the birds were singing their pretty songs of the forest back and forth to each other. The whole day was a memory that would last a lifetime, and Mary was glad she had come.

As the afternoon faded into twilight, a chilly wind blew down from the mountain and Jack and Mary snuggled up in the blanket. They watched as the bright orange sun set in the west and gradually slipped beyond the distant mountain peaks, leaving behind the most beautiful silvery-orange sky, which shadowed the still white clouds and gave the effect of that forever-sought-after silver lining.

Nightfall was fast approaching and as reluctant as they were to leave behind their day in the mountains, they knew they needed to make their way back to the van before darkness overtook them.

As they started down the rocky trail, they turned to take one last look at the beautiful sanctuary of nature where they had spent this special day. As they looked back, they saw something they had missed before. Standing on a rocky cliff just above the grassy knoll where they had made love, was a big buck deer and at his side, his doe. They watched in passionate silence, as the two deer stood side by side gazing out at the sunset and sharing the beauty and wonder of God's world.

* * * * *

It was almost dark as they made their descent down the mountainside. Only the soft radiance of the harvest moon lit their pathway. There was a chilly bite in the air, as the brisk autumn breeze blew through the trees. The wind in the crisp, dry leaves made strange sounds and the hazy moonlight created haunting shadows around them. Fog was beginning to rise from the valley below, and the mountain that had been so tranquil during the day now seemed eerie and threatening.

Mary gripped Jack's hand tighter as they felt their way along the rough, dark pathway. We should have started back earlier, she thought.

He sensed her nervousness and drew her closer.

"It's okay babe. We're almost there."

And she was no longer afraid. She thought about how gentle Jack was. He was strong and tough, and in some ways callused to the world, but he was also kind and caring and sensitive.

Just a short distance farther they spotted the van, and soon they were headed out of the mountains and on their way home. They were both very quiet, apparently lost in their own thoughts as they returned to what they knew was 'the real world'. Occasionally their eyes met as they simultaneously turned to look at each other, and it was obvious that they were both wondering if this day had actually happened or if it had been only a dream.

Jack placed his hand on Mary's.

"Are you okay?"

She nodded and was about to speak when Jack continued.

"No regrets?"

"Only that it's over." Her voice was a trifle sad.

They drove on in silence until they reached the outskirts of Atlanta. He felt her hand relax in his and turned to see that she was asleep. He stopped for a traffic light and watched her as she slept. She was tired and a bit unkempt from the soaking in the pool, but she was still the most beautiful woman he had ever known.

As he pulled into her driveway she was still sleeping. He reached into her purse and found her keys and went to open the door. Then he came back and gently picked her up. The movement awakened her, and she looked up and smiled as she realized she was in Jack's arms.

"Are we home?" she yawned.

"I'm afraid so."

"Would you like some coffee?" She asked once they were in the kitchen, "or maybe a glass of wine?"

"I'll pass tonight. We're both tired, and you didn't get much sleep last night. Remember?"

She smiled, "It's been such a wonderful day, Jack. Thanks for sharing your mountain with me. I'll never forget this day."

"Neither will I, but when I remember it, it won't be the mountain I'll think about." His eyes were solemn as he looked at her. Then he bent down and kissed her softly on her forehead. "Good-night. I'll call you tomorrow."

He paused at the doorway to remind her to lock the door and grinned as he added, "Some bad guy... like me... might try to get in."

And then he was gone.

She wished he would stay the night, but she knew he would not. He would not spend the night in another man's house with another man's wife. Jack Roberts would make his share of mistakes in life, and later he might decide that today had been a mistake, but he was not without honor, and as much as she had wanted him to spend the night, she knew without asking what his answer would be.

But he had given her today, and what a day it had been! Throughout all the tomorrows of her life, she would always have today. Nothing could ever take it away.

CHAPTER 16

SUNDAY

She went about her normal Sunday morning routine, yet nothing seemed normal. After yesterday, she wondered if life would ever be normal again.

She showered and dressed for church, but today the thought of going to church seemed strange... Maybe it was guilt that she was feeling, but it really wasn't that. She had not yet dealt with the guilt or wrongness of yesterday. Eventually she would have to, but right now yesterday didn't seem wrong. Instead, it seemed like the most right thing she had done in years... Yesterday she had felt loved... something she hadn't felt in a long time... That couldn't be so wrong... Could it?

She didn't know what would happen next or even what she wanted to happen. For some reason though, church seemed like the place to be on Sunday morning.

As she started to put on her earrings the phone rang.

"Hello."

"Mary, what are you up to?"

"Hi, Jack. I'm getting ready for church. What are you doing?"

"Missing you."

She smiled at his sincerity.

"Me too."

Her words brought a smile to his face and a relief to his heart. As much as he had hoped, he was unsure she would feel the same after having a night to 'sleep on' their day in the mountains.

"I've got an idea." He hesitated. "Why don't we go to church together?"

She thought of the times they had attended church together as teenagers. They sat on the back pew and he flirted, she blushed, and neither of them got very much out of the sermon.

"Jack, I don't think it would look exactly right if I brought a date to church while my husband's out of town."

It was the first time she had mentioned Garrett all weekend and even now she didn't say his name.

"We don't have to go to your church. There are plenty of churches in Atlanta. You know what they say about Atlanta. There's one church for every bar."

Mary laughed. She had never heard that one, but it was probably true. Atlanta had a lot of both.

"Where do you want to go?"

"I don't know. We'll just drive around until we find one that suits us. How about that?"

It sounded crazy, but the idea of spending another day with Jack was exciting.

"Okay. Why not?"

"Good. I'll pick you up around ten."

*   *   *   *   *

The dashboard clock showed 11:05 as they pulled up in front of the Antioch Baptist Church. They parked alongside the road since the parking lot was already full. Apparently services had already begun, as there was no one standing outside chatting or finishing that last cigarette.

The sign out front read:

HOMECOMING TODAY
11:00 A. M.
VISITORS WELCOME

The beautiful white church was situated in a grove of oak trees, and the entire setting was peaceful looking. It was as if the church could have a ministry of its own, even if there were no congregation inside. It seemed to reach out to you and welcome you in, and they knew they had found the right place.

They quietly opened the front door, trying not to disturb the service already in progress. Then as they entered the sanctuary it hit them... Everybody in the church except for them was black... They had hit homecoming at an all black church!

Mary's immediate reaction was to turn and leave, but Jack had already accepted a bulletin and shook hands with one of the ushers.

All the pews in the back were filled, and as they made their way down the aisle in search of a seat, an older black gentleman stepped out into the aisle.

Every eye in the church was fixed upon this man who stood there blocking their passage. It was so quiet you could have heard a pin drop as everyone waited to see what was about to happen. Although Jack and Mary had no way of knowing, the older man was the head deacon. He slowly reached out his hand and smiled and welcomed them to the service. A few others also smiled and nodded toward the Caucasian strangers to let them know it was okay, and that they were more than welcome in the House of the Lord.

The deacon motioned them to seats about halfway up on the left side, and they slipped into the pew and joined in singing the chorus of *When the Roll Is Called Up Yonder I'll Be There*.

Mary wondered if there were others who had made the same mistake, and if so, had they chosen to stay or had they turned and left immediately. After all this was the South and the churches, unlike the schools, were for the most part still segregated.

She felt a touch on her elbow, as the lady seated next to her handed her an open hymnal. The woman's gracious smile eased Mary's uncertainty and made her feel welcome.

The choir looked regal in their glistening white robes and red stoles with gold embroidery, and as the congregation joined in singing the familiar lines of Amazing Grace, both Jack and Mary were glad they had come.

They stood and repeated together the Lord's Prayer as they had done so many times in their own church, and it all seemed very comfortable and very right. Mary found herself remembering the simple words of her father during all the unrest of the civil rights movement of the sixties...

"I don't think Heaven will have one side for whites and another for blacks. So why should we be segregated down here... After all we're all God's children."

The Reverend Alonzo Driggers made the announcements and extended a cordial welcome to "all those who are worshipping with us today," after which a large black woman stood up to sing. Mary looked at her bulletin. The soloist's name was Cassandra Upshaw.

She had a lovely resounding voice and as she began to sing, Mary and Jack's eyes both met. The song was his daddy's favorite... *Peace in the Valley*. Mr. Roberts was no singer and rarely even tried to join in the singing in church, but he loved this song.

> *There'll be Peace in the Valley someday,*
> *There'll be Peace in the Valley, Oh Lord I Pray,*
> *There'll be no sickness, no sorrow,*
> *No trouble, I see.*
> *There'll be Peace in the Valley for me.*

Jack's eyes were fixed on the singer and his lips silently formed the words she sang. Mary could tell he was deeply moved by the beautiful rendition.

As the soloist took her seat, there were a number of reverent "Praise the Lord's" uttered, and it was obvious the congregation also had been inspired by the poignant words of the hymn.

"Wasn't that beautiful, people? Now let's take a few moments to shake hands and greet each other," Rev. Driggers instructed as he made his way down from the pulpit to greet his parishioners.

Mary and Jack immediately felt a touch on their shoulders and turned to see a frail black hand extended to them. The lady had to be ninety, if she was a day. A bright red pillbox hat was perched on her head, and she wore thick-lensed glasses, but she had a smile that would light up a Christmas tree. She looked first at Jack and then at Mary and said, "I'm Emma Shropshire. I sure am glad ya'll come today! We're just so glad to have you."

Seeing the unprejudiced love in this lady, Mary reached across the pew and hugged her affectionately.

Jack saw the moisture in Mary's eyes, and he knew she was enjoying the service as much as he was. And although this was not exactly how they had planned it, it was nice.

The preacher then continued. "Again, I'd like to welcome our visitors. Your presence adds so much to our service."

As the offering was taken, Cassandra Upshaw again stood to sing, and the words of *How Great Thou Art* seemed to reach beyond the congregation and through the open windows of the small country church, proclaiming its magnificent message to all who passed by.

The Reverend Alonzo Driggers took his text from the 40th Chapter of Isaiah.

"But they that wait upon the Lord shall renew their strength; they shall mount up with wings as eagles; they shall run and not be weary; and they shall walk and not faint."

The sermon was eloquent and powerful, and one they would think about and draw strength from in the days ahead.

As soon as the benediction was pronounced, they were approached by first one and then another, who insisted they stay for lunch.

Mary was hesitant to stay since they had not brought food, but Jack said, "We'll hurt their feelings if we don't."

They enjoyed a wonderful dinner under the huge oak trees, which no doubt had provided shelter and shade for many homecoming crowds. They met so many nice people, shook hands, laughed, swapped stories and thoroughly enjoyed this special Homecoming day.

They had thought nothing could surpass yesterday, but today was just as special in its own way.

As they started to pull out of the driveway and head back toward I-20, the afternoon service had just begun. They paused for a moment to once more hear the choir, knowing they would long remember this day and this homecoming service. And they truly felt that today, they had 'come home' to a place they had never been before.

          *   *   *   *   *

Mary took a couple of aspirin for her headache, and wished she could deal as easily with the pain in her heart.

The weekend ended as it began... quickly. It had been hard saying good-bye, as neither of them knew what the future held or even if they had a future. She fiercely clung to Jack, not knowing when, if ever, she would feel his loving arms around her.

Finally, he broke the embrace and with a look of uncertainty said, "I'll call you in a couple of days."

She could only nod through the tears. Then he kissed her once more and drove away.

She tried to sleep, but it was no use. She couldn't get him off her mind. She stared blankly at the green fluorescent numbers of the clock on her nightstand. There was something about a digital clock that bothered her. It was like seeing your life flicking away before your very eyes, only tonight the numbers changed slowly. The minutes were like hours and it seemed dawn would never come.

Finally around three o'clock, realizing that sleep was not to come for her tonight, she pulled on her fleece robe and went to the kitchen to make coffee.

After pouring herself a cup, she turned off the kitchen light and went out on the deck. The night was dark except for a few stars, and the early morning air sent a chill up her spine. She pulled her robe closer and sat on the back step, trying to sort out all that had happened. Again and again she asked the question, "Why?" Why after all these years had Jack suddenly reappeared in her life? There had been no problems until he came back.

But she knew that was not true. There had been many problems in her marriage, problems that had nothing to do with Jack or his reappearance in her life. His presence, however, had reminded her how nice it was to smile and laugh and be happy again, but mostly it had forced her to look at the pathetic state of her life and marriage.

But the truth was that Jack had not 'reappeared' in her life. She had 'reappeared' in his. When she had first seen him at *Kelly's*, she had promised herself that she would not stay for the entire performance. She would only listen to a few songs and then quietly slip out without him knowing she had been there... But she had stayed. And she had gone back a second time, and that time he had known, and they had talked, and they had ended up spending the better part of a weekend together.

Now she didn't know what she felt.

Guilt?... Perhaps.

Confusion?... Very much.

Uncertainty?... Definitely.

However, the one thing she knew beyond the shadow of a doubt was that her feelings for Jack had not changed. She still loved him. She always would.

She had believed that what she had once felt for Jack had been relegated to the past when she married Garrett, much like the items in the hatbox.

Over the years she had busied herself in the role of wife and mother, and although she had thought of Jack from time to time, she had not allowed her mind to dwell on him. Now she could think of nothing else. Earlier as she tossed and turned trying to get to sleep, she had tried to force herself to think of Garrett and her present life, but the mind has a strange way of doing its own thing, and try as she might, there was no changing its direction.

Her thoughts drifted back to Chattanooga and to a time when she and Jack were young and terribly in love. It didn't matter that he was playing in the minors and not making much money. She didn't care! She didn't need fancy things. All she needed was him. She had never known anyone like him, and all she wanted was to marry him and be with him forever.

He had loved her too. She never questioned that. But he was older and perhaps a little wiser. He wanted to wait until he could make a decent living for them. He knew she couldn't travel with him, not on the money he was making. At one time she had even suggested that he give up baseball and get a regular job that they could live on, but after seeing the look on his face, she was sorry she had mentioned it.

Baseball was Jack's life, and she realized that whether or not he ever made it to the majors, he had to try. He was good, real good. She knew that. The Jazz had signed him out of a tryout camp, and that didn't happen often... She remembered the telephone call so well. He was half-laughing and half-crying as he told her they had offered him a contract.

She was happy for him. He was fulfilling his dream. But somehow 'their dream' was getting lost in the shuffle.

All summer long they argued about it.

She would say, "Jack, please, it doesn't matter to me that we don't have much money. We'll get by. I just want to be with you."

And then Jack would counter. "But honey it does matter. You just can't live like that. Being broke isn't any fun, and it's certainly no way to start a marriage. I'll save every dollar I can, and you do the same, and maybe by next year, we'll have enough to get started." He would then pause and say, "After all, a year isn't very long."

But she was young and in love and to her a year seemed like forever.

After signing with the Jazz, Jack was assigned to their minor league team in Savannah. Savannah was almost four hundred miles from Chattanooga, and when he had an occasional day off, the team might be between series in Florida or the Carolinas. In fact, he only got home three times all summer.

Mr. & Mrs. Roberts always invited Mary to go with them when they went to visit Jack. And although they treasured those times together, they were few and far between and always so rushed.

It was during this time that Garrett had walked into her office and, subsequently, into her life. He had called on her boss twice and each time had spoken briefly with her. A few days later, he called and asked her out. He brought her flowers and took her to a dinner theater. The entire evening was very nice, and for the first time, Mary realized how nice it was to 'live the good life', and understood what Jack meant about being broke.

When she arrived at work the following Monday, she found a single yellow rose on her desk. The card read: *"Thanks for a lovely evening. Garrett"*

They saw a lot of each other the rest of the summer. It was a fairy-tale courtship with more flowers, candy and frills. Garrett was charming and romantic, and Mary was walking on 'Cloud Nine' from all the attention.

In late July Garrett went to Boston for a weeklong investment seminar. He called her every night, and when he came home, he continued to wine and dine her. And she was not surprised when two weeks later he asked her to marry him.

Jack was shocked to hear that Mary had met someone else and was going to be married. He made one attempt to see her. However, she and Garrett had already made plans for the evening, so she and Jack spoke only briefly.

His words now came back to haunt her.

"I hope you know what the Hell you're doing. You're flushing everything we had down the drain, just because this guy flashes money and fancy baubles in your face."

Then he took a deep breath and added, "I just hope he's worth it... If not, you'll have the rest of your life to think about what you threw away."

In defense, Mary countered. "You were the one who insisted money was so all-fired important. I was willing to settle for being poor... remember?"

For a moment neither of them spoke. They only stared intently at each other and watched the tears mount in the other's eyes. Then Jack broke the silence. "Good luck, Mary... I have a feeling you're going to need it."

That was the last time they had spoken until last week.

Just before dawn she cut off the coffee maker and climbed the stairway to her bedroom. Weary of mind and body and chilled from the cool night air, she slipped out of her house shoes and into bed. All the thoughts, which had flashed across the screen of her mind, had not provided the answers she sought. Only time would do that. But sheer weariness took its toll and finally she slept.

As she opened her eyes, the light filtering through the window told her it was morning. The clock showed 11:15. She had not slept so late in years. Suddenly she was overcome with panic. She had been away from the phone for almost two days. What if something had happened to Jody? What if he had gotten hurt and they had tried to call? Whatever possessed her to take off with Jack like this? What if her child had needed her or simply wanted to talk to his Mommy? She reached for the phone, her fingers shaking so she could scarcely dial the number. There was a numb sensation throughout her body, and as she waited for an answer, she realized she had not even shed her robe when she went to bed.

Finally a small, excited voice said, "Hel-Woah."

"Hey, Baby! How you doin'?"

The sound of that little voice, always so animated and so 'high on life', brought a calmness to Mary.

Words were tumbling end over end as Jody related all the things he and his grandmother had done. "We went to Lake Winnie... Gramma, what is it called?"

Mary smiled, as she remembered the many times she had gone to Lake Winnepesaukah as a little girl. It was an amusement park just across the state line from Chattanooga. Her mama and daddy had taken her there to ride the merry-go-round, the little cars, and bright shiny boats. Afterwards they fed popcorn to the ducks on the lake. It was one of those amusement parks that seemed as if it would always be around. And it was plain to see that in his mind, the local amusement park had completely overshadowed Opryland.

Her mother was now on the phone, and Mary could tell she had enjoyed the day as much as Jody.

"I thought you might have tried to call. I went shopping Saturday and spent Sunday at Madeline's." Mary lied.

"No. Everything's been fine. We've had quite a weekend ourselves... You should have seen your son when we got home last night. He was covered with coke and cotton candy, and I bet we had to wash off two layers of mustard."

Mary was now laughing. Everything was okay. Jody was fine. And she would never again spend another weekend like this. She must have taken leave of her senses. She was a wife and a mother, and Jack no longer had a place in her world. Seven years ago she had made a choice and put him in the past. You can't resurrect the past... Yesterday's gone... You can only remember it for what it was... a memory... But that's all it can ever be.

CHAPTER 17

It was quarter 'til five when Mary arrived at the airport only to learn that Garrett's flight had been delayed. The attendant at the Delta desk assured her everything was fine. The plane had not been cleared for departure as scheduled because of early morning fog and was now due to arrive in Atlanta at 5:50 instead of 5:00.

During her weekly trips to the airport, she had looked through every gift shop in the entire complex many times over, and she didn't care to do it again. She went to the restroom, checked her appearance and decided she looked all right, and returned to the lobby to wait. It had been two weeks since she had seen her husband, and things had not been good between them when he left. She was apprehensive as she waited. Lately she never knew what to expect from Garrett. He was either pleasant and utterly charming or he was cold and remote, and he could change like the wind.

As she continued to wait, her mind drifted back to the weekend and the time she had spent with Jack. All week long her emotions had vacillated between the rightness and wrongness of what she had done.

At times she felt gloriously happy, as if she had been offered and had taken, a small portion of the happiness to which she felt rightfully entitled. At other times she felt the burden of guilt. She had done something totally selfish with little regard to those whose lives were intertwined with hers. This was not the way she did things, and she felt shame and remorse for her foolish actions.

Nevertheless, try as she might, she had been unable to keep her mind off Jack, and she continued to be haunted by the question, "Where do we go from here?"

Every time the telephone rang, she thought... she hoped... it would be him... but it never was.

Now it was Friday and she still had not heard from him. Maybe he had not intended to call in the first place, but he had said he would. Why would he say such a thing if he had not meant it? She knew he would not call on the weekend and risk Garrett being home.

Once again she tried to put the whole thing out of her mind. She was here to meet her husband. The clock on the wall said it was now 5:35. Again she went to the restroom, ran a brush through her hair, and nervously returned to wait for Garrett to arrive.

Garrett left the plane with a spring in his step and seemed glad to see her. He held her close for a moment and then smiled warmly. "You look great. It's good to be home."

On Saturday he played golf with John Lewis. He got home about four and suggested they go out for dinner, just the two of them. Mary arranged for a sitter for Jody, but she would have preferred some place where the three of them could go together. Jody got to spend so little time with his dad.

They drove across town to *The Plantation* and enjoyed an elegant meal. It was a beautiful restaurant with dim lighting and soft music. He was extremely complimentary of her appearance and was making every effort to make the evening special.

It was almost as though he were trying too hard... But she was trying hard too... She often wondered when Garrett was like this if he were somehow trying to make amends. Now she was doing the same.

"What did you do last weekend?" he asked.

"Not much. I had some good books, and with both you and Jody gone, I had a chance to catch up on some reading... How about you?" She quickly reversed the question.

"Not much either. George and I had dinner and a few drinks on Saturday night, and then I came back to the hotel and caught up on some reports I needed to get done."

Mary knew Garrett was lying. She didn't know how, but somehow she always knew. Tonight, though, she wondered if he knew she was also lying. He had no reason to. She had never lied to him before.

They came home early and listened to a classical album he had bought in Boston. Then he watched the eleven o'clock news while she read.

"I guess you're not sleepy yet?" he said, as he got up to go to bed.

"Not really. I think I'll read awhile if you don't mind."

"Stay up as late as you like. I'm kind of tired. See you in the morning, my love," and he bent and kissed her lightly on the forehead.

She was glad he had not wanted to make love. Normally they did on Saturday nights, especially when he had been away all week. Sometimes she wondered if his Saturday night lovemaking was initiated more out of guilt than out of real desire for her.

She read for awhile and then went upstairs to bed, and having spent many sleepless nights of late, she was soon asleep.

Morning dawned and Garrett was eager for that which he had passed up the night before, and his ardent advances awakened Mary. She wished he wouldn't. She had not wanted him last night and she did not want him now. For a long time now she had been unable to make love to Garrett without remembering the condoms she had found in his briefcase.

That had been a long time ago and she had tried to accept his explanation and put it behind her, but she had never been able to forget it.

He removed her nightgown, and as she lay there naked beside him, she knew it was pointless to object. He was her husband and he had certain conjugal rights. He took her passionately, holding her and possessing her completely, and though he professed his love for her, it was difficult for her to respond.

When it was all over, she reached out and held his hand for awhile as they lay beneath the damp and twisted sheets and tried to pretend that everything was all right... But it was not... It had not been for a long time.

Garrett closed his eyes and dozed. As he slept, she couldn't help thinking that this man, who had just made love to her with such fervor, would no doubt make love to someone else with the same passion before they shared this bed again.

She crept quietly out of bed and went downstairs to make breakfast. Then she went to wake Jody so they could have at least one meal together as a family.

After breakfast Jody and Garrett romped together on the living room carpet while she cleared the dishes. Jody enjoyed having his daddy play with him and today Garrett seemed to enjoy it too.

Before they knew it their time together was gone and it was time to make the usual Sunday trip to Hartsfield International. Garrett would board his plane to Boston and his 'other world', and Jody and Mary would come home alone.

* * * * *

WEDNESDAY

Mary and Jody had spent most of the day by the pool. The water made Jody relaxed and sleepy, and she knew he would be no problem to get to bed tonight. The day had been one of mixed emotions and had left her with a feeling of loneliness. She delayed supper as long as she could, knowing that as soon as Jody ate, he would be out like a light and she would feel even more alone.

When she put him to bed, she tucked the cover snugly around him. If he were too warm, he would throw it back in a little while. She could never resist the maternal instinct of 'tucking him in', and as she looked down at her little boy, already in the early stages of peaceful sleep, she felt a unique closeness to him. She hoped to have other children, but he was her firstborn, and she knew that whatever the years might bring, there would always be a special bond between the two of them.

Feeling tired and a little sleepy herself, she got ready for bed earlier than usual. Sleep did not come for her as easily as it did for Jody, so she usually read for awhile. It seemed to help her relax.

At ten o'clock the telephone rang.

It was probably Garrett, but why would he be calling on Wednesday? He usually called on Thursday to let her know what time to meet him at the airport or to say he would be staying over in Boston for the weekend... Perhaps it was her mother. No one else ever called this late... But it was neither Garrett nor her mother.

She had already decided that for whatever reason, he was not going to call. All last week she had waited... afraid he would call... and at the same time, afraid he would not. When Monday passed, and then Tuesday, and then an entire week and she had heard nothing, she resigned herself to the fact that for him the weekend was only a pleasant re-creation of the old times and nothing more. But for her it had been far more than that. It had shaken the foundation of her very being, and she knew her life would never be the same. But men are different, she reasoned, and long ago she had come to realize that things are not always what they seem.

"Did I wake you?"

"No, I was just reading... How are you?"

"Okay, I guess... How about you?"

This was not the same Jack Roberts she knew... not the one she had so recently spent a weekend with... not the one she had loved for the better part of her life. The conversation was strangely formal, like an exchange between two people who scarcely knew each other.

"I'm okay. I'm just a little surprised to hear from you."

"I told you I'd call."

"I know you did, but I hardly expected you to wait ten days."

"I didn't expect to either. I had a lot of thinking to do."

"And I suppose you think I didn't?"

The conversation was terrible. All last week she had waited to hear his voice and had imagined what he would say to her and what she would say to him and it certainly wasn't anything like this.

He ignored her question.

"I wanted to call earlier, but I knew how you would react after you had time to think things over. And I wasn't ready to hear you say it was all a mistake, and it never should have happened."

"I haven't said that. I haven't even thought that." Mary snapped back. "Those are your words, not mine."

"All right, let's face it. Regardless of which one of us has the guts to say it, it was a mistake. I had no right to infiltrate your life and your marriage as though it was my God-given privilege. And you had no right to let me. We were a couple of fools trying to roll back the years, conveniently forgetting that you're a married woman and a mother. For God's sake, Mary, it's 1978 not 1970. Things have changed. They're not the same, no matter how damn much we would like for them to be. Yesterday's gone."

At least he had finally called her name. The tears slipped silently down her cheeks and dripped one by one on the polished mahogany nightstand. She reached for a Kleenex and wiped them away only to have them replaced by more.

Jack heard her gently blow her nose and knew she was crying. He hadn't meant to hurt her. God, that was the last thing he wanted to do, but there were things that must be said.

"I've spent a Hell of a week trying to sort it all out, and the only real conclusion I've come to is that several years ago you made a choice. You couldn't settle for the precious little I had to offer and you chose someone else." He hesitated and then continued. "Apparently you made the right choice. You have a successful husband who obviously provides quite well for you, far better than I could have, and more importantly, you have a child who needs both his mother and father."

At least this was the real Jack talking now. She should have known he would react this way. He was a man of principles... Sometimes bullheaded... Sometimes independent... but never without honor. He had always been a decent, caring human being, and she had never known him to deliberately hurt anyone.

"I couldn't compete with Garrett Davenport then, and I sure as Hell can't now. I could never settle for some back street affair, a stolen weekend now and then, dark glasses and cheap motel rooms. I can't handle that sort of thing. When I play, I play for keeps... It's too late for us, Mary... Our time was long ago. We had our chance and we blew it. We can't go home again." He paused, as if spent from the outpouring.

"Jack, 'we' didn't blow it. I blew it. I was the one who didn't wait. But I did try. All I wanted from you was the chance to be your wife. But you wouldn't let me. You had to do it all on your terms. It was your career, your decision as to how we would live our life. You weren't willing to listen to me. I would have pitched a tent with you if you had only let me. I didn't need the big wedding at the Presbyterian Church. The preacher's study at the Methodist Church would have been fine with me. I didn't have to have an engagement ring. All I wanted was a simple band of gold... and you."

He started to interrupt, but she wouldn't let him.

"You've had your say. Now it's my time. I don't know where this thing with us is going... probably nowhere because you won't let it. But there's something you need to know, Jack... I'm not a whore! I don't fool around. Until last weekend I had been completely faithful to my marriage vows. I'm not proud of what happened last weekend. Perhaps you're right. Maybe it was a mistake. I haven't yet come to terms with that. Maybe in time I will. I don't know, but right now I can't see it as a mistake. I know I'm never going to have you because you're never going to let me. You'll always come up with a hundred thousand reasons why we can't be together. But for one brief weekend you were mine... completely mine... and if that's all I'm ever going to have, at least I had that." She hesitated. "I'm not trying to justify what I did. There is no justification for adultery. It's wrong. God, I know it's wrong, and I know firsthand how much it can hurt." Again she hesitated, unsure if she should go on. Then she continued. "Garrett was the first to cheat, and he has done it with regularity over the last few years. I don't love Garrett. I don't even respect him anymore. Our marriage is a farce. He would divorce me right now except that being divorced would tarnish his business image. The company frowns upon it."

Jack breathed a sigh as he listened quietly on the other end.

"Our marriage was in trouble long before last weekend. I talked to a lawyer over a year ago. I was ready to go forward with the divorce at that time, but he encouraged me to give it some time because of Jody. I cannot stay in this marriage. I reached that decision a long time ago and you had nothing to do with it."

There was silence on the line. Then Jack heard her take a deep breath. She had poured out her very soul, and he knew it had taken a lot of courage.

"I didn't know all this. I guess it hasn't been easy for you. I'm sorry, Mary. But what the Hell are you saying to me? Where do I fit into the picture? Am I supposed to wait around until you finally decide the time is right to end your marriage?... And by then maybe you'll change your mind again. I thought you were mine before, remember?"

"That's not fair, Jack!" He could hear the anger rising in her voice as she continued. "I guess what I'm trying to say to you, damn it, is that I love you. That wasn't good enough for you seven years ago and apparently it's not good enough now. Tell yourself last weekend was a mistake if you want to... Keep on telling yourself that... Maybe it was for you. But it wasn't a mistake for me."

And she hung up the phone.

* * * * *

It had been another sleepless night. She seemed to have a lot of them lately. Something was wrong with the coffee. It tasted horrible. She hadn't changed brands. Maybe she was just drinking too much of the stuff. But she poured another cup anyway and was about to sit down with the morning paper when the telephone rang.

"Could we talk?"

She hesitated. She wasn't sure she even wanted to talk. Maybe he had been right. Maybe it was all over for them. But the person who had uttered those three words was a different person from the one she had tried to talk to last night.

On the other end of the line, Jack waited, wondering if he would once more hear the click of the receiver. He breathed a sigh and picked up the cold cup of coffee he had poured ten minutes before and stared into it. "God, this coffee is awful," he thought... Still no click of the phone, but there was no response either.

He tried once more. "Please, Mary, could we try to talk, just for a few minutes?"

"I don't know... I don't know anything anymore."

At least she was still on the line and she had finally responded, but maybe she had rather not talk to him. Maybe she had decided in spite of what she had said last night that it was a mistake.

"Honey, I don't want to upset you. Maybe I shouldn't have called... If you don't want to talk, I understand."

He waited for her to say something, to let him know she was willing to continue the conversation, but there was only silence. Finally he could contain his feelings no longer. He felt such desperation, such confusion. "Just tell me what to do, Mary! For God's sake, tell me what to do!" His voice broke, and this person who had always demonstrated such strength in the face of life's adversities was no longer strong.

She wanted to reach out and touch him, to assure him that everything would be all right, much as she did with Jody when he had a problem. But Jack was not Jody, and neither was she sure that everything was going to be all right.

Again there was only silence. They were two people a hundred miles apart, joined only by a telephone line, reaching out to each other for answers, which neither of them could provide.

Finally Jack spoke. "Will you answer me one question?"

"What is it?"

"Did you mean what you said last night?"

She wasn't sure what he was referring to. She had said a lot last night, a lot more than she had intended. It had all spilled forth as though she might never have another chance.

"Did I mean what?"

"Did you mean it when you said you loved me?"

"Yes, Jack. I meant it. I never stopped loving you!"

"If I'm only sure of that, the rest can wait. It's the not knowing that eats away at me... I've been to Hell and back since I saw you. It has been awful! Seeing you after all these years, spending one gloriously happy weekend with you, and knowing that was probably all it would ever be, then trying to find a way to put it all behind me as if it had never happened."

"I know. I've been there too."

They had both wrestled with uncertainty, neither with any assurance that when they worked through their own feelings, the other would feel the same.

"Jack, I need some time. There's a lot I have to do." She paused and breathed a deep sigh, which he could hear over the phone. "I think it would be better if we didn't try to see each other..."

He interrupted. "I understand. I've got shows in the Carolinas for the next couple of weeks, but you've got my number at the apartment. If I'm not there, there's an answering machine." Jack paused and his voice quietened. "Just promise me one thing... if you change your mind, you'll let me know."

"I won't change my mind. Just let me do what I have to and I'll call you in a couple of weeks. Okay?"

"Take whatever time you need. I'll wait. Just say it one more time."

This time she knew what he wanted to hear, and this time her response was immediate. "I love you, Jack... I always have... I always will."

"And I love you... Give yourself a hug from the one who loves you most."

Mary smiled. She had heard those same words many times. It was how he closed almost every phone conversation they had ever had.

"I'll wait to hear from you." Jack repeated. "It's probably best that way."

Mary agreed, and when they finished talking, they said good-bye and each reluctantly hung up the phone.

CHAPTER 18

October in Georgia is Mother Nature in all her glory. The sky is azure blue and the clouds look like huge balls of white fluff. The sun shines warmly down and everything seems to slacken its pace, and people turn instinctively to the outdoors, realizing that the long, dreary days of winter are simply biding their time.

Georgia winters aren't usually terribly cold, but they are wet and dismal. Whoever wrote *A Rainy Night in Georgia* had certainly experienced the dreariness of Georgia's wintry rain. Because of this, fall is a season to be treasured and savored in all its splendor.

Garrett was in Boston, and Jody and Mary were taking advantage of the beautiful fall weather by spending every available moment outdoors. Jody was riding his tricycle in the driveway while Mary potted geraniums to take inside for the winter.

It was one of those near-perfect days. Jody was providing his own entertainment and occasionally would call out, "Hi, Mommy," as he circled round and round on his tricycle.

Big Charlie had come over from next door, and Jody had stopped to play with him. The huge Saint Bernard, who would make two of Jody, had endeared himself to everyone in the neighborhood. No one seemed to mind that the friendly, good-natured animal thought the entire neighborhood was his domain. He was gentle and loving and seemed to bring out the best in people.

Jody would often say, "Mommy, look, Big Charlie's smiling."

And, indeed, it seemed he was. Maybe it was because of his huge size, but sometimes he seemed almost human. Jody and the dog played together for awhile, and then something else caught Big Charlie's attention and off he ran.

Mary called to Jody, "Would you like some milk and cookies?"

"Uh-huh!" Jody exclaimed.

She did not correct his grammar. It was too nice a day for scolding.

"Okay, get off your trike and meet me on the patio."

She poured two glasses of milk and reached into the pantry for chocolate chip cookies, keeping a watchful eye out the window on Jody.

It hadn't taken Big Charlie long to make his rounds and, as usual, he was already back with Jody. Jody was still on his trike and was petting the large dog when a butterfly came along, and Big Charlie took off down the driveway in hot pursuit of the butterfly.

"Come back, Big Charlie," Jody cried out, "Don't go out in the street," but the big dog paid no heed.

Jody followed him down the driveway, pedaling as fast as he could.

"Please, Big Charlie, come back. You'll get run over!"

Mary ran outside and called to Jody, as she hurried down the driveway.

"Jody, come back! Don't go out in the road!... Jody!... Jody!"

Then suddenly she heard a loud roaring sound coming from the end of the street, and she caught a glimpse of a young man on a motorcycle. She looked at the motorcycle and then back at Jody, and knew she could not get to him in time.

She let out a blood-curdling scream and Jody turned to see what was wrong.

As she watched the accident unfold, it seemed as though it were happening in slow motion. The biker was trying to avoid hitting her son, but as he jerked the handlebars to one side, the bike went out of control and slid along the pavement. Sparks flew, tires skidded, brakes squealed, and then the back wheel crashed into the tricycle and catapulted both Jody and the tricycle into the air.

Mr. Snider, who lived across the street, was raking leaves and was the first to get to Jody.

He yelled to his wife. "Call an ambulance!" Then he added, "Better tell them to send two," as he looked at the motorcycle rider, lying motionless on the pavement, blood running from his face.

Mary was now in the middle of the street kneeling over her son's crumpled little body, trying to awaken him from his unconscious state, but he would not respond. Her screams ceased as she pulled his lifeless little body to her.

"Jody, it's mama. You're going to be okay. We're going to get you to the hospital. You'll be fine."

And then from somewhere in the distance she heard the sound of sirens piercing the fall air. Jody would be frightened if he heard them, but he did not hear.

Then emotion overtook her and she could say no more. As she bent over him, her tears fell making dark circles on the bright blue sweater he was wearing. She had tried so hard to get to him... to save him. If only she hadn't stumbled coming down the driveway, maybe she would have made it.

* * * * *

She was scarcely aware of the other people in the trauma waiting room. She saw them only as a part of the furnishings. They were not real. Nothing was real. The day that had started out on such a perfect note was no longer real. The only thing real in her life was that her child lay somewhere on the other side of those double doors, fighting for his life. She could not see him or hold him. She could only wait.

She had never felt so alone in her life. Garrett was in Boston and her mother had gone to Asheville to visit her sister. And as she tried to pray, even God seemed far away.

They were taking very good care of him, and everything possible was being done to stabilize him, and she was not to worry. The doctor would be in to talk with her later. That was what they had told her.

She had no idea how long it had been since she had heard those words. Time was without meaning. She couldn't even remember who had told her this. Was it a nurse or the lady in the admitting office? The whole afternoon was one big blur.

The paramedic had been kind. He had sat beside her on the narrow seat in the ambulance as it sped down Piedmont Street. The young man talked back and forth with the hospital and followed their instructions for immediate attention to Jody, and it was obvious that he was not only proficient, but he was also very caring.

He had seen the sheer panic on her face and had turned to her and gently touched her hand. "Hang in there. He's going to be all right."

He wasn't supposed to tell her that. One of the first things you're taught in any medical training is that you don't promise things that are beyond your control. She knew that, but it was the only positive thing she had heard since the accident and she was grateful.

She tried to remember the name on his badge. She would write him a note when Jody was better and thank him for his kindness, but like the rest of the day, his name was a blur.

She got up from her chair and walked to the window. Night had fallen on the city and a glance at her watch told her it was 9:15. When would they tell her something? She could not bear the waiting much longer. But what else could she do? She no longer had control of anything. Everything was being handled by someone else and all she could do was wait.

She would not call Garrett or her mother until she had talked to the doctor. There was no need to alarm them if his injuries were not severe.

Jody had looked so good as he lay on the stretcher on the way to the hospital. There was not a scratch on his face. Apparently it had not hit the pavement or the motorcycle. There were abrasions on his arms and legs, and she suspected he had a broken leg, but all this could be fixed.

But why was the 'fixing' taking so long? If there were complications, why didn't someone tell her?

"Don't they realize I'm his mother? That I have a right to know what's going on behind those doors?"

She could not stand it any longer. She had to know something. She would go to the desk and ask, beg, plead, whatever it took, for someone to tell her something about her child.

Finally she heard a female voice saying, "Mrs. Davenport, the doctor wants to talk to you."

She anxiously looked up into the face of the tall grayish doctor.

"Mrs. Davenport, I'm Dr. Avery. I've been working with Jody. At this point we don't know the full extent of his injuries, but we have him stabilized and he's resting comfortably. His left leg is broken and he has suffered a traumatic blow to the cranium. We've done x-rays and scans, and we'll know more when we get the results in the morning."

"We've immobilized his leg. Later we will need to operate and insert a pin to hold the bone together while it mends, but that's no problem. Right now I'm more concerned about the head injury. I want to call in a neurologist. Do you have one you would like me to call?"

She said she did not.

"Then I'll contact Dr. Bowen. Dr. Bowen is the finest neurologist in the state, if not the whole country. After we've studied the tests, we'll let you know what we've found and what course of treatment we recommend... Do you have any questions?"

"Yes, I do. I assume from what you've said that Jody isn't conscious yet."

"No, I'm afraid not, but at this point that's not unusual."

"How long do you think it will be before he comes to?"

"It's hard to say. It could be soon or it could be tomorrow or maybe the next day. We'll know more after Dr. Bowen examines him."

"Can I see him?"

"Yes, but only for a few minutes. The nurse will take you back."

"Dr. Avery," she hesitated, "he will be okay... Won't he?" Her voice was quivering. She had waited so long to learn so little.

"Mrs. Davenport, we are going to do everything possible to assure that he will. He's young and healthy, and I would say he has an excellent chance. I don't want to minimize the extent of his injuries. He's got a lot of mending to do, and we've got a lot to do to help him. I can promise you this. I'll do the very best I can and so will Dr. Bowen. Meanwhile, he's in excellent hands. This hospital has the finest intensive care unit in the area. He will be monitored constantly, and I've left word with the nursing staff to call me if there is any change."

Dr. Avery looked at the anxious young mother and felt deep compassion. While it was never easy to deliver uncertain news to loved ones, it was particularly difficult when they were waiting alone. As he turned to go, the thought came to him. He would soon be home and would sleep tonight, but Mary Davenport would not.

She fumbled through her purse for her AT&T card. She had to call Garrett and her mother and tell them what had happened.

It was strange... once you told even one person, it seemed all the more real. As long as no one else knew, it remained more like a dream, and you could cling to the hope that at any moment you would awaken and everything would be all right.

On second thought, she decided to wait until morning to call her mother. If she called tonight, her mom would not sleep. At least this way she would get a good night's sleep before making the trip to Atlanta. But Garrett was a thousand miles away, and he had to be told tonight so he could make arrangements to get home. But she had no idea where to reach him. He always said, "Just call the office if you need me."

She had no choice but to call his secretary at home.

"Mrs. Davenport, I am so sorry, but I'm sure your son will be fine... Let me see..." Phyllis was hesitant. "I'm not sure if he's at the *Briarcliff* or the *Beacon Towers*. There are two large conventions in town. He may even be at the *Regency*." She was stalling again. "Let me locate him, and I'll have him call you back right away."

The same old record, Mary thought. I wonder how much these ladies get paid to 'locate' all their missing representatives. This was not the first time, nor the second, she had needed to get in touch with Garrett and he had to be 'located'. And she wondered just what they were trying to cover up.

She was angry. Why couldn't Garrett have told her where he was staying? Why couldn't she have dialed him direct and heard the sound of his voice without having to go through some stranger and then wait for him to call?

She needed him now. She needed him to say, "It's okay, Honey. Everything's going to be all right. I'll get the next flight to Atlanta and be there before you know it."

Just a few reassuring words from someone would mean so much. She had sat alone in the trauma unit all afternoon, not knowing if Jody would live or die, and now she had to wait again while they 'located' Garrett.

* * * * *

Mary paced the hall, anxiously awaiting Garrett's call and wondered why it was taking so long. Then she realized it had been only ten minutes since she had talked to Phyllis.

"Can I get you some coffee?" a friendly voice asked.

The halls were mostly vacated at this time of the night, and she had not realized anyone was around until she heard the voice and felt a gentle touch on her arm. Her nametag read, *Sally Knox, R.N.*

The attractive black nurse appeared to be about thirty, and there was something about her that immediately told Mary she cared. Maybe it was the gentle way she touched her arm or the softness of her voice, but she seemed to understand the agony Mary was going through. Perhaps she was a mother herself.

It was only a cup of coffee, yet it was more than that. Sally Knox had reached out to her and had shown that she cared. And never in her life had she needed someone to care as much as she did right now.

She would never forget Sally Knox, as she would never forget the young paramedic who had attended Jody in the ambulance. They were two perfect strangers who, by their simple acts of kindness, had reached out to her when no one else was there.

"I'm expecting a call from my husband, and I'm going to wait down the hall by the pay phone. Will you let me know if Jody should wake up?"

"Certainly." And seeing the tiredness in her eyes, Sally said, "There are some chairs around the corner if you care to sit down. You can hear the phone from there. It rings loudly."

Mary had just settled into a chair when the phone rang, and even though she was expecting the call, the loud ringing startled her. Garrett would get a flight early in the morning and should be in Atlanta by noon.

"I wish I could be there tonight." There was a pause, and he asked, "Are you all right?"

"I'm okay. I'll be here at the hospital all night. If there's any change, I'll call you."

"Mary, is Jody in a lot of pain?"

"No, Garrett, Jody is unconscious. He doesn't feel pain. He doesn't feel anything."

She was sorry she had been so blunt, but he had to know. It had been almost twelve hours since the accident, and Jody had shown no signs of regaining consciousness. Their son was in a coma!

Tears welled up in her eyes, but she quickly dried them and reminded herself that this was no time to go to pieces. Jody needed her strength.

The clock on the wall showed it was almost midnight. A new staff of nurses was reporting in and those who had just completed their shift were preparing to leave.

In the hushed silence of the grim waiting room, Mary observed those who had no doubt been waiting for days with critically ill loved ones. They drank coffee, closed their eyes and eventually nodded in shallow sleep. They looked very tired, and most of them were expressionless, and no one seemed to care to talk. It was as though they waited, not knowing the day or the hour, only knowing that ultimately the news would come. And when it came, it was not likely to be good.

She saw little sign of hope on their faces, and she wondered if her face looked the same to them. But she had not given up hope. Jody would get better! She knew he would!

Perhaps there was a time when these people also had felt equally optimistic about their loved ones, but as the days had vanished, so had their hopes. She wondered if there would come a time when she would sit as these, marking time, devoid of all hope. And then she quickly banished the somber thoughts from her mind.

In a few days Jody would be better, and they would be at home with the hospital scene behind them. She would read him a bedtime story and tuck his favorite blue blanket snugly around him and all would be well. He was young and healthy. Dr. Avery had said so. The other patients, whose families waited silently, were probably old and in poor health or perhaps the victims of strokes or heart attacks or cancer. That was why their loved ones held little hope for their recovery. But Jody was different. He would be all right. He just needed time. Surely God would not be so cruel as to take him from her.

* * * * *

She stirred from her thoughts each time the double doors to the ICU swung open, as she waited anxiously for some word about Jody. A group of strangers had complete access to her child and she could only wait on the outer side of those doors, hoping that eventually someone would come to tell her that Jody was awake and asking for her. He had not been in a hospital since his birth, and he would be frightened if he awakened and she was not there.

When she could stand the waiting room no longer, she paced the halls, being careful not to get too far away. It was well past midnight and unlike earlier in the day, everything was deathly quiet. The halls were deserted except for an occasional nurse who crept quietly in and out of a patient's room.

At the end of the hall, she saw a lady standing alone, staring out a window. She appeared to be middle aged, and Mary wondered what her story was. Perhaps her husband or a parent was gravely ill, and she was keeping vigil. She, too, had probably had all she could take of the waiting room, and the window and the world outside provided a temporary means of escape.

She thought how much pain and heartache there is in the world. Someone is always grieving over someone and facing the possible loss of that person who they don't believe they can live without... a husband... a wife... a father... a mother... a child... How abruptly life can change.

She and Jody had been having such a wonderful morning. The beautiful October day seemed made to order for doing whatever made you happiest. And that was precisely what they were doing. Then in the twinkling of an eye everything changed.

As she wandered through the halls, she noticed a small room to her left, which appeared to be some sort of private waiting room. She stopped to look in and saw a nurse who was apparently taking a break.

Sally Knox looked up. "Would you like to sit in here for awhile, Mrs. Davenport? It would at least be a change of scenery."

She accepted Sally's offer and sat down across from her. The room was attractively furnished in soft shades of peach and green, and was comfortable and almost cozy.

"This room is provided for those families who have been here for awhile and need a little privacy. No one was using it tonight, so I thought I'd take my break in here rather than in the nurses' lounge."

"I thought you got off at eleven."

"I was supposed to, but one of the nurses has a sick child, so I'm working over tonight."

"Do you ever go back in the Intensive Care Unit while you're on duty?"

Sally Knox knew immediately why she was asking.

"Sometimes. I used to work back there, but I transferred out here a few months ago. When they're short a nurse, I'm usually the first one they call." She took another sip of Coke and continued. "I don't mind now and then, but it's not quite as exhausting out here."

"He's such a little boy to be back there alone. If he were in a room, I could sit by him. If he wakes up back there, he'll be frightened." It was almost as if Mary were talking to herself.

Sally saw the dejected expression on Mary's face and imagined how she would feel if it were one of her own children. She wished it was within her power to relieve the anxiety of this young mother waiting alone through the endless night, but she could not. This was one of the limitations of the job she had chosen. She could relieve some pain, but not all.

"I know it's hard, Mrs. Davenport, but your son is where he needs to be right now. They're monitoring him closely and taking very good care of him. The nurses back there are the finest in the hospital. I've worked with most of them and they are top notch. As soon as Jody wakes up, someone will come and get you."

Mary nodded, but the sad look on her face did not go away.

"I'll be on duty until three and I'll go back and check on him before I leave and give you a report... Okay?... Meanwhile, why don't you stretch out here and try to get some rest. Don't worry about dozing off. If you do, I'll wake you before I leave. I promise... Now just get some rest."

Mary thanked her for her kindness and felt somewhat relieved. At least she would be able to hear from him in a little while.

Three o'clock in the morning seemed like a strange time to get off from work. Mary hoped Sally's car was parked near the building and that the parking lot was well lit.

The effects of sheer weariness had laid hold of Mary, and the soft chair felt good. She kicked off her shoes, stretched out in the over-sized recliner, and closed her eyes.

At exactly ten minutes 'til three, Sally Knox aroused her to tell her she had just looked in on Jody and he was resting peacefully. She had checked his charts and his vitals were very good.

"Try to go back to sleep now. I'll see you tomorrow."

Mary thanked her again and as she watched her leave she wondered about Sally Knox. Would she go home to a husband and children or perhaps to an empty apartment? Mary couldn't remember if she had worn a wedding band.

And as once again she closed her eyes, she thought of the nurse who had gone above and beyond the call of duty. Sally Knox was a good woman. She was kind and caring and Mary hoped that life in turn was kind to her.

*   *   *   *   *

It was eight A.M. and in the hallway outside the intensive care unit people waited anxiously for a chance to see their loved ones. Some wore clothing wrinkled from a night of trying to curl up in a lounge chair in the waiting room. Others had gone home for the night and wore fresh clothes and were better groomed. But the expression on each face was the same as they waited for that moment when the double doors would open and they would be allowed to enter. Their loved ones had made it through the night. Some had not been so lucky.

It was ten minutes after eight when the doors finally opened. Mary lost no time in getting to Jody's bedside, hoping that perhaps he had just awakened and they had been too busy caring for other patients to let her know... but such was not the case.

Nothing appeared to have changed. He looked the same as when she last saw him. A nurse was doing something to his I.V. and she smiled gently at Mary.

"His vitals are good, and he hasn't lost any ground. Did you talk with the doctor last night?"

Mary said she had and asked what time the doctor would be in.

"He should be here soon. Dr. Avery usually makes rounds before he goes to the office. I believe Dr. Bowen is scheduled to see your son today. She's usually early too."

So Dr. Bowen was a woman! Mary could not help wondering how Garrett would react to this. There were a lot of women in the investment business, and he dealt with them on a regular basis, nevertheless she was not sure how he would feel about a woman doctor.

Mary bent over to kiss the soft little forehead of her son. The room seemed cold, but she supposed it had to be. She wondered if Jody was warm enough. She would like to ask for a blanket to wrap around him, but he was attached to so much equipment.

"Jody, mommy's right here beside you. Please wake up and talk to me. I love you so much."

There was not the slightest indication he heard her, and she could only stand in silence staring at the face of this little one that she loved more than life itself. She yearned for the slightest sign of movement... a sigh... a moan... a cry of pain... anything to let her know that he heard or felt or sensed anything. But there was nothing.

Then the announcement came over the intercom. Visiting time was over and the families would have to exit the ICU. She glanced at her watch. Families were only allowed to go back to ICU for fifteen minutes at a time, four times each day, provided there was not an emergency at visiting time. Last night, just before time to go back, one of the patients suffered a stroke and visiting time had to be canceled.

She understood the rule. Jody and the other patients in ICU were there for a reason. They needed around-the-clock attention and monitoring, and the doctors and nurses could not provide this degree of care if the family was constantly standing around the bed. Still, she was his mother and she needed to be with him, maybe even more than he needed her.

An hour or so later, Dr. Avery came out and told her Jody's condition was stable and there was no change since last night.

"Dr. Bowen is with him now and is ordering further tests. I know this all seems painfully slow to you, Mrs. Davenport, but we need to know as much as possible about your son's condition before we start treatment."

"When do you expect to have the reports?"

"I hope we'll have them later today."

"Thank you, Dr. Avery. Just please take care of him for me."

Dr. Avery nodded and looked at his watch. He needed to see two more patients in the hospital and if it didn't take too long, he wouldn't be more than a half-hour late getting to his office. Although his patients were accustomed to waiting, they knew that once they did get to see him, they would have his undivided attention. He was that kind of a doctor.

There were two great loves in Richard Avery's life, his family and his patients. And sometimes Diane Avery thought his patients came first. She had been a nurse and had known her husband for four years before they were married, so she knew what she was getting into when she married Rick. There were the unfinished meals and those that he never showed up for at all because he had an emergency or a desperately ill patient, but she did not complain. She was married to one of the finest human beings she had ever known, and she loved him very much. The quality of the time they shared together was what was important to her. While he was busy caring for his patients, Diane cared for their two children, and in her heart she knew that when he had done all he could for them, he would come home to her. And that was what mattered most.

Sometime later Mary heard someone call her name and looked up to see an attractive lady standing at the entrance to the waiting room.

"Mrs. Davenport, I'm Dr. Bowen," she said, extending her hand.

"I've just seen Jody and I need to get a little more information from you."

Mary answered her questions and after talking further with Dr. Bowen, felt quite secure with her. She was very professional and like Dr. Avery, was kind and compassionate.

"I've ordered some additional scans and a few other tests. He's going to be pretty busy for awhile. Why don't you use the time to go get yourself some breakfast?"

Ignoring the reference to breakfast, Mary answered, "I need to go home and change clothes. I know I look terrible. I was potting geraniums when Jody... when the accident happened. Do you think he would be okay if I went home just long enough to get a shower and change?"

Mary looked down at the old blue jeans and faded polo shirt she was wearing and wondered what Garrett would think if he saw her like this.

"Sure! We'll take good care of him while you're gone. Take your time and remember to get something to eat. Okay?"

* * * * *

As Mary crossed the patio to the back door, she saw the two glasses of milk and the cookies, stark reminders of a picnic that never happened.

She turned the shower down low so she could hear the phone if they called from the hospital. The warm water pelting against her tired body felt good, but there was no time to linger. She finished her shower and slipped into a pair of navy slacks and a white blouse, and laid out a red cardigan. Then she brushed her teeth and threw the toothbrush and some personal items into an overnight bag along with her makeup. She could do her face after she got back to the hospital. She did not want to be gone long. Jody might need her.

She checked the front door to make sure it was secure, quickly folded another blouse and some underwear, placed them in the overnight bag and locked the back door.

She was almost to the car when she thought of Felix. There was still some feed in his bowl, so he had not gone hungry. Quickly she filled the bowl again and got him some fresh water. Poor old cat! She hadn't even thought of him.

Then she heard him. The big orange cat with eyes the same color of his fur had the softest "Me-ow" she had ever heard. He was at her feet, purring gently as he rubbed against her legs.

She had had Felix longer than she had had Jody, and he was just as much a part of the family. The soulful look in those big yellow eyes told her he didn't understand what was going on. He must have waited at the back door last night, but no one had come to let him in.

Instinctively she reached down and picked up the cat, who had been her constant companion during the early years of her marriage when Garrett was working and before Jody came along.

For a moment she held him close and stroked his head.

"Felix, Jody got hurt. He's in the hospital and I have to be with him. Take care of yourself, big fellow. We'll be home as soon as we can."

Maybe Felix didn't understand what she was saying, but he was her friend, and he deserved to be told something, whether he understood or not. Besides, it brought a measure of comfort just to hold him close for a moment.

She pulled into the *Hardee's* drive-thru and ordered a sausage biscuit and some orange juice. She couldn't face another cup of coffee. It was almost eleven o'clock and she was beginning to feel a little queasy from all the coffee she had consumed during the night. The food tasted good, and she was glad she had eaten, even though she had not wanted to take the time.

When she reached the hospital she went to the restroom and applied her makeup and arranged her hair a little better. Her eyes showed the weariness, but other than that, she supposed she looked all right. The shower and food made her feel better.

Then the waiting started all over again. Garrett should be somewhere between Boston and Atlanta by now, and her mother was on her way from Asheville. Mary hoped she would drive carefully. She said a prayer that God would watch over them and take care of Jody. Then once again she fixed her eyes on those double doors. In another hour she would be able to see Jody. She tried to read the morning newspaper, but she couldn't concentrate.

When twelve o'clock came, Jody was still in x-ray, and when the other family members went back to visit their loved ones, she sat alone in the waiting room. She changed chairs, walked the corridors, and looked at her watch. She went to the bathroom, not because she needed to. It was simply something to do.

It was three o'clock and she hadn't seen Jody since the eight o'clock visit. The nurse had told her she could go back and see him when he came back from x-ray. She wondered if he was still going through tests or if they had simply forgotten to come and get her. She was almost beside herself with worry.

Across the room sat the lady Mary had seen staring out the window the night before, at least it looked like the same lady. Mary didn't know why she couldn't talk to any of these people, but the words just didn't come, and apparently it was the same for them. They all seemed to be caught up in their own private misery.

Finally, the nurse came to get her. They had finished the tests and Jody was back in ICU. They had turned him on his side, but other than that, he looked the same as before.

She stroked his cheek gently and again tried to evoke some response. "Jody, it's Mommy. Please wake up. Daddy will be here in a little while and Grandma too." Her voice was trembling and she could say no more. She bent to kiss the soft cheek and whispered, "I love you."

Once more the tears formed in her eyes, as she asked the nurse, "Could I sit with him for a little while?"

"I'm sorry," the nurse replied. "We have so much to do for the patients that we can't allow visitors except during regular visiting periods. It will be visiting time again soon. You'll see him then."

Mary walked down the hall. She could not go back to that waiting room, not now anyway. A door opened and she observed the familiar quick steps of the nurse making her rounds.

She walked to the end of the hall, and this time she was the lady who stood staring out the window. Another door opened and closed, but she did not look around. Then she was aware of someone beside her and a soft voice saying, "Hey, Mrs. Davenport, how are you?"

Mary managed a weak smile.

"Sally, I'm so glad to see you... Is it all right for me to call you Sally?"

"Sure. Everybody does, except my kids. They just think my name's 'Momma'."

She asked about Jody, and Mary told her there was still no change.

"I'll be around until eleven, that is, if I'm lucky. If there's anything you need, just let me know. Is your husband here yet?"

"No, his flight was delayed because of the fog, but he should be here soon, and my mother is on her way from Asheville.

"That's good."

Sally smiled and was on her way to check on another patient.

*   *   *   *   *

Mary had never experienced Atlanta so quiet. It was 2:30 a.m. as she made her way back to the hospital. The night people had apparently called it a night, and the day people had not yet started their day's activities. Garrett had insisted she go home and get some rest. He would stay at the hospital in case there was any change in Jody.

She had gotten in bed around eleven, but by 1:00 she was wide-awake, and try as she might, she could not get back to sleep. The tossing and turning was only wearing her out more, so she got up and dressed and headed back to the hospital.

When she was away from the hospital, even for a little while, it was as if she had left part of herself behind. Dr. Bowen had said that in cases like Jody's oftentimes the patient would awaken suddenly. When this happened, Mary wanted to be there.

She knew Garrett was tired, so she would relieve him and let him go home or simply sit with him until dawn if he wanted to stay. He had been away from Jody a lot because of his work, and there was not the same bond between them that she and Jody shared. Nevertheless, she knew he loved Jody, and not being able to talk to him or let him know he was there was tearing him apart as much as it was her.

After all, he was flesh of their flesh and blood of their blood, and whatever else might have been lacking in their marriage, Jody was the one wonderful thing they had created together.

As she stepped out of the elevator, she saw Garrett making a call from a pay phone at the end of the hall... Who would he be calling at this hour of the night?... Then it hit her!... Oh, God, no! Had something happened to Jody? Was Garrett trying to reach her at home?

She hurried toward him to let him know she was there and to find out what had happened, but when she got within a few feet of him, she heard him speak into the receiver.

"Gloria?"

Mary stopped in her tracks. Then she quickly slipped into an alcove to conceal herself and to find out who 'Gloria' was. Never before had she eavesdropped on Garrett's conversations, and she knew she shouldn't now. She tried to walk away and pretend she had not heard anything, but she couldn't! It would probably be better if she didn't hear this, but she had to. She had to know!

At first his voice was quiet, and she could barely hear what he was saying.

"Honey, he's bad. He still hasn't regained consciousness. We just wait and wait... It's a bad scene... Poor little guy."

She could hear Garrett's voice start to break. Then he continued. "He has a broken leg, which they'll operate on later, but that's not the main problem. It's his head, and even with all the testing they've done, they still don't know when he'll regain consciousness, nor the extent of the damage.

Gloria was now talking, and Mary watched as Garrett's expression changed.

"I miss you too, babe."

He paused again to listen.

"Gloria, there's no way I can leave now. Don't you understand? My son may not make it."

Apparently Gloria was talking again.

"Look, Gloria, you don't understand. You've never had a child. That little boy is part of me. He's my son and I love him." His voice cracked again.

What is she trying to do, insist that he leave us to be with her? Damn whore!... Mary wanted to scream out in anger, but she could not.

"Gloria, I can't come to Boston now. I have to be here."

It was obvious that Gloria didn't understand and apparently didn't care. She was used to getting what she wanted, and what she wanted right now was Garrett, and the fact that his son was in the hospital fighting for his life didn't matter to her.

"Look, I've got to go. I'll call you when I can."

There was a pause.

"No, I don't know when." His voice was no longer subdued, and it was evident that he could not handle much more of her whining and begging.

Where did he find this one? Mary wondered.

Whatever Gloria had just said had moved him to rage.

Mary watched his face grow red and heard him raise his voice.

"Just do whatever the Hell you want! I don't give a damn!" And with that he slammed the receiver.

She pressed herself tightly against the wall, aware that he would step right in front of her and would know she had been listening. Instead, he turned toward the men's room, and she saw him reach for his handkerchief to wipe his eyes.

She didn't know why, but she almost felt sorry for him.

Why are women like this? She thought. They always hate the 'other woman' and make excuses for their own husband.

What she had overheard tonight only confirmed what she had suspected for a long time, but there was no way she could deal with it now. One crisis was enough. There would be time later to address this and all the other problems that had been swept under the carpet for much too long. However, now was not the time. The only thing that mattered now was Jody. Right now they must put aside their own problems and do whatever it took to see that Jody got well.

*   *   *   *   *

THREE DAYS LATER

Clouds hung heavy over Atlanta as Mary left for the hospital. In the distance there was the mournful sound of a rain crow, foretelling the day's weather. Garrett had never heard of rain crows or toadstools or lightning bugs, but then he had not grown up in the South.

She wondered why she was thinking these irrelevant thoughts. Perhaps it's the inexplicable effort the mind makes to insulate itself against the unbearable circumstances of the present moment.

For days she had made this trip each morning, hoping this would be the day she would walk into his room and Jody would be awake and would say, "Hi Mommy!"

But as each day passed with no change, her hopes grew dimmer. What if he never regained consciousness? What if she never again got to see his smile or hear his bubblesome laughter? What if when she held him in her arms, he never again reached up and wrapped his arms around her neck? What if he died?

No! This could not be! He would come out of it! She knew he would. And he would do all of those things again and more. He would be Jody again! It was just a matter of time.

Then the inevitable thought ran through her mind. Was this some sort of punishment for her wrongdoing... for the weekend she had spent with Jack? Surely God would not visit her sin upon her child. Jody had done nothing wrong. She was the one. As she groped for some understanding of why Jody was still in a coma, even this irrational reasoning seemed to serve some crazy purpose.

How anxiously we search for answers in our times of desperation, she thought, and how seldom we find them. Now she was able to understand the hopeless expressions on the faces of the people she had seen in the ICU waiting room that first night.

It happens slowly, almost unnoticeably at first, but when each passing day brings no improvement, your mind gradually adjusts, and as much as you resist it, a certain acceptance seems to set in.

She was angry with herself for thinking such dismal thoughts. It was the miserable weather. If the sun would only shine, she wouldn't feel so despondent.

The morning commuter traffic was worse than usual and 'usual' was bad enough. Suddenly she was aware that the man in the silver Honda behind her was blowing his horn. She must have done something wrong. While she had no idea what it was, she realized she must clear her mind of everything else and concentrate on the traffic. The last thing she needed was to wind up in the hospital herself.

As she walked into Jody's room, she noticed how tired Garrett looked. The strain of the last few days was showing. Perhaps he should get back to his job. Changes in their routine would ultimately have to be made. He was staying at the hospital every night, and she was staying during the day. This could not go on indefinitely. Eventually, he would have to go back to work.

"Is there any change?" she asked.

He only shook his head and looked at her as if searching for something to say. Finally he asked, "Did you get some rest?"

"A little. Sometimes I think it would be easier just to stay here. I can't get Jody off my mind when I leave."

"Mary, don't even think about staying here all the time. You would go nuts! You've got to get away."

"I suppose so."

"I think I'll go home and get a shower and go to the office for awhile. There are a few things I need to follow through on."

As he started to leave, he put both arms around her and pulled her close. "It's so hard... Just watching him... He doesn't even know we're here."

This was the first time he had really talked to her in months, and even though she would not have had this happen for anything, it was good to share something with her husband, even this terrible pain.

She felt moisture on her face and looked up to see the tears roll unashamedly down his cheeks. Whatever else he had done or had not done, she knew he loved Jody. In their seven years of marriage she had seen Garrett cry only twice... once when they moved into the house in Atlanta and last week when he got off the phone with Gloria.

She had not yet come to terms with that. There would be time for that later, but right now he needed her... They needed each other... And Jody needed them both.

As they stood clinging to each other in their shared anguish, Mary said softly, "He's going to make it. I just don't know if we are."

She was smiling weakly and trying to give some reassurance, perhaps to herself as much as to Garrett.

"I wish you didn't have to go to the office. You look so tired."

"I'll be fine. Maybe doing something productive will be good therapy. I won't be there all day. I'll get some rest this afternoon. When your mother comes by, why don't you let her stay with Jody and come home for awhile?"

"We'll see." She appreciated his concern, but knew she would not leave. It was hard enough to tear herself away at night.

* * * * *

FOUR DAYS LATER

Mary all but dropped into the chair. Her body ached from head to toe, and her legs seemed incapable of supporting her any longer. Since 9:30 she had stood by Jody's bed literally trying to pull him out of the coma he had been in for nine days. She had talked, begged, pleaded, screamed and used every tone of voice she could to try to get his attention. It was no use. It wasn't going to work.

Except for his comatose state, Jody was stable, and Dr. Bowen had moved him out of intensive care and into a private room. She had instructed Mary to talk to Jody in a firm, loud manner, insisting that he wake up.

"Yell at him! Demand him to wake up. Whatever it takes! Medically, we have done all we know to do. At this point this is his only chance."

She was to do this over and over for as long as it took. Dr. Bowen said sometimes this method worked when all else failed.

It was all so strange. There was no medical reason why Jody had not come out of the coma. The doctors said that while the blow to the head had been severe, it should not have produced such prolonged unconsciousness.

She glanced at her watch. It had been five hours since they brought him to his room. He had been somewhat restless during the night, and according to Dr. Bowen, this was often an indication a patient might be on the verge of coming out of a coma. But during the long hours she had stood by his bed, there had been no sign of movement or stirring. He lay perfectly still, totally unaware of his surroundings. She would try again after awhile, but right now she could stand on her feet no longer. And for the first time since the accident, she gave vent to her feelings. Deep uncontrollable sobs enveloped her, and all the emotion and weariness of the past several days rolled over her like a mighty river as tears poured from her eyes. She was no longer strong or brave, but a broken woman without hope.

She thought of the parents of Karen Ann Quinlan, and how they watched their beautiful young daughter gradually curl up in a fetal position, never regaining consciousness. She had read that for seven years Mrs. Quinlan had gone daily to the nursing home to visit her daughter, who apparently never knew her mother was there.

"Would this happen to them?"

The tears, which had almost subsided, now came in torrents again.

"Oh, God, please help me! I can't handle it any longer."

Finally, crumpled up in the chair, her body spent from the emotional outpouring, she slept.

Once she thought she heard a sound, but when she opened her eyes and looked at Jody, there was no change. She was so tired, and once more she closed her eyes. She would rest a few minutes more and then try again.

Then it happened!

At first she thought she was dreaming... Then the sound grew louder... It was Jody!

"Big Charlie! Come back! You'll get run over!"

Mary was out of her chair and leaning over his bed, kissing his forehead.

"Oh, Jody! Jody! Mommy's right here and you're going to be okay!" Jody looked around, unsure of where he was, while she tried to explain that he had been in an accident and was in the hospital, but everything was going to be fine.

"Is Big Charlie all right, Mommy? He ran out into the street, and I was trying to get him back."

"Big Charlie's fine, baby. He didn't get hit."

Mary pushed the light for a nurse and heard the desk clerk answer, but she could not answer back. She could only hold onto the metal rails of Jody's bed with all her strength. The room seemed to be spinning. Then everything grew dark and she knew she was going to faint.

The head nurse was coming up the hall and saw the light go on over Jody's doorway. She stepped into the room just in time to see what was happening and ran to Mary. Realizing there was no way to get her to the chair, she eased her down onto the floor and grabbed a cushion from the chair to elevate Mary's head. Then she pushed the button for the desk.

"May I help you, please?" The desk clerk answered.

"Yes, get me a nurse in 214 STAT."

"Is it a Code 99?"

"No! Damn it, Ginger! Just get me a nurse. Jody's mother has fainted. All I need is a little help."

CHAPTER 19

From her kitchen window Mary watched Jack leave. They had said their good-byes and she had started to follow him outside, but he had said, "Please don't. I want to know you are safe inside when I leave." There was a moment's hesitation, then he continued. "And I'm not sure I could drive away seeing you standing alone on the patio."

For a moment they looked deep into each other's eyes, each trying to capture a mental image of the other, realizing it would have to last for a long time.

At last Jack reached for the doorknob and sighed.

"If you ever need me..." He tried to continue, but he could not.

She would need him... She needed him now. But they both knew she wouldn't call... She couldn't call... just as Jack could not stay.

"Take care of yourself and remember, I'll always love you."

"I'll always love you too."

As he started the van, she waved to him from the window and then watched him drive away. He was gone, and it seemed that a part of her had gone with him.

It had been only a few weeks ago that he drove up that same driveway and into her life once more. Their time together had been so brief, and now he was gone. When he left this time there were no promises, no future plans... just Good-bye. It had to be this way. They both knew it... but it wasn't easy.

The last couple of weeks seemed like a dream, as her thoughts traveled back. Jody was home and doing much better. Garrett had gone back to work, and her mother had left earlier in the day to return to Chattanooga. The house seemed strangely quiet for a change.

She thought of Jack. She must call him. He was in Charlotte when it happened and had no way of knowing about Jody. She was sure he must have wondered why he had not heard from her.

As she dialed the phone she wondered if he thought she had changed her mind.

"Jack?"

"Mary! How's Jody?"

Apparently he knew.

"He's home and he's doing much better."

"And you? Are you okay?" He continued.

She could hear the distress in his voice.

"I'm better. It has all been a terrible nightmare. Jody was in a coma for over a week, and we didn't know if he would make it. There is nothing like fearing you may lose your child." A shiver went over her body as she said the words. Then she asked how he had known about Jody.

"When I didn't hear from you, I broke my promise and called. It was late one night after a show. The phone rang and rang, but there was no answer. The next night I tried again and it was the same. I knew something was wrong. On the third night your husband answered. It was 1:00 a.m. and I'm sure I woke him. I didn't know what to say, so I asked if Mike was there."

"First he told me to go to Hell. Then he said I should 'check the damn number' before I disturbed someone in the middle of the night. But he did stay on the line long enough to say his son was critically ill and in the hospital, and a call at that hour of the night was very alarming. I felt terrible, but at least I knew something."

"I came home from Charlotte to try to find out what had happened. I continued to call, hoping I might catch you at home. I didn't dare call again at night, and no one was home during the day. I knew if I called the hospital there was no telling who might answer the phone. The last thing you needed was having to explain a call from a strange man to your husband."

"I drove by the house a time or two hoping to see you, but no one was home. Finally, I stopped across the street. The man was raking leaves, and I told him I was supposed to put out some shrubbery for you and hadn't been able to get in touch with anyone. Then he told me about the accident."

"Jack," Mary interrupted, "Could you come over for awhile?"

"Are you sure it's okay? I don't want to cause any problems."

"It's okay. There's only Jody and me, and he's already settled in for the night."

They talked far into the night, and she told him all that had happened. Tears welled up in his eyes when she told him of the first night she waited alone, not knowing if Jody would live or die.

"I know it has been so hard for you, baby. The worst part for me was that after I finally found out what had happened, there wasn't a damn thing I could do. It was a family crisis and I wasn't family. I couldn't be there for you. But I cared, Mary. I cared so much."

"I know, honey, I know. After Jody finally came out of the coma and things seemed to be under control, I thought of my promise to call you. I knew you were wondering why you hadn't heard from me, but Garrett and mother were both here."

"I understand."

She told him that Jody would start therapy on his leg as soon as the cast came off, and the doctor had said it would be long drawn out and quite painful in the beginning, but that it had to be done to prevent him from winding up a cripple.

"Hopefully, he will be fine some day, but they say we can expect at least a year of rehabilitation. If we get the anticipated results, he should have only the slightest limp. Fortunately, there's no brain damage. As long as he was unconscious that was a possibility we had to face. At least we have good insurance. The hospital and doctors bills have already exceeded $100,000.00."

They talked about all that had happened, both with them and subsequently with Jody.

Then finally Jack spoke the words, which they both knew were true.

"I don't have to tell you where your priority lies. It's not with me. It's not even with yourself. It's with that little fellow upstairs."

She nodded through tear-dimmed eyes and whispered, "I know."

And then she fell into his arms and wept while he held her close. All the stress of these past weeks was being unleashed, and he was glad he was there to comfort her.

He would be in Greenville next week for five shows, and after that he had an offer to do an extended engagement at a club in Florida. He had not yet made up his mind if he would take the Florida offer.

"I can think of a lot of places I would rather go than Florida, but it's a big club and the pay is good. A couple of friends of mine are playing in the area and they want to try to put a band together. It would give us a chance to get together and see what we can come up with. I'd rather be on my own, but right now there's a lot more demand for bands than for solo acts."

"When will you make up your mind?"

"I have to let them know something by the first of next week."

"Will you come back to Atlanta before you go?" She hesitated, "If you decide to."

"I'll be back next weekend. If I decide to take the job, I'll give up the apartment here."

She understood. If he took the job, he would be leaving, not just for a week or two, but for good.

Perhaps it was better that way. There was nothing they could do now. Jody needed her more than Jack did. He had to walk again and be made whole, and she would be there to help him every step of the way.

But knowing that she was never going to see Jack again was almost more than she could bear. She told him this, and he reminded her that 'never' is a long, long time. While there was a remnant of hope that someday things might work out and they might be together again, that was all that it was, and remnants tend to grow weaker with the passing of time.

When Jack came back from Greenville, he had made his decision. He was going to take the job. He would leave early Tuesday morning for Orlando. He called Mary and asked if he could come by before he left.

On Sunday night Jack came by. Mary took him upstairs to see Jody. He had already taken his last dose of medicine and had drifted off to sleep while she read to him.

Jack could only shake his head, as he looked down at the little fellow whose entire left leg was encased in a massive cast, which seemed almost bigger than he was.

She had mentioned last week that the one thing Jody had wanted for Christmas was a ball glove, but she couldn't bring herself to buy one now. What if he was never able to play ball? It would serve only as a constant reminder of what he could not do. But when Jack entered the door tonight he was carrying a package.

She laughed. "I was always told to beware of strangers bearing gifts."

"Well, I'm no stranger and the gift is not for you, so you have nothing to beware of. It's an early Christmas present for Jody."

She knew without asking what it was.

"It may be a little large now, but it will be just right a year from now, and he'll be the best left fielder in the league."

Mary smiled as she looked at the beautiful leather glove with the big red "R".

"Why left field?"

"It's a good position. That's where I used to play. Remember? Before some fool coach decided I could pitch."

Jack placed the glove on the bed beside Jody where he would see it in the morning when he awoke.

"Just tell him Santa came a little early this year." Then he turned to her. "He's going to be fine. He has a mommy that will take good care of him and make sure that one day he's as good as new. He's a lucky little guy in that respect."

Jack put an arm around Mary's waist and as they stood by Jody's bedside, he added, "I just wish I were as lucky, but he needs you more."

"I know... I wish the three of us could be together. But it can't be, not now anyway," and she felt a sadness creep over her that she knew would linger for a long time to come.

Jody needed her more, but there was someone else who needed her, and who she needed, and there was nothing they could do about it... absolutely nothing.

They sat in the den and talked for hours, knowing that when they said good-bye tonight, it would really be 'good-bye'. There would be no tomorrow.

It was comfortable and pleasant and seemed very right. They held hands and sometimes laughed and sometimes cried, but mostly they talked, trying hard to say all the things that needed to be said.

Just before Jack left, he reached in his pocket and pulled out a square velvet-covered box and handed it to Mary.

"I have one more early Christmas present."

As she opened the box, she beheld the most beautiful gold bracelet she had ever seen. It was etched in roses, her favorite flower.

"Oh, Jack, it's so beautiful. I will wear it often and think of you... and love you."

Her arms were around his neck, and once more he held her while their hearts beat in unison.

"I wanted to have it engraved, but I guess you'll just have to remember who it's from."

She understood why he could not have it engraved. An inscription might one day require an explanation.

"What would the inscription have said?"

He thought for a moment.

"Maybe, *Jack to Mary, October 7th, 1978. Try to remember.*"

"I'll always remember. How could I ever forget that day in the mountains?"

It was a memory she would carry with her throughout all eternity. Nothing would ever take it from her. The years might erase many things from her memory, but she would always have that.

She stared down at the gold bracelet on her arm and wondered what the future held for Jack. She hoped the Florida venture would be the beginning of something good for him. She could not share his success, but it would come. She knew it would. And when it did, no one would be happier for him.

CHAPTER 20

MAY 29, 1982

"It seems I've spent half my life on the road." Jack thought as he drove south on I-75.

For the better part of the last seven years he had crisscrossed the Southeast, moving from town to town, playing his music and hoping to make enough money in one town to get him to the next, all the while trying to keep body and soul and his '69 Volkswagon van together until his break came.

During his baseball days the endless stretches of highway were as much a part of his life as the green grass of the outfield or the smell of the ballpark. There were no plane rides for minor leaguers. While the major leaguers went first class, the minor leaguers traveled the cheapest route possible, which meant buses, not modern luxury buses, but usually some worn-out vehicle that had already seen its better days.

Jack grinned, as he remembered the times he had stood in line with twenty-four other players outside the men's room at some local *Shell* station, while some 'shade tree mechanic' tried to figure out how to get a few more miles out of an engine that should have been put out to pasture years before.

His thoughts drifted back to '71 and Columbus, the day Mary had gotten married and he had lost the no-hitter in the ninth inning. He remembered the stupid street sign just outside the stadium... *VICTORY LANE*... What a stupid name!... And how on that hot August night eleven years ago, he felt he had lost everything.

One thought led to another, and he realized how true the saying is, "LOSING HURTS MORE THAN WINNING FEELS GOOD."

It had been three years since he left Atlanta, and he had not seen nor heard from Mary. Once his mom had run into Mrs. Howard at the mall and had learned that Jody was doing better, and that Mary and Garrett had another child, a daughter, she thought.

After leaving Atlanta he played solo for awhile. Then one night in St. Petersburg he ran into Buddy Bowers. After the show they went back to Jack's motel and sat up half the night jamming together and talking about old times. And in the wee hours of morning they came up with the idea of forming a band.

Both Jack and Buddy had played the circuit long enough to know who was good and who was better left alone, and they soon put together a group that seemed to click from the start. Jack was the lead singer and played rhythm. Townes Hurley played bass. Bobby Caldwell played drums, and Buddy played lead guitar and sang background vocals. Buddy and Jack had been friends since first grade, but after high school they had gone in different directions, each chasing his own dream. Buddy had done well with his talent. He was the best lead guitar player Jack had ever seen. There was no doubt about it, but he was also a borderline alcoholic.

For the next three years their band had been one of the fastest rising groups in the South, and they were never without playing dates. Jack managed the group and wrote a lot of their material. They were all talented musicians, and they quickly established their own unique sound and style. They sounded natural and new and fresh and the people liked it.

However, during the last few months they had begun to get a reputation for showing up to play with some of their musicians missing.

Jack had always tried to run a tight ship, and he wasn't at all happy with the situation. But what can you do when your lead guitarist keeps showing up drunk, and you can't find your bass player because he hasn't come in from his late night date with some groupie he met the night before.

Townes had always been a lady's man, and although he had only missed the bus for the next city a couple of times, Buddy's problems had not been as easy to handle. Buddy drank all the time... He drank before the show... He drank after the show... He drank when he got up in the morning and until he went to bed at night. The only time he didn't drink was during the show. That was the one thing Jack could control and would not allow.

Finally it had gotten so bad Jack was forced to fire him. It was tough firing a guy who was probably the best picker in the business... a guy who had been his best friend since they were kids, and who, at times, seemed to be his only friend... And realizing that firing him was going to end that friendship forever... All because he had some so-called 'disease' he couldn't control.

Jack was a strong person and didn't have a lot of patience with weak people. He had never bought that stuff about drinking being a disease that the drinker couldn't help. Rather, he saw it as a weakness that Buddy could control if he wanted to. The trouble with Buddy was he didn't want to.

Buddy reacted exactly as Jack thought he would when he told him he was fired. First he laughed. Then when he realized Jack wasn't kidding, he cursed, and in a fit of anger broke a chair across a table.

"You can just go to Hell, Jack! I don't need you anyway! But you need me! You sure as Hell need me if you're gonna keep this damn band together!"

He stared at Jack through bloodshot eyes and waited for a reaction, but Jack gave none. Finally, he lowered his head, stuffed his few belongings in a bag and stumbled out the door.

Firing Buddy was one of the toughest things Jack had ever had to do. He knew it was the right thing, but that didn't make it any easier. However, the straw that broke the camel's back, as far as the band was concerned, was not the firing of Buddy, but the chain of events that followed.

That night after the show, Jack and Bobby went out for pizza and tried to put some things in perspective and decide where to go from here. It was at this time Bobby told Jack something that he had known was coming, but hadn't expected so soon.

Bobby Caldwell was one of the finest drummers in the business. He had played sessions for several big name recording artists before he joined Jack.

"There's more money in the studio," Bobby had said, "but it's so dead. No real people to play for, to watch them respond and let you know they love what you're doing. Man, that's what it's all about."

Jack knew Bobby had received offers from other bands, several of which could pay a lot more than he could, but Bobby felt a loyalty to Jack. Not only did he believe in the material Jack wrote, but he respected him for the way he hung in there with Buddy and Townes, and carried them at times when they were just dead weight to the band.

However, this time Bobby had received an offer he could not refuse, at least that's what Jack told him.

"Jessi McCrae!" Jack exclaimed. "She's good... really good! It's the chance of a lifetime. You've got to take it, Bobby!"

Jessi McCrae had won the "SOUTHEASTERN STAR SEARCH COMPETITION" a few years back and was a finalist in the national competition. Jack had never seen her in person, but he had seen her do a couple of songs on a public t.v. fundraiser.

She was young and seemed a little nervous, but when she started to sing, you forgot all about that. She had more natural talent than anybody he had seen in years. Someday, with the right promotion and the right song, she would make it big, and Bobby would be perfect for her. Lord knows Bobby deserved this chance. He was the dependable one who never caused any trouble, while Townes and Buddy were raising all the Hell they could.

As he tried to convince Bobby that he couldn't pass up this opportunity, Bobby poked the last piece of pizza in his mouth and mumbled around it.

"We'll talk about it later. We've got to get some sleep now. We're pulling out for Macon pretty early."

To no one's surprise, Townes hadn't come in when Jack and Bobby got back to the hotel around 2:30, and when the alarm went off at 10:30 the next morning, Townes' bed had not been slept in.

"Damn!" Jack greeted the morning when he spotted Townes' empty bed.

"What are you going to do?" Bobby asked, seeing a frustration in Jack's eyes he had not seen there before.

"I'm not going to do anything! He knows the bus pulls out at 12:00 with or without him." Jack paused. "And, frankly, I don't care which!"

Jack showered and shaved, nervously cutting himself in the process, and at 12:00 o'clock he and Bobby got on the bus and pulled out of the parking lot and onto I-75 without a word spoken between them.

Finally about an hour down the road, Bobby pulled a thermos out from under the seat and broke the silence.

"You want some coffee?"

Jack shook his head and several more minutes of silence passed before he finally spoke.

"Bobby, it's over. We'll go on to Macon and play the show tonight, but that's it."

Bobby knew Jack meant what he said, and there was no use trying to change his mind. Nonetheless, he tried to ease the tension.

"Ah Jack, you know Townes. He'll show up. Matter of fact, if you check your rear view mirror, you'll probably see him running down the highway now, pulling his pants on, carrying his shoes and chasing the bus." Bobby grinned, picturing the scene, and added, "probably with some half naked redhead chasing after him."

Jack only stared straight ahead and said quietly, "Not this time!"

As they drove on, Bobby asked, "What will you do?"

Without taking his eyes off the road Jack answered. "I don't know. I'm tired of the road. I might just quit."

Bobby knew Jack was not about to give up music, but he understood his frustration. One night Buddy had gotten really loaded and told him the story about the girl in Atlanta. He had never mentioned it to Jack or let him know that he knew, but he did know, and he understood the frustration Jack now felt.

Somehow it seemed the consequences of other people's actions always affected him more than it did them, and Jack was always having to turn loose of a part of himself so that somebody else could be better off.

Bobby looked across the seat at the solemn man behind the wheel and thought to himself, "It's not fair!... Damn, it's just not fair."

*   *   *   *   *

After the band broke up, Jack traded the bus in on a '74 Dodge van. It was all he needed and it was not as expensive to operate.

It was now May 29th. The air conditioner was busted and the man on the radio said it was a scorching 90 degrees as Jack pulled out of the McDonald's parking lot in Ringgold, Georgia, and headed south on I-75 to Daytona Beach.

Jack and the band had played a lot of gigs in Florida, tourist traps, as they call them. And that was where he was headed. Only now, for the first time in three years, he was going solo.

CHAPTER 21

AUGUST 1982

DAYTONA BEACH, FLORIDA

"Man, it's hot!" Jack thought, as he sipped a Michelob on the back deck of *Sharky's Beachside Saloon* and stared out at the calm waters of the Atlantic. The smell of coconut oil blew in from the beach, and for lack of anything better to do, he boringly watched the beach crowd.

It was only eleven o'clock, and he didn't have to be at the club until two. He had already read the sports section. The Braves had a shot at the playoffs and maybe the World Series, if they didn't blow it.

Contrary to what he had imagined, he missed the camaraderie of the guys in the band. Sometimes they would shoot baskets, and always there were the card games. Buddy loved to play hearts and generally won, but at least it had been something to do. When Townes hadn't had a late night and could roust himself out of bed before noontime, the two of them played tennis or jogged if there wasn't a basketball goal handy.

He didn't miss the hassles of trying to keep the band together and making sure they had enough bookings and enough money to pay the guys and meet expenses, but he did miss the guys.

The summer had been endlessly long. One boring day followed another, short meaningless conversations with people he had never seen before and would never see again, patrons of the club who came in mostly to get out of the ninety-plus heat, not to hear the music.

Mornings he usually ran on the beach to keep in shape, sometimes pausing to remember the wonderful beach vacations he had shared with his parents when he was a kid. After the last show he would swim laps in the motel pool 'til the wee hours of the morning, then it was back to the loneliness of a motel room, hoping he was sufficiently tired to go to sleep without doing too much thinking.

A couple of times he had played golf with the club owner, but most of the time Mark was too busy with his own work or filling in for one of his employees who didn't bother to show up.

Sharky's paid well and it was nice to sleep in the same bed every night and not have to get up the next day and drive ten or twelve hours to do another show in another town.

Playing at *Sharky's* was different from playing at *Kelly's* or the other clubs he had played for the last seven years. In those places, the people came to hear you. They listened to your music and related to what you sang about, and at the end of the show you felt good about what you were doing. But it was not that way here.

Sharky's featured two afternoon shows... one at three and one at five. Since the club was right on the beach, most of the afternoon patrons were beachcombers and sunbathers, who had grown tired of the sun and come into the air-conditioned club to get out of the heat and have a couple of drinks, not to listen to the music.

The night shows weren't much different. The same people, dressed in their fashionable summer attire, came to drink or 'pick someone up' or 'get picked up'. Few actually came to listen, and most of the time he felt as if he were singing to the walls. It was depressing and although he was making good money, this was not why he had gotten into the music business.

He smiled as he watched a young couple with two children enjoy what appeared to be their first family trip to the beach. The boy was six or seven and wide-eyed with wonder. He ran as fast as his little legs would carry him to get to the white foamy surf, but his mom quickly caught up with him and hauled him back to apply another layer of sun screen. Then with his dad holding his hand, they made their way together into the cool blue water. Mom helped the little girl build a sandcastle, although mom did most of the building, as the little girl quickly grew tired of the castle and found it more fun just to play in the sand.

At other times he watched lovers walk arm in arm down the beach. Some were newlyweds and showed signs of being on their honeymoon. Others were older and appeared to be retired, but the warmth of their smiles and the look in their eyes spoke of a love that though far from new, was even stronger than when they walked this same beach as newlyweds.

Daytona was a wonderful place, but it was a place to be shared, not a place to be alone. As he watched the happy couples on the beach he thought of Mary and wondered how she was. He wondered if she was happy or simply coping with the hand life had dealt her?... He wondered about Buddy. No doubt Buddy would find other bands to play with. He was that good... But finding a place to play was not the problem. Buddy's problem was far more than that, and Jack wondered if he would ever conquer it. He smiled as he thought of Townes. Townes would be fine. He wasn't the most responsible person in the world, but he loved life and lived it to the hilt. Wherever he landed, he would be okay.

Then his thoughts returned to himself... Was this what life was about? Was this all there was to it... day after day of boring aloneness? But he knew better. He had seen far more with his own parents. They were not wealthy, but they had each other and their family, and they had love. Everything else was a bonus... What he wouldn't give for that kind of life.

CHAPTER 22

The summer of 1982 was finally over and after his closing Labor Day performance, Jack loaded his belongings into the van and in an hour's time was on the interstate headed home, happy the summer at Daytona was over. He had one stop to make before he returned to Chattanooga. Bobby had called a couple of weeks earlier and said they would be playing in Jacksonville the following week, and Jack wasted no time accepting his invitation to "Stop and spend a few days". It was just the break he needed from a summer he thought would never end.

He arrived in Jacksonville shortly before seven and had just enough time for a quick shower and shave before heading over to the club for the nine o'clock show.

Bobby was better than ever on the drums, and everything Jack had heard about Jessi McCrae was true. He had heard how very talented she was, but in this business you can hear that about a lot of performers, and many times those with "STAR" written all over them turn out to be the biggest flops. But not this time! This lady could sing.

Jessi had never heard of Jack Roberts until Bobby joined her band. One day while setting up the equipment for a show, she walked into the sound room and Bobby was listening to a tape. She was captivated by the words and style of the unknown voice coming from the speakers.

"Who is that?"

A look of fascination filled her eyes, as if she had just stumbled across a yet unknown Bob Dylan in Greenwich Village.

"That's Jack Roberts... the guy I played with before I came here."

"Who wrote those lyrics?"

"He did. He writes a lot of his own material."

She sat down next to Bobby and listened to the rest of the tape. Her mind never wavered from the first song to the last.

"Wow!" She spoke when the final song ended.

It was a simple comment, but it expressed her sentiments completely.

    *   *   *   *   *

The following day the three of them were sharing a pizza by the pool when the motel manager came out.

"Mr. Caldwell, there's a phone call for you in my office."

Bobby went to answer the phone, leaving Jack and Jessi to visit in the warm Florida sunshine. Jack found it easy to talk to Jessi. They seemed to relate well. Maybe it was their common interest in music, but it was nice to talk to someone about something real and something that was so much a part of his life. He had had few opportunities to do either the last three months.

Yet, there was something different about her... something mysterious... Outwardly she was nice, but there was a distance... almost like a wall she refused to let down. He couldn't tell if she was uppity or if she was simply a private person.

She expressed interest in his writing, and told him that Bobby had played one of his tapes for her, although she didn't mention that she had performed a couple of the songs in her own show.

"*Simple Case of Lonesome* expresses so much emotion, so much hurt and pain. It makes you feel as if you're there and it's happening to you." Jessi looked deep into his eyes as she continued. "How do you write like that?... I've tried to write a little myself, but I can never seem to capture that kind of feeling... How do you do it?"

A look immediately came over his face... a mixture of pain, sadness and possibly a trace of anger, and she realized she had hit a nerve.

Jack had written *Simple Case of Lonesome* during the first year after he left Atlanta... after he had left Mary. It was one of the hardest times in his life, harder even than losing baseball. For a long time nothing seemed to matter. He tried to move on, to focus on his music, on the new band he had formed, on anything he could. But though he forced his thoughts away from her, his heart refused to let go. It was out of that time and that terrible emptiness that he had penned *Simple Case of Lonesome*.

He was surprised Jessi knew about the song. The lyrics were probably the most personal he had ever written. It had taken several months before he could bring himself to share it with the guys in the band. They loved it from the start and insisted they incorporate it in their show. It received tremendous audience response everywhere, but the gut-wrenching despair in his eyes was apparent each time Jack sung the song, and it came as no surprise when one night he said, "We're not going to do that one tonight."... And they had not done it since. They understood the reason... It hit too close to home.

"Where did you hear that?"

"Bobby had a tape of one of your shows and we listened to it one night on the bus."

Suddenly he seemed miles away, and she knew his thoughts were not of this place nor of her. Finally, for lack of something better to say, she simply voiced her thoughts.

"I'm sorry if I said something I shouldn't have. It's a beautiful song. It touched me deeply." She hesitated for a moment, then decided to tell him anyway. "I've even sung it a few times in my show."

"You what?" He couldn't believe it. Who did she think she was? It wasn't her song. It was Mary's... And she had no right. What was Bobby thinking to share something like that?

Jessi watched, as his eyes grew cold and distant. She wasn't sure what to say.

"The lyrics convey such pain and despair, such loss and loneliness, and wondering if you could go on and if there was a reason to... Maybe it's because I've been there myself and have known that kind of pain, but I..."

He interrupted her. "What do you know about pain?"

She was patronizing him, and if there was anything he hated, it was being patronized. He had seen her type before... Blonde and beautiful, with that innocent 'girl next door' smile... Head cheerleader... probably Homecoming Queen... blessed with extraordinary talent... soaring her way to the top... What could she possibly know about pain... about losing... and having to start over with only loneliness to keep you company?

All of a sudden she didn't like this guy's attitude. Did he think he was the only person in the world who had ever known trouble? No doubt he had experienced pain and loss. It was reflected in the songs he wrote, but nobody has a monopoly on trouble. Sooner or later it comes to everyone.

"Maybe I haven't walked in your shoes, but I have known sadness and sorrow. Everybody has, you know. Pain and disappointment come to all of us at different times and in different ways."

Jack was in no mood for a lecture and without waiting for her to finish, he interrupted with a touch of sarcasm.

"So, what do you know about pain and disappointment?" His eyes rested on her, challenging her, assuming that probably the worst disappointment she had experienced was having to wait until her senior year to be elected Homecoming Queen.

She resented his sarcasm and wondered how Bobby could have such respect for this guy. He was talented, but he was extremely arrogant.

He watched the anger building in her eyes.

She was ready to walk away, but first she would answer his impertinent question.

"I'll tell you what I know about pain and disappointment!... On March 4th, 1969, I stood at the altar of the little country church I grew up in and became the wife of Pvt. James T. McCrae. Two weeks later I kissed him good-bye at the bus station as he shipped out for Vietnam. Then on October 5th, 1970, there was a knock on my door and there stood another marine, one I had not seen before. There was a somber expression on his face, and he was holding a telegram. I didn't have to read it. I knew what it said... Jimmy was dead... I was nineteen years old and a widow."

Her voice trailed off as she turned away and stared into space.

Jack felt like a complete jerk. He had misinterpreted her pain for conceit and had taken his own frustration out on her.

"I'm sorry. I didn't know."

He had no further words. He had been unintentionally cruel, and she didn't deserve it. It was a part of the moodiness that had crept over him at the beginning of summer and continued to build until finally it reached a point where he perceived the whole world as a bunch of phonies.

For a few minutes they were both quiet. Then Jack asked, "Did you re-marry?"

"No. Jimmy and I were high school sweethearts. He was the boy down the street, and we had known from the time we were twelve that someday we would be married." She paused, remembering. "I was not his wife for very long, but I had loved him for a long time. I felt robbed... cheated. All I had left were memories, and I clutched them to me with a passion."

"You don't ever really get over something like that. You function and go on with life, although at times you really don't know why." Again Jessi paused, as her mind replayed the scenes and emotions she had experienced. "I worked. I paid the rent. I thought if I was old enough to get married, then I was old enough to support myself... and I made it."

"It must have been rough. Did you ever consider moving back in with your parents?"

"My parents are dead. They were killed in an accident when I was seven."

Compassion covered Jack's face. He had been so wrong, so very wrong about Jessi McCrae.

"I'm sorry."

"You had no way of knowing... By the time I finally let go of my grief, I was trying to get started in this business, and there was little time or opportunity for relationships. You know how it is when you play a different city every night. You meet everyone and get to know no one." She paused. "My career is very important to me. Maybe someday I'll marry again, but right now I'm not concerned about it."

He listened without taking his eyes off her as she told him the cold hard facts of her life. Quiet settled around the poolside as they sat under the large floral umbrella lost in their own thoughts.

Finally Jack broke the silence.

"Do you have brothers or sisters?"

"No. I was an only child and so was Daddy. Mom's only brother had three boys, so I've got cousins, but they live in Michigan and I've only seen them three or four times."

"I guess that means you're all alone in the world, as far as family goes."

"My grandmother is still living. She's the one who raised me. I moved in with her after Mom and Daddy died."

"Where does she live?"

"Ft. Payne... Ft. Payne, Alabama."

Jack's eyes lit up and a bit of a smile crossed his face.

"I know where Ft. Payne is. I'm from Chattanooga."

What a small world it was. Chattanooga, Tennessee and Ft. Payne, Alabama were about forty-five miles apart, separated only by Lookout Mountain.

"Tell me about her."

The look on his face told her that he wasn't just being courteous. He really wanted to know. Few people she was now associated with even knew her grandmother, and it was nice to be able to tell someone about her. She was a very special lady.

"She's short and a little plumpish, although she would never admit it. She's fun to be around and has more energy than a twelve-year old. And she loves baseball... Since she got cable, she never misses a Braves game... She's a good cook and she cooks everything from scratch. At least she did until the last couple of years. Then she discovered corn dogs and all the other microwavables. Now she eats more junk food than a kid." The smile on Jessi's face was warm and animated as she spoke of her grandmother. "She would rather work outside than in the house. She hates to dust. Her thing is digging in the dirt, whether it's setting out azaleas or hoeing in her vegetable garden... She's seventy-four years old and still uses a garden tiller."

"She sounds like quite a lady." Jack smiled as he pictured the little lady tilling her garden.

"She is!"

Jessi loved her grandma. She knew she had given up a lot to take in a little seven-year-old girl after she had already raised her own family.

Jessi appreciated the interest he had showed in her grandma, and now he didn't seem as brash and indifferent as he had earlier.

They watched as Bobby walked through the hedged archway surrounding the pool.

"That was Dave Palmer. I played drums on a recording session for him last week, and the producer's not happy with two of the songs. So they're getting everybody back together this afternoon to re-cut them. The singer's leaving town tomorrow and this is the only chance to do it."

He apologized for having to leave and then said, "If I'm going to make it by two, I'd better be on my way. I'll see you guys tonight."

"I've had about all the sun I need," Jessi said, as she gathered her sunscreen and pool supplies into her tote bag. If she stayed out much longer, the sun would zap her energy, and it would show in her performance tonight. It might be September, but the heat in Jacksonville paid no heed to the fact that summer was officially over as the temperature was still in the nineties.

"Could I buy you supper?" Jack asked almost hesitantly, not sure she would accept.

"You don't have to do that. I'm used to eating alone when the guys get involved in a recording session."

She was about to say more, but Jack interrupted.

"I know I don't have to." His voice was gentle and a trifle sad. "But I would like to... if you'll let me."

Jessi got the message. He was trying to make amends for coming on so heavy earlier, and while he had been hard as nails, something told her that was not the real Jack Roberts.

"Okay, if you really want to."

A smile crept across Jack's face. "I really want to."

They went to *Nikki's* for barbecue. It was quiet and relaxed, and neither of them could remember when they had enjoyed a meal so much, and they were both glad they had chosen not to eat alone.

*　　*　　*　　*　　*

The last few days had been fun. It had given Jack the 'shot of life' he needed after a summer of Daytona tourists. He almost hated to see Saturday come. Bobby, Jessi and the band would leave for the Carolinas, and he would head back to Chattanooga.

The instruments, sound system, and luggage had already been loaded on the bus, and the lead guitarist and the bass player, who also doubled as the bus driver, were already on board. Jack and Bobby chatted on the hot asphalt parking lot, while they waited for Jessi to finish packing.

"Jack, you ought to go with us."

"It's tempting, but right now I've got some songs that need to be put down on paper." He had already told Bobby he was taking the fall off to work on his writing. "But I don't think we've played our last song together."

"No way! I'll be in Nashville for a recording session in November. Maybe you can drive up."

"Sounds good to me. Give me a call when you get there."

About that time Jessi came across the parking lot with a tote bag in one hand and an overnight case in the other.

"It was really nice to meet you, Jack." Jessi spoke in a reserved, almost professional manner as she shifted the tote to her left hand and reached to shake hands.

There was a story behind this man, a very involved one, she suspected. But he had chosen not to reveal it, and she respected that, although she was curious.

After having spent some time with him, she knew he was not as callous as he first appeared. He was hurting or he had been hurt. She could tell that much. She also assumed the reason he didn't care to talk about it was he didn't want to expose himself to the pain it extracted.

She understood the feeling. She felt that way for a long time after her parents were killed. It was a lot easier to act as if you were like the other kids who went home to their mommies and daddies every night, than to try to explain that she had no parents. They didn't understand anyway. They couldn't. They had not experienced that kind of aloneness. They could imagine all they wanted, but it was only imagining, and there was no way they could really understand.

Although she didn't know the details of his story or why he chose not to talk about it, she knew he was not the jerk he had seemed on Wednesday. He had not meant to hurt her. His thoughts and harsh words weren't even aimed at her, but had been hurled recklessly at life and the bad hand it had dealt him. She had simply gotten caught in the crossfire of Jack's cold war.

"It was nice to meet you too, Jessi." He took her hand in his and for a moment their eyes met. "You know you've got the best drummer in the business right here." He smiled, as he tried to change the somewhat formal mood.

"I know. I'm lucky to have him." Jessi looked over at Bobby, who could tell they were both trying to say more than their words were conveying.

"Take care of him for me... and yourself too."

"I will." She noted Jack's focus was as much on her as on Bobby.

As she turned and started up the steps of the bus, Jack called to her.

"Jessi... Ever since we talked the other day..." He paused, wondering if the remembrance would make her sad, but it didn't seem to. "I've had these lines running through my head. If I can put them together, I'd like to call you and see what you think."

She saw something she had not seen before, maybe hints of it a few times, but not as completely as she saw it now. And although she didn't fully understand, she wanted to know more.

Jack's eyes were filled with uncertainty as he searched her face for a response.

"It sounds great. Just give me a call."

Bobby watched as both Jack's and Jessi's smiles lasted a little too long. Then she disappeared into the bus, and Jack stared at the empty doorway where she had just stood.

The bus driver honked the horn and could be heard complaining about Bobby holding everybody up.

Jack grinned. "Hey, you better get on that bus or like you said about Townes, you're gonna be chasing it."

They laughed and shook hands.

"Take care of yourself, man."

"You too. I'll see you later."

Then the door closed and the bus pulled out. And Jack stood in the empty parking lot... Alone again.

CHAPTER 23

ONE MONTH LATER

"Hey, Jack! It's good to hear from you. How are things going?"

"Fine. How about you guys?"

"We're okay... How did you manage to track us down?"

The band was on the seventh day of twenty-two back-to-back one-nighters... Greenville today... Knoxville tomorrow... then north into Kentucky.

"The same way I always do. I called your Mom. You know Mrs. Nora knows every move you make."

"Yeah, I never could pull anything off without her knowing. And usually she knew before I even did it."

Bobby covered the receiver and whispered to Jessi, who was sitting at the table playing solitaire.

"Hey Jess, it's Jack!"

"Tell him to come see us, if he can catch us."

Her attention quickly turned from her card game to thoughts of Jack. By the end of the week Jack spent with them in Florida, it was plain to see she had more than a casual interest in the quiet songwriter. She had asked Bobby about him, and he had grinned suspiciously.

"Don't tell me you, too, have succumbed to the Jack Roberts charm."

"What do you mean, 'me too'? Is he a 'lady killer'?"

"I wouldn't say that. Women just seem to be attracted to him... I'm not sure why they go for him so. He's not really a flirt."

Jessi knew why. There was something about the tall, quiet man that made you want to know more. While at times he seemed distant and almost cynical, she had also seen a warm, gentle side of him.

Bobby had answered some of her questions, but the rest she would have to find out for herself. He told her about his tragically shortened baseball career, but he did not tell her about the girl in Atlanta. Whether or not she was to know that would be up to Jack.

Bobby and Jack chatted for a few minutes. Then he handed the phone to Jessi.

"He wants to talk to you."

"Hey, Jack, why don't you come up and see a good show?"

"By the time I got there, you'd be somewhere else. You guys cover more miles than a Greyhound."

"I know. Sometimes it's hard to remember what city we're in... How about you? What have you been doing lately?"

"I've been doing what you told me to do."

She had no idea what he was talking about. "What do you mean?"

"You told me to write you a song, but I'm hung up on the third verse... You got time to listen?"

"Sure, I'd love to."

As she listened, her thoughts were transported to another time and another place... a long way from the small motel room in Greenville, South Carolina.

When he finished the song, she did not reply. Instead she sat in silence, overwhelmed by the poignant lines she had heard.

The song was about a young soldier who had gone off to war, only to have his life so quickly stripped from him and those who loved him. It spoke of the waste of war and how the sacrifice of this young life had not changed anything, not really.

It told of the young widow and the dreams that would never come true. It spoke of the sorrow and resentment she felt for a system that had taken him away from her and from his small hometown, where he had never even seen a Vietnamese, much less had a problem with one. He wasn't old enough to vote, but he was old enough to die.

It was a sad story, but it was a true story... It was Jessi and Jimmy's story, and the story of so many others. The feelings expressed in the lyrics were accurate and real. It was beautiful the way he had captured the gamut of emotions.

"Jess, are you still there?" His voice was soft and searching.

"Yes." She paused to wipe away a tear. "That's exactly how it was."

She was amazed at his perception of what she had felt thirteen years ago when she first read the telegram.

"How did you do it? How did you write something like that without experiencing it firsthand? Did you know someone who did?"

"Only you... only what you told me in Jacksonville."

"But I don't understand how you captured the range of emotions... the pain... the anger. I didn't tell you those things. I've never told anyone. I only told you what happened, not the confused, lonely feelings I had in the days and weeks that followed."

"You didn't have to. I saw them in you eyes and heard them in your voice."

She didn't know what to say, and her silence made him afraid he had hurt her.

"Jessi, I didn't mean to make you sad."

"You didn't."

He could hear her sigh over the phone.

"It's beautiful. It's the closest anyone has ever come to understanding what it was like for me and for countless other wives and mothers who have given up husbands and sons. Thank you for writing it, Jack."

Bobby left the room, aware she was overcome with emotion and would probably like to be alone. He didn't know what was going on, but it was not his place to listen.

As he walked down the hallway to the Coke machine, he remembered the day in Florida when they were leaving... Jack and Jessi were saying good-bye, and their smiles had seemed to linger a little long... Now he knew why.

* * * * *

Autumn in Chattanooga is the one season that year after year seems to outdo itself in its quest for beauty. This year was no exception. The leaves on the trees were various shades of red and gold, and while the mornings were cool, the afternoon sun shed its warmth upon the earth, extending an open invitation to come outside.

Jack was glad to be home and off the road. The money he had made during the summer afforded him the opportunity to spend the fall working on his writing. He spent most of his time on the patio out back, his guitar across his lap, and his pad and pencil close at hand, developing song ideas. Some days were more productive than others, but each day he woke up with a new desire to make his thoughts come alive.

The last four years had been filled with frustration. Although his musical talent had improved, and he had gradually made the move from roadhouses and bars to larger, classier clubs, the hassle of managing a band and trying to keep his musicians out of trouble long enough to get from one city to another had overshadowed whatever personal success he had attained.

He went to bed at night worrying about the problems of the day, and by the time he took care of those problems, there was a new set waiting for him. It never seemed to change. There was always something. And when the band broke up in the spring in many ways it was a relief.

He hadn't been sure if going solo was the right direction or not, but there was one thing for certain. He wasn't ready to deal with another band. He had had it with musicians.

The members of the band were all very talented, but Bobby was the only one that showed any responsibility. Jack had finally reached the point that he could no longer put up with Buddy's drinking and Townes' womanizing. They took no responsibility for themselves, and he was tired of being their caretaker. The band was good and they could have made it, if Buddy and Townes had just cared. But you can't make people care.

He knew the breakup had been the right thing. The summer in Daytona, though frustrating itself, had made him aware of what he wanted to do and the steps he needed to take to achieve his goals.

While he had enjoyed playing the guitar and singing, his real love was songwriting. There was no greater satisfaction than reaching deep inside himself and drawing upon feelings and emotions and weaving them into a song.

He had spent countless afternoons by the pool, working on songs and ideas, which had been in his head for many years, but until now he hadn't had the opportunity to transpose into real lyrics, and not just lines stored in the back of his head or scribbled on a barroom napkin. He felt good about the songs he was writing. He was developing a unique style, and it was becoming easier to express himself and say the things he wanted to say.

He wasn't sure why he was able to do this so freely now, when it had been so hard in the past. Maybe he had finally put the hurt of the past behind him. He hadn't forgotten it, but maybe he had let go of it, and instead of allowing it to control him, now he controlled it.

Whatever the reason, the lyrics and the melodies now flowed from his pen. It was very tiring work and by the end of an afternoon of writing, he felt as if he had been digging ditches for hours. The intense concentration and outpouring of emotion took a lot out of him, both mentally and physically, but even though it was tiring, it was fulfilling. And he knew what he was doing was right for him at this point in his life.

Bobby came by one afternoon on his way back from Nashville. They visited for awhile, and then Jack played him a couple of the songs he had written.

"Be honest, Bobby. If you think they're terrible, tell me. I need your opinion."

Bobby didn't think they were terrible. He thought they were great.

"Jack, this is some of the best stuff I've heard in a long time. I think you just needed to get away from me and Buddy and Townes," he grinned.

Bobby knew Jack had found his niche, and with the right promotion and contacts, it was only a matter of time before these songs would penetrate the airways of American radio.

When Bobby rejoined the band, he told Jessi about his visit with Jack and the songs he had written.

"I always knew he was good, but this latest stuff is great writing."

Jessi wasn't surprised. She knew he was good when she heard the song he wrote about Jimmy. She had never known anyone who could feel the anguish and sorrow of others so deeply and express those feelings so completely in the lines of a song.

* * * * *

OCTOBER 1982

"Jack, telephone!" Virginia Roberts called from the back door.

"Mom, can't you get a number? I'm busy right now." He stopped strumming his guitar only long enough to make notes on the ever-present pad.

Virginia walked out to the deck. "I think you ought to take this one."

"Who is it?" He again jotted some words on the pad.

"It's a girl, and she sounds nice."

Virginia had sensed the hurt Jack had tried so long to conceal, and she had hoped for a long time that he would meet someone nice.

"I don't know any girls around here... Just tell her something... anything... I'm busy."

"She's not from around here. She's calling from Huntsville."

"Huntsville? I don't know anybody in Huntsville." He continued to strum his guitar, "Did she say who she was?"

"Jessi... Jessi McCrae... Never mind. I'll just tell her you're not here."

She started toward the house, realizing the girl was spending her money while she and Jack were arguing over whether he would take the call.

Suddenly, he quit playing his guitar. "No, wait, I'll take it." He laid his guitar aside and started to the back door.

A slow smile stretched across Virginia's face, as she noted the sudden change in Jack's willingness to take the call.

"Apparently you know this Jessi."

"Yeah... She's the singer Bobby Caldwell's playing with now."

"She sounds kind of nice."

Jack only smiled, but the smile revealed more than words.

* * * * *

Jack got a Coke from the refrigerator and went to his room to take the call.

"Hey, Jess. Is everything okay?"

"We're fine. Just staying busy... I thought I'd call and say 'Hello.'"

"That's great. It's good to hear from you."

"So, how are things with you?"

"Fine. I'm just living the good life. Eating my mom's home cooking and getting fat."

Jessi couldn't imagine that Jack had ever been fat in his life or ever would be for that matter.

"Are you guys playing in Huntsville?"

"Yeah, we're still doing one-nighters... Huntsville tonight, Birmingham tomorrow, and Columbus and Panama City over the weekend."

"Sounds like you're logging the miles."

"Yeah, we're covering Alabama, South Georgia and the Carolinas between now and Thanksgiving, but we're going to take off the whole week of Thanksgiving. So I think we can make it 'til then."

She paused a moment and her voice took on a more serious tone, as if she were ready to end the small talk and move on to whatever she had called about.

"Bobby tells me you've had that magic pen of yours going again."

"Well, I wouldn't say that." He smiled at the way she had phrased her comment, "but I have been doing quite a bit of writing since I saw you."

"I hope you're saving a few of them for me."

"I don't know if you'll want any of them. They may not be that good." He was being modest.

"That's not the way I hear it. Bobby thinks your new material is some of the best he's heard in years."

"Well, maybe. I don't know." He was always cautiously optimistic about his writing.

"So when do I get to hear them?"

He could hear the smile in her voice. He wasn't sure if she was flirting, but she seemed to have more than a professional interest in the songs he had written. In fact, she hadn't asked anything specific about the songs. Rather, it was as if she were using the songs as an excuse to call.

Jessi was okay, and he was glad she had called, whatever the reason.

"Whenever you like. Are you coming home for Thanksgiving?

"Yes, for a whole wonderful week."

He understood her sense of relief. How well he understood. He had done his share of one-nighters and knew how good it was to get off the road for a few days.

"I've got an idea. Why don't you have Thanksgiving dinner with us? Mom always cooks a big turkey with all the trimmings, and there's just the two of us now. It would be nice to have company." He hesitated, "Unless you already have plans with your Grandma... or someone else."

Jessi sensed an air of questioning in the "or someone else" line.

"No, Grandma is flying to Michigan to spend Thanksgiving with her sister. She has never been on a plane in her life, and she can't wait. I'm free, but are you sure your mom won't mind having an extra guest?"

"Mom's in all her glory when she has company. She'll be delighted."

"Okay. Then I'd love to come."

Jessi's normal reserved manner could not contain the excitement she was feeling. "I'm looking forward to seeing you, Jack."

"Me too! Give me your number and I'll call you after you get to Ft. Payne." He paused for a moment and added, "I'm glad you called, Jess."

She hung up the phone and thought about him. She had not expected the invitation for Thanksgiving dinner, but she was glad he wanted to see her. In spite of their somewhat rocky beginning, she felt comfortable and happy and secure when she was with him, and she had not felt this way with anyone since Jimmy.

A few minutes later Bobby returned. He took one look at the expression on her face and remarked, "Why are you grinning like a Cheshire cat? Looks like you've been up to something."

She was only slightly embarrassed that her excitement was so easily detected.

"I just talked to Jack."

"Jack Roberts?"

"Yes." The smile on her face grew wider.

"That explains it. I figured he would be calling soon. He sure asked enough questions about you the other day."

"He did?" She was surprised, but pleased. "What did he say?"

"Oh, I don't know... You know just the normal stuff."

"Like what?" She asked eagerly.

"Like, wHat you were like... If you shaved your legs regularly." He kidded. "I don't know. Ask him. He's the one calling you."

Bobby saw the mischievous look on her face.

"He did call you? Didn't he?"

"Well, not exactly... I called him."

"Jessi McCrae! You wild woman!"

He would have a field day with this one. He was giving her a hard time and would continue to, but inside he was happy for her. In the seven months he had known her, he had never seen her with a guy or show any interest in dating. He hadn't given it much thought because he knew she was completely dedicated to her career, but now he wasn't sure music was her only interest.

"It won't be long now," Bobby teased.

"What won't be long?" Jessi grinned, knowing he was up to something.

"Until Jack takes you home to meet his Mom... You see the one's he really likes, he takes home to meet her, while the ones that are just 'time to kill' never meet Mrs. Virginia." Bobby laughed good-naturedly. "So when are you two getting together?"

Jessi smiled. "Thanksgiving... at his Mom's."

* * * * *

Jack hated parades, yet here he sat watching the annual Macy's Thanksgiving Day Parade. Bryant Gumbel and Sarah Purcell were this year's hosts and vividly described every float that came down 34th Street. There were the usual ones that were there every year: Mickey Mouse, Donald Duck, Fred Flintstone, and all the characters from cartoon land. Bryant and Sarah told how tall and how wide each float was, how many pounds of air it contained, and the fact that it had been under construction since June.

Then came the high school marching bands. Not only had they spent endless hours on the practice field preparing for their thirty second spot on national t.v., but they had also spent the entire year doing fundraisers to pay their way from Iowa or Oregon or wherever it was they had come from. Jack thought about the parents, who had bought countless numbers of three dollar candy bars and had cooked gallon upon gallon of home-made chili for the band boosters' big chili supper only to go down to the school cafeteria and buy the same chili back again.

He watched as one marching band after another proceeded down 34th Street. Other than the different colored uniforms, they all looked the same. Each group was led by two girls in short skirts carrying a huge banner decorated in their school colors, which told everyone in America who they were and where they were from.

They all wore those stupid hats with the bills pulled down low over their eyes and the chin strap worn high above their upper lip. You couldn't tell what any of them looked like as they moved down 34th Street in synchronized motion.

Even the parents had difficulty telling which was their child unless their kid was six foot-eight or the class heavyweight.

"Why don't they have numbers?" Jack wondered. It made perfect sense. Then the people could pick out their son or daughter. Football players had numbers, otherwise the people in the stands would have no idea who was on the field. So why not band members? But that would never happen. Tradition would not allow it. It was a shame though, after all the candy bars and chili tickets those kids had sold, that nobody could tell them apart.

He changed the channel, but to no avail. CBS was also carrying the parade, the only difference being it was hosted by *Dallas'* Larry Hagman and Linda Gray.

About that time he heard his Mom call from the kitchen.

"Jack, how about setting the table for me?"

He didn't mind the interruption. He had seen about all of the parade he cared to. It was just something to do while he waited for Jessi. He took the plates from the cabinet and started toward the dining room to set the table.

"Jack, not those! They're for everyday. Let's use the good china."

He shook his head and returned the 'everyday' dishes to the cabinet and took out the 'company' china.

"I don't see what difference it makes. They'll be covered with food, so nobody will know what they look like anyway."

Virginia looked at him with a half grin, realizing he was trying to give her a hard time.

"I just want things to look nice for your girlfriend."

"She's not my girlfriend!" Jack quickly defended. "She's just someone I met... She's Bobby's boss." He weakly countered.

"All right, if you say so. I just don't remember that we normally invite Bobby's boss for Thanksgiving dinner, especially when we haven't invited Bobby." She smiled back at her son, knowing she had won this little exchange.

"Should I set a place for Aunt Velma?"

"There's no telling. You know Velma. She has such a busy social calendar that she can't ever let you know for sure... Go ahead and set a place. I expect she'll be here."

"Wonder what game we'll have to play this year? I hope it's not Monopoly."

"Oh my gosh, I hope she doesn't start that this year. It's bad enough when it's just the three of us, but with a guest coming, it would be embarrassing." Virginia wanted things to be nice, and sometimes Velma could be a pain with her ever-present board games.

"Don't worry, Mom. I imagine Jessi has seen her share of Aunt Velmas."

Virginia wasn't sure. It had been quite awhile since Jack had brought a girl home or showed any serious interest in anyone and she didn't want her sister to spoil things.

*   *   *   *   *

FRIDAY

The day was crystal clear as Jack drove down Interstate 59 toward Ft. Payne. Tall, ancient pine trees lined the highway, and there was little traffic, unusual for an interstate.

He was excited about seeing Jessi. Although they had spent the day together yesterday, today would be different. There would be just the two of them, and they wouldn't have to play monopoly or listen to Aunt Velma's constant chatter.

Jessi had seemed to enjoy Thanksgiving at his house and appeared unruffled by his Aunt Velma. When Velma brought out her monopoly board, Jessi exclaimed, "Oh, I love to play monopoly."

Jack grinned, and his mom shrugged her shoulders, as if to say, "Well, it's only once a year," and Jessi and Velma sorted the play money and set up the board.

He was in Fort Payne before he knew it. The rest of the way was the challenge. As he waited for the light to change, he glanced at the map Jessi had drawn for him. The next thing was to find the gristmill just south of town.

He soon spotted the old building, and just past it he turned onto a twisting two-lane road. About two miles down the road he saw an old barn with a rusted roof and kudzu covering one side. Again he looked at the map... He was right so far. Then he turned onto a narrow dirt road that led to God knows where.

Soon the house came in sight. It was a two story white frame house with green shutters and a big front porch, a typical old southern farm house, and everything around the place was neat and well kept.

Jessi heard Jack's car pull into the driveway and came out to greet him. She was dressed in jeans and a blue chambray western shirt, and her hair was caught back at the neck in a soft blue bow. The sight of her almost took his breath. He had never seen her this casual, but she was beautiful beyond words.

"I'm almost surprised you found me. I'm not very good with directions," she smiled.

"Neither am I, but I stopped a few miles back and asked a bear for directions, and after I passed the Seven Dwarfs' house, I knew I must be close."

"We're not that far out in the boonies," she defended.

"Pretty far, but I love it. Some day I'm gonna have a place like this, away from the hustle and bustle of city living."

He opened the trunk of the car and retrieved a picnic basket. "This is from Mom. She didn't want you to go hungry with your grandmother gone."

"How nice," she replied, as they entered the kitchen, "but I've got to show you something." Jessi opened the refrigerator, which was laden with ham, potato salad, slaw, green beans... you name it.

"The only way grandma would leave me here alone on Thanksgiving was to fix Thanksgiving dinner before she left." She hesitated, trying to figure out what to do with all the food. There was no way the refrigerator would hold it all. "Tell you what. We'll put the things away that need to be refrigerated and leave the turkey and dressing in the microwave and the pecan pie on the table. I want to show you the place first, and then we'll come back and 'pig out'."

"You do ride horseback?"

"It's been awhile, but I think I still remember which side to mount from," Jack smiled, realizing how little he knew about this lady, but liking the things he was learning.

"Sometimes grandma rides Kit. She won't give you any trouble. She's as gentle as a lamb."

Jack grinned. "Your grandma or the horse?"

"Both." She was quick with her response.

For a long time they rode and surveyed the beauty of the gently rolling hillside. It was so peaceful. He could understand why Jessi loved it. She counted heads to see that all the cows were there. Most of the older ones she knew by name. Then they rode down to the creek where as a child she had waded and tried to fish.

"I could never quite get the hang of it. Grandma said I couldn't be still long enough. I suppose she was right."

Pointing to her right, she said, "See that smoothed out area over there where there's no grass? That was my ball field."

"You played ball?"

"Sure. The neighborhood kids used to come here on Sunday after church, and we'd play all afternoon."

Jack stared at the smooth area that had obviously been well used. "I can't believe you had your own ball field."

"Grandma said this old farm wasn't worth very much anymore with grandpa gone. She only used it to raise a few cattle and make a garden. I suppose she figured it wouldn't do any harm to use part of it for a ball field."

"Okay, tell me more about you. Were you Golden Gloves champ, as well?" Jack kidded.

"No. However, I grew up surrounded by boys, and I learned early on how to pack a few punches if it became necessary. For some reason, everybody on this road had boys. I was the only girl around, except for Patsy Holmes, and all she wanted to do was play with dolls."

"So you were a tomboy?"

"I guess so."

"What position did you play?"

"Left field."

"You must have had a pretty good arm to beat out the boys in left field."

"Well, I didn't exactly beat them out. But it was my ball field, so that gave me the right to play wherever I wanted. At least I thought so."

"Yeah, I would say it did." Jack grinned and shook his head at the gutsy side of this girl he was just beginning to get to know. He wanted to know more. He wanted to know everything there was to know about her. And so far, he hadn't found anything he didn't like.

"I played shortstop on the high school softball team."

Jack laughed, "I guess you didn't own the field?"

"No, unfortunately... I got beat out in left field by a tall blonde named Vivian. She had a good arm, but I could out hit her. We were state champs my senior year."

"Keep talking. I'm making notes. Someday I may write a book and call it *Jessi*."

She liked him. He was light and easy, and could give as well as take the kidding. She thought of their first encounter and how cynical he had been, but that was not the same person she had come to know since that time. Something had made him that way. Maybe in time he would tell her, maybe not, but today was not a day for dwelling on bygones. It was a wonderful day, and she was spending it with a special friend, and she wondered if he knew how happy she felt.

And as they rode along together, Jack was having similar thoughts.

Finally, Jessi broke the silence.

"I'm about to starve. I'm ready for some of your mom's turkey. How about you?"

"Sure... Race you to the house?" He challenged.

"It wouldn't be a fair race. You'd lose. Old Kit is a good one, but she's been around a long time and isn't up to racing anymore."

In his wildest dreams, he could not have imagined the girl that was unfolding before his eyes. She was natural, and relaxed and real. There was no pretense about her. She was just a small town girl, who had grown up on a farm, reared by a loving, caring grandmother, played with the neighborhood boys, and learned to be assertive when she had to. But deep down inside she was as gentle and warm as the soft fall breeze that caressed their faces as they made their way back to the house.

Jessi poured iced tea, and Jack heated the turkey and dressing, and hungry from their long ride, they feasted on the food Virginia had sent.

"We'll get into grandma's fixings for supper."

They spent part of the afternoon riding around the small town where she had grown up. She showed him where she had gone to school including the ball field where Vivian Austin beat her out for left field. Then she showed him the neighborhood theater.

"Growing up in a small town, all there was to do for fun was play ball and go to the movies... and play monopoly... By the way, I've got the board set up for later," she teased.

"Not on your life. I'm not playing monopoly today."

They rode out past Randy Owens' place, and she smiled once more. "Few people outside the area had ever heard of Ft. Payne until the group *ALABAMA* made it big. They've done so much for the people around here. In addition to their musical success, they're a great bunch of guys. We're proud of them."

Finally, she drove out to the cemetery where her parents were buried.

"I don't come here very often... It makes me sad... I try to honor them in other ways."

"I think you do honor to them simply by being the person you are. I'm sure they are very proud of you." Jack spoke as if her parents were not far away and knew all about her.

She smiled ever so slightly and their eyes met. "Thank you for saying that."

Then she took him by the hand and they walked to another section of the cemetery, where a modest military headstone marked the final resting place of Pvt. James T. McRae. This time it was Jack who felt sad. Here in this small cemetery on the edge of town lay the people she had loved the most. They were all gone except for her grandmother.

He slipped his arm gently around her shoulder and spoke softly. "Thank you for sharing them with me."

They made their way back to the car just as the sun was setting and headed home, and for the first time all day they were both very quiet.

Finally, Jessi spoke. "Are you hungry?"

"Yeah, I think I could handle a ham sandwich."

When they got back to the house, Jack lit a fire in the fireplace while Jessi got out the food. Although it was not really cold, the house seemed a little chilly and the fire felt good.

"Well, now you know the story of my life," Jessi said, as they sat down to supper. "I hope I haven't bored you."

"Not at all. It has been one of the nicest days I've known, spent with one of the nicest people I know."

"You should be a poet. You're great with words."

"I'm a songwriter, at least I try, but those were not just words. I meant them. I like you, Jessi McCrae, very much. I think the luckiest day of my life may have been the day I stopped off in Jacksonville to see Bobby."

"I'm glad you came today," she said softly.

"So am I."

For a long time they sat by the fire and sipped coffee.

"Jack, there's something I've been thinking about lately."

He looked at her, unsure of what she was about to say, but aware that it was more than trivial conversation.

"Come on the road with us!" The enthusiasm showed on her face, and was reflected in her voice.

"Whoa!" He smiled as he tried to get over the initial shock of her proposal. "I just got off the road. I don't know if I'm ready to go back this soon."

"But you will go back, won't you?"

"I suppose so, eventually. Right now home feels real good. I couldn't write if I was out there traveling and performing every night, and my writing is very important to me."

"I understand."

He knew she did. She was a pro, but he also knew she was disappointed. And so was he. The idea of performing with a group as good as they were was exciting, and it would give him more time with her, something he found very tempting, but he was not yet ready to go back on the road.

"Well, it's an open invitation, if you should change you mind... I guess I'm being a little selfish. I'm trying to get the best songwriter I know to travel and perform with me."

Jack grinned. "Thanks for the endorsement. Right now I feel the need to write. My creative juices are flowing, and I've got a lot of thoughts running around in my head... Who knows? Maybe out of all the jumble, I'll come up with something good, but I can't do it if I'm performing every night."

"I understand." She couldn't entirely read his reaction, but she realized now was not the time to pursue it. Maybe in time it would happen... if it were meant to be. He was good, and she knew he would add solidity to the band and selfishly, she liked the idea of being able to spend more time with him.

Finally it was time for him to go. Neither of them was ready to say good-bye. It had been a truly wonderful day, but it had gone by much too quickly. Next week Jessi would be back on tour, and she wouldn't be home again until Christmas.

"See you Christmas?" he asked.

"I'd like that."

"Then save some time for me."

"I will."

"Well, I better go. Maybe I can find my way out of the boonies after dark."

"I think you'll make it back to civilization," she kidded.

Once more their eyes met and he drew her to him. She was soft and warm in his arms and offered no resistance. Instead she lifted her face to his, and their lips came together in a loving kiss.

He didn't want to leave, but he knew he must.

"Lock your doors," he cautioned. He hated leaving her alone.

"Don't worry. I'll be fine. This is probably the safest place in the whole world."

As he headed home, he carried with him warm thoughts of the day with Jessi. He would not have guessed that she was a country girl when he first saw her in concert. She had the appearance of a thoroughly modern woman, who could handle herself well in what was still mainly 'a man's world'. Yet today he had witnessed the simple, unpretentious side of her. She was modern, yet old-fashioned. She was tough and could take care of herself, yet gentle and easy to be with.

And for the first time since Mary, he had found someone he cared for. Where the relationship would lead he had no idea. Time, as it always does, would tell. All he knew was that right now being with Jessi was good... real good.

CHAPTER 24

The month between Thanksgiving and Christmas had been a long one. The band had played twenty-three shows in twenty-three cities and the sudden change in weather had left her with a touch of bronchitis. She went on with her shows in spite of feeling bad, and although the guys in the band said it didn't affect her singing, she knew that it did. She breathed a deep sigh of relief when she walked off the stage in Memphis Saturday night. It was their final show before Christmas, and was she ever ready for the break. Before the guys could get the equipment on the back of the bus, she was asleep in the back seat, her nose red from the cold she had been fighting. She didn't wake up until early the next morning when the bus pulled off the main road and onto the gravel drive that led to her grandmother's house.

She said good-bye to the guys and told them she would see them Thursday in Chattanooga, and then headed inside to the big sawmiller's breakfast she knew her grandmother would fix. The smell of coffee perking and sausage frying made her realize how nice it was to be home.

It was good to be off the road and away from the band for a few days. They were a great bunch of guys, but after traveling inseparably with three fellows for an entire month, she was ready for some time to herself.

They would all get together on Thursday at Jack's. He had called a couple of weeks earlier and invited them to his house for Christmas. He knew they would want to be with their own families on Christmas day, so he had planned the get-together for the twenty-third. This way they could all celebrate Christmas together and still have time to get home by Christmas Eve.

She was surprised to learn that Jack was such a 'Christmas' person. Most men could take it or leave it, but not Jack. Although he was somewhat of a loner and treasured his privacy, she could understand why he felt Christmas was not a time to be alone, but rather a time to be with family and friends and share the special joy of the season. She shared his sentiments and was looking forward to seeing him. They had talked on the phone several times since Thanksgiving, and each time she was drawn closer to him.

It was nice to sleep late each morning and engage in womanly conversation with her grandmother. Sometimes it seemed she lived entirely in a man's world. Mrs. Hughes was entertaining her Sunday school class for their annual Christmas dinner on Wednesday night, and Jessi enjoyed helping her clean and decorate. It was a tradition she had followed as long as Jessi could remember, and everything had to be 'just right'.

As the week went by, she thought more and more about Jack, and how nice this Christmas was going to be. He told her they would trim the tree early Thursday afternoon, then go caroling through the neighborhood, and come back to his house for hot chocolate and homemade cookies. Later they would all sit down to his mother's lavish Christmas dinner.

Virginia had said not to bring a thing, but Jessi was not about to go empty-handed. She had baked a large batch of cinnamon rolls, which her grandmother had taught her to make years ago.

Just as she was starting out the door the phone rang. It was Danny, her lead guitar player. While Danny was a great guitarist, he was not known for his congeniality, so she knew he was not calling just to wish her a Merry Christmas.

"Jess, I'm leaving the band," Danny announced abruptly when Jessi asked, "How are you?"

"You're what?"

"I'm getting married... I hate to do this to you. I know it's short notice and it's right before Christmas, but I've made up my mind."

She sat down on the end of the couch and wondered what had brought about this sudden decision. Danny had dated the same girl for several years, but that ended last summer, quite emotionally, as she recalled. He had not mentioned the girl in months, and marriage seemed to be the last thing on his mind when they broke for Christmas.

"Well, who is she?" Jessi finally asked.

"It's Beth."

Jessi could hear Danny sigh, almost as if he felt he needed to explain why he was marrying her.

"Jess, I lost her once, and I'm not going to lose her again. I haven't said anything, but we've been writing for about four months and I spent Thanksgiving with her. I'm tired of the road. I want a home and family, and I want Beth. I'm going to work in her dad's hardware store 'til something else develops."

He paused as if waiting for Jessi's reaction.

"I hope you're not mad."

"Of course I'm not mad, Danny... I'm happy for you. We'll miss you, but I understand." She was trying not to let her frustration show. "Listen, you have a good Christmas and send me an invitation to the wedding. Okay?" Knowing Danny, they would probably find the nearest justice of the peace to take care of it.

He thanked her for understanding, wished her a Merry Christmas, and hung up the phone.

She sat back on the couch and wondered what she was going to do. They had two months of bookings starting New Year's Eve, and now she didn't have a lead guitar player... What a way to begin Christmas!

As she pondered her dilemma, she thought of Jack. He would be perfect. He was just as good a guitarist as Danny, but she doubted if he would do it. When she had asked him to join the band and go on the road with them before, his reaction had been less than ecstatic. If she kept after him about something he apparently didn't want to do, she might drive him away completely, and that was the last thing she wanted to do.

Finally, she got up and went to the kitchen to tell her grandmother about Danny.

"Try not to worry, Honey. You'll find someone. I've never seen you strike out yet. You're on your way, Jessi, and it will take more than losing Danny Dawson to stop you."

She appreciated the vote of confidence, and only hoped her grandmother was right.

* * * * *

As she drove along the highway, she searched her mind for a replacement for Danny. There were some talented pickers around, but they were in such demand and commanded such a high salary, she doubted she could get any of them. And those who might be available were not the caliber she wanted.

She tried to erase these thoughts from her mind and concentrate on Christmas, but it was impossible. She had to come up with a good guitar player, and she didn't have much time to do it. New Year's Eve was only eight days away.

* * * * *

"Come on in," Virginia called to Jessi from the kitchen. "I'm baking cookies."

"Merry Christmas, Mrs. Roberts... Let me get my things out of the car, and I'll help you."

When Jessi returned, she was carrying a shopping bag of gifts and a baking sheet of delicious-looking cinnamon rolls. Then she went back to the car for another box.

"This is for you from my Grandma. It's her 'CARE PACKAGE'."

The deep cardboard box was filled with jars of home canned green beans, bread and butter pickles, and strawberry preserves.

Virginia stared at the beautiful assortment of canned goods, and envisioned the little lady spending most of her summer planting and harvesting her garden, and then canning jar after jar of vegetables and fruit, most of which she gave away. The gift in the unwrapped cardboard box touched Virginia deeply. She had never met Jessi's grandmother, but she knew instinctively that Mrs. Hughes had probably given her life to loving and caring for others.

"It's lovely. I don't know what to say except 'Thank You'... I used to do a lot of canning for my family, and I know how much work goes into it..." Virginia paused, "and how much love."

The two ladies stood side by side and stared down at the cardboard box, each lost in her own thoughts of the little lady from Fort Payne, Alabama. Finally, the silence was broken as Virginia reached out and gave Jessi a warm hug.

"Merry Christmas, Jessi."

Jessi responded with the ageless greeting that could be either a few words spoken as a casual greeting with little real feeling or a warm and loving exchange of good wishes. And between Jessi and Virginia, it was the latter.

Jessi then accepted Virginia's offer of a cup of coffee and helped herself to some warm cookies, fresh from the oven. Being with Virginia was like being with family.

She could wait no longer. "Where's Jack?"

"He went to cut the Christmas tree. He should be back in a little while."

"Since he was a little boy, almost too small to carry the ax, he and his dad would go up on the side of the mountain and search for hours for the perfect Christmas tree. Then they would return, carrying their prize possession with the pride of a hunter who had just landed his first buck."

"The two of them never admitted it, but I think the thing that made those Christmas tree expeditions so special was not the search for the tree, but the time they shared together."

"A couple of years after John died and Jack was on the road so much, I bought an artificial tree. I thought it would make things easier. Jack had a show to do in Atlanta on the 23rd and wouldn't get home until Christmas Eve. But when he came in and saw the tree in the box in the living room, he looked at it with the most forlorn expression."

"Finally, he said, 'Mom would it be okay if I went out and cut a tree and we saved this one until next year?'"

"He said it wouldn't seem like Christmas without tromping through the woods to find a Christmas tree or sitting around the tree on Christmas morning and smelling the fragrance of a live cedar tree. I saw how much it meant to him, and said 'sure', and explained I was only trying to make things easier for him. That was six years ago and the artificial tree is still in the box in the attic."

"I think there must be something about going up on the mountain and looking for that perfect Christmas tree that makes him feel close to his father. Each year he comes in with a bigger tree than the year before and with the same gleam in his eye he had as a little boy. Once I spotted a tear in his eye as he dragged the tree across the back yard, but I think it was a happy tear, and I didn't let on that I noticed."

Jessi stopped drying the dish she had taken from the drainer and considered what Virginia had told her. She didn't know Jack that well, but somehow this did not seem out of character. He felt deeply about a lot of things. It was revealed in his writing. He just didn't let everyone know what he was thinking.

"Jessi, please forgive me. I haven't let you get a word in edgewise. I guess I'm all caught up in Christmas."

"That's okay, Mrs. Roberts. Thank you for sharing that with me. We always have a fresh tree too, and like Jack, my grandmother goes out and chops one down off the farm."

As the last of the cookies were baking, Virginia realized Jessi had grown quiet and seemed troubled about something.

"Jessi, are you okay?"

"I was hoping it wouldn't show… It's nothing earth shattering. I just got a Christmas surprise I could have done without. My lead guitarist called this morning to tell me he is quitting the band to get married."

"Surely there's someone you can get?"

"I don't know. Most of the good ones are taken, and we don't have long to look."

She saw the concern on Virginia's face and wished she hadn't burdened her with the problem.

"It'll be okay. We still have a week before we go back on the road. We'll work something out." She paused and then looked directly at Virginia. "Mrs. Roberts, do you think Jack might consider playing with us, at least until we can get someone?"

Virginia breathed a deep sigh. "I don't know. When he came home from Daytona, he had had about all he wanted of the road." She opened the oven door to check on the last batch of cookies and continued. "Jack's not through playing music, but I'm not sure he's ready yet... But there's no harm in asking."

*   *   *   *   *

The temperature had dropped into the lower teens the night before, and Jack turned up the collar on his blue jean jacket as he made his way back down the mountain. The wind had picked up since he left home earlier in the morning, and it would feel good to get back to the warmth of the living room fireplace.

He was really looking forward to Christmas. He always loved the holidays, but this year would be even better. He remembered a lot of good Christmases when his dad and little sister were with them. The Roberts were modest people, and although they always had gifts and a big ham or turkey dinner, they didn't go overboard with the toys and gift giving... What made Christmas special for them was simply being together.

John Roberts had been raised very poor. He was born in the midst of the depression and was the tenth of twelve children. His family farmed for a living, and by the time the kids were fed, and the landlord was paid his share of the crop, and new shoes and school clothes were bought, there wasn't much left. Yet during those tough times in which John Roberts had grown up, he learned the important things of life. He learned that true happiness comes from your heart and not your pocketbook... Although he knew full well that an empty pocketbook and a hungry family made it hard to smile.

As a little boy, John's Christmas gifts were usually a few pieces of fruit and a candy cane or maybe a small metal truck, but he learned that Christmas was much more than the material things he did or did not receive. It was Jesus' day, the celebration of His entry into the world. It was a time of reverence and joy and excitement. The whole month was filled with secrets and each member of the family had his own special project that he was working on... usually a home-made gift, which always seemed to mean the most to their mother.

John Roberts knew the real meaning of Christmas and had passed it on to his family, and instilled in them the same excitement and reverence that his parents had passed on to him.

Jack missed his dad. Many times since he died Jack had wished he could talk to him... to share his victories... to find solace in his defeats... and to seek his guidance and understanding in facing the future. But the time Jack missed his dad the most was at Christmas... Yet, it was also the time he sensed his presence the most.

As he walked out of the woods and onto the trail leading down to the back yard, he noticed how dark the sky had become.

"I hope it doesn't rain," he thought to himself.

There were very few 'white Christmases' in Chattanooga. As a matter of fact, it had been thirteen years since Chattanooga had seen a white blanket on Christmas day, and folks still talked about the Christmas snow of '69. Yet no one wanted rain on Christmas Day.

He carried the tree across the back yard to the basement, where he trimmed the lower branches and fitted it into a stand. As he started in the house, he saw Jessi's car in the driveway. He must have lost track of the time. He hadn't expected her for several hours.

He took the tree inside and set it in the corner of the living room, the same place the Roberts' Christmas tree had stood for as long as he could remember. Then he headed to the kitchen where he heard the ladies' voices.

"Are you two eating all the Christmas cookies?" Jack teased as he stood in the kitchen doorway.

"We saved a few." Jessi smiled back, and thought how ruggedly handsome he looked in his jeans and flannel shirt.

"Ah, this tastes good!" He shivered as he took a sip of the hot coffee his mother handed him, and helped himself to some of the cookies fresh from the oven.

The three of them sat around the kitchen table visiting and munching on angel-shaped Christmas cookies. It was a relaxed, easy time. They told stories, one after the other, of favorite Christmas memories. The stories flowed naturally and so did the laughter, especially when Virginia told of a particular Christmas when Jack was seven. Before they knew it, it was three o'clock. The rest of the group would be there before long.

"We've sat here and talked away the afternoon," Virginia said.

"It's Christmas, Mom. That's what we're supposed to do. Enjoy it! Especially when you've got family and good friends to share it with." He smiled at Jessi as he said it, and she smiled back. "But I guess we had better get a move on. Bobby and Danny will be here before long."

Suddenly Jessi and Virginia were very quiet, and the smiles that had covered their faces only moments before were gone, and Virginia waited for Jessi to tell Jack about Danny.

Finally, Virginia spoke, "I don't think Danny is coming."

"What's wrong?"

This time it was Jessi who spoke. "Danny quit the band."

Jack wasn't surprised. He didn't have any problem with Danny, but he was different from the others in the band and seemed to think mainly of himself, which was evidenced by his quitting on such short notice. He was a good guitarist, though, and would be hard to replace.

"When did you find out?" Jack asked quietly, concern showing in his voice.

"This morning. He called just before I left. When we broke for Christmas, everything was fine. Now all of a sudden, he has decided to get married. He's going to work in her dad's hardware store until something else turns up."

"How much notice is he giving you?"

"He isn't giving any notice. He's gone."

Jack could hear the despair in her voice. This was just another example of the lack of responsibility he had experienced in trying to keep a band together.

"I guess that means you need a guitar player?" His tone was matter-of-fact and gave no indication as to whether he was interested in the position himself.

She only answered a dismal, "I sure do."

He realized what a bind this put her in with the two-month tour scheduled to start in a week. A slow grin then came across his face.

"Does that sneaky little grin mean you've finally decided to join us?"

"Not quite."

His smile broadened.

"Jack, we need you! I think we're right on the verge of making it, but I've got to have a good lead man to make it work. You play the guitar, you sing and you write great lyrics. You would be perfect. You don't have to work for me. We'll work together... I need you Jack."

"You're right. You are on the verge of making it. And I'll write for you. I'll even sing with you if you want, but you need the best guitar picker in the business."

"Jack, you're good! You're real good!"

He interrupted her. "Jess, you need the best. And that's not me, but I know who is."

The disappointment showed on her face. She couldn't imagine who he had in mind or if he could possibly be as good as Jack.

"Let me make a phone call."

The two women sat at the table while Jack went to make his call.

"What's he up to?" Jessi asked Jack's mother.

"I'm not sure, but I have an idea... And if I'm right, you'll have a guitar picker, a good one, and Jack will have his best friend back."

Jessi had no idea what was going on, but the smile on Virginia's face told her not to worry.

A few minutes later Jack returned.

"Did you talk to him?" Virginia asked.

"No. He wasn't there, but I talked to Edna and she told me where to find him... By the way, she said she baked you a fruit cake, and she'll bring it by tomorrow."

Then Jack looked at Jessi and said, "Get your coat, we've got to go."

"Where are we going?" She asked as she slipped an arm into the sleeve of her jacket.

"We're going to get you a guitar player."

* * * * *

Although it was only sixty-five miles, the drive to Rome seemed farther. A light mist began to fall shortly after they left Jack's house. It was half rain and half sleet, and the dismal weather mirrored Jessi's feelings.

Jack was quiet, as if his mind was preoccupied with what he would encounter in Rome. He told Jessi the guitarist they were going after was Buddy Bowers, and that Buddy had been the lead guitarist in every band he had ever formed, as well as being his best friend since childhood. He also told her about Buddy's drinking problem, and that last spring it had gotten so bad that he had been forced to fire him. Jessi could tell from the expression in Jack's eyes that it was one of the hardest things he had ever had to do. She also gathered that their parting had been far from pleasant.

He wasn't sure how Buddy would react to his visit or the invitation. He remembered the morning eight months ago when he told Buddy he was letting him go.

"I'm sorry, Buddy, but you're not going on stage again half-stoned... I've got a band to run, and I'm tired of being your nurse maid."

"I don't need a damn nurse maid, and I don't need you!" As Buddy started to leave, he turned and glared at Jack. "You can just go to Hell!"

And that was the last time they had seen each other.

Buddy had no problem connecting with other bands, but he hadn't been able to stick with any of them. He would get drunk and miss a couple of shows, and get fired or just quit. He was a top-notch musician, and he knew it, and because of that he thought he could drink whenever he pleased, and someone would always cover for him. However, he quickly found other performers didn't have as much patience as Jack, and by the time he realized he had to straighten up and take some responsibility for himself, he had gained a reputation as a drunk and a 'no show'. All the talent in the world didn't matter then. Nobody trusted him, and they were through giving him 'one more chance'.

Buddy's mother told Jack that he had hit the bottle pretty hard after he realized no one would hire him, but that he had done a little better the last few months.

Buddy had married when he was nineteen, but the marriage lasted barely two years. However, one good thing had come from it. They had a daughter, who was now eleven. Buddy had visitation rights, and although he and his former wife were far from being on good terms, Donna had never tried to keep him from seeing Amy. He had always spent as much time with his daughter as he could, even though it wasn't easy being on the road so much.

After Buddy had drunk himself out of music, one day he went to see his little girl. He wasn't drunk, but he had been drinking, and Donna knew it. She refused to let him near Amy, and later went back to court and petitioned to have his visitation rights terminated. The judge reviewed Buddy's recent work record and his blatant alcohol abuse, and declared him unfit to see his child and revoked his visitation rights.

It was then that Buddy realized he had to do something. He had hit bottom and had lost everything. At that point his prowess on the guitar didn't seem to mean much. He checked himself into a rehab center and stayed for six weeks. He had his chances to drink. Liquor was sneaked in every day, and even though daily urine testing was required, one guy could pee in the cup for six others. He still hungered for the booze, but he wanted to see his daughter more. The judge said he would review his case in a year and unless he had turned his life around, he would make the ruling permanent.

After leaving the rehab center, he got a job as a mechanic in Rome. He honestly tried, but he didn't know a thing about cars, and although his boss understood Buddy's situation and wanted to help, he finally had to let him go and hire someone with experience. Afterwards, Buddy picked up odd jobs here and there, and although they bought a few groceries, he knew this type of employment would not impress the judge when it came time to review his fitness case. All he knew was music. It had been his life... it and alcohol.

Finally, he got the job at the mall. It wasn't much, but it paid enough to keep a roof over his head and beans in his stomach. He was hoping that maybe after Christmas he could get on at the textile plant.

It was just before dark when they pulled into the Midtown Mall. This was where Edna Bowers said they would find her son. They went directly to the information desk at the north end of the mall to inquire about Buddy.

"I'm looking for a friend of mine who's supposed to be working here. His name is Buddy Bowers. Can you tell me where to find him?"

The security guard scratched his head as he thought, and then answered, "Buddy Bowers?... No, that doesn't ring a bell... Are you sure he works here? I know most everyone that works in the mall, unless he's one of the extras some of the stores have hired for Christmas. Do you know which store he works in?"

"No, I don't. He's a musician. I assumed maybe he was playing in one of the restaurants here."

"Not here!" The heavyset security guard laughed.

"We don't have any fancy night spots here. The fanciest restaurant we've got is the Burger King... What's he look like?"

"Well, he's about five foot six, skinny, like he hasn't eaten too good in awhile... He's got a thin moustache and he grins a lot."

"How old a fellow is he?"

"He's about thirty."

The security guard started to smile.

"Now, I know who you're talking about... 'Chris'."

"Chris?" Jack didn't understand.

"Yeah, that's what we call him around here. Just go down to the center of the mall in front of Sears. You'll find him."

Jack flashed an uncertain look at Jessi. 'Buddy' was a nickname. His real name was Walter, but he had never heard anyone call him Chris. He wasn't sure the security guard knew what he was talking about, but it was the only lead they had. They made their way through the last minute Christmas shoppers and worked their way down to Sears. Maybe Buddy had been hired to play Christmas carols in the mall. The main entrance to Sears was in the center of the mall, but Buddy Bowers was nowhere to be found. On one side of the mall, a little gray-haired lady stood next to her kettle, ringing a bell for the Salvation Army. Across the way they heard the laughter and excitement of kids waiting to have their picture taken with Santa.

Jack's eyes searched the crowd in vain. He asked the lady at the popcorn stand, but she had never heard of Buddy or this 'Chris' guy. Apparently the security guard didn't know what he was talking about. Jessi saw the disappointment in Jack's eyes. She knew how much it meant to him to find Buddy. She also sensed that he felt he had let her down.

He was so sure that getting Buddy would be the perfect thing for everyone. It would give Buddy a great opportunity to get on his feet again and do what he did best, and it would provide her with the caliber guitarist she needed.

Suddenly they heard a clamor from the crowd waiting to see Santa. The photographer had just made an announcement.

"It's six o'clock and time for Santa to feed his reindeer."

Santa would return at six thirty, and neither the kids nor their mothers, who already had waited a long time, appreciated the additional delay.

Jack looked at Jessi and smiled.

"Maybe you should go sit on Santa's lap."

"Do you suppose he would bring me a guitar player?"

"I don't know, but he couldn't do any worse for you than I've done."

"Don't worry, Jack. Something will work out. It always does." She was trying to convince herself, as well as ease Jack's mind, but her words were of no more comfort to her than they were to him. "Let's just go home. Your mom has planned a nice Christmas dinner. There will be time to find somebody after Christmas."

He didn't want to leave without what he had come for, but he knew she was right. Buddy could be anywhere. If he was as bad as his mom said, he had probably already lost this job and moved on somewhere else.

"I guess you're right. We're not doing any good here, so there's no need to miss out on Christmas. Let's go home."

Before they left, Jack went to the restroom, while Jessi walked across the mall to view the Coke and Sprite cans, which had been stacked to the ceiling in the shape of a giant Christmas tree.

Jack flushed the commode and walked out of the stall just in time to see Santa Claus standing at the sink. He was in no mood for 'Jolly Ole St. Nick' and started for the door. Santa hadn't realized there was anyone else in the bathroom and pulled his wig and beard off to splash some cold water on his face.

"I'll be damned!" Jack exclaimed, as he saw Santa's reflection in the mirror. "What are you doing in that monkey suit?"

There was no mistaking the voice. Buddy would recognize it anywhere, and as he turned around, still holding the wig and beard, a slow grin covered his face.

"Jack Roberts! What in the devil are you doing here?"

Buddy was laughing and reaching out his hand to Jack.

"Looking for you! Although I'll admit you make it pretty tough. Your mom told me you were working here. She just didn't tell me you were working undercover."

Jack was laughing, as he looked at the skinny little guy with all the padding in the bright red suit.

"You're about the puniest Santa Claus I ever saw."

Buddy looked down at his outfit and shook his head.

"It ain't much of a job, Jack, but it buys a few groceries and pays the rent. And right now it's the best I can do." He took a deep breath and continued. "After you fired me, I drifted for a while, but mostly I drank... I didn't have any problem getting jobs playing, but I'd get drunk and lose them almost as fast as I got them. Then it got to the point nobody would hire me, so that just gave me another excuse to drink... and to make a long story short, I hit bottom." Buddy took a deep breath and his voice cracked as he spoke. "Jack, I lost Amy. The court took her away. I can't even see her. I can't call her... Nothing. They said if I get anywhere near her, they'll put me in jail."

Tears welled up in Buddy's eyes and rolled freely down his cheeks and onto the white fleece collar of his Santa suit. Jack moved closer and put his arm around Buddy's shoulder. "I know. Your mom told me about it."

"I'm trying, Jack. I'm really trying. I checked myself into one of those rehab centers. I was there for six weeks. That was two months ago, and I haven't touched a drop since." He looked down at the big fur trimmed black boots. "I still want it. I crave it every day, but it ain't worth it. I can't live without her Jack... If I could just get a decent job."

Buddy was sobbing loudly and Jack pulled him close to try to comfort him. About that time the door opened and an elderly gentlemen started to walk in, but when he saw Jack and Santa Claus in their embrace, he apologized for interrupting and quickly left the room.

"Lord, Buddy, now they're gonna' think Santa Claus is gay."

Buddy's tears quickly changed to laughter and everything was all right. Maybe not everything, but at least Jack was here, just like he had always been.

"I've got somebody I want you to meet."

Buddy nodded and put his wig and beard on so he could go back out into the mall.

Jessi couldn't believe her eyes when Jack walked up to her with an arm around Santa.

"Well, it wasn't easy, but I found him... Here's your new lead guitarist."

She looked first at Jack, then at Buddy, with an expression that said, "You've got to be crazy!"

When Buddy heard Jack's words, he was almost in shock. Then Jack explained the situation and Jessi's need for a guitar player.

Quite a crowd was gathering around them, growing more and more impatient that Santa was not back 'on his throne' listening to the want lists of the children. The mall manager soon made his way through the crowd and suggested that "Feeding Time was over", and it was time to visit with the children. Buddy ignored him.

"When do we start? I mean, if Miss McCrae likes my playing." The excitement mounted in Buddy's voice and could be seen on his face even through the Santa beard.

"Right after Christmas!" Jack answered. "But right now we've got to get home and celebrate. You know how Mom does Christmas."

"Boy, do I ever! Nobody makes peanut butter fudge like your mom."

"Then go back with us! What time do you get off?"

Buddy took one long excited look at Jack and then at the mall manager, who looked like steam would come out of his ears at any moment.

"Right now! Let's get out of here."

The manager was flabbergasted. It was the 23rd of December. Santa Claus couldn't quit! Not now! They had no one to replace him. Besides, there was a long line of kids waiting to sit on Santa's lap, not to mention some angry parents who would take their shopping elsewhere.

"You can't quit! I won't pay you!"

"Keep your damn money. I don't care." Buddy turned and started to walk toward the door.

"I'll sue!" The manager screamed after him.

But Buddy only laughed. "Hell, he wouldn't get much. Would he Jack?"

Jack was laughing too. "Don't you think you ought to at least give him back his Santa suit?"

"I would, but I ain't got a thing on underneath it. These things are hot."

They were all laughing, as Jack and Jessi and Santa Claus walked out of the mall with the mall manager in hot pursuit as he screamed for the security guards to "Arrest that man!"

"You two are a couple of nuts," Jessi said, as they hurried to the car.

The three of them were giggling like a bunch of silly teenagers, and they knew this would be a Christmas they would long remember.

*　　*　　*　　*　　*

Before heading back to Chattanooga, they went by Buddy's apartment to turn in his key and pick up his belongings. The sign out front was faded and most of the paint had chipped off, making it hard to read.

ROOMS FOR RENT
WEEKLY AND DAILY RATES

The place was run down and located in a bad section of town. Jack had not expected The Ritz, but neither was he prepared for what they found. Buddy apologized for the paper and beer bottles that were strewn up and down the hallway.

As Buddy opened the door, a small brown rat dashed across the floor and into a hole in the baseboard. No one said anything, although the embarrassment on Buddy's face was apparent.

The apartment was only one room. It was small and dirty, not untidy, but dirty from years of neglect. The walls, which appeared to have been white at one time, were now a dull gray, and it was doubtful that a new coat of paint would cover up the dinginess.

There was a box of soda crackers and half a jar of peanut butter on the kitchen table, which appeared to be the only food in the house and an empty Coke can sitting on the sink.

Buddy picked up a brown grocery sack and opened the top drawer of his dresser. He pulled out two pairs of tattered jeans and several tee shirts that were almost threadbare, and placed them in the paper bag. Then he stuffed a couple of pairs of socks, which could use some darning, into the bag.

As he pushed the drawer closed with his knee, he picked up a small framed picture of Amy, which was the only picture or decoration in the room. He looked intensely at the picture for a moment, then placed it in the bag and took one final quick glance around the room he had been calling home.

"Let me go turn in the key and I'll be ready."

There was little expression on Buddy's face, and it was apparent he wanted to get out and put all this behind him, just as much as did Jack and Jessi.

"I'll pack the rest of your things while you do that," Jessi offered, as she pulled open a second and third empty drawer.

"This is everything," Buddy stated quietly, and without waiting for a response, turned and walked down the hallway.

"I didn't know it was this bad," Jack muttered, when Buddy was out of hearing distance. He seemed to be half talking to Jessi and half talking to himself. And she knew he had not been prepared for what they had found.

She moved closer to him, keeping a watchful eye on the floor in case the rat should emerge from his hiding place.

"Jack, are you sure this is such a good idea... I mean he seems like a nice guy... but I just don't know."

Jack could see the concern in her eyes. She didn't mean to be judgmental. She had just never lived like this or been exposed to anyone who had.

He reached out and put his arm around her and pulled her close. "Jess, maybe he needs us as much as we need him."

And after one final look at the room, Jack and Jessi closed the door behind them and started down the hall to meet Buddy.

*   *   *   *   *

Jack called his mom and told her they had located Buddy and were on their way home. He could hear the delight in her voice when she said, "Tell Buddy I'm expecting him for dinner."

She had always had a special place in her heart for Buddy. He had spent almost as much time at their house when he was growing up as he did at his own. Buddy's father had left them shortly after Buddy was born, and his mother had not had an easy life. Edna Bowers was a good lady and worked two jobs just to make ends meet. Consequently, she had not had as much time to spend with her son as she would have liked. She was a proud person and, like many of her generation, did not accept charity or welfare, but was determined to make her own way.

Virginia had a lot of respect for Edna and realized she had had a 'tough row to hoe'. Therefore, she had tried to do whatever she could for Buddy, whether correcting him when he needed correcting, bandaging his skinned knees or simply drying his tears when he got hurt... And over the years, Buddy had come to regard her as his 'Second Mom'.

Although Jack did not go into details over the phone, she sensed everything was all right between him and Buddy, and the prayer she had said when he and Jessi left for Rome had not gone unanswered.

Bobby had arrived earlier, and Virginia told him that Danny had quit the band, and Jack and Jessi had gone to Rome to try to get Buddy.

"Damn!" He muttered. Then quickly apologized to Virginia for his swearing. "I suppose he has a right to get married or do whatever he wants, but he could have given us a little more notice."

Bobby was putting a string of lights on the tree, and Virginia was taking the ham out of the oven when the car pulled into the driveway.

"Mrs. Roberts, they're here!" Bobby announced.

She hurried from the kitchen, still wearing her apron, and looked out the window as they got out of the car.

As the three of them came up the sidewalk and into the glow of the front porch light, Bobby exclaimed, "That's not Buddy! That's Santa Claus!"

Virginia and Bobby burst into laughter. They had seen Buddy in some outrageous situations over the years, but this one had to take the cake. They could not contain their laughter when Jack opened the front door and Buddy, alias Santa Claus, came strolling in. Virginia gave the skinny little guy in the red suit a big hug. Then Buddy looked over her shoulder and saw his own mom and reached to embrace her. Virginia put her arm around her own son and told him that after he called, she invited Edna to join them.

After an enormous meal, with second helpings of ham, potato salad, and home made rolls, and all sorts of holiday fixings, and then sampling the various desserts Virginia had prepared, they moved to the living room to continue their celebration.

Buddy had changed into a pair of jeans and a flannel shirt, and Jessie was surprised to see how small he was. He and Jack looked like *Mutt and Jeff* as they stood by the fireplace. She wondered how a person of his size ever convinced anyone to hire him to play Santa Claus. Perhaps the mall manager was as desperate for a Santa Claus as she was for a guitar picker. She still wondered if he could play as good as Danny, but if he didn't work out at least it would buy her some time to find someone else.

After decorating the tree, they sat around the fireplace roasting marshmallows and singing carols in the warm glow of the fire. Finally, after too many verses of too many songs, Virginia pointed to the brightly colored packages under the tree. "Don't you think it's time we opened the gifts?"

"Hey Buddy, since you're our experienced Santa, why don't you pass out the presents?" Jack kidded.

An embarrassed grin crossed Buddy's face, as he got up and began passing out the packages.

Jack's mom had told them not to bother with gifts. "It's just too much trouble," she had said.

But they had brought gifts anyway, and she had something for each of them, except Buddy. By the time she knew he was coming, it was too late to get anything.

"I'm sorry, Buddy, but I promise to bake you a chocolate cake after the holidays." It was his favorite.

Buddy smiled.

"Mrs. Roberts, I don't need anything else. You and Jack have already given me the best Christmas I've ever had."

Buddy then took his mother by the hand and continued, "I don't know of anything else you could give me that could make this day any more special."

Jack had left the room a few minutes earlier, unnoticed by everyone except Jessi. Now he came down the steps holding something behind his back.

"Not even this?"

Buddy turned to see what Jack was talking about. He was speechless, as slowly he began to run his fingers down the neck of the timeworn guitar, smiling as if he had just rediscovered a long lost friend.

"I can't believe it!" Buddy finally spoke. "Where did you get it?"

The guitar Buddy was holding was his own. He had pawned it six months earlier for whiskey money, and by the time he had enough money to get it out of hock, it had been sold.

They all looked at Jack, as though waiting for an explanation, but he only said, "Aren't you going to show Jessi what you can do with that thing?"

Buddy continued to stare at the guitar... He had never expected to see it again... At last he looked up at Jack.

"Thanks, Jack... I don't know what to say."

Jessi listened intently as Buddy began to play. Jack had said he was the best around and he was.

As Buddy continued to play, Jack went to the kitchen for a cup of coffee, and Virginia followed him.

"Where did you get it?" she asked.

"Get what?"

"The guitar."

He hesitated. Then after pouring a cup of coffee, he explained the story behind Buddy's guitar. "This wasn't the first time Buddy pawned his guitar. Usually he manages to get it out before they sell it, but this time he left it too long and the guy at the pawnshop needed his money. He knew I had paid it out of hock a couple of times before when Buddy didn't have the money, so he called to see if I wanted it. He didn't know I had fired Buddy, and that we were no longer working together... I don't know why I did it. I just did."

Virginia smiled proudly at her son. She knew why he had done it. Buddy was his friend. She thought how much like his father Jack had become, and she knew John would be very proud of him.

They sat around the living room and played for hours. Buddy was every bit as good as Jack had said, and Jessi knew it had been a day well spent in many ways.

Edna and Virginia watched and listened with the pride that only mothers have. Edna hadn't heard Buddy play in several years, and she didn't realize how good he had become.

Finally, around two o'clock, Edna decided it was getting too late for her and she went home. Virginia also went upstairs to bed. It had been a long day for her as well, but a good one.

About five o'clock she awakened and tiptoed downstairs to see if everyone was still there. The music had ceased, but they were all there, sacked out in various places around the living room. Jessi was on the couch. Jack was under the Christmas tree. Bobby was stretched out in front of the t.v. and Buddy was curled up in front of the fireplace. The fire had burned low, but still left a cozy glow, and Virginia felt a warm contentment as she went back to bed. She set the alarm for seven thirty so she could fix breakfast, but when the alarm went off, she went downstairs to find the living room deserted, except for Jack, who was still sleeping soundly under the Christmas tree. The others had left to spend Christmas with their families. The house seemed empty without them, but she knew they would be back.

Someone had turned the thermostat down and the room was cool. She got a blanket from the hall closet and spread it over Jack. There was no need to start breakfast yet. He would sleep for several hours, and she could use some more sleep as well.

And as she once more climbed the stairs to her room, she heard the chimes at the Methodist church down the street, pealing out *I HEARD THE BELLS ON CHRISTMAS DAY.*

CHAPTER 25

"Man, is it cold!" Jack thought as he sat by the small fireplace in the lobby of the Asheville Inn. It was 3 a.m. and he couldn't sleep. So he ventured out of the room he shared with Bobby and Buddy and came here for some hot coffee and solitude.

Although it was late March, winter still held the mountains of North Carolina tightly in its grip. Six inches of snow had fallen since they arrived two days earlier, and having spent his entire life in the deep south, he was unaccustomed to this kind of weather.

As he sipped the coffee by the dim firelight, he reflected upon the first three months of their tour. The group had played their first show on New Year's Eve in Jackson, Mississippi. There was a lot of tension and nervousness backstage before they went on, but the opening night jitters proved unwarranted and the show was a tremendous success.

The band seemed to jell from the beginning. They got along well and each respected the others' talent. They were pleased with the music they were making and the direction the band was taking. They were drawing on the strength of each other and improving both individually and as a group.

Even Buddy was doing well and had not drifted back into his old habits. He was taking responsibility for himself, something he had seldom done in the past.

Jessi was perfect! She loved to sing the songs Jack had written, and the feeling with which she sang gave added meaning to the lyrics.

Much to his surprise, he found that he was enjoying performing again. The only thing that bothered him was there was so little time for writing. They were always performing or travelling or practicing. Gosh, how that woman loved to practice! They practiced all the time, or at least it seemed they did.

"It's the only way we can get better." Jessi repeated over and over again. "We're good... real good, but I want us to be the best we possibly can. And to do that, we've got to practice."

He knew she was right, but it left him virtually no time to write. That was the reason he had turned her down the first time. He had done some of his best work last fall when he had been able to devote himself completely to his writing.

He could no longer concentrate on his writing. There were too many distractions and it was frustrating. He would get a really good idea, but before he could find some uninterrupted time to develop it, the lines were gone. He had tried to write and perform in the past, but it just didn't work. He could not give either one the attention it required, and when he tried, both usually suffered.

Nevertheless, he was glad he had chosen to go on the road with Jessi. He had hoped they could spend more time together. And while they spent a lot of time together, it was usually with the group, leaving little time for themselves. He realized things had to be this way, but he yearned for some private time with her. They had shared some quiet times, just the two of them, and it had been wonderful. However, those times were few and far between, and the daily demands of the band overwhelmed their personal time.

As he mulled these things over in his mind, he heard footsteps on the stairway and turned to see who else was up at this late hour.

"Is there any coffee left?" Jessi asked as she walked through the lobby and over to where Jack sat.

"Sure, let me get you a cup."

The coffee had been brewed an hour or so earlier and was strong and bitter, but it was hot, and on a night like this, that was what mattered most.

The lobby of the small hotel was cool, and Jessi wrapped her hands around her coffee cup and stared into the fire. Jack knew something was wrong but, like himself, Jessi was somewhat private, and whether she would choose to share her problem remained to be seen.

He watched her as she sat beside him on the couch. She was wearing gray sweats and white sneakers and her hair had not been brushed, but she still looked good. She made no effort at conversation, but appeared to be absorbed in her thoughts.

Finally Jack broke the silence.

"Well, what do you think so far?"

"About what?"

"About the band."

Jessi loved her new band, and they had quickly become her pride and joy.

"It's the best group I've ever been a part of. They're all good, and they put so much of themselves into everything they do."

"So you have no regrets about this bunch of vagabonds you've put together?"

"None at all... if I can just keep them together." Her voice quietened and grew more somber.

"From the enthusiasm I've seen out of Bobby and Buddy, I don't think you have anything to worry about, and you know I'm not going anywhere."

"It's not that... The problem is we're running out of bookings. We only have one more week booked. I've tried everyone I know, but no one wants a band. They all want a soloist. They can pay a soloist a third of what we have to get just to break even."

She paused as she thought about her dilemma.

"I know how good you guys are, but if I can't get jobs, then I can't keep the group together, and I'll never have another group like this."

Jessi was a strong person, and the tears in her eyes were not typical. He had sensed something was bothering her lately, but he didn't realize they were running out of work.

"Don't worry about it. I'll make some calls tomorrow and see what I can do. I've played a lot of places these last few years and in most of them I'm still welcome. We'll find something."

"I hope so. I don't want to lose you guys."

She settled back in her seat, not feeling quite so alone in her dilemma, and Jack put his arm around her and pulled her close.

"You're not going to lose anybody. I've been down to my last show before, and something always opened up, and it will now. So don't worry."

She smiled at him through the mist that clouded her eyes and nodded, and then curled up under his arm and in peaceful silence they watched the red glow of the warm embers, which had all but burned out in the old fireplace.

CHAPTER 26

There were no fireworks... No one final round... Just a phone call... Garrett wanted a divorce.

Although it had been a long time since their marriage was good, she was surprised to hear Garrett mention divorce. He had the best of both worlds, and seemingly enjoyed it to the hilt. She knew there were other women, but that was nothing new. There always had been.

She had been the first to suggest divorce, but he thought the idea ridiculous. He insisted their marriage was no worse than countless others, and that they had a responsibility to the children to maintain their marriage.

Now and then there had been a glimmer of hope that things would change and they would be a real family again. Garrett had been very shaken by Jody's accident. After Jody came home from the hospital, he called every night to check on him and came home every weekend. He seemed to understand what she was going through and was kind and caring. Jody underwent daily therapy, which was exhausting and often painful, and even with that, there was no promise of what the final outcome would be. But the therapy had worked, and now Jody walked with only the slightest limp.

Then Katie was born, and they had another reason to make their marriage work. Garrett had always wanted a little girl, and he was so excited about Katie. While Jody had been the spitting image of his father, Katie looked more like her mother. Yet from the beginning she had been a daddy's girl. She even preferred for him to hold her, and it was Garrett who had suggested she be named Emily Katherine, after her two grandmothers.

He was a doting father to Jody and Katie, and for the first time in a long time Mary believed he had truly changed. They would not have other children. They had decided two were enough, especially since she had such a difficult pregnancy with Katie. Garrett continued to treat her with kindness and affection, and she was willing to forget all that had gone before if only it could continue like this. Although still cautiously optimistic, she was happier than she had been in a long time.

Before long, however, she realized that nothing had really changed and that it never would. Garrett was frequently away for weeks at a time, and his calls were perfunctory, with several days and sometimes as much as a week passing between them. When the children asked, she told them their father had a very important job which demanded a lot of his time and attention, and he would be home as soon as possible.

She knew she could not keep up the charade forever. The time would come when she would leave Garrett, but right now she had to do what was right for the children. Yet ultimately she would have to do what was right for her.

Now it was Garrett who wanted a divorce... Office gossip has a way of making its rounds, and his latest conquest was apparently different from the rest. Her name was Lauren Smythe, and she came from a long line of New England aristocracy. Her father was in banking and real estate, and her mother's side of the family had accumulated considerable wealth in the steel industry. Her uncle was a United States senator and was very influential on the Washington scene. Apparently her credentials were so ostentatious as to cause even Anderson-Walton to look the other way regarding divorce.

Mary had seen her picture in a magazine. She was attending a Washington gala. She was tall and statuesque and very chic, but not the raving beauty Mary expected.

She would not stand in Garrett's way. It was time to end the pretense. Tomorrow she would tell the children. She would do it as gently as possible and would encourage Jody and Katie to love and respect their father, but she would not make him out to be something he was not. There had been enough of that. As the years went by, they would make their own assessment of their father, and that was as it should be.

In one way, she felt a strange sense of relief. Yet on the other hand, she realized her life would be very different. She would be on her own, and while she welcomed the freedom and challenge, she was uncertain about what lay ahead or how she would cope.

She would have to get a job. The part-time job she had taken at the library when Katie started kindergarten would not be enough. She had to support herself and the children. Garrett would pay child support. She didn't worry about that, but she didn't want alimony. It would be hard, but she would make it on her own. She refused to be dependent on him any longer.

Again her thoughts turned to the children. They would miss their father. They had not seen a great deal of him for a long time, but they were always glad when he was home.

For the first time tears welled up in her eyes and she felt very alone. The tears were not for Garrett nor for the marriage that had died years ago, but for Jody and Katie. They deserved better. They deserved parents that loved each other and wanted to spend the rest of their lives together. This she could not give them, and that hurt most of all.

Garrett had failed them, but so had she. Maybe if she had done all the right things, she could have somehow made it work. But deep in her heart, she knew it never would.

Try as you may, you cannot make someone love you. Garrett had never loved her as much as she had loved him, and little by little, he had killed the love she had for him.

* * * * *

Mary took a deep breath as she climbed the steps of the imposing gray stone courthouse. It was by no means the happiest day of her life, yet neither was it the saddest. It was simply the day her marriage would officially end.

All the details had been worked out. The house would be sold and the equity split between the two of them, and she would receive a cash settlement as permanent alimony. It was not a lot, but it would help bridge the gap until she could find a job. Her lawyer had insisted on this.

She would have permanent custody of Jody and Katie, but Garrett could visit them or have them visit him on weekends and during summer vacation. She had no problem with lenient visitation rights. She hoped the children would have a good relationship with their father. Yet in her heart she somehow knew that while he would shower them with gifts and cards on special occasions, his visits would be few and far between. This saddened her because both he and the children would be the losers. Yet this, as had been the case with so many things, was beyond her control.

She hoped to buy a smaller house in Atlanta with the equity she received from the sale of the house. It was the only place Katie and Jody had ever lived. They were happy here and the schools were good.

She was wearing a turquoise linen suit with gold tone buttons. Her only jewelry consisted of simple gold earrings and a gold bracelet. She had dressed with care. If she looked nice, she would not feel intimidated by Garrett's always immaculate image. She took a last look in the mirror before leaving home and was pleased with her appearance.

The quickness of her step and the unruffled look in her eyes eschewed confidence and control. She could easily have passed for one of the growing number of young women lawyers seen regularly in courts throughout the land, reflecting the changing winds of time.

As she reached the second floor, her lawyer met her outside the judge's chambers. He told her what the proceedings would be like, and asked if she had any questions. Then they went in together. Garrett and his attorney were already present. They both rose to their feet when she entered the room and Garrett managed a pleasant hello.

Promptly at ten o'clock the judge entered his chambers and wasted no time getting on with the hearing.

Several times during the brief session she noticed Garrett cast his eyes surreptitiously at her. She had no idea what he was thinking nor did she care.

It was over quickly. The judge asked a few questions, confirmed that the property settlement they had worked out was agreeable to both of them, and assured himself that the child support stipulated in the final decree was adequate to provide for the children.

He thereupon took off his glasses and looked directly across his desk at Garrett and admonished him that he was to be prompt and regular with his child support payments.

"This court does not look kindly upon fathers who don't support their children. The children are our first priority, and you must make them yours, else you will be prosecuted to the full extent of the law. Do you understand?"

Garrett was not accustomed to being scolded.

"Yes, sir. I understand. They are my first priority too."

Then with a final flourish of the pen, the judge signed the papers. And that was it. The marriage contract previously entered into between the parties hereto was now null and void.

Mary's lawyer shook hands with her and wished her well. As she thanked him for his help, he quickly scribbled a telephone number on the back of one of his business cards and handed it to her.

"A friend of mine is looking for a secretary. If you're interested, give him a call. He's in court in Savannah this week, but he should be back in the office on Monday. You may use my name as a reference."

"Thank you very much." Mary replied, as she carefully placed the card in her purse.

She waited a moment for the elevator and then decided to take the stairs instead. She was anxious to get home to her children. This was the first day of their summer vacation. Madeline was looking after them, and they were probably still asleep. She wanted to hold them in her arms and tell them how much she loved them. They were all she had now, but they were enough. The three of them would make it. She didn't need Garrett. She didn't need anything but Jody and Katie... and a job.

Suddenly she was aware someone had caught up with her and was walking beside her. She glanced around. It was Garrett.

"Could we talk for a moment?" he asked.

She stopped, and without responding, waited for him to continue.

"How are the children?"

"They're fine."

"And you?"

"I'm okay."

"Mary, I have no idea how you'll react to a compliment from me, but you look beautiful."

He was staring directly into her eyes, but she was unaffected. What they had once shared was over, and she had no interest in reviving it.

"Thank you."

She was polite, but it was obvious the compliment made no more impression upon her than had if it been offered by a total stranger. In fact, that's how Garrett felt right now, like a total stranger. She made no effort to further the conversation, and he realized that whatever she had once felt for him was gone, and it would never return.

"Give Jody and Katie a hug for me and tell them I'll see them soon." He then paused as if searching for words, and finally added, "Take care of yourself."

They had reached the sidewalk, and Mary saw the familiar silver Mercedes parked across the street. Her car was in the back parking lot. So it was here they would each go their separate ways.

She extended her hand, almost as if concluding a business deal, and said simply, "Good luck, Garrett." Then she turned and walked away.

Garrett hesitated for a moment as he watched the pretty lady in the turquoise suit walk quickly out of his life. Then he crossed the street to the silver Mercedes. Once he looked back, but she had already turned the corner.

CHAPTER 27

The next year was lean at best, but they were paying the bills and, more importantly, they were still performing. Jessi continued to worry, but the jobs came. There were times when they were down to their last booking, but something always opened up.

Gradually, they made the transition from taverns and dance halls to nicer clubs and an occasional concert booking as opening act for some of the bigger, more recognizable names.

They talked to a number of record companies, some of whom seemed impressed with their work, but the story was always the same... "They didn't need another band right now."

Jessi frequently asked the bigger named performers how they got their breaks, and she was always open to advice, but sometimes it seemed they were just spinning their wheels. One night before a show in Roanoke, she was talking to Justin Blaylock, who played lead guitar for *Stillwater* and also did a lot of session work in Nashville. He suggested that they cut a professional demo.

"It was the best money we ever spent. We got the same rhetoric from the record producers... 'You've got a good group, but right now we don't need another band'. And by the time they did, we were long forgotten."

According to Justin, being able to put a studio tape in the right people's hands proved to be the key to their first recording contract.

"I'd suggest you give it a try. You guys are good. All you need is the right break."

She mentioned it to Jack. "What do you think?"

"I agree, but can we afford to do it?"

"According to Justin, we can't afford not to."

Jack sighed and nodded in agreement. "He's probably right, but we need a high tech studio. Otherwise, we'll just be throwing our money away. The demo has to be first quality, and good recording studios don't come cheap."

"I know. But I think we can handle it, if it's not too expensive. We've got a little money in the bank. I'm convinced we really need to do this."

"So am I." For a moment he said nothing more, but she could tell the wheels were turning. Then he spoke. "I've known some people who've made demos and, like us, they couldn't afford the big Nashville sound. If you'd like, I'll make some phone calls and see what I can find out... It's going to be expensive at best, but there are some smaller studios with very good equipment. I just hope we can afford them."

After weeks of waiting on calls that were not returned, and calling again and again to no avail, Jack finally reached a friend of a friend, who managed a studio in Columbus, Georgia. It was a small studio, but their equipment was hi-tech.

Although the band had played in Columbus several times, memories of the place still haunted Jack, and as Golden Park came into view, his blank stare bore witness to the fact.

They had worked out a fantastic deal for the studio. However, to get this price, they had to record between midnight and dawn and be cleared out by 7 a.m.

Like most musicians, they were night owls and not accustomed to getting in bed early, so this presented no problem. The Monday through Wednesday schedule also worked out well, as their next gig wasn't until Friday night in Macon.

Although it wasn't easy, Jack had found time to work on some new material. He would seclude himself on the back seat of the bus, his guitar across his lap and pad and pen at his side, as they rode for endless hours from town to town.

Sometimes the words came to him in the wee hours of the morning in a deserted hotel lobby while the rest of the world slept, but nonetheless they came. And by recording time Jack had eight new songs, which Jessi and the guys felt were his best yet.

Buddy and Bobby could see the influence Jessi's presence was having on Jack's writing. His lyrics, while as deep and direct as ever, were happier and embodied an air of hope and promise.

Over the year and a half they had known each other, Jessi and Jack had grown very close. It was apparent to everyone who knew them. There was a caring and unification of spirit between them that few couples ever find, and an inner communication rarely shared by two people.

The demo would contain twelve songs, the eight new ones Jack had just written and four he had penned in Chattanooga two years earlier. They would record four each night and should have distribution copies in three weeks.

The first night went great. They had been able to get into the studio a couple of hours early and get used to the equipment and the recording process.

By seven, they had surpassed their goal of four songs, and had six in final form except for some minor mixing and over-dubbing, which would be done later by the sound technicians.

Tuesday night started out equally productive. By 3:30 they had completed two songs and were working on the instrumental track for a third, when one of the technicians tapped on the glass that separated the control room and studio and motioned for Jack.

Several times the night before, Jack had been called to the control room for his opinion on a particular aspect of the recording, so no one thought anything when he left the room.

Bobby watched through the glass as the technician pointed toward the phone. And although he couldn't hear through the soundproof glass, the expression on Jack's face told him something was wrong.

A couple of minutes later, he hung up the phone, took a deep breath and turned toward the studio door. Neither Buddy nor Jessi had noticed the phone call. They were busy working on a line they 'just couldn't get right'. But when Jack returned, the look on his face told them there was a problem.

"Jess, that was Mom."

She looked directly at him, then glanced at the clock. She knew a phone call at this time of night could not be good news.

"What's wrong?"

Jack searched for the words to tell her.

"Jess, it's your grandma... She's in the hospital."

"Oh, Dear God, no. What happened? Is she all right?"

He put his arm around her. "They think she has had a heart attack, but they've got her stabilized."

She leaned against him, as all the strength seemed to flow from her body. "Jack, I've got to go to her. She's all alone."

He nodded understandingly. "I knew you would... We'll need to rent a car. Why don't you go back to the hotel and get your things packed? I'll pick up the car and meet you at the hotel... And Jess, she's not alone, Mom's there with her."

Jessi thought how much Virginia Roberts reminded her of her grandmother. She had not waited to be asked. She had just done what she could, which was to go and be with Mrs. Hughes until Jessi could get there.

Jack was right. She would have to get a rental car. She couldn't drive the bus. He and the boys could finish the demo. Jack was a good singer and though they hadn't planned it that way, it would be good for him to do a few solos.

Jessi gazed at the traffic from the window of the hotel lobby. She didn't want to waste time by having Jack come to the room. She had hurriedly packed her bags and turned in her room key, and now sat on the edge of her seat, anxiously rising to her feet each time a car pulled into the lot.

Finally a bright red Ford Escort pulled up near the 'NO VACANCY' sign, and Jack got out.

She picked up her luggage and headed to the entrance, almost colliding with him as he came through the door. He loaded her bags in the hatchback, as she sat down behind the wheel to acquaint herself with the car.

"Jack! This is a straight shift! You know I can't drive a straight shift!"

He walked around to her window and said simply, "But I can."

"Jack, the recording! It's already paid for! You've got to stay here and finish the demo. It's too important not to!"

He opened the door and motioned her over into the passenger seat. Then he looked deep into her troubled eyes and said softly, "Your grandmother is what's important, not the recording. Now, let's go see about her."

And as she settled into the seat beside him, she realized how much he loved her... and she knew how much she loved him.

*   *   *   *   *

By Friday morning, Mrs. Hughes was much better, and Jessi insisted that Jack join Bobby and Buddy for the show in Macon. She would stay with her grandmother until she got back on her feet and make whatever arrangements were necessary for her care. Then if things continued to go well, she would join them in a few weeks.

As she watched the red Escort pull out of the parking lot and disappear in the distance, she thought how wonderful Jack had been through the whole ordeal. She had not even suggested he go with her to Ft. Payne, but he would have it no other way. She felt bad about messing up the recording. The guys had worked so hard. Jack had told her not to worry, and Bobby and Buddy were both very understanding. They had called every day to check on Mrs. Hughes and had sent flowers, which she knew they really couldn't afford. The band had become family and except for her grandmother, they were her only family.

As they often did, her thoughts quickly drifted back to Jack. She remembered the first time he kissed her. It was here two Thanksgivings ago. What a special day that had been! She remembered her secret thoughts and dreams on that day, and realized how many of them had already come true.

She loved him so much, and she knew he loved her. This was not the first time he had been there for her. He was always there... never crowding, never pushing, but always there when she needed him. And she needed him more than she had ever needed anyone.

*　　*　　*　　*　　*

By the time she rejoined the band three weeks later, the demo tapes had arrived. As she listened to the tape, she understood what Justin Blaylock meant.

She had known the studio recording would make a difference, but she had no idea it would make this much. Maybe this was the break they were looking for. They sent copies of the demo to every promoter they knew, and in July they took a week off and went to Nashville. It seemed as if they knocked on every door in town, but to no avail. Some listened to the tapes and agreed they were good, but said they 'didn't need another band'. Others promised to listen later and placed the tape on a large stack of unsolicited material. Although Jessi held a glimmer of hope, Jack knew those would never be listened to.

Even though the tapes had not accomplished their main purpose of a recording contract or a national tour, they had spurred more regional interest. The band no longer had to beg for jobs. As a matter of fact, it was all Virginia could do to sort through the offers and organize their schedule. The job, though time consuming, was very exciting. She had come to be 'Mom' to the entire band, and when the scheduling became too much to do from the back seat of the bus and a pay phone in a motel lobby, she was glad to help out.

During the summer they played county fairs from Mississippi to Kentucky in addition to their regular club and concert dates. Autumn found them in the mountains of North Georgia and Southeast Tennessee playing arts and crafts festivals. Although they had the opportunity to work straight through Thanksgiving, Jessi refused. She was going to spend Thanksgiving with her grandmother.

The following Monday they left for Myrtle Beach, where they would perform six shows in three days, and then begin a swing through Florida which would keep them busy until Christmas break.

Their schedule was back breaking, but it sure beat the old days, when they had scarcely been able to keep gas in the tank, food in their stomachs, and pay for lodging in third-rate motels.

CHAPTER 28

They finished their last show in Miami around midnight, and all Jessi wanted was to grab a few hours sleep and head home for the holidays.

Although she barely remembered Christmas with her own parents, she had fond memories of Christmas with her grandmother.

Mrs. Hughes had made an amazing recovery from her heart attack, and the doctor said she was doing fine and could do whatever she wanted as long as she took her medicine.

Jessi could almost smell the fruitcakes and pecan pies baking in the oven, and the fresh fragrance of the cedar tree that no doubt had already been put up in the corner of the living room. The doors and windows would be decorated with wreaths made from fresh greenery gathered from the nearby woods and adorned with red velvet bows. The mantle would be festive with holly and nandina. And on the coffee table, there would be the ceramic manger scene, which she and her grandmother had made when Jessi was twelve. This was going to be their best Christmas ever, and the very thought of it caused her to tingle with excitement.

When Jack mentioned that he wanted to stop in West Palm Beach, she was noticeably disappointed. She had assumed they would drive straight through. She hadn't done any shopping and was anxious to get home. They had scarcely traveled fifty-miles and this would only delay them.

"It won't take long," he assured her. "Then we'll be on our way."

As they turned onto the narrow city street with the lyrical name, Wyandotte Circle, it looked strangely familiar. She had not been here before, yet, in her mind's eye, she had been here many times, and she knew immediately where Jack was going.

This was it! This was the place where he had come as a young man, full of excitement and dreams. And it was here that he had met Mr. Bradshaw, and a special, though somewhat unlikely, friendship had begun.

She had never wondered why Jack called the old black man 'Mr. Bradshaw'. She knew. It was the way he had been brought up. Virginia Roberts had taught her son that if someone was older than you, you addressed him as 'Mr.' or 'Mrs.', out of respect, regardless of their color or status.

A couple of weeks ago Jack mentioned Mr. Bradshaw. He spoke of the old man's love for fishing and regretfully said, "I never got to go fishing with him. He always wanted me to, but I was trying so hard to make the team, there never was time." Then, as though lost in his own personal reverie with the past, he had continued. "This is Robert's senior year at Florida State. I hope the scouts give him a chance. He's got a better arm than I ever had."

He had mentioned Robert before. He was Jack's favorite of Mr. Bradshaw's grandchildren, probably because of their mutual passion for baseball.

As they turned the curve, Jessi spotted the rusting mailbox bearing the faded name *JACOB BRADSHAW*. Jack stopped the car, but for a moment he seemed uncertain if it was the right place.

"This is it, I'm sure, but I don't remember that yellow siding."

Suddenly from out of nowhere two little black boys came around the corner of the house in hot pursuit of another, who had just taken cover under the front porch.

"Bang! Bang!" They yelled, as they shot the little boy with their 'tree limb' guns.

"You can't shoot me. I'm invisible," he shouted.

Almost simultaneously the two boys spotted Jack's car and quickly abandoned the invisible one under the porch to check out the two strangers in their front yard.

The taller boy, who appeared to be seven or eight, walked up to Jack and without hesitation, asked, "Who are you?"

Before Jack had time to answer, the other little boy took one look at him and shouted, "That's Jack!"

"Jack who?" The first boy scowled back at his little brother, as if he were stupid.

"Jack, the baseball player! You know... that used to live with us before we was born."

The little one no doubt remembered the picture of Jack, which Mr. Bradshaw kept on the table among those of his grandchildren, and apparently had heard the story.

Jack and Jessi smiled at the candor of the boys, who had now been joined by the invisible kid and four dogs, who deemed it their sole mission in life to announce the arrival of company by loud barking.

Then the front door opened, and the old man Jessi had heard so much about stepped out onto the porch.

"Norman, who's that out there?" The old man asked, as he adjusted his bifocals and started down the steps.

"It's Jack!" The older boy hollered back.

"The baseball player, Grampa!" The other boy added.

224

"Jack? Jack Roberts, is that you?"

"It's me, Mr. Bradshaw. It's me."

As the man reached out his weathered hand to shake hands, Jack moved closer and put an arm around the old man's shoulder and gave him a warm hug. A handshake between these two was not enough.

Jessi watched Mr. Bradshaw's face break into a wide grin and then saw him wipe a tear from his eye. It was evident the two were glad to see each other. And suddenly she no longer felt so anxious about getting home. There would be plenty of time to get everything done. This was Christmas, seeing the two of them standing side by side... the one young, the other old... the one white, the other black... but each with a genuine fondness for the other that neither time nor distance could ever erase.

Once more her mind wandered from the present, and she remembered the first time she had seen the picture. She and Jack had been thumbing through an old photo album on her first visit to his house. The album contained mostly family pictures. There were school pictures of Jack and Jenny, pictures taken at Christmas time, birthdays and vacations... the kind usually found in a family album.

Then there was a picture of a very young Jack standing in the front yard of a beat-up old house, which hadn't seen a coat of paint in many a year. And next to him, with his arm around Jack's shoulder, was an old black man.

This was the same place she had seen in the picture, just fancied up a little with the yellow vinyl siding. Now she realized why that picture had been included in the Roberts family album. To Jack, Mr. Bradshaw was family.

She wondered what Jack was like back then and wished she had known him during his baseball days. However, there was someone else in his life at that time, someone he loved very much. Jessi had seen her picture in that same family album. She was beautiful. He had told her about it once, but after that it was a closed subject.

Sometimes she wondered about the girl called Mary. Was she happy? And how could she possibly have given up someone like Jack?

"Who've you got with you, Jack? Did you bring me a wife?"

"No sir." Jack grinned. "She belongs to me."

He introduced Jessi to Mr. Bradshaw, and then Mr. Bradshaw introduced the three boys they had met earlier.

"These two are Vernon's boys, and this little one here is Rocky. He belongs to Earl. They stay with me while their mamas work."

"I almost didn't recognize the place, Mr. Bradshaw. I like that siding."

"Yeah, Thamon did that. I still can't get used to the idea of living in a plastic house, but he wanted to do it. He's got a good job with IBM.

Said he wanted to do something for me. I told him to put his money in the bank, but you know these young folks. They think they gotta' spend it fast as they make it."

Mr. Bradshaw downplayed it, but it was apparent he was very proud of his grandson, and the fact he hadn't forgotten where he came from.

"Well, come on in the house. I was just gettin' ready to fix these boys some breakfast. I let 'em sleep as long as they want to, and then cook breakfast when they get up. I hope you and Miss Jessi haven't eat yet. I'd be mighty pleased to have you join us."

Jack grinned and looked at Jessi.

"No, sir. We just had some coffee and juice, and I can't think of any place I'd rather sit down to breakfast." Then he turned to Jessi. "You're in for a treat. I always thought Mom was a good cook, but nobody can make hot biscuits and scrambled eggs like Mr. Bradshaw."

The living room reminded Jessi of her grandmother's. There was a crocheted sofa cover on the couch and knick-knacks and do-dads all over the place. It appeared Mr. Bradshaw never threw anything away. Pictures lined the walls and covered every shelf in the room. The pictures were of his children and grandchildren at various stages. There were six different wedding pictures, the oldest of which she assumed was Mr. & Mrs. Bradshaw.

As she continued to look around the room she saw another group of smaller photographs on top of the t.v. Some were framed. Others were not. Directly in the center was a picture of Jack in his *Memphis Jazz* uniform with his arm around a small, shy-looking black boy. The kid was wearing a battered baseball cap. And she knew it must be Robert.

Jack was right about Mr. Bradshaw's cooking. She had never eaten such a good breakfast. There was fried ham, scrambled eggs, grits and those wonderful biscuits, not to mention the homemade blackberry jelly.

"I can't claim credit for the jelly." Mr. Bradshaw confessed. "Juanita, Rocky's mother, makes the jelly and keeps me supplied."

After breakfast Mr. Bradshaw and Jack and the boys went fishing. Jack had been about to decline the invitation, aware that Jessi was anxious to get home, but she insisted that he go.

"I'll go into town and start my Christmas shopping. Just be sure you catch enough for supper."

"If we don't catch 'em, I've got plenty in the freezer. We gonna have us a fish fry tonight."

Jack smiled. The very thought of anything else to eat after such a hearty breakfast seemed ridiculous.

Jessi shopped all afternoon. She bought a jacket for Bobby, and boots for Buddy, and then she went to the bookstore and selected books for her grandmother and Virginia. She spent most of her time with the guys, and it was nice to have an afternoon all to herself. Then she bought Christmas stockings for the boys, the biggest ones she could find, filled with toys and all kinds of candy and treats.

The day's catch was slim. Norman said Jack and Mr. Bradshaw talked too much. "Fish won't bite when they's a lot of talking going on."

She was glad Jack had gotten the chance to go fishing with Mr. Bradshaw. It was obvious they had enjoyed being together, and the frozen fish was just as good.

After supper she helped Mr. Bradshaw with the dishes, while Jack and the boys played ball in the back yard. It was plain to see that he was having as much fun as the boys. It must have been hard for him to face giving up baseball. He was a talented musician, but music was not his first love. Jessi knew that.

It was easy to talk to Mr. Bradshaw. He was gentle and easygoing and didn't seem to 'sweat the small stuff'. She was glad Jack had brought her here. Her life would be richer from the experience.

They chatted comfortably like old friends, as they dried and put away the dishes, and watched the backyard game from the kitchen window.

"I never knew he was so good with children," Jessi observed out loud.

"Oh, he's just a kid himself... Always was... It was the same way when he was here before. I had as much trouble getting him in out of the yard at night as I did my own grandkids... I never did see nobody want to play baseball as much as he did. It was a shame... the accident."

Mr. Bradshaw's voice almost quavered with the last statement, and then he grew quiet.

Jessi continued to watch how Jack interacted with the boys. She had never seen this side of him and thought what a good father he would make.

"You gonna marry him?"

She smiled at the directness of the old man, but she was not offended by his boldness.

"Oh, I don't know, Mr. Bradshaw. I'm not sure Jack's the marrying kind."

"Every man's the marrying kind when the right woman comes along."

"You think I'm the right woman for Jack?"

"Could be." He was smiling as if he knew more than he was saying. Then he repeated himself. "Just could be."

She wondered what Jack and Mr. Bradshaw had talked about on the creek bank. Mr. Bradshaw did not say, and she dared not ask, but she wondered. In fact, she had wondered a lot about Jack lately. She knew he loved her, but he had loved baseball, and he had loved Mary, and neither had loved him back... at least not enough.

She wasn't sure he would ever commit himself unconditionally to anyone or anything again. What they had was special and real, and she loved him as he was, and she knew he loved her... And time would tell what lay ahead.

Before leaving West Palm Beach the next morning, they stopped by to say good-bye to Mr. Bradshaw and the children. Jack had bought a new baseball glove for each of the children and a new rod and reel for Mr. Bradshaw. And Jessi had bought him a new red tie.

The old man stood there smiling down at his new fishing pole and the red tie, and then his countenance grew sad as he looked at Jack.

"Son, I haven't got anything to give you."

"Mr. Bradshaw, you've given me more than I could ever give you."

And with that the old man looked away and wiped his eyes before looking back.

"But I have got something for Miss Jessi."

He looked down at the little black and white puppy, who had been at her side constantly since she arrived. It was almost as if the dog had adopted Jessi. Then Mr. Bradshaw picked up the puppy and handed him to her. "Merry Christmas!"

The old man smiled as the little dog snuggled in Jessi's arms.

"Take good care of him, Miss Jessi... His name's Toby." It was Rocky who always seemed to be the spokesman for the group.

She looked first at Toby and then at Mr. Bradshaw and the children, and then handed the puppy to Jack, while she hugged each of them and wished them a Merry Christmas.

As Jack pulled out of the driveway, the four of them stood in the front yard, waving, surrounded by the rest of the dogs.

A few miles up the highway he said something to Jessi and got no response. When he turned to look, both she and Toby were fast asleep, the puppy nestled comfortably in her lap.

CHAPTER 29

It was late in the day when they arrived home. The porch light was on and Buddy's car was parked in the driveway.

"Wonder what Buddy's doing here?" Jessi asked.

Jack grinned. "He probably just dropped by to see Mom."

Jessi didn't know that Buddy came and went at the Roberts' house as though it were his own. He always had. One Christmas Jack's mother had bought Buddy a pair of pajamas, but he never took them home. They were washed with the Roberts' laundry and folded and put away to be ready whenever Buddy decided to spend the night.

Virginia met them at the door, clutching a brown manila envelope in her hand.

"Where have you two been? I've been trying to reach you for the last two days."

"We stopped to see Mr. Bradshaw... What's the matter, Mom? Is something wrong?"

"No, no. Everything is wonderful."

"Well, what is it?" Buddy asked anxiously.

Virginia had called him earlier and said she had great news, but she refused to tell him until Jack and Jessi got home.

She opened the brown envelope and read aloud the first two lines.

They couldn't believe it! Jessi cried... Jack shook his head in disbelief... and Buddy just stood there grinning and repeating, "Well, whatta' you know?"

R C A had offered them a recording contract.

It was almost Christmas, but Christmas was the farthest thing from their minds. They had finally made it. At long last someone wanted to record them, and that someone was the biggest in the business... It had been a long time coming, and there were times they wondered if it would come at all.

Even the demo, which had seemed like such a good idea, had failed to produce. But finally, when all else had failed, fate intervened.

A record producer's wife had dragged her husband to "Another one of those damn craft festivals", as he put it. And after hours of looking at all the 'absolutely gorgeous' handmade items with his wife and mother-in-law, he finally wandered over to the grandstand to listen to the music, which, for the most part, wasn't much better than the crafts.

However, there was one band that got his attention. The lady had one of the purest voices he had heard in a long time, and their material was fresh and unique and not the typical Nashville clone. He planned to speak to them when they finished performing, but Miriam and her mother sought him out and insisted he come look at some stained glass, which 'would be just perfect' for the new sun room. By the time he got back to the grandstand, they were gone.

He found out who they were from the festival director and borrowed a tape the PR man had recorded to use in next year's promotion. When he got back to Nashville, he played it for his boss.

"Whose label are they on?" The record executive asked.

"Nobody's."

"They are now! Get them on the phone!"

And the rest, as they say, is history.

The album was released on Valentine's Day and by early April, their first song broke into the Top Ten. By late summer they had repeated that success with two other hits, both of which went to "Number One".

Jack would never forget the first time he heard one of their songs on radio. He was driving home from the grocery store, and he had to pull off to the side of the road. The initial shock of hearing it was unreal. He was half-laughing and half-crying, and the tears made it impossible to drive.

The band had been on the road continually since March. They no longer played the clubs and small theaters they had played in the past. Now they performed to sell-out crowds in the largest concert halls and stadiums from coast to coast.

It had all happened so fast! Sometimes it didn't seem real.

People called constantly... old friends... people they hadn't heard from in years... people they hardly knew, and some they didn't know at all... booking agents, promotions people, and wardrobe managers. Overnight they had moved from relative unknowns to household names, and suddenly they were hot commodities.

An article in *NASHVILLE HITMAKER* described them as an overnight success. As Jack read it, he thought... If only they knew what a 'long night' it had been.

CHAPTER 30

As Jack and his mother entered the magnificent Opryland Complex, they found themselves surrounded by celebrities. Everybody who was anybody in country music was here tonight adorned in all their flashy splendor. It was the event of the year, the annual Country Music Awards.

Virginia Roberts felt she was attending the fashion show of the year as she looked about her at the vast array of finery. Everyone was dressed to the nines, and the outfits and hairstyles ranged from the sublime to the ridiculous.

She felt somewhat overwhelmed by it all, as she looked nervously at Jack and asked, "Do I look all right?"

"You look perfect." He assured her.

She was wearing a blue satin ankle-length dress with silver accessories, and she looked very chic. Virginia Roberts was a very attractive lady, but she had been too busy working and raising her family to concern herself with the world of high fashion. She had wondered all week if the dress she had chosen was right for the occasion. The clerk who had helped her said it was perfect, and Jack had said the same thing... She hoped they were right.

The band had been nominated for the *Newcomer Award*, an honor given each year to the best new group or individual in country music. Jack had known about the nomination for several weeks, but only recently had learned that he was also nominated for writing the *Song of the Year*. The three other nominees were all seasoned songwriters, each having won the award in the past. Jack was still very new to the Nashville scene and did not expect to win, but just being nominated was quite an honor.

Many thoughts raced through his head as they were ushered to their seats. He thought about his dad. How he wished he could be here tonight. John Roberts had always encouraged him to do his best and never give up, and Jack knew that whether or not they ever gave him an award, his dad would be very proud of him.

He remembered his dad's words of long ago. "Son, it's nice when others think well of you, but what matters most is that you think well of yourself."

He thought of his mom. It was only fitting that she be here sharing this special night. She had been the one constant in his life. She had loved him and had been there for him every step of the way, through the good times and the bad.

What bothered him most was that Jessi was not here. Her grandmother had suffered another coronary, and although she was doing better and had been moved to a private room, Jessi would not leave her.

*   *   *   *   *

Jessi could not have been more excited as she and her grandmother watched from Mrs. Hughes' hospital room. They listened as the emcee opened the envelope and announced:

"The winner of the Newcomer Award... The Jessi McCrae Band."

She couldn't believe it! They had worked so hard, and now it was finally happening. She waited anxiously for their reactions, as Jack, Bobby, and Buddy made their way to the stage. Seeing Buddy in a tuxedo made her smile. She remembered the cold Christmas Eve she and Jack had driven to Rome to get him. Jack had told her he was the best "damn guitar picker" around, and he had been right. They were all so good!

She listened as Jack spoke first.

"The reason we're here tonight is a lady named Jessi McCrae. She should be here sharing it with us, but instead she's at her grandmother's bedside in a hospital in Birmingham. Jessi's grandmother raised her after her parents were killed in a car wreck." He hesitated, still trying to gain his composure. "I talked to her this afternoon, and she said, 'There'll be other awards shows, but I only have one grandmother.' I wish all of you could know Jessi as those of us who work with her day in and day out do. That's the kind of person she is."

Buddy and Bobby nodded in agreement.

Jack paused for a moment as he thought of the lady he had fallen in love with.

"Jess, this one's yours. We love you."

Tears welled up in Jessi's eyes as she sat beside her grandmother's bed and held her hand.

"You should have been there, Jessi. I would have been all right."

"No, Gramma. I'm right where I want to be. You're the one who taught me to sing. You're the one who has loved me and taken care of me all my life and there's no one in the world I'd rather be sharing this with."

Soon it was time for the presentation of the *Song of the Year Award*, given annually to the writer of the year's best song. Jack was still thinking of Jessi, and he didn't hear the announcer call his name. Suddenly his mom grabbed him and was hugging him, and those seated around him were reaching to shake his hand. He couldn't believe it! And as he made his way to the stage, he had no idea what he would say.

The song, which had won the award, was called *"Best Friends"*, and as he stood behind the podium and looked out over the cheering crowd, he thought of the many best friends he had had. There was his Mom, and Jessi, and Buddy, and Bobby, and Mr. Bradshaw, and Susan. Each of them at different points in his life had been his best friend, but more than anyone else, he thought of his dad.

"The best friend I ever had was my dad... He never lived to see me get into music. He never got to see me pitch in the majors, but without him, I never would have done any of it." He could say no more. He was too overcome with emotion... But as he raised the crystal accolade, he managed to say the words, "Dad, this is for you."

Tears rolled down Virginia Roberts' face as she listened to her son's acceptance. It wasn't the award that made her cry, but rather the son she and John had raised. If only he could have known about this... Then she realized that perhaps he did. And as she sat among the thousands of cheering fans there in the Grand Ole Opry house, she felt John's presence in a very real sense.

CHAPTER 31

JUNE 22, 1986

A glance at her watch told Mary it was three o'clock. It almost seemed that she and the chair had become one. The room was so quiet. Visitors were not allowed except for family. She got up and stepped to the side of the bed. He slept quietly and there was no visible sign of pain. Softly she called his name, hoping for even the slightest response, but there was none.

She walked out into the hall for a drink of water and then returned to her vigil. The straight-backed chair was strategically positioned between the bed and the window. From this position she could watch and listen for any sign of change and could also look out the window at the hospital courtyard. The flowers and shrubbery were neatly kept, and small children played carefree on the freshly mowed lawn while their parents visited with sick loved ones.

She thought of the day she first met Bill Johnson. It was only a few days after her divorce, and at her lawyer's suggestion, she had called for a job interview.

She had arrived at his office in the midst of a summer shower. He was crouched over the typewriter at his secretary's desk, laboriously trying to type a brief. He looked up over his spectacles and saw her trying to manage a wet umbrella which the wind had all but turned inside out, and which was trailing a stream of water on the carpet while she searched for the umbrella stand.

Recognizing her dilemma, he smiled and motioned down the hall.

"The ladies' room is in the back if you want to dry off. When you're finished, we'll talk."

She dried herself and tried unsuccessfully to fluff her damp hair. She thought of the man she had not officially met, but who she presumed to be Bill Johnson, and immediately liked him. It had been several years since she had worked for lawyers, but she knew she could do the job if he would give her the chance.

She had gotten the job, but more than that, she had gained a friend.

And for the past three years, she had worked for William T. Johnson, Attorney at Law. In addition to her job, and trying to be both mother and father to her children, she had been attending law school at night. There was barely enough time for the things she had to do and little time at all for herself, but it had been worth it. In May she had graduated from Emory University School of Law, and now all that stood between her and practicing law was passing the bar exam.

Over a year ago, Mr. Johnson had been diagnosed with terminal cancer. The cancer was attached to the top of his spinal chord and was inoperable, which Bill considered a blessing. He did not want an operation. He wanted to spend the time he had left doing what he loved most, practicing law. He didn't want to waste whatever time he had waiting for hours in doctors' offices and lying in a hospital bed, when either way the end result would be the same.

The first six months had not been bad. He looked good and was as active as ever, and sometimes Mary wondered if the diagnosis might have been wrong. Then one morning he called and said he wasn't feeling well and would be late coming to the office. He didn't come in at all, and she left work early to check on him. When he came to the door, he was still in his pajamas, and she could tell he was very ill.

The last six months had taken their toll. The tumor had grown and the cancer had spread. He no longer had the stamina to work the large caseload he had always prided himself in doing, and as the months went by, his cases seemed to interest him less. The weight loss and his general failing health were apparent. He tired easily and his attention span lessened.

Since late winter, the only thing that seemed to matter to him was her law degree. It had become his sole obsession. He knew he was dying, but that was unimportant. What was important was seeing Mary get her degree and pass the bar.

He had been sick the morning of her graduation... throwing up, diarrhea, etc... but he had made up his mind that nothing was going to keep him away. He willed himself well long enough to attend the commencement exercise and watched with pride as she walked across the stage to accept her diploma. All the hard work and sacrifice had paid off and she had graduated tenth in her class.

Bill Johnson had been like a father to Mary. There had been rumors of an affair, as there always are when an older man and a younger woman share a special friendship, but there was no affair. That was not the nature of their relationship. They had simply come to love and care for each other as two very dear friends.

Chip and Sandy, Bill's children, understood this. They appreciated all that she had done and was doing for their father, and considered her part of the family. For the last two weeks the three of them had rotated shifts sitting at the hospital and caring for Mr. Johnson, and supporting each other, as they dealt with the impending loss of someone they loved.

* * * * *

JUNE 23, 1986

The large, circular clock at the end of the hall showed 8:30 as Mary walked past the nurses' station to relieve Sandy. She had sat up the night before worrying about Mr. Johnson and trying to study for the bar exam she was scheduled to take on Thursday.

Mr. Johnson had lived long enough to see her graduate from law school. Now all he wanted to do was see her pass the bar. However, during the night he had taken a turn for the worse.

He had told her the day before, "Mary, I want you there Thursday morning acing that bar exam, no matter what's happening here! And Mary... You're going to be one Hell of a lawyer!"

With those thoughts conveyed, he closed his eyes and drifted into peaceful sleep. He slept all through the afternoon with a look of contentment on his face that had taken the place of the pain that had been etched across his face for the last several weeks.

Her mind drifted back to another hospital vigil. The setting was the same, only the characters were different. She thought of the grueling days she had spent in that small hospital room with Jody. It was so white, so cold and sterile, so damn clean! Her mind was blocking out the intense problems and concerns of today with far-removed thoughts of yesterday, as minds sometimes do when the present day pressures are more than they can bear. Why was she thinking about the hygiene of Jody's hospital room, she wondered, as she shook herself from the trance-like state.

The nurse had entered the room so quietly that Mary had not heard her. She was leaning over Mr. Johnson's bed checking his vital signs. For days they had gone through this ritual every few hours. After checking his pulse and blood pressure, the nurse would usually look at Mary, and with a strained smile say, "His vitals are stable," before moving on to another room and another patient in the oncology unit.

She had grown accustomed to the procedure and no longer rose to her feet or slid to the edge of her seat as she had the first few days, hoping to hear some encouraging words. The scene had been the same for days, the checking of the vitals, the half-smile, and that damn "His vitals are stable" line, which told her absolutely nothing.

Mary sat back in her chair and watched the nurse go through her normal routine, but this time she repeated the procedure. Finally, she lifted the stethoscope from Mr. Johnson's chest, straightened up, and walked around the bed to where Mary sat.

She knew what had happened. Every nerve in her body ached at once. She longed to hear the nurse repeat that previously monotonous statement, "His vitals are stable," but this time it was not to be... Bill Johnson was dead.

As the nurse walked around the corner of Mr. Johnson's bed, Mary stood to her feet to face her, still somehow grasping at a thread of hope that she was wrong about what she knew she was about to hear. But she wasn't.

The nurse reached out and gently took Mary by the hand.

"Mrs. Davenport, I'm sorry."

Then she put her arm around Mary and led her from the room, pausing to pick up a box of tissues as they left. Through tear-filled eyes, Mary thanked her for her kindness and turned and slowly walked down the hallway, knowing she had just said good-bye to one of the best friends she would ever have.

*   *   *   *   *

A slow drizzle had begun to fall around eight in the morning and lingered on throughout the day, as summer rains often do. The chapel was filled with those who had come to pay their final respects to Bill Johnson... business colleagues, friends, and clients who had come to regard him as their friend, as well as their lawyer.

The brief eulogy delivered by the Presbyterian preacher, the Reverend Don Harwell, was a fitting tribute. For many years Don Harwell had preached to Bill on Sunday and played golf with him on Wednesday. The only music was the soft tones of the organ and a solo sung by Carrie Mae Jones, who had worked for Bill and Ruth during most of their married life. When Ruth died, Carrie Mae had stayed on to take care of the house.

On one occasion, she had invited the Johnsons to her church for a special service, and it was there they had first heard her sing *Amazing Grace*.

They both agreed they had never heard a more beautiful rendition, and when she came to work the next day, Bill said to her, "Carrie Mae, when the Good Master sees fit to take me home, I want you to sing that song at my funeral."

"Oh, Mr. Johnson, don't say that. I'll be gone long 'fo you... But if I'm still around, and that's what you want, I'll do my best."

The black woman's powerful, yet mellow, voice touched the hearts of all those present, just as it had touched Bill the first time he had heard her sing.

> *Amazing Grace, how sweet the sound*
> *That saved a wretch like me.*
> *I once was lost, but now I'm found,*
> *Was blind, but now I see.*

> *When we've been there ten thousand years,*
> *Bright shining as the sun,*
> *We've no less days to sing His praise,*
> *Than when we first begun.*

It was beautiful, as was the entire service. Chip and Sandy had planned it exactly as their dad would have wanted. Although the chapel was full for the funeral, only a few braved the weather and went on to the cemetery for the interment, most of whom were family and a few close friends from the neighborhood where the Johnsons had lived for over thirty years.

The darkness of the cloudy sky and the slow drizzling rain reflected the somber mood of those assembled at the spot that was to be Bill Johnson's final resting place. Chip and Sandy had insisted that Mary sit with the family, and the small group congregated under the green funeral home tent.

Following the reading of the 23rd Psalm and the final prayer, Mary stepped aside to allow Chip and Sandy some time with the rest of the family. After shaking hands with the minister and thanking friends and relatives for coming, Chip looked around for Mary. When he spotted her, she stood motionless under a tall pine tree with a black umbrella over her head. He and Sandy walked over to where she stood.

Chip was forty-five and a successful lawyer himself. After law school, he had practiced with his father for a few years, but his real interest was corporate law. Several years ago, he had moved to New York to join a large firm, which specialized in that field.

Sandy was a speech therapist and also lived in New York with her husband, Steve, and their two sons, Nick and Billy.

Chip reached inside his coat and handed Mary an envelope. She looked first at the envelope and then at Chip, her eyes questioning the meaning of it all.

"Mary, Dad asked me to give you this. He loved you very much."

She wasn't sure if she should open it now, but both Chip and Sandy appeared to be waiting. Her fingers trembled nervously as she attempted to open the sealed envelope. As she unfolded the letter written in Bill's own scraggly handwriting on the firm stationery, something fell out and dropped to the ground. Chip stooped to retrieve it and handed it to her. It was a check.

*Pay to the Order of Mary Davenport
the sum of FIFTY THOUSAND DOLLARS*

After regaining her composure, she looked at Chip and then at Sandy, and with the loss showing deep in all of their eyes said, "I can't accept this."

"Dad said you would say that," Sandy smiled through the tears. "Mary, Dad wanted you to have it, and so do we. We know how much he thought of you."

Then Chip spoke. "Dad took care of his money, and he left us well provided for. He wanted you to have this to help you get established in your practice, and he made us promise not to let you give it back."

"I don't know what to say... except thank you. Your father was one of the best people I've ever known. And I'll miss him, so very much."

Tears rolled unashamedly down her face for this man who had been much more than her employer. He had been a trusted friend, and there would never be another like him.

Sandy hugged Mary tightly and went to join the others waiting in the family car. Chip also gave her a hug and said he would call her next week about closing his father's office, and he, too, was gone. They were all gone... Bill, Chip and Sandy.

And as she stood alone in the cemetery under the black umbrella, the rain started to come down harder, and she could almost hear the words:

"The ladies room is in the back if you want to dry off. When you're finished, we'll talk."

LOS ANGELES TIMES

July 26, 1986

JESSI McCRAE COLLAPSES ON STAGE

LOS ANGELES - AP - Country music star Jessi McCrae collapsed on stage last evening during a performance at the Los Angeles Civic Center. Although unconscious for less than a minute, the show was halted and Miss McCrae was transported to Los Angeles Medical Center for further evaluation.

CHAPTER 32

"I'm fine, Jack. I just haven't been eating right or getting enough sleep. Go back to the hotel and get some rest yourself. I don't need you passing out too."

But he refused to leave the hospital until all the tests were complete.

Following a three-day hospital stay, in which she underwent every test imaginable, Jessi was released, and the press report confirmed what she had claimed all along... FATIGUE.

As with any case where a performer goes down on stage, rumors circulated quickly. It had happened to Loretta Lynn, Tammy Wynette, and a host of others, and the released report was always the same... Fatigue, caused by too heavy a schedule... But, as always, rumors abounded. Drugs... Alcohol... even AIDS.

She had expected the rumors, and while she hated having her name and reputation dragged through the muck, she knew that the more she said, the guiltier she would appear. Besides, she had more to be concerned about than what the media had to say. They would report what they wanted to anyway. The doctors in L.A. agreed she had been overdoing it with her schedule and not taking proper care of herself, but they also found that she had a slightly enlarged heart. And with her family medical history, they felt it would be in her best interest to do further testing.

She talked the doctors into giving the phony 'fatigue report' to the media and convinced them to let her go home and have the tests done in Birmingham. They realized she was putting them off, but they also knew that Birmingham had one of the finest cardiac care units in the country. Since she lived as close as she did, they agreed it would probably be a good idea to have the tests done there.

After returning home she continued to excuse the collapsing as fatigue.

"Jack, I know how it is! I'm not stupid enough to think we'll stay on top forever. This is a tough 'dog-eat-dog' business. Today you're the star... Tomorrow they don't remember your name... You've got to perform while you're hot. There will be plenty of time later to rest."

"You don't have to tell me how it is! I know how it is! But I also know you've got to take care of yourself! Nobody else will! The public thinks they own you, and that you should sign every autograph and pose for every picture."

"Jack, you don't understand. Everybody has been so good to me, the fans and the promoters..."

"The promoters! Hell!" Jack interrupted. "The promoters don't give a damn about you. They don't care if you fall over dead on the stage. As long as they've sold their tickets and collected their money, they don't care what happens to you." He paused long enough to get his breath and then continued. "Matter of fact, they would probably find a way to make more money out of it. They'd paint a square on the stage and charge thousands of idiots twenty bucks a piece to have their picture made where the great Jessi McCrae fell over dead!"

As he raged on, she began to smile.

"What are you grinning about?" Jack asked, frustrated that she wasn't taking him seriously.

"Do you know how cute you are when you get mad?"

He stopped and shook his head. "I'm not mad. I just care about you."

He put his arms around her, and she snuggled close to him.

"I know you do. Don't worry, though. Everything's going to be okay."

*   *   *   *   *

Jack insisted that they cancel the rest of the summer tour to give Jessi a chance to rest. She thought it was ridiculous, but he would hear of nothing else. If everything went well, they would resume their tour in September.

After spending a couple of weeks at home, she found it to be quite nice. She slept late and did exactly what she wanted. She spent most of her time in a tee shirt and cut-offs, cleaning house, working in the yard and playing with Toby. Toby loved being at home. He had logged a lot of miles traveling with them on the bus, and he enjoyed having plenty of space to run and play, and bark at anything that caught his attention.

Once Jessi got home, she again put off the testing. There had been no further problems since the incident in L.A., and if she did have a heart problem, she simply was not ready to deal with it. She knew she was probably being foolish, but somehow not knowing seemed safer than having it confirmed.

She had watched the disease slowly kill her grandmother and she knew it was a massive heart attack, and not slick road conditions, that caused her dad to lose control of the car, taking both her mother and her father to their deaths.

There was no urgency in getting the tests done. She felt better than she had in a long time. The extra rest and reduced stress showed on her face. Her cheeks were rosy, and she felt wonderful, and she was glad Jack had insisted on the hiatus.

It also gave the two of them more time together. Even though they managed to find time to be alone when they were on tour, it was not the same. The guys were never too far away, and the demands of performing and practicing often preempted their personal time together.

She finishing washing the car and came inside to fix a sandwich. It was fun to get up in the morning and be able to choose what she wanted to do, and today washing the car seemed like a good idea.

Toby had been out in the yard with her, but he followed her inside, obviously thinking it was time for his lunch too. She had come to really love the little dog Mr. Bradshaw had given her. No matter how tired or depressed she was, he always cheered her up. He didn't scold her or remind her what a cold, hard world it was, like Jack did.

Toby didn't know what negative was. He thought life was just loving and playing with everyone he came in contact with, but most of all, Jessi.

She could tell him things she couldn't tell Jack, and he seemed to understand what she said. Usually their conversations were about Jack.

She loved Jack so much, but sometimes she had trouble putting her feelings into words. Maybe she was afraid to admit love completely. It seemed everyone she had ever loved had died. But she could tell Toby how she felt, and he listened attentively, and the wag of his tail and the sparkle of his shiny black eyes seemed to reassure her that Jack knew.

Sometimes she didn't know who she loved more, Jack or Toby. Maybe it was like trying to decide who you love more, your mate or your child. She loved them both. The two of them were her family... her only family.

She kicked off her tennis shoes and went to the pantry to get some food for Toby. As soon as her back was turned, Toby made a quick leap onto one of her shoes, grabbed it in his mouth, and took off to the den. After turning a couple of flips on the den floor with the tennis shoe clinched firmly between his teeth, he rolled into the end table, knocking over a lamp in the process. It didn't break, but the commotion brought Jessi running from the kitchen to see what was going on, as if she didn't have a pretty good idea.

From the dining room she spotted him lying on the carpet, the lamp and the contents of an over-turned magazine rack strewn all around him. He was on his back, vigorously pawing up into the air at the sneaker he still held firmly in his mouth.

Her aggravation grew when she saw the mess he had managed to create. In addition to the other clutter, he had turned over a plant, and dirt was scattered all over the carpet she had just vacuumed this morning. Yet, she couldn't help but grin when she saw Toby's expression when he spotted her, and realized he had been 'caught in the act'.

There was a split second of silence as they each eyeballed the other... Jessi plotting her attack, and Toby planning his escape... Then suddenly, with lightning speed, Toby bounced to his feet, still holding onto Jessi's shoe.

She lunged for him, but he was too quick. In less than a heartbeat, he hurdled the overturned lamp and took off, pausing at the far end of the table to look back at her, taunting her, eagerly waiting for her to chase after him... It was all part of the game. He had pulled the trick before.

She stared at him with a playful "I'm gonna get you!" look on her face, and both were totally engrossed in this little game of cat and mouse.

Toby stared back at her from a safe distance with a "What's taking you so long?" look in his eyes. Then he dropped the shoe and let out a short loud bark, again challenging her to chase him.

She obliged and started around the coffee table after him, and Toby quickly picked up his prized possession and darted behind the sofa.

Then it hit her! It was as though something had stabbed her from within. Like a huge hand had reached into her chest and grabbed her heart, wrenching it, squeezing it unmercifully, and trying to wrest it from her body!

She grabbed at her chest as her entire body flinched. She gasped for air, but the air would not seem to go into her lungs. She tried to speak, but the words would not come. Then her knees buckled, and she fell to the floor, her last thoughts being the terrifying realization of what was happening, and the sheer panic that she was about to die.

*   *   *   *   *

SOMETIME LATER

Slowly she opened her eyes. At first she did not realize where she was or what had happened. Then she felt something wet and coarse upon her face, but she was not sure what it was. She lay crumpled on the carpet. The overturned lamp and magazine rack and the broken coffee table, which she must have hit when she fell, surrounded her almost lifeless body. As her eyes slowly started to focus and an awareness of her whereabouts returned, she recognized the source of the cold damp coarseness on her cheek. It was Toby. He was standing beside her with his front paws on her shoulder, licking her face, feverishly trying to revive his master and friend.

He was frightened too. She had never done this before. It was not part of their game. He whimpered quietly, and she could see the fear and distress in his eyes. Slowly and painfully she reached out a hand to the little black and white dog and then lay motionless, her hand across his back.

Toby sat next to her in silence, the worry and concern he felt for his human friend showing in his sad eyes. Slowly he pulled his paw out from under her arm and laid it on her hand, as if to comfort her and let her know he was there.

Exhausted from her ordeal, Jessi drifted off to sleep. When she awakened, Toby was still at her side, only now he was holding her shoe in his mouth... He whimpered softly, as if apologizing for all the trouble he had caused.

A tired smile came across her face, as she looked up at the little dog and reached to rub his head. Toby unclenched his teeth and let the gnawed-upon tennis shoe fall to the floor next to Jessi's hand.

Finally, she managed to get to her feet and slowly made her way to the bathroom with Toby still at her side. She ran cold water in the sink and splashed it over her face. Then she wet a towel, wrapped it around her neck and dabbed the wet ends over her forehead and face. The cold water felt good, but the energy she had expended getting to the bathroom had sapped her strength. She needed to get to the telephone, but she wasn't sure she could make it, not until she rested. She eased herself down onto the commode and continued to apply the wet towel to her face. The portable phone was normally on the dressing table, but she had taken it outside when she washed the car and had forgotten to bring it in.

After resting awhile, she was eventually able to get to the bedroom phone, and with trembling fingers dialed Jack's number.

The phone rang several times, and with each ring, she grew more frightened. What if he wasn't home?

Finally on the fifth ring she heard his voice.

"Thank God," she whispered inaudibly.

"Jack..." Her voice trembled and she started to cry.

"What's the matter, baby?"

Jessi was not given to tears, and he knew something was terribly wrong.

"Jack, I'm so sick." Her voice was weak and frightened.

"I'm on my way, Jess. Just stay where you are!"

And she heard the click of the phone.

CHAPTER 33

Her client was obviously a happy young man. He had expected to do time, most likely a year to eighteen months minimum. Instead, he was walking out of the courthouse a free man. Mary had won her first case against the illustrious District Attorney.

Dan Kelley had offered Mary a job when she passed the bar, but she had declined. He was probably the best district attorney in the state, and she had been told she was a fool to pass up the opportunity, but she wanted to see what she could do on her own.

It had been extremely hard in the beginning. A few of Bill Johnson's clients had continued with her, but most moved their business to other 'more experienced' attorneys. She drew wills and deeds and was not too proud to accept court-appointed cases. At a hundred dollars for a misdemeanor and twice that for a felony, she didn't get rich, but she did get seen.

Bill Johnson had told her to camp out on the courthouse steps if she had to. "You won't get a lot of money for these cases, but you will get exposure, and that's what's important."

Bill was right. The key to getting established was being seen and showing what you could do in court. And somehow, with the deeds and wills and the 'petty' cases, she had managed to pay the rent and keep the doors open.

Dan Kelley didn't lose many cases, but he got a little too eager on this one and attempted to prosecute the case with illegally obtained evidence. She pounced on the state's wrongful procurement of evidence, and the judge ruled favorably on the defendant's motion to dismiss. The young man, who was barely eighteen, shook her hand and thanked her for what she had done for him. He knew he was guilty, and she knew he was guilty. They had won the case on a technicality. He was extremely lucky and Mary told him so.

"You've gotten a break. Take advantage of it. Drop by the office sometime and let me know how you're doing, but don't ever let me see you back in this courtroom again... Okay?"

He assured her she would not, but they all say that. She hoped Randy would straighten up his act and do something worthwhile with his life. He was a fine looking young man and could have a good future if he would stay away from the drugs, but whether he would only time would tell.

She placed the familiar yellow legal pad in her brief case, looked at her watch, and quickly left the courtroom. It was nice to walk away the winner for a change. In most court-appointed cases, the defendant was guilty beyond a doubt, and there was little defense to be offered.

It was three o'clock when she reached the office. She signed the letters she had dictated earlier in the day, returned some phone calls, did some more dictation, and was about to leave the office when the phone rang. It was Ken Wardlaw, an old colleague of Bill Johnson.

"Mary, I've just been hired to represent a young man charged with rape. He's the son of a prominent Fulton County family. They've authorized me to hire co-counsel if I feel the need. It's a big case, and there's a lot of work to be done, but I think there's a chance of acquittal. I've been observing you in the courtroom, and I want you to work with me on the case. There's a substantial fee involved."

She tried to conceal her surprise at the offer. It was a big case, and it would be an opportunity to work with one of the best lawyers in the business. Of course, she would take it! As she hung up the phone, a proud smile broke across her face. It had been a good day.

CHAPTER 34

The day had been frustrating, and it was nice to be home. Jody was spending the night with a friend, and Katie was finishing her bath as Mary sat down to look at the evening paper. Too tired for heavy reading, she turned to the entertainment section.

She had almost forgotten. Tonight was the night for the country music awards. She couldn't believe she had let it slip her mind, but she had been so focused on the rape case. She was grateful for the opportunity to work with Ken Wardlaw, but there was so much evidence to procure and sift through, and try to come up with a strong defense, that there was little time for anything else. Katie and Jody were growing up fast, and it seemed that lately she had so little time for them.

She remembered the wonderful times she and Jody had spent together when he was Katie's age. They had gone to the park, swam in the pool and enjoyed long, leisurely days together, but since that time things had changed in all of their lives.

She had worked during most of Katie's life and, consequently, had not been able to spend as much time with her as she had with Jody. Nonetheless, it was evident that Katie felt loved and secure.

"Mommy, I washed the tub, so you don't have to do it," Katie announced as she crawled up on the couch, carrying her favorite doll.

"Well, that's nice. Thank you. How was school today?"

Katie was a beautiful little girl. Her long brown hair was naturally curly, and her warm brown eyes were both serious and at the same time a bit devilish.

The children had handled their parents' divorce well. Katie had been Garrett's favorite, there was no mistaking that, but it had not embittered Jody toward Katie. They were very close and extremely protective of each other.

They had seen little of their father since his marriage last December, and while the support checks arrived each month without fail, he had allowed both of their birthdays to slip by unnoticed. Each time a check had arrived a couple of weeks later with a note saying he had been 'out-of-town', and asking if Mary would buy a belated gift and give them a hug, and he would see them soon... which he had not.

"I'm glad Jody's spending the night with Kevin." Katie said, as she settled herself close to her mother on the couch. "Tonight we can watch television together, just you and me," she paused, "and Ellie."

The doll had been named after Katie's friend, Ellen, who had moved to Wyoming last year.

"I'd like that. Would you like to watch the country music awards?"

"The one we watched last year where they win all the trophies, and wear pretty clothes, and they tear open the envelope and say, The winner is...?"

"That's the one."

"I liked that program." Katie hesitated as she thought about the program they had watched last year. "Those people are famous, aren't they?"

Mary nodded. "Yes, they are."

"Did you ever know anyone famous, Mommy?"

"Sure, a few people."

"Did they win any trophies?"

"One of them did. He had a whole shelf full."

"Oh, boy! A whole shelf full of trophies?" Katie's eyes sparkled. "He must have been really famous. Did he sing songs and make records?"

"Not when I knew him," Mary hedged.

"Then how did he win all the trophies?"

"He was a baseball player."

"You knew a baseball player?"

Mary nodded and smiled.

Katie was at a very impressionable age. "I like baseball players... I think I may marry one."

"Not soon, I hope." It was fun to just relax and talk small talk with Katie.

"No," Katie giggled, "I have to grow up first."

"Okay. Once you're all grown up, I guess it might be okay for you to marry a baseball player, but he better be a good one."

She reached for the remote control and smiled at the innocence of her daughter. Life was so simple to Katie right now. She dreaded the time when Katie would find out how wrong her childish assumption had been.

The awards show was about to begin, and she lifted Katie and Ellie into her lap. She knew Katie would not watch long. The sleepiness was already creeping into her eyes. She held her close and whispered "I love you."

"I love you too, Mommy."

As always, the ceremony was an elegant affair. Many recognizable faces were evident throughout the huge auditorium. Some were this year's nominees, hoping this would be their lucky night. Others were the music greats of years gone by, who had come to see old friends, and applaud the new winners.

They were all fashionably dressed in the latest, most chic styles. Mary thought of the conservative business suits her profession demanded, which she wore day in and day out. While she was impeccably dressed for the office and the courtroom, there was no sparkle nor glitter in her attire, and she wouldn't dare try some of the hairstyles she saw tonight, although it might be fun.

Katie was noticeably impressed with the beautiful dresses the women wore. She loved pretty clothes, although in a few years, this would probably give way to the sloppy sweats and faded jeans considered high fashion by the teen set.

"Oh, Mommy, look at the pretty lady in the blue dress!"

Mary had already seen her... Jessi McCrae was indeed beautiful, and she had a smile that seemed warm and real. It was obvious she had the full attention of the man at her side, and it wasn't hard to see why he was in love with her.

Mary's glance quickly shifted to him. He had not changed a great deal... but he had changed. He was still ruggedly handsome, but in a more polished way. He smiled often as he talked with Jessi, and there was no mistaking his feelings for her.

"Mommy, I like him. I hope he wins a trophy. Do you think he will?" Katie looked earnestly into her mother's eyes.

"I wouldn't be surprised, sweetheart. He's nominated for several awards." She turned her head so Katie would not see the tears in her eyes.

"Well, you can tell me in the morning. I have to go to bed now. I'm sleepy." Her voice ended in a slow yawn.

As Mary tucked her in, Katie murmured, "Goodnight, Mommy." Then she drew Ellie close and said, "Goodnight, Ellie," and as her voice trailed off, Mary heard her whisper, "Goodnight, Jody".

It was another big night for Jack and Jessi. They won every award for which they were nominated. At one point she almost turned off the television. It pained her to see the love in Jack's eyes for someone else... a love that once had been hers.

Not once, but twice, she had lost him... Once because of her own foolish impatience, and once because of a horrible twist of fate. She would not get another chance... She knew that... Now he belonged to Jessi... heart and soul.

Yet, she could not turn away. She had to watch... She tried to block out Jessi McCrae's face and make this her own private reverie with Jack, but she could not. Jessi was always there. There was no removing her from the picture. She was a very real part of what was happening in Nashville tonight, and she was a very real part of Jack's life.

When Jack stepped up to the podium to accept the award for *Song of the Year*, the cameras focused on him, and for a moment it was as though he were looking directly at her. And she saw him, not as he looked tonight, but in a baseball uniform on a pitching mound in Chattanooga, as she cheered from the stands... They were young and terribly in love, and the world was theirs for the taking.

Quickly the scene changed... It was the last time she had seen him... He had come to bring the baseball glove for Jody, and they had stood by Jody's bed, realizing that had it not been for the accident, they would have had a second chance.

But that was a long time ago. Now there were no more chances for her and Jack. It was all over except for one thing, and no matter what happened in either of their lives, that would remain.

She cut off the television, removed the tape from the v.c.r., and climbed the stairs to her bedroom. She carefully placed the tape in the back of her dresser drawer and then went to look in on Katie.

As Katie slept peacefully, Mary silently observed each feature of her delicate face. Finally, she pulled up the blanket and kissed the smooth forehead of her daughter.

And, although Katie was sound asleep and did not hear, Mary leaned over her and whispered, "Katie, your daddy was just named *Entertainer of the Year*."

CHAPTER 35

MARCH 12, 1987

For three days the Minnesota snow had fallen without ceasing and showed little sign of stopping. The daytime temperature barely got above zero, and each night new record lows were set. The street crews were working around the clock to keep the main highways clear, but the streets were still virtually impassable. It was one of the worst snowstorms Minneapolis had seen in years, and almost the entire city had been shut down.

The band had been scheduled to do a concert the previous evening at the Metrodome, but like everything else in town, it had been canceled. The way she felt right now, she really didn't care. Her sinuses were giving her a fit, and the last thing she wanted to do was go on stage before fifty thousand screaming fans. Earlier in the day, she had run down to the corner drug store to get something for her sniffling aching head, and the harsh arctic wind beat upon and burned her already red face. She was not used to this kind of weather, as it rarely snowed in Ft. Payne, and when it did, it was nothing like this frozen city they call Minneapolis.

She couldn't ask for her career to be going better. She had been named Female Vocalist of the Year, and her last album had two songs that had gone to number one on the charts and another that had broken into the top ten. The band had just finished recording their third album, which would be released in early June. She was so proud of the new album and felt it was their best work yet. Jack had written most of the songs and had sung with her on three of the cuts, including the title cut, *ALWAYS*.

She missed him so much. She had become spoiled by his constant presence with all the touring they had done the last few years. He had taken a couple of months off to work on the songs for the new album, and following the recording, he had stayed in Nashville to tie up a few loose ends.

It had been a year and a half since her heart attack, and everything was going fine. The doctor said it had been a mild one and with proper medication and regular checkups, she should live to 'be an old lady'.

She had just gotten back to her hotel room and was staring out the window, trying to figure out something to do with herself. She turned the radio on in time to catch the latest weather report. The meteorologist said it was -8 degrees with a wind chill factor of -37. The Minneapolis airport was shut down, and the airport officials had no idea when they would re-open.

As she stared out at the frozen city, her mind started to wander, and as it often did, it quickly found Jack. He was never far from her thoughts, and as she thought how nice it would be to be snowed in with him, the phone rang.

"I was just thinking about you!" She spoke into the receiver.

Just the sound of his voice lifted her from her wintry blahs.

For weeks he had pleaded with her to take some time off, and it appeared that finally he had caught her at the right time. He told her he had the chance to rent a beach house for a whole month on a private beach in Florida.

"Would you like to join me?"

"Florida?" Jessi laughed. "I'm a big star now... remember? Make it Malibu and I might consider it."

"It's either Florida or Minneapolis, Miss Feisty, and I know you really love all that snow... Don't worry about it. I'll call Tanya Tucker or somebody that's not 'too big a star' to go to Florida."

She could almost see the grin on his face.

"Well, Jess, I'll call you when we get back. Bye!"

"You're not going anywhere without me, especially with her." She pretended to be mad.

"Do I hear a hint of jealousy?"

She did not validate the question with an answer. The thought of a sunny beach and Jack, after having been stuck in this frozen igloo for the past three days, was pure heaven. She yearned to feel his arms around her and the warm caress of his lips as he drew her close.

"If I can just get out of this snowbank of a city, you've got a deal."

*　　*　　*　　*　　*

Her plane touched down at Tampa International Airport at 4:45 Saturday afternoon. It was a beautiful Florida day, with balmy temperatures in the upper eighties. Jack watched from the observation deck as the passengers debarked. Some were businessmen in light summer suits, but most were vacationers in shorts and tank tops, looking as if they were ready to walk right out of the plane and onto the beach... Then there was Jessi.

Standing at the foot of the steps Jack saw this little homesick Eskimo, or so it appeared. She was wearing an off white turtleneck sweater, a long plaid wool skirt and fur lined designer boots, and draped over one arm was a full-length leather coat. She was clutching the big bag she always carried in one hand and a fur-trimmed hat in the other. Jack started to smile, and as he approached her, he couldn't help laughing out loud.

"Wasn't sure if it was you or Davy Crockett."

"It was 8 degrees when I boarded the plane in Minneapolis, I'll have you know, and I was very properly dressed, and if you'll just stop laughing, maybe no one will notice."

She had changed planes in Nashville, and the rest of the passengers headed south had no reason to dress so warmly. Jack pulled her close and hugged her, still laughing at the sight she made. It didn't make any difference to him how she was dressed. She was here, and he loved her, and that was all that mattered.

She was aware of the strange glances from the properly dressed Florida travelers, as she waited for what seemed an eternity before her luggage made its appearance on the revolving track.

Jack moved close to her as they stood waiting while the rows of luggage moved past them, and discreetly whispered, "That security guard over there has his eye on you. I think he believes you're an Iranian spy."

She gave him a smirk. "I'll take care of you later, smart guy. Right now all I want is my luggage and a ladies room."

A short time later, she emerged from the ladies room wearing white shorts, a nautical striped top, and multi-colored sandals, and looking very much the proper beach vacationer.

Jack smiled approvingly. "Hey, pretty lady. What happened to Suzy Snowflake?"

Once more he put his arm around her and they headed for the parking lot. The Florida sun shined warmly down upon them, and they were tremendously happy, and Minneapolis seemed far away.

As they drove along Highway 60 between Tampa and Santa Laurel Beach, Jessi felt a peacefulness she had not felt in months. It was good to be out of the city and away from the crowds... God, she loved this man in the seat next to her. He was so giving, so warm and tender, so gentle.

Little was said as they drove along the coast on the narrow two-lane blacktop. Their communication was the warm, loving smiles they from time to time exchanged, as they held hands between the seats. The sun setting in the western sky looked like a huge orange ball of fire in the distance, as it separated the harsh ocean waves from the soft blue sky. The horizon was painted various shades of yellow and orange, and while it signaled the close of the day to most, to Jack and Jessi it was the beginning of a beautiful vacation together.

The beach house was cozy and inviting. It sat on a hill overlooking the Gulf of Mexico and had a large kitchen with an old fashioned round dinner table in the center. In the living room there was a mantle which framed a fireplace that would be perfect for those still cool nights. It was quaint and romantic. They could lie in bed with the windows open on warm nights and hear the gentle roar of the ocean. And on cooler nights, they could cuddle up on the big Indian rug in front of the fireplace and spend the night in each other's arms, watching the red and gold embers slowly melt away, long after the flames had died down.

After giving her the tour of the house, he took her hand in his and led her down the winding row of steps that led to the beach. He untied his tennis shoes, so he could feel the soft sand under his feet, and she slipped out of her sandals and slid her arm through his as they strolled down the beach. She felt a peaceful sense of well being as she leaned her head on Jack's shoulder.

A gentle breeze blew in from the ocean, and the pale moonlight reflected off the waves, forming an aura around two lovers, who stopped from time to time to kiss and cling to each other.

* * * * *

The first day of their vacation was relaxed and carefree. There were no schedules, no telephone calls, just the two of them alone in their own private paradise.

Jessi was feeling a bit of jet lag, and they were both tired from the day before, so they slept until mid morning. She was usually the early riser, but today Jack awakened first. He brought her a glass of pineapple juice and sat beside her on the bed.

"Hey, Goldilocks. You're sleeping away your vacation."

Slowly, she rolled over on her back and smiled up at him. "What time is it?"

"It's 10:30."

She took the glass of juice and grinned. "I could get used to this." She was strong and self-reliant, and didn't expect to be waited on, but today it was nice to be pampered.

She brushed her hair, tied it back, and slipped into a royal blue bikini, and they headed for the beach. Jack was wearing aqua trunks, and his body was golden brown from the Florida sun.

The night had been cool, but the mid-day sun warmed their bodies as they walked hand in hand down the beach. It was a slow 'do-what-you-will' kind of day, and they were enjoying it to the fullest. It was a time for being together... for sharing and loving... just the two of them, as though the rest of the world didn't exist.

Jessi was usually surrounded by people and she couldn't remember when she had known such blissful privacy. Being alone here with Jack was the nearest thing to heaven she could imagine. Santa Laurel was a private beach on the gulf. They saw no people and only an occasional fishing boat, almost too far out for the naked eye to see.

Once she stopped and pressed her body close to his and reached up to kiss him.

"Watch that stuff," he smiled down at her. "It gives me lewd thoughts." Then he wrapped her in his arms and pulled her close and kissed her again as the sun caressed their bodies, and the gentle ocean breeze played in their hair.

After the long, peaceful walk on the beach, they sat in the glider on the back deck, sharing a pitcher of limeade and eating cashews. Jessi's nose was as red as a beet, and Jack called her 'Rudolph'.

"I should have worn my beach hat. I think I'll go in and use some lotion and take a nap."

"Are you okay?" He asked, as a look of concern crossed his face. It wasn't like Jessi to take a nap in the middle of the day.

She smiled. "I'm fine. I'm still a little tired from the flight, and that crazy man in my bed last night didn't let me get much sleep."

He followed her into the house and turned down the bed for her while she covered her nose with cream.

"Now you look like Bozo, The Clown."

She looked up at him and wrinkled her white nose, and smeared some of the cream on his chin.

"Stop playing around, pretty lady or your plans for a nap might get put on hold."

It was tempting, very tempting, but there would be time for that later.

"Now get out of here," she smiled and playfully tossed a pillow at him as he ducked out the door.

She slipped out of her bikini and slid between the smooth sheets. She had never slept nude in her life, but it felt wonderful. She felt such complete freedom here in this place. She would get a quick nap. Then they would have the rest of the day together with no one to interfere... something that didn't happen often... There was always someone around or at least not far away. And as she fell asleep, her thoughts were of Jack and how much she loved him.

*　　*　　*　　*　　*

A warm breeze blew in from the ocean as he set the table. They were both outdoors people, and it would be nice to have dinner on the back terrace, surrounded by the beauty of the sea, and silhouetted by the golden sunset over the waves.

He had planned this dinner for weeks and wanted everything to be perfect for Jessi. The steaks were marinating, and he put the potatoes on the grill to bake slowly, then finished preparing the salads and went inside.

Jessi was still asleep, and he paused in the doorway and gazed at her. She looked so beautiful as she slept, so peaceful, and content. This was what he wanted to give her, a lifetime of peace and contentment.

As if sensing his presence, she opened her eyes and smiled.

"I smell food and it smells wonderful."

"I hired a chef from the other island, but I was beginning to think you planned to sleep through dinner." He replied facetiously.

"Not on your life." She started to get up and then remembered she was naked and hesitated.

Jack grinned. "I'm learning more about you all the time."

"Go away, smart guy," she teased back, "and let me take a shower and get dressed. I'm ready for those steaks."

A little while later as he lit the candles on the dinner table, he heard the hinges of the screen door creak and turned to see her. She looked like a princess. Her light blue, pinstriped sundress was gathered at the waist, emphasizing her trim figure. The dress was light and cool, and cut low, revealing the top of her ample breasts.

Her hair was swept up in a loose French braid, exposing her neck and bare shoulders. Wisps of soft curls framed her face, highlighting her beautiful smile, a smile that seemed to come from within. He stared at her, wondering if she had any idea how much he loved her.

She felt his awestruck eyes upon her. There was something in the way he looked at her... something different... a strange look of uncertainty.

The back of her neck tingled, and she shivered as goose bumps ran up and down her spine. She had known him for a long time. She had seen him hurt, and she had seen him indifferent, and sometimes 'mad as Hell', but she had never seen him unsure of himself.

"Honey, what's wrong?" She reached over and laid her hand on top of his.

For a moment he said nothing. In the background the steaks sizzled, and an ice cube jiggled in the tea pitcher.

All the things he had planned to say had left him, but the look on his face said it all. He looked deep into her eyes and said, "Jess, I love you...

I want to spend the rest of my life with you." Then he pulled a small velvet box from his pocket. "Will you marry me?"

The words were simple, but profound.

A smile spread across her face. Now she understood what this evening was all about. "Oh Jack!... Yes! Yes!"

And he slipped the ring on her finger.

She looked first at the beautiful diamond ring, then at Jack, and with tears glistening in their eyes, they clung to each other, both ecstatically happy.

* * * * *

Today marked the midpoint of their month long vacation. She could hardly believe they had been here two weeks. The time flowed gently by... long, leisurely days of contentment. She could not remember when she had felt so at peace with life, so safe and secure, and so loved.

They had made a lifetime commitment to each other... a commitment that knew no limits, and while they were not yet married, they felt a deep sense of oneness, and she knew she would never be alone again. She was part of someone... someone she loved with all her heart and soul.

While they were never far apart, each realized the need of the other to have some time to themselves, and that was what she was doing this morning. Jack was still asleep. It was a habit he had acquired from many years of late baseball games and shows that ran far into the night.

She had performed just as many late night shows and had every reason to lie in bed long after the morning sun showed its face, but she seldom did. She was a morning person... Jack was a night person. But it presented no problem, as it gave each of them their quiet time to think their own thoughts and dream their own dreams, and being the strong individuals they were, this was important.

As she sat on the deck overlooking the ocean, she was still dressed in the thin Vanity Fair nightgown that fell to just above her knees. The early morning breeze felt wonderful upon her body. It blew her hair back from her face, and she tasted the salt on her lips, as she sat with one golden leg stretched out in front of her and the other dangling over the banister.

Some days she went for an early morning walk on the beach, strolling along the edge of the water, allowing the white foamy surf to run over her feet. She liked to stand in the drift and look out to sea, and watch the sun rise in the distance and begin its daily trek across the sky. It was fun to stand with her feet planted firmly and feel the sand wash out from between her toes, as the undertow carried the white foam back out to sea.

The cold water rippled across her feet and splashed upon her legs, inviting her to wade out farther. Sometimes she accepted the invitation of the sea, and holding her nightgown up, she waded out deeper until an unexpected wave rolled in and broke upon her, soaking her. Then she swam along in the gentle water, her gown drifting up over her shoulders and her blonde hair drawing up into wet corkscrews, while chill bumps covered her body. It made her feel exhilarated and alive.

And then, realizing Jack would be worried if he knew she was out there alone, she would wade out of the water and head back to the house with the filmy nightgown plastered against her body. Once Jack had awakened earlier than usual and was standing on the deck watching her as she came back to the house looking like a drowned rabbit.

"You'd make a nice centerfold for Hugh Hefner," he grinned, as he watched. The wet nightgown clung to her, revealing every curve of her smooth firm body. Her brown nipples, made hard by the cold seawater, protruded from underneath the thin wet gown, and suddenly she felt very sensuous.

But this morning the lure of the ocean was not as strong, and her thoughts were not of action, but of reflection.

It seemed ages since she was snowed in in Minneapolis, and since the recording session in Nashville. It seemed like another world... another time. This was her world now... this wonderful 'place in the sun' with Jack. She knew it could not go on forever, but she wanted it to. The rest of the world and its problems seemed far away.

It was their world that mattered... hers and Jack's, and here on this tranquil island she had found a happiness that before she had only dreamed of.

She had loved Jack for a long time, but they had not always had complete freedom to express their love. Here there were no restrictions. They were free to love and laugh and play as they wished. Sometimes they played Lover's Tag and chased each other through the sand and waves until one finally caught the other. Then they would collapse together on the warm sand, their hearts racing as the cool ocean breeze glided gently across their bodies. Then he would take her in his arms and kiss her slowly, passionately. First her lips, then her neck, which gave her the strongest sensations. Then they would make love... uninhibited love, each giving of themselves completely, until at last, their passions satiated, they lay in each other's arms.

This morning she did not care to walk on the beach. She only wanted to sit on the deck and sense the nearness of the man she loved so much, and later hear the creak of the screen door when he came out to join her, and look up into his face and feel the warmth of his lips on hers.

* * * * *

March 29 was Jessi's birthday, and they went into town for dinner. It was the first time they had left the island since their arrival, and when Jack first mentioned it, she had been reluctant to leave. But as the day wore on, she found she was looking forward to it... It was like a real date. She dressed in her prettiest spring dress and wore white sling pumps and white, gold-trimmed earrings with a matching bracelet.

"Wow!" he exclaimed when he saw her, and the look in his eyes told her how beautiful he thought she looked. She splashed her neck and shoulders with his favorite fragrance, and they were on their way.

Jack had chosen *The Light House* for Jessi's birthday dinner. It was elegantly furnished and just the place for a romantic dinner date. They sipped champagne and held hands across the table while they waited for their food to arrive. The prime rib was delicious and the tiny, cloverleaf rolls covered with real butter reminded her of her grandmother's.

To the right of the main dining room was a dance floor with a band playing both contemporary and golden oldies music. When they had finished their dinner, she folded her napkin and said, "Jack, let's dance."

"You'll be sorry. I'm a real klutz," but seeing how much she wanted to dance, he smiled and said, "What the heck."

He led her out onto the ballroom floor, and they flowed with the music as he held her close.

"You are not a klutz. You're a very good dancer. I can't believe in all the years we've known each other that we've never been dancing."

"I can... We never had time. We had to practice."

They stopped to rest and get something to drink, and Jessi continued the conversation. "Did you ever think during those early days on the road that one day we'd do something crazy like getting married?"

A serious look came across his face, and his answer was a question, "Truth?"

"Truth," she responded.

"I didn't want to marry anybody. I just wanted to see you go to the top. I knew you could do it, and I wanted to be around to see it happen. I was just as ambitious as you were. I wanted us to be the best in the business. I admired your talent, and you were pleasant to work with. But marry you? No way! I wasn't the marrying kind."

She was grinning mischievously as he revealed all.

"Then one day I realized I was involved in more than a business venture. I was crazy in love with you. I don't know how or when it happened, but I'm glad it did."

Then it was her time.

"I'm not sure when I first knew I loved you either, but I think that Christmas at your house was the beginning. You stood in the doorway drinking a cup of coffee and talking to your mom. Then there was the night we sat alone in that chilly hotel lobby in Asheville. I was down to my last booking, broke, with no money to pay the band. And you assured me everything was going to be all right. Suddenly I was the richest girl in the world because you cared, and I hoped in time that you would come to love me as I loved you."

They sat out the next dance, but when the band began to play *Stardust*, Jack led her back on the floor. They danced slow, and he held her close and nestled his chin in her hair. Once he thought he felt a tremor go up her spine as their bodies touched in graceful movement.

When the song ended, she said, "Let's go home, Jack... Thanks for such a special evening."

When they reached the car and were safe inside, once more he took her in his arms and whispered, "Happy Birthday, Jess."

They drove in silence along the moonlit beach road, holding hands between the seats. Once Jessi yawned.

"Tired?" he asked softly.

"A little."

"We're almost home."

*   *   *   *   *

It was finally working out. After all the hurt and heartache in his life, he was truly happy. He was in love with the most beautiful woman in the world, and she loved him back. They had known each other almost five years, and they were best friends, as well as lovers. Their love was real... the kind from which marriages and families are made, and he knew they would love each other until their dying day.

It had been a special day. They had not done anything spectacular, just the simple things that life is all about. She had made lasagna covered with Mozzarella cheese for dinner, and he had helped clear the table and wash the dishes.

They went out on the deck, but the late evening air was too cool to linger. So they came back inside and Jack lit the gas logs and turned on the stereo. They sat on the rug in front of the fire and listened to the strains of Harry Chapin's *Cats in the Cradle* and hummed along. Jessi thought how wonderful things were. She loved this man sitting beside her with all her heart and knew he loved her. She did not need to worry about that changing or about him being unfaithful. Jack Roberts was a 'lifer'. When he loved, he loved forever!

They sat in silence as the music continued, her hand in his. His eyes were fixed on her engagement ring, and as he softly stroked her fingers, she looked up at him and spoke.

"I was thinking of our early days together on the road... the hard times."

Jack shook his head. "What brought that on? Most of those I'd like to forget."

"No you wouldn't, not really. They are part and parcel of who we are. And looking back, they weren't so bad."

He grinned. "Pretty bad, I would say. We didn't even get chicken on Sunday, maybe pickle and pimento loaf, and sometimes we couldn't even afford that."

Jessi burst into a laugh as she remembered the pickle and pimento loaf days.

Few bands were making any money in those days, and they were no exception to the rule. Hopefully you made enough to cover your expenses and buy enough gas to get to the next town. Your biggest goal was to do well enough and get enough exposure where you were playing to get your next gig in a little bigger place where more people would see you, and hope that someday you'd get discovered.

Usually the club or tavern where you were playing furnished your supper, and everybody stayed out half the night and slept through breakfast, so breakfast was no problem, but the big challenge of the day was lunch. Occasionally the club or tavern might feed you a hamburger for lunch, but most of them weren't open that early, so they usually had to fend for themselves.

There was not enough money to go to McDonald's every day, although in those days McDonald's hardly cost anything. So they would go down to the local Winn Dixie and ante up their change in the parking lot. Then they would buy a loaf of bread and a pack of bologna or a jar of peanut butter to make sandwiches for the whole band.

On Fridays, if they could come up with an extra dime or fifteen cents from each band member, instead of bologna, they would splurge and buy pickle and pimento loaf.

"Yeah, but the worst part was while you guys went to the store to buy the bologna, you sent me to McDonald's to ask for the little packets of mustard and mayonnaise to go on the sandwiches."

"Well, why not? They gave them away for free," he teased.

"Yeah, to their customers... Their 'paying' customers!"

"Well, they never turned you down. Did they?"

"No, but I hated to do that worse than anything. I still don't know why I had to be the one to beg for mustard." She frowned, recalling the embarrassment she had felt long ago.

"You looked better in those tight shorts than me and Bobby did. Besides, I think he and I were the only people in history to be banned from McDonald's for stealing mustard."

"You should have been!"

They smiled as they thought of the crazy times they had shared on the road, while Jim Croce's *Photographs and Memories* played softly on the stereo.

"Do you remember the time Buddy pawned his guitar for a case of beer?" Jessi grinned, knowing the remembrance of that incident would get Jack's goat.

"I should have killed him! We had a show to do that night, and he comes in drunk as a skunk, with no guitar. I said, 'Where's your guitar?' and the fool had pawned it... It hadn't been long since I bought the thing back for him, and here he goes out and does the same thing again. I should have killed him."

"You probably would have if I hadn't been there to settle you down." She paused as she thought to herself. "You should have been ashamed of yourself, after what he did for you!"

"What he did for me!... He was the one that got drunk and pawned his damn guitar... He never did anything for me, but make my life a living Hell... Bailing him out of jail... Trying to sober him up long enough to do a show."

"Maybe so, but, even drunk, Buddy was the best guitar picker in the band."

"I'll give you that! And if he could ever stay sober long enough, he could be the best picker in Nashville." Even in his anger, Jack could not help but defend his friend's ability. "But what's this stuff about 'after what he did for me'. All he had done was get drunk, pawn his guitar and was once again about to blow the show for all of us."

A serious look came over her face. "You don't know, do you? You really don't know?"

Jack stared back at her, frustrated by the remembrance of Buddy's lack of responsibility, but more frustrated that the remembrance of those distant times had seemingly spoiled the wonderful time he and Jessi had been sharing only moments before.

He looked at the stunned expression on her face, as she repeated, "You really never knew!"

"Never knew what?" He didn't have a clue to what she was talking about.

Then she told him the story behind the story, which he had never known before.

"Jack, Honey... The case of beer wasn't the only thing Buddy pawned his guitar for."

He waited for her to continue.

"He bought you a present!"

"He never gave me a present." The confusion was apparent in his eyes, and Jessi was loving every minute of it.

"He was too scared to! And I don't blame him. The way you were hollering at him and calling him a drunken fool for selling his guitar. I wouldn't have given you a present either."

"Okay," Jack said calmly. "What was this present that Buddy pawned his guitar for that I never got?"

"Buddy had heard you guys talking baseball and somehow the subject of baseball cards came up. He overheard you say you didn't have any of your cards from your playing years. You know Buddy, he thought it was a shame that you pitched in the Major Leagues and didn't have a single one of your baseball cards. So he went out and bought you one."

"Okay. That's nice of him, but a *'74 Jack Roberts'* baseball card probably wouldn't cost over a quarter, if that much. Why did he have to pawn his guitar?"

"Well at first, he was just going to buy the card, but the man at the card shop told him he could take both cards from the two years you were with the *Jazz*, laminate them, and mount them on this big walnut plaque, with the *Jazz* mascot in the center and your name and the years you played engraved in gold at the bottom."

Jack sighed as he thought how this sounded exactly like something Buddy would do. "How much did it cost him?"

"A hundred bucks." Jessi answered the question in the same somber tone he had asked it. "You know Buddy. He's always wanting to do something for somebody, especially the people who've helped him." She paused as she saw the troubled look in Jack's eyes. "He said he knew he shouldn't have spent that much money, but you had always done so much for him. You bailed him out of jail. You got him the job with me, even knowing he still drank. But, mostly, you believed in him when no one else did. He knew he had caused you a lot of trouble, and it was his way of saying thanks for being his friend... He really respects you, Jack."

"So why did he have to go get drunk? Why didn't he just explain it?"

"You know Buddy. He acts without thinking a sometimes. He told the man he was a struggling musician and as much as he wanted to get you the plaque, he didn't have the money. Then the man told him he could pawn his guitar, and he would give him the plaque and fifteen dollars to boot... Buddy couldn't turn it down, especially when the man offered to throw in an extra *'74 Jack Roberts* card for Buddy."

"After he left the card shop with your plaque and his hero's card securely in his wallet, he walked back towards the hotel. He was so proud of what he had done. He had finally found a way to do something special for you. Then it hit him... He had pawned his guitar, and he knew you would kill him. He got scared and didn't know what to do. He knew the man at the card shop wouldn't let him have it back, not without a hundred bucks, and if he'd had a hundred bucks, he wouldn't have pawned it in the first place. He just wanted to do something nice for you, and now he had blown it... Big time!... So he did what he always does when he gets scared. He got drunk."

"Why didn't he just explain it?"

"Would it have mattered if he had?"

"I don't know." Jack shook his head in frustration, and then admitted, "You're right. I probably would have been the same way."

She smiled at his honesty.

"But he could have at least explained it."

"He did. He explained it to me."

"Yeah, and that's when you took the next month's grocery money and paid his guitar out of hock." The remembrance of that night rang clear.

Jack sat back in silence, looking at nothing in particular, seeing only the allegiance of a true, yet sometimes misguided friend.

"So whatever happened to the plaque?"

"Buddy sent it to your Mom and explained to her what had happened. She said she would give it to you when you settled down." Jessi started to smile and added, "I guess you've never settled down."

As the evening continued, so did the stories. They had shared so many experiences. They had starved together in the early days, as most young musicians do. They had shared the happiness when success finally came their way. They had shared the loneliness of living on the road and being away from their families, and they had experienced the warmth and closeness that comes with traveling and living day in and day out with the people in the band until they became family as well. They had shared the good times and the bad... the successes and the failures... the happiness and the hurt. And tonight seemed to be a time for reminiscing. As Jess had said, it was all part of who they were... a very real part.

Again she spoke of Buddy. "I think that incident may have been the turning point for him. I made him pay it back, every penny of it. I took it out of his check, $25.00 a week. After he paid his part of the lodging, that didn't leave a lot. So he had to choose whether he wanted to eat or drink. I'm proud of him, Jack, and one day he'll get the recognition he deserves in Nashville. I'm sure of it."

"I hope so. In spite of all our problems, he's still the best friend I've got in the world, except for you."

Jessi started to yawn. It was almost 4:30. Where had the evening gone?

He smiled at her. "Hey, pretty lady, I think it's past your bedtime."

She returned the smile.

He wrapped his arms around her and picked her up, and as he held her there in front of the sofa, he kissed her.

"I love you, Jack," she whispered, as tears of joy welled up in her eyes.

"I love you too, Mrs. Roberts."

She looked surprised.

"I just wanted to see how it was going to sound."

The glow on her face brightened, and she wrapped her arms tighter around his neck and whispered. "It sounds nice... very nice." Then she yawned once more and said, "Let's go to bed."

He carried her to the bed and laid her down softly, and she pulled him down beside her, and they held each other, as though they would never let go.

As usual, she drifted off to sleep first. He had often told her she could go to sleep in the wake of an approaching hurricane, while he, on the other hand, had to unwind and let go of the day.

He slipped his arm out from underneath her tiny waist and watched her as she slept, and smiled as he remembered the first time they had slept together. It was at his house on Christmas Eve, except she didn't sleep in his arms. She slept on the couch, while he slept under the Christmas tree and Buddy and Bobby stretched out on the living room floor.

Then he thought of other times the four of them had shared sleeping quarters during the early days when they did well to afford one room in some dinky motel. She got the bed, and the guys slept on the floor.

He could hear her now... "Okay, fellows, don't any of you get cute. I'm too sleepy to defend my honor." And she had never had to.

The moonlight shining through the window gave their bedroom a soft glow, and in its light he noticed the sparkle of her engagement ring. He longed for the time when he would place another one beside it, a simple band of gold. She emitted a sigh, like the soft purring of a contented kitten, and as he turned on his side, he heard the gentle patter of rain against the windowpane. And it soon lulled him to sleep.

*   *   *   *   *

The call had come early Tuesday morning. It was Graham Price.

"I'm sorry to bother you, Jack, but there's a problem with the album... Can you come to Nashville?"

Graham explained that while it wasn't a major problem, they couldn't continue with the release until they worked it out.

Jack wanted Jessi to go with him, but she declined.

"That's your territory. I don't know anything about production... Why don't we fly to Atlanta together? Then I'll check on things at home and go by and see your Mom."

They kissed good-bye at the airport in Atlanta, and she transferred to a flight to Chattanooga, and he to a flight to Nashville.

"I'll miss you," he whispered.

"Me, too," she whispered back, as they clung together, resenting the brief separation.

The problem was a question of mixing on a couple of songs on the album. The producer had one idea, while the engineer had another. It was soon solved, and by midday Thursday Jack was on a plane back to Florida. He had talked to Jessi earlier, and he would pick her up at the airport on Friday.

Thursday night was the longest night of his life. He was lonely, and the bed seemed cold and empty without her. He and Jess weren't even married yet, but how quickly they had become as one, and without her, it was as though a part of him was missing.

Just before dawn he was awakened by the sound of thunder and rain coming down in torrents, and the day dawned gray and dreary. The morning dragged endlessly on, and the beach that was so beautiful only a few days before, now seemed cold and ugly. And the ocean, which was pleasant and peaceful when Jessi was there, now seemed to roar at him, as the waves crashed violently against the shore, as if preparing for battle.

Finally, about mid-morning the clouds disappeared, and the sun, which had felt so warm upon their bodies as they played together on the beach, now burned his skin and almost blinded his eyes in its intensity, as he stood silently and watched a lone sea gull slowly crawl across the sky.

He had done some fishing, using the nets and cages just as the man at the tackle shop had told him, and had caught enough for a clambake on the beach. It would be Jessi's 'Welcome Home' dinner, and after they ate, they would sit in the warm glow of the fire and hold each other and watch the sun slowly sink beyond the horizon. He wanted it to be a night neither of them would ever forget, not for the rest of their lives.

Her plane arrived ahead of schedule, and she was waiting in the lobby when he walked in. When she spotted him, she ran to him and hugged him tightly.

It was so good to be with him again and feel the warmth of his love. She never imagined how much she would miss him. They had been apart before, but it was different now. It was almost like they were married, and soon they would be. She had picked out a wedding dress in Chattanooga. She hoped he would like it.

The midday sun shined brightly overhead, as they pulled off the main highway onto the dirt road that led to the beach house. The sky was soft blue, interspersed with white fluffy clouds, the kind God decorates the sky with to create a perfect day. The storm was over, Jess was home, and everything was beautiful again.

It was the most wonderful day of her life... but now every day was wonderful. It must be true what they say... Happiness comes from within... and within, she was gloriously happy.

"How did things go?" She finally mentioned the reason for their separation.

"Fine. It wasn't really necessary for me to be there. They could have fixed it themselves. It was just a matter of deciding which sounded best, but you know Graham... It's a great album, Jess. It will get you another award. Mark my word."

"Jack, stop! I didn't do it by myself. I'm nothing without you and Buddy and Bobby. Whatever success I've had is because of the three of you. It's our album."

"Don't be so modest. You're the star. And this one's gonna go straight through the ceiling. I'm not kidding. It's the best one yet."

"Well, good. I'm glad. Now let me tell you what I've been doing." Once Jessi got started, there was no stopping her. It was plain to see she had had a good time with his mother. "She's happy about us, and she sends you her love. We went to the Catfish House for supper last night."

"My mom ate catfish?" Jack knew his mother better than that. She had never eaten catfish.

"No, but I did. She had fried chicken. We had such a good time. Jack, when it comes to moms, you picked the best."

"I didn't pick her. She picked me."

"I'd say she had to settle for what she got with you. But I picked you. So, I guess that makes us both winners."

"Yeah, some people have all the luck."

"I suppose so." She snuggled close to him and kept talking.

He had not seen her so full of herself in a long time.

"I slept in your bed."

"So, what's new?" He grinned mischievously. "I haven't been able to keep you out of my bed lately."

"I mean at your house."

"You didn't mess with my baseball cards. Did you?" He chided.

"I didn't dare. I know how cranky you are about 'your things'."

"I'm not cranky."

"Yes, you are, so I didn't touch a thing. I just lay there and stared at a poster of Mickey Mantle until I went to sleep."

Jack grinned. The poster had been on the wall since he was eleven.

Like the Energizer Bunny, Jessi kept on going. It was as if she was on a roll and couldn't stop. Suddenly she realized that Jack had pulled off the road and stopped the car. "Why are we stopping? Is something wrong?"

He didn't answer her question, but instead asked one of his own. "Did anyone ever tell you you're a chatterbox?"

"You have, lots of times... But why are we stopping?"

"Because I want to kiss you, and it's the only way I can get you to stop talking long enough to catch your breath."

"You already kissed me at the airport."

"Do I only get one a day?" He teased.

She smiled. "Well, maybe two on Sundays."

He pulled her into his arms, and she smiled up at him and continued to tease. He covered her mouth and drew her close, and she melted into his arms. For several minutes they held each other and kissed and whispered, "I love you."

Finally, she looked up into the warm brown eyes of the man who held her, and said softly, "Jack, let's go home."

When they reached the beach house, he came around to her side of the jeep to help her out. As he took her hand, he saw her in a strange, new way. He had noticed her at the airport and had 'listened to her' all the way home, but as she stepped down from the jeep, it was as though he were seeing her for the first time.

She was wearing a new spring dress in pastel shades of aqua, pink and violet. It had a white lace collar, and was light and dainty, flowing gently over the curves of her young, sensuous body. She was so beautiful. She always had been, but especially right now.

He could not take his eyes off her. What innocent sexuality she possessed. She could put on the scantiest nightgown or the sheerest teddy and still not appear as seductive as she did right now. She was so fresh and lady-like, so soft and pretty, so delicately refined.

She was well aware of the spellbinding effect she was having on him, and she felt like a young girl in love for the first time. She had never known anyone like him, and had never experienced such a deep, mature love.

She reached out to him and took him by both hands, breaking his dream-like state. Then warmly and passionately, she looked deep into his eyes and whispered, "Jack... Make love to me."

Then she fell into his arms and they held each other close. Finally he picked her up and carried her to the house. One of her white pumps fell off in the yard, but they did not stop to pick it up. The shoe was not important... Being together and sharing their love was all that mattered.

CHAPTER 36

The reflection of the love they had made radiated from their faces as they came down the path to the beach, carrying the last of the supplies for their clambake.

They had gotten a later start than they had planned, and the first signs of darkness were approaching. The sun was making its descent, and they paused to watch the huge orange ball gradually sink beyond the horizon and drop into the sea. Many evenings they had watched the sun set on Santa Laurel and each time it seemed more beautiful than before. And today was no exception. As the last tinge of orange disappeared from the horizon, Jessi slipped her arm around Jack's waist and breathed a soft sigh.

"Are you glad I brought you here?" He spoke softly.

"It's the most beautiful place I've ever seen. I hope we can come here again and again."

"We will," he promised. For a moment he hesitated. He had planned to surprise her, but sometimes the excitement of looking forward to something is even better than the surprise. "I've already reserved it for next year."

A look of pure delight showed in her eyes. "That's wonderful. I'd like to come every year on our anniversary."

She nestled her head on his shoulder and sighed once more, and he knew the sigh was a revelation of the happiness she felt. He always knew when she was happy. She would snuggle close, like a contented kitten, and a dewy mist would cover her eyes ever so slightly.

He held her close and kissed her.

"I love you," she whispered.

"I love you too, Babe."

For what seemed an eternity they clung to each other, listening to the peaceful lull of the ocean waves. There were no words to express the depth of their love, but their souls seemed to unite to express that which words could not.

After awhile and without warning, Jessi tickled him under his ribs, and as he laughed and tried to escape her playful mischief, he stumbled and fell in the sand, pulling her down with him.

For several minutes they giggled and frolicked in the sand like a couple of carefree teenagers. It was one of the things he loved about her.

She could be serious and romantic one moment, and mischievous and kittenish the next.

Finally, he pulled away.

"Now, if you'll behave yourself, I'll get a fire started so we can eat."

"You don't like to play in the sand?" She grinned impishly and pretended to pout.

"I love to play in the sand, but I also like to eat."

They prepared dinner and then sat on the blanket and enjoyed the delicious clams and broiled shrimp. After dinner they went for a walk down the beach. The stars had come out in all their heavenly splendor, and for a moment Jessi was reminded of some lines she had learned in school...

God's in his heaven, All's right with the world.

They strolled in silence in the soft moonlight, holding hands and engrossed in their own private thoughts of each other.

Finally, tired from the walking, they returned to the campsite and stretched out on the blanket. The fire had burned low, leaving only a bed of warm coals. The night air was cool and Jessi shivered. Jack put a couple of logs on the fire and wrapped the blanket around the two of them. The fire responded to the logs and crackled and soon cast a warm romantic glow.

As they stared into the fire, she spoke. "Jack, I've never been this happy in my life. Sometimes I can't believe all the good things that have happened to me, and the best part of all is loving you and knowing you love me." She paused a moment as a log shifted. "I want to get married as soon as we get home."

"I hoped you would say that." He smiled down at her as she snuggled closer under the blanket.

"Your mom and I picked out a wedding dress. I hope you'll like it."

"I'm sure I will. You would be my beautiful bride if you wore a tow sack."

They both giggled.

"Get serious, honey. I want to look beautiful."

"You are." And for a moment he tried to remember when he first knew he was in love with her.

"I want to have a church wedding... You don't mind, do you?"

"Of course not. I just want to marry you, babe. The 'where', 'when' or 'how' doesn't matter. I want you to be mine, forever."

"I already am," she assured, "I'm a 'lifer', so count on keeping me around a long time."

Again he kissed her, long and loving, and she snuggled close, lost in the love of the man she had waited a lifetime for.

Finally, she looked up, again misty eyed, and said, "Jack, I love you so much, but don't kiss me again like that or we'll never get this wedding planned."

"You said you were mine."

"I am."

"Then why can't I kiss you?" He teased.

She didn't answer. Instead, she reached out to him and pulled him close, kissing him and allowing him to kiss her, each knowing they had found that 'once-in-a-lifetime' love.

Finally, he spoke. "Do you want to get married in Fort Payne?"

"I don't think so. I don't have anyone left there anymore, except for a few school friends... I'd like to get married in Chattanooga, if that's okay with you... Your mom said she would take care of the reception."

So they had it all worked out. He grinned as he thought of the two women he loved most in the world planning his wedding. Now he knew why she had wanted to go see his mom. Whatever they did was fine with him. He was just glad the two of them were such good friends.

"And Jack, I want to have a baby as soon as possible, a little girl."

"What's wrong with a boy?"

"Nothing," she grinned coyly, "but I already have one of those... He's six foot two, good looking, and he gives me goose bumps every time he kisses me." She paused, and the look on her face, though impish, clearly showed the unreserved love she felt for him. Then she continued. "I just thought a little girl would be nice."

"If that's what you want, then we'll have a little girl... Help me get this stuff gathered up, and we'll go to the house and see what we can do about it."

"Jack, is that all you think about?"

"Mostly," he teased, "except, sometimes I think of you."

It was easy being with Jessi. They could love, and they could laugh, and they could tease.

They sat in the soft glow of the fire and continued to make plans for the wedding and their future... Then suddenly he saw a look of terror come across her face.

"Jess, what's wrong?"

She did not answer... She was trying, but the words would not come... Fear showed in her eyes. Her skin was pallid, and she was sweating profusely.

He tried to lay her back on the blanket, but she resisted, and he realized it made her breathing more labored. Finally, she motioned toward the pocket of her jacket, and he found the bottle of pills, which apparently she went nowhere without.

She held up two fingers, and he quickly placed the two white tablets under her tongue, and waited for the nitroglycerine to do its job. He knew the medicine usually worked quickly to dispel the pain. When he was with the Jazz, he had a coach that had suffered a heart attack. He carried the pills with him all the time, and all the fellows knew what to do if there was a problem... But Jessi had never mentioned that she carried the medicine.

She had said she was fine, and the doctor had said she was fine. But she wasn't fine. She was as white as a sheet, and her breathing was shallow and difficult.

Huge beads of sweat formed on her brow, and he tried to wipe them away. She still couldn't speak. Finally, she placed her hand over her chest, and her grimace told him the pain was severe.

"Hold on, Baby. The pills will relieve the pain in a few minutes. Then I'll go for help."

And with all the effort she could muster, she whispered, "Don't leave me!"

"I'm not going to leave you, Baby... I'm right here beside you... You'll feel better in a few minutes, and we'll get some help."

Although she was still pale, she seemed less anxious than she had earlier. Once she tried to smile, but she never took her eyes off him. All the strength seemed to have drained from her body, and as he held her hand, it was weak and limp.

He needed to go for help, but he couldn't leave her. Maybe in a few minutes the nitroglycerine would take effect. And then he would carry her to the house and call an ambulance. He tried to smile to reassure her and hoped the panic he felt inside did not show on his face. He had never felt so helpless in his life.

Then almost as quickly as the attack had come on, it began to subside. She was tired and spent from her ordeal, but her breathing seemed to be leveling off. He still wasn't sure she was out of danger, but her pain was easing. She was exhausted and lay almost motionless on the blanket as he patted her forehead with a wet beach towel.

Finally she turned to him and repeated. "Don't leave me!" It was almost as if she were pleading with him.

"Baby, I'm right here. You're going to be okay."

She looked up at him, relieved that he was there and had not left him to get help.

"Just lie here and rest, and after you're feeling better we'll get a doctor, but don't worry, I'm not going to leave you... I'll never leave you."

While it had been only a few minutes since the onset of the attack, it seemed like an eternity. He gently stroked her face and hair, as she clutched his other hand. As her breathing became more regular, she looked up at him and tried to smile.

"Jack, thanks for staying with me."

"Baby, don't try to talk right now. Just save your strength.

She ignored his warning and continued. "You've been so good to me," her breathing shortened, "and to Grandma... She loved you Jack."

"I know she did, Honey." He tried to quieten her to save her strength. "Just try to rest, okay? And then in a little while we'll drive into town and see a doctor."

But she spoke again.

"Nobody ever cared about me like you." Tears flowed from her eyes and spilled down her cheeks. "Nobody ever loved me like you do."

He struggled to hold back his own tears and bent close to whisper, "I love you."

As he did, her body jerked violently. She sat up suddenly, almost knocking him over. A look of terror filled her eyes. She turned toward him and tried to speak, but she couldn't. Her voice would not work. She struggled to speak, as if what she had to say was more important than the pain she was feeling. Finally, as if she had blocked out the heart attack for a few brief seconds, she began to move her mouth. There was little sound, faint whispers at best, but slowly and painfully she moved her lips to say what she had to say.

"I... love... you... Jack..."

Then she fell back onto the sand and she was gone.

*   *   *   *   *

He was in shock!... He couldn't believe it!... It was all a horrible dream!... It couldn't be true!

He tried her pulse... There was none.

He listened for a heartbeat... He heard none.

He started CPR immediately... He tried and he tried, begging her to respond... First for ten minutes... Then for twenty... Then, finally exhausted, he fell over on her.

It was no use... Jessi was gone.

The sight of her lying there on the sand was more than he could bear, so he gently gathered her up and held her there on the blanket where just moments before they had sat planning their wedding.

He cradled her in his arms and held her close, and wept openly. Deep, wrenching sobs came forth from his tortured soul... And there was only a sea gull to hear... and no one to care.

For a long time he rocked her lifeless form back and forth in his arms, as one gently shakes a no-longer-working timepiece, hoping the motion will start it to ticking again... Yet it never does.

The diamond on her finger sparkled in the glow of the fire, as tears dripped from his chin and onto her face... He tried to wipe them away, but it was no use. They trickled across her forehead and dampened her beautiful hair... But Jessi wouldn't mind. She had felt the dampness of his tears before.

She was gone... He knew it... There was no need to hurry... No doctor, no hospital could help... It was too late.

He would hold her awhile longer, and then do what had to be done... Once they came, they would take her from him, and he would never hold her again.

CHAPTER 37

The days following Jessi's death were the worst of Jack's life. He had gone back to the house he rented on the outskirts of Nashville. It was near Hendersonville, far removed from Music City Row. In the past the simple country setting had provided the peace and quiet he needed to write, but now there was no peace anywhere for him, only bleak emptiness that never seemed to go away.

And the dreams drove him crazy... He would toss and turn until the bed bore no semblance of ever having been made, and in the wee hours of the morning, he would finally doze off. Then the dreams would set in - crazy unreal dreams.

One time it would be Jessi. She was in the street, and a transfer truck was headed straight toward her. He was trying to cry out to warn her, but he couldn't make a sound. It was as though his vocal chords were paralyzed, and no sound would come... He was trying to get to her, but his legs refused to move.

Sometimes it was the huge eighteen-wheeler bearing down upon her and other times it was a motorcycle and the driver with the Hell's Angels jacket. But try as he might, he could never do anything to save her, and he would wake up screaming and wet with sweat.

Then there were the dreams that started out so pleasantly. They were children, and they were walking in the woods, and she was his little sister, except the face was always Jessi's. Suddenly he would look around to find she had disappeared. He would run frantically through the woods calling her name, but he couldn't find her.

Or they would be sitting on the steps of the house in Chattanooga, watching the fireflies and talking about their future together. Jessi would go inside to get them a coke or a glass of lemonade, and he would wait, and wait, and wait... but she would not come back. And then the house, where only moments before they had sat together, would be gone... And he would be standing alone on a pitcher's mound in Columbus, Georgia.

He had thought he could bury himself in his writing, but the words would not come. It all seemed so pointless now. Even if he could write beautiful lyrics, Jessi wasn't here to sing them, and without Jessi, the words were meaningless, hollow thoughts.

Sometimes when sleep would not come, he would get up in the middle of the night and try to write. He would play with words on paper all day long, and when the day was over, all he would have to show for his efforts was an overflowing wastebasket of crumpled paper. The ashtray would be filled with half-smoked cigarettes, and he wouldn't have eaten breakfast or lunch.

Though not really hungry, he would go to the kitchen to fix himself some supper only to find he hadn't been to the grocery store in weeks, and everything was stale or molded. Sometimes he would get in his truck and drive to the Waffle House for a hamburger and a glass of milk, or a waffle and more coffee, having already drunk a dozen or more cups during the day. Other times he would find a box of vanilla wafers that didn't appear to be molded, spread them with peanut butter and make another pot of coffee, and that would be supper. It didn't matter what he ate anyway. Nothing seemed to satisfy. Nothing could.

All of his life it seemed he had been stalked by loss. First Mary... then his baseball career... and now Jessi. In the past when one door closed, eventually another one opened, but this time he had lost everything. Jessi had been his reason for living, and now that reason was gone. There were no more doors to open.

Sometimes his mail went unopened for days. He had tried to read the notes of condolence, most of which were from friends he and Jessi had known in the music business. He wasn't sure if reading them helped or simply made his loss seem more acute. Finally he reached the point he could not bear to read them every day, and would let them accumulate until he felt better able to cope with the constant reminder that Jessi was gone.

There was one with a return address that read simply 2700 Sunbeam Avenue, Chattanooga, Tennessee. As he opened the note, he realized the handwriting looked strangely familiar. The stationery was the palest shade of pink and had a single white rose ensconced in a silver frame in the upper lefthand corner. The message read simply:

Jack,

> *I am so sorry. I know you must have loved her very much.*
>
> > *God Bless You,*
> > *Mary*

He wondered what she was doing in Chattanooga, and then remembered that Mary's mother had moved. The new address was probably hers. He read the note once more and placed it on the stack with the others. Maybe one day he would be able to thank all those who had expressed their sympathy. Right now he could not.

The days crept slowly by. Occasionally he would come up with some lyrics which seemed pretty good at the time, only to read them the next day and decide they were 'no damn good', and they would join the other crunched up paper previously consigned to the wastebasket... It was no use. The well was dry.

In the past he had done some of his best writing in times of personal despair, the long nights of the soul, they call them, when loneliness seems to be the only friend you have. A songwriter often draws from the intense emotions evoked by desperation and unfulfilled dreams to produce his best lyrics. It was out of such a time when Jack had felt isolated from and rejected by the world that he had written *A Little Bit of Me*. He had written it in a single sitting and had known from the start it was good. And it had been a big one for him.

It was at the close of another day when he stared at the wadded-up pages of nothingness which filled his wastebasket and spilled over onto the floor that he finally realized he could not make himself be creative. Either he was, or he was not. Right now, he was just banging his head against the proverbial brick wall. It was no use. Maybe someday the words would flow again, but right now they were all dried up inside him.

The next day he made no attempt to write. Instead, he began his day with a decent breakfast, and then started to clean house. He vacuumed and mopped and carried out garbage, and busied himself with simple household chores. It felt good to do something physical. He had been a bachelor for a long time and could look after himself rather well. He simply hadn't been doing it lately.

He had rented the house from another songwriter, who had told him it was a wonderful place to live, as well as to write.

"Nobody bothers you out here. They have too much trouble finding you." Curt had said.

Jack had spent a lot of his life on stage performing for one audience after another, and while he appreciated the fans, he was in many ways a private person. And this had proved to be a good place to withdraw from the world and the noise and clamor of the stage.

Jessi had loved to come here when she had the time, but Jessi had so little time. She had given herself so completely to her music and her fans, and had taken so little time for herself.

It had happened to Elvis, and Hank Williams, and Patsy Cline. They had all worked so hard and had devoted themselves intensely to their music. Then suddenly they were gone, and someone else enjoyed the fruits of their labor.

Life isn't fair! He thought. It just isn't fair!

Later that evening he sat on the porch. He had taken his tape player out, intending to listen to some Kristofferson and Harry Chapin tapes, but he never turned it on. Instead he listened to the myriad night sounds, and lost himself in his thoughts.

He thought of the long trip his life had taken from the south side of Chattanooga to Columbus, Memphis, Atlanta, and now this place they call Music City U.S.A. In many ways life had been good to him. Financially, he was set. The royalty checks came every month and would continue, whether or not he ever wrote another song.

He had invested his money well and should never have financial worries. He could have whatever he wanted in the way of material things, but sadly, the things he had wanted most in life were the things that money could not buy... And it was these he had been denied.

There were times when he felt a little bitter... A little bitter?... Hell, he felt a lot bitter... He hadn't been an evil person. He had tried to treat people right. He had never deliberately hurt anyone or anything.

Isn't there some justice in the system? He thought. If you do right by the world, isn't the world supposed to do right by you? Isn't there some unwritten law to this effect?

He remembered the words of his childhood Sunday School teacher, 'Miss Delores'. "Do unto others as you would have them do unto you." She didn't say that if you did right by others, everything would be all right for you, but at the time it had seemed it would.

Over and over the questions came, but the answers did not. For a long time he sat with his head in his hands pondering the whys and wherefores of life.

Finally he lifted his head. The night was beautiful. The lightning bugs had come out and their tiny lanterns lit up the darkness, and the full moon shone brilliantly down on all it surveyed.

In the distance he could hear the haunting sound of a freight train as it huffed and puffed its way down the tracks, and then the wailing whine of the whistle as it approached the crossing.

He thought of his Dad and how he loved trains. In fact, his Dad loved a lot of things. At his funeral the preacher had said that John Roberts was more in love with life than anyone he had ever known. But mainly Jack's dad had loved his family. They had been his life and his love, and he had never failed to let them know it. And Jack missed him very much.

Then he thought of his mother... He would call her tomorrow. No doubt she was worrying about him. She always had. She always would. And the thought that somewhere in the world there was someone who cared enough to worry about him was tremendously comforting.

The birds were chirping their evening calls, and there was one that he thought he could distinguish from all the rest. As he listened again, he knew he was right. It was the lonely call of the whippoorwill.

Almost without thinking, he reached for his guitar, and there on the front porch with only himself and God to hear, Jack sang the words:

> *HEAR THAT LONESOME WHIPPOORWILL*
> *HE SOUNDS TOO BLUE TO FLY.*
> *THAT MIDNIGHT TRAIN IS WHINING LOW*
> *I'M SO LONESOME I COULD CRY.*
>
> *I'VE NEVER SEEN A NIGHT SO LONG*
> *WHEN TIME GOES CRAWLING BY.*
> *THE MOON JUST FELL BEHIND THE CLOUDS*
> *TO HIDE ITS FACE AND CRY.*
>
> *DID YOU EVER SEE A ROBIN WEEP*
> *WHEN LEAVES BEGIN TO DIE?*
> *THAT MEANS HE'S LOST HIS WILL TO LIVE*
> *I'M SO LONESOME I COULD CRY.*
>
> *THE SILENCE OF A FALLING STAR*
> *LIGHTS UP A PURPLE SKY.*
> *AND AS I WONDER WHERE YOU ARE*
> *I'M SO LONESOME I COULD CRY.*

* Words and Music written by Hank Williams, Sr.

The haunting loneliness expressed in the song created its own special kind of beauty, and Jack wondered about the loneliness Hank Williams must have experienced that inspired him to write those words. It was probably the classic 'lonely' song of all times, and Jack knew that as long as there were people left to sing, each new generation would record its own version of the song, and each new generation would feel the poignant reality of loneliness.

Later that night as he closed his eyes to sleep, somewhere in the distance he again heard the haunting call of the lonesome whippoorwill.

*   *   *   *   *

The lightning that earlier had lit up the sky was gone, and he could hear only the distant rumble of thunder. The storm had spent its fury, and all that remained was the gentle patter of raindrops falling on the tin roof. When Curt bought the old house he re-did the interior, but left the outside unchanged. He had loved the place from the first time he saw it, and would still be here had it not been for his mother's failing health. He had moved back to Jackson to be near her, but when she passed, he and Lisa would come back to this house.

The two story white house was built in the 1850's and had tall columns, a large front porch and lots of windows. The old tin roof had been beyond saving, but Curt had replaced it with one as close to the original as possible. And Jack was glad he had because tonight the rain tapping softly on the metal roof served as a gentle reminder that the storm was over.

The house sat back from the road apiece nestled among several huge oak trees that seemed as though they had stood there since the beginning of time. A winding driveway lead from the road, and to the right of the driveway stood an old buckboard with the hand-carved name *"ELLISON"* on the side. Lisa had discovered the buckboard covered with dust and spider webs in the barn, and had it cleaned and restored.

One day Curt came home and found the 'thing' sitting austerely in the front yard.

"Is there something you'd like to tell me about that strange looking thing in our front yard?" He had asked.

"Not really," Lisa said, as though what she had done was perfectly normal.

"I just thought if F. B. Ellison liked it enough to carve his name on it, that it shouldn't be hidden away in some dusty old barn... You know, this farm was his long before it was ours, and he probably raised a flock of kids and grandkids on this land."

Lisa paused as she imagined the old man who lived here and farmed this ground more than a century ago.

"I suppose this place is actually a lot more his than it is ours. So I thought the old buckboard should be fixed up as sort of a memorial to him... He may not even have a headstone at his grave," Lisa added in justification of what she had done.

"Well, he's got a monument now, and it's sitting right out there in my front yard." Curt shrugged his shoulders... And the buckboard stayed.

Curt explained this to Jack when he rented the house.

"I've kind of grown to like it. After all, I guess the old man deserved to have his buckboard preserved. I'm sure he put a heck of a lot more sweat into this place than I ever will."

"Doesn't bother me," Jack replied. "Maybe I'll write a song about it someday."

Curt had been right. It was a nice place to live, and in the past it had been the perfect place to write. Maybe it would again. One thing he knew... He would write when the words came, and not before. Without a song in your heart, it's hard to put one on paper.

Jack looked at the clock once more. It was 1:15. And in the cool aftermath of the summer storm, he wondered about the man and the buckboard. Jack imagined he was a big man, tall anyway, and his wife was probably small and quite pretty. She had borne him a large family, and they had been quite content here. Perhaps they had slept in this very room. He had found an old fishing pole in the barn, and he wondered if it had belonged to the old man or one of the boys.

Then with the cool breeze blowing through the open window, Jack felt the tension gradually leave his weary body, and he slept. And that night he did not dream of Jessi, but rather of an old man, and a buckboard, and fields white with cotton.

* * * * *

The rain that had fallen steadily throughout the night continued into the noon hour with little hint of ceasing. The walls of the hundred-year old house seemed to close in on him as the weather trapped him inside. It had been three days since he had attempted to write. He didn't know if the well was dry or if it was just so deep and encumbered by his pain and his thoughts of Jessi, that he could not draw the words to the surface. Someday he would write again... At least he thought so. He didn't know when, and right now the 'when' didn't hold the urgency it had a week ago. Right now he just needed time. Time... that great healer of all things... that somehow bears you through the raging tempest and restores hope that life does still hold promise. Time doesn't change the facts or alter the situation, but with its passing, you change and you adjust, in whatever way you must to move on with your life. The passing of time allows you to accept those things you cannot change and change the things you can.

There were days when the memories were not so poignant, when Jack could momentarily think of other things, but ultimately his memories would return to the one he had loved and lost.

Time was the answer. He had come to terms with that, but it moved so painfully slow, and he wondered to himself, "If time is supposed to be the answer, what do you do while you wait for it to pass?"... And to that he had no answer.

It was as if some unseen hand had followed him all his life and guided his pathway in the direction it chose, rather than in the direction he had planned. Had he not torn the rotator cuff, he would not have gone into music. He would not have come to Nashville. And he would not have met Jessi... Looking back he wouldn't take anything for his experiences in life, even the hard times. They had been Hell at times, but without them he wouldn't be the person he was today, and he was proud of that person.

If there was anything he had learned over the years, it was that life can be a series of disappointments... You handle them the best you can and move on... And he knew this was what he had to do now.

* * * * *

A strange sense of contentment came over him, so unlike what he had felt earlier in the day. Maybe time was indeed passing. Today had not been the most grand day of his life, far from it, in fact. The rain had finally stopped about mid-afternoon. The sun had come out, and he had gone for a walk down by the creek. The grass was high and wet, and his boots and pants were saturated by the time he returned. He listened to the croaking of the bullfrogs, and thought how much louder they were after a summer rain. The birds were flying about, chirping their songs of gratitude that the rain was over, and expressing the simple joy of being alive.

The steady summer rain seemed to cleanse all it fell upon, and now as the late afternoon sunshine came out, it brought with it a promise of newness and freshness... and hope.

* * * * *

As darkness fell upon the backyard, the silver glow of the full moon illuminated everything below. The gentle wind blew through the ancient trees and stirred the shadows, bringing an eeriness to the old farmhouse.

Once again Jack sat on the porch and contemplated the sights and sounds of the night. His first peaceful night since Jessi's death had begun here, and maybe subconsciously he had returned to the top step in an effort to recapture the peacefulness he had discovered the night before.

He sat alone and stared into the night for a half-hour or more, and then reached back and pulled his tape player next to him. He had planned to listen to some of his old favorites the night before, but for some reason had never turned it on.

He opened the lid and deposited a John Prine cassette and listened as the music broke the quiet night.

ONE RED ROSE
By John Prine

THE RAIN CAME DOWN ON THE TIN ROOF,
HARDLY A SOUND WAS LEFT FROM THE BIRTHDAY PARTY,
KITCHEN LIGHT FELL ASLEEP ON THE BEDROOM FLOOR.
ME AND HER WERE TALKING SOFTER,
ALL THE TIME BEFORE I LOST HER,
HER PICTURE SAT ON TOP OF THE CHEST OF DRAWERS.

ONE RED ROSE IN THE BIBLE
PRESSED BETWEEN THE HOLY ALPHABET.
PROBABLY WOULDN'T BELIEVE YOU, IF YOU TOLD ME,
BUT WHAT I NEVER KNEW, I NEVER WILL FORGET.

* * * * *

The song reminded him so much of Jessi. The one red rose in the Bible... Why had he picked up that single rose from Jessi's grave, and then pressed it between the pages of the Bible?... Maybe he was trying to hold on to something... anything.

He listened again to the final lines of the chorus:

"PROBABLY WOULDN'T BELIEVE YOU, IF YOU TOLD ME,
BUT WHAT I NEVER KNEW, I NEVER WILL FORGET."

It made him sad... sort of melancholy. He had known Jessi better than anyone, but their time together was so short. There was so much they had planned to do, and now they never would.

"BUT WHAT I NEVER KNEW, I NEVER WILL FORGET."

* * * * *

As Jack sat alone in the darkness, the music continued...

SOUVENIRS
By John Prine

ALL THE SNOW HAS TURNED TO WATER.
CHRISTMAS DAY HAS COME AND GONE.
BROKEN TOYS AND FADED COLORS
ARE ALL THAT'S LEFT TO LINGER ON.

AND I HATE GRAVEYARDS AND OLD PAWN SHOPS
FOR THEY ALWAYS BRING ME TEARS.
I CAN'T FORGET THE WAY THEY ROBBED ME
OF MY CHILDHOOD SOUVENIRS.

MEMORIES, THEY CAN'T BE BOUGHT,
THEY CAN'T BE WON AT CARNIVALS FOR FREE.
IT TOOK ME YEARS TO GET THOSE SOUVENIRS
AND I DON'T KNOW WHY THEY SLIPPED AWAY FROM ME.

BROKEN HEARTS AND DIRTY WINDOWS
MAKE LIFE DIFFICULT TO SEE.
THAT'S WHY LAST NIGHT AND THIS MORNING
ALWAYS LOOK THE SAME TO ME

AND I HATE READING OLD LOVE LETTERS
FOR THEY ALWAYS BRING ME TEARS.
I CAN'T FORGET THE WAY THEY ROBBED ME
OF MY SWEETHEART'S SOUVENIRS.

MEMORIES, THEY CAN'T BE BOUGHT,
THEY CAN'T BE WON AT CARNIVALS FOR FREE.
IT TOOK ME YEARS TO GET THOSE SOUVENIRS
AND I DON'T KNOW WHY THEY SLIPPED AWAY FROM ME.

* * * * *

WHEN I LOVED HER
By Kris Kristofferson

WELL, SHE DIDN'T LOOK AS PRETTY
AS SOME OTHERS I HAVE KNOWN,
AND SHE WASN'T GOOD AT CONVERSATION
WHEN WE WERE ALONE.
BUT SHE HAD A WAY OF MAKING ME
BELIEVE THAT I BELONGED,
AND IT FELT LIKE COMING HOME...
WHEN I FOUND HER.

CAUSE SHE SEEMED TO BE SO PROUD OF ME
JUST WALKING HOLDING HANDS.
AND SHE DIDN'T THINK THAT
MONEY WAS THE MEASURE OF A MAN.
AND WE SEEMED TO FIT TOGETHER
WHEN I HELD HER IN MY ARMS,
AND IT LEFT ME FEELING WARM...
WHEN I LOVED HER.

CAUSE SHE BRIGHTENED UP THE DAY
LIKE THE EARLY MORNING SUN,
AND SHE MADE WHAT I WAS DOING
SEEM WORTHWHILE.
IT'S THE CLOSEST THING TO LIVING
THAT I GUESS I'VE EVER KNOWN,
AND IT MADE ME WANT TO SMILE...
WHEN I LOVED HER.

I KNOW SOME OF US WERE BORN
TO CAST OUR FORTUNES TO THE WIND,
AND I GUESS I'M BOUND TO TRAVEL DOWN
A ROAD THAT NEVER ENDS.
BUT I KNOW I'LL NEVER LOOK
UPON THE LIKES OF HER AGAIN,
AND I'LL NEVER UNDERSTAND...
WHY I LOST HER.

CAUSE SHE BRIGHTENED UP THE DAY
LIKE THE EARLY MORNING SUN,
AND SHE MADE WHAT I WAS DOING
SEEM WORTHWHILE.
IT'S THE CLOSEST THING TO LIVING
THAT I GUESS I'VE EVER KNOWN,
AND IT MADE ME WANT TO SMILE...
WHEN I LOVED HER.

* * * * *

"When he loved her..." Jack thought... He still loved her! Just because somebody dies doesn't mean you stop loving them... Maybe he loved Jessi too much... Then he realized you can never love someone too much.

* * * * *

FIRE AND RAIN
By James Taylor

JUST YESTERDAY MORNING,
THEY LET ME KNOW YOU WERE GONE
SUZZANNE, THE PLANS THEY MADE PUT AN END TO YOU.
I WALKED OUT THIS MORNING,
AND I WROTE DOWN THIS SONG
I JUST DON'T REMEMBER WHO TO SEND IT TO.

I'VE SEEN FIRE AND I'VE SEEN RAIN
I'VE SEEN SUNNY DAYS THAT I THOUGHT WOULD NEVER END.
I'VE SEEN LONELY TIMES WHEN I COULD NOT FIND A FRIEND,
BUT I ALWAYS THOUGHT THAT I'D SEE YOU AGAIN.

WON'T YOU LOOK DOWN UPON ME JESUS,
YOU'VE GOTTA' HELP ME MAKE A STAND.
YOU'VE JUST GOT TO SEE ME THROUGH ANOTHER DAY.
MY BODY'S ACHING AND MY TIME IS AT HAND
I WON'T MAKE IT ANY OTHER WAY.

I'VE SEEN FIRE AND I'VE SEEN RAIN
I'VE SEEN SUNNY DAYS THAT I THOUGHT WOULD NEVER END.
I'VE SEEN LONELY TIMES WHEN I COULD NOT FIND A FRIEND.
BUT I ALWAYS THOUGHT THAT I'D SEE YOU AGAIN.

* * * * *

By the time the tape clicked off, Jack's mind had escaped the music. The songs that once had been his dearest companions now only echoed the pain he felt inside. There were too many lines with too much hurt that was still too fresh and painful. As hard as Jack tried to block out the pain of losing Jessi, her memory seemed to infiltrate everything he did. She went with him everywhere, whether consciously or unconsciously, until finally his heart had all it could stand and somehow temporarily blocked out any more pain.

CHAPTER 38

As Buddy steered the blue mini-van off the highway and onto the narrow winding road, he thought about the last time he was here. The band was in Nashville recording what proved to be Jessi's last album. They had worked all week trying to get it exactly right, and Jessi had never sounded better. Jack left the studio early on Friday, having already finished his part of the recording.

"I'm going to get some steaks for supper. When you guys get through, come on out."

When they finished the last number, Jessi had said, "I think we did okay, don't you?"

Buddy smiled. Jess always did okay. She was the best he had ever heard, and he had heard a lot of them.

They loaded up their instruments and headed for the country and the steaks Jack had promised. Recording sessions were hard work and everyone was glad it was over, none of them knowing it would be their last together. After a wonderful weekend of relaxing at Jack's place, Buddy, Bobby, and Jessi headed to Cincinnati to begin another tour. Jack would remain in Nashville to see the album through and then join them after it was released. Buddy remembered them waving good-bye to Jack as he stood on the end of the porch, and how alone he looked.

* * * * *

Then the call had come. It was two o'clock in the morning and Buddy had just gotten in bed. It was Jack, and Buddy knew immediately something was wrong.

"Buddy, I'm sorry to get you up, but Jess is gone... Her heart just gave out... I knew you would want to know."

His voice broke.

"She thought the world of you, Buddy. You know that, don't you?"

Buddy could hear Jack sobbing.

"Jack, I'm sorry. I'll be there just as quick as I can... Where are you?"

He didn't even know where Jack was calling from, but it didn't matter. They were family, and at a time like this, families were there for each other, and he would be there for Jack... and for Jessi.

"If you're busy, it's okay. I just wanted to tell you myself. I didn't want you to hear it from the press."

Jack paused and Buddy could hear his deep sigh over the phone.

"I'm still in Florida. That's where it happened. We'll take her back to Nashville in the morning. They haven't released the..."

Jack couldn't bring himself to say "the body"... not yet.

Buddy listened on the other end and heard not only Jack's words, but the unspoken pain between his words.

He was sobbing again, only now more profusely.

"Jack, why don't I meet you at Jessi's apartment?"

Jack would have to go back there to get her things and make the arrangements, and Buddy knew how hard it would be for him to be there alone.

"Okay, I'll meet you at Jessi's." Jack mumbled into the receiver.

"I'll be there, hopefully by noon."

Buddy quickly put a few things in an overnight bag, grabbed the only suit he owned, and headed for Nashville to say good-bye to one of the best friends he had ever known.

The last time he had seen Jack was at Jessi's funeral, as they stood together at the grave. Tears flowed unashamedly down their faces, each grieving for a lady they had loved and lost. She had been Jack's love and soon-to-be wife, but she had been Buddy's friend and confidante. There had never been a romantic relationship between them, but Jessi had always cared about Buddy and looked after him. She tried to keep him out of trouble, but when her efforts failed, she was there to bail him out and help him get back on his feet again. She had loaned him money during the lean days, and picked him up when he was down.

He wondered if Jack knew that he had a key to her apartment. He always had, wherever she had lived. She used to worry about him getting drunk or being broke and not having a place to stay. Many years ago she had given him the first key and said, "Just remember, there's always a spare bed here if you need it."

Only once or twice over the years had he used it, but that was Jessi's way of taking care of him. There would never be another like her, Buddy thought, as they walked away from her grave. And as he shook hands with Jack and prepared to leave, he remembered all the times that Jack, too, had looked after him. Jack fussed at him more than Jessi, but he had always been there when he needed him, and Buddy hated to leave the tall, grieving man, who had always seemed so alone, and now seemed more alone than ever.

He could hear Jack now. "You're the best darn guitar picker around. Why do you have to go out and get drunk and cause all this trouble?"

He no longer blamed Jack for firing him. Jack had put up with him longer than most would, and even then he had known if worse came to worst, and he needed him, Jack would be there. Jack was that kind of friend and had proved it later when he took Buddy back, knowing full well he hadn't quit drinking.

As he headed in the direction of Jack's house, he wondered what it would be like. Would Jack be glad to see him or would the sight of him only bring back sad and painful memories? Whatever the case, he could not come to Nashville without seeing Jack.

*   *   *   *   *

It was almost noon and Jack had not eaten breakfast. When he awoke it was such a pretty day that he couldn't wait to get outside and feel the warmth of the sunshine. Not only had the rain been depressing, but the cool, damp air reminded him of his old baseball injury. The shoulder had pained him a lot these last couple of days, but with the change in weather, he scarcely noticed it today. He busied himself picking up the limbs that the storm had left strewn around the yard until finally he got hungry. He went inside and put on a pot of coffee, and was about to get the bacon and eggs going, when he heard a car coming up the driveway. This surprised him. The one thing you could count on out here was that no one just 'dropped in'. Then he saw the blue van and the little guy emerging therefrom, and he had never been so happy to see anyone. He was quickly on the porch, and the smile that Buddy saw on Jack's face was definitely a smile of welcome.

"Damn! It's good to see you."

Jack reached out his hand, and smiles lit up both their faces.

"Man, that coffee smells good," Buddy said, as they made their way into the kitchen, and he reached for a cup to help himself.

"I was just about to fix breakfast, and I sure could use some company."

Jack put the bacon back in the refrigerator and took out a package of ham instead. Ham and eggs were Buddy's favorite food. He remembered the old days when they were playing the bar circuit in Florida and barely making enough money to pay the rent. They ate whatever they could afford, which was definitely not ham.

Buddy would say, "If I ever make the big time, there's one luxury I'm gonna' have."

And Jessi would ask, "What's that Buddy?"

Then Buddy would reply, "Ham and eggs... three times a day."

"How many?" Jack asked as he started to break eggs into a bowl.

"As many as the skillet will hold." The smell of the coffee and ham whetted Buddy's appetite. "Besides, you look like you could use some extra nourishment yourself."

"Yeah, I guess I could." Jack acknowledged.

And the two old friends sat on the back porch at high noon enjoying a breakfast of ham and eggs and biscuits... And once again, life was good.

* * * * *

It was good to have someone to talk to, and with Buddy, Jack could 'spill his guts'. They knew just about all there was to know about each other. They had laughed and had fun together... They had worn each other's socks and underwear when one or the other had forgotten to go to the laundromat... There had been times when they were mad as Hell at each other, but those times had never lasted. They shared a kinship born of years of struggle when the only way they could make it was by hanging in there together.

After Jessi's death most of the members of the band made new connections and went their separate ways, and now only Jack and Buddy remained. Jack didn't realize how much he had needed someone to talk to. As much as he had thought about Jessi, he had not shared his feelings with anyone. Buddy needed to talk about her too. He had known Jessi almost as long as Jack had, and he had cared for her deeply in his own way.

"I thought if I could come out here and get on with my writing, I could get over her. But I can't write, Bud, I just can't. The words don't come anymore... Sometimes I wonder if they ever will."

"You'll write again. It just takes time. One day the words will come... You're a songwriter, Jack. You haven't forgotten how. You're just burdened down with grief and loneliness, and that's got to pass... I don't know how long it will take. Maybe awhile... Everybody doesn't love the same. Some love a lot deeper... You're one of those. You just can't let her go that easy. I loved her too, but in a different way. She probably cared more for me than anybody ever did, and I ain't ever gonna forget her." A tear rolled down Buddy's face. "But you and her were going to get married. You had your whole life laid out before you. You were two good and decent people in a world where there ain't a lot of those kind left, and you got robbed, man!... You just got robbed!... And it ain't fair!" Buddy could say no more.

Jack looked at the little guy sitting in the rocker staring out at nothing in particular and felt compassion for him. He had lost Jessi too.

For awhile they sat in silence, each absorbed in his own thoughts. Finally, Jack broke the spell.

"What brings you to Nashville?"

"Another recording session. Steve Puckett called me last week and asked if I'd be interested in playing guitar on an album. Some new guy - name of Jackson - comes from down around Atlanta. He's supposed to be pretty good. You wouldn't believe what they offered me to play for him."

"Yeah, I would. It's not the old days, Buddy... Thank goodness! Then we had to pay our dues and work our way up and hope we could survive long enough to make it. These days if you're good, it's not hard to find a backer who's willing to front the money to promote you. They're looking for a good investment, and they would rather gamble on a good singer than put their money in the bank." Jack paused. "I don't know if the guy can sing or not, but he's got a good guitar man. When do you start?"

"Tuesday. I thought I'd come up early and see you and get me a place to stay."

"Don't worry about a place to stay. The rent's paid and you've slept here before. You know where your bed is. Right now I need to go get some groceries. Want to ride into town?"

"You get the groceries, and I'll mow the yard... It looks like it could stand it."

"Yeah, I know. I was going to mow yesterday, but it rained all day... I didn't ask you to stay just so you'd mow the yard."

Buddy was grinning that little mischievous grin.

"Just go get us something to eat, and I'll mow the damn yard. You never did do it right anyway."

Jack was grinning too. He knew what Buddy was talking about. When they rented the place in Florida, Buddy always did the mowing because he insisted Jack didn't 'do it right'. He also cleaned the house because the others just gave it a 'lick and a promise'. It struck Jack as funny that a guy like Buddy, who had so much trouble keeping himself straight, always wanted everything clean and neat around him.

After supper Jack and Buddy sat on the front porch and jammed for hours. They did some of the old numbers they played when they were starting out. Sometimes they couldn't remember the words, and they made them up as they went. It was fun, and Jack hadn't had fun in a long time. This had been a good day for both of them, and finally around midnight, they called it a day.

Jack was almost asleep when he heard Buddy snoring down the hall, and for once the snoring didn't bother him. It was a nice reminder that tonight he wasn't alone.

CHAPTER 39

Jack hadn't been to *Tootsie's* in years, and as he deposited his money in the parking lot slot, he wondered if coming had been such a good idea. Buddy would probably wind up getting 'drunk as a skunk', and he would have to half-carry him out of the place in the wee hours of the morning, with Buddy insisting he needed just 'one more drink'.

Buddy wasn't mean or violent when he got drunk... He was more like a little kid, but he could get so sloppy drunk that it was disgusting. If you could get him away from the place, he would usually pass out and sleep it off... Getting him to leave was the problem.

It had been Jack's idea to come to *Tootsie's* tonight, and Buddy had said, "Why not? I've got some fond memories of that old place."

"You probably spent a few Saturday nights there you don't remember at all."

"I guess so. There's not too many places in this town where I haven't got stoned a time or two."

As they approached the familiar nightspot, Jack realized why he had come. There was a certain yearning inside him to remember the old times... the times when he and countless others had hung around this place, hoping the success of those whose pictures decorated the walls of *Tootsie's* would somehow rub off on them. Perhaps coming here tonight had been a means of escape from the reality of the present to the hopes and dreams of the past.

For whatever reason, they were here, and as they stepped inside there was a comfortable familiarity about the place... It hadn't changed... It never did.

The bar to the left was the first thing that caught your eye, and then the collage of pictures that covered every inch of every wall, and were displayed under the glass on the tables and counters. Everywhere there was an inch of space, there was a picture... from Roy Acuff, Jimmie Rodgers, Kitty Wells and Patsy Cline to Randy Travis, Trisha Yearwood, Vince Gill and Reba McEntire. Everyone who had ever been anyone in country music had their picture plastered on the walls of *Tootsie's*. There were pictures of Johnny Cash, Hank Williams, Little Jimmy Dickens, Merle Haggard, and George Jones... Everyone!... It was a unique place.

In the old days the Grand Ole Opry stars came here between shows at the Ryman to grab a beer and mingle with fellow musicians. And in turn it had become the place for the 'would be' stars to hang out, hoping to be heard and perhaps discovered.

Over the years many stories had grown out of *Tootsie's*, some exaggerated, as stories tend to become with the passing of time, but many were true, at least in part. Legend had it that Kristofferson wrote *Sunday Mornin' Comin' Down* one Saturday night in the back room upstairs at *Tootsie's*, and the song had gone on to be Single of the Year.

The walls of *Tootsie's* told the story of country music all the way from the days of Vernon Dalhart and the Original Carter Family to Garth Brooks and Travis Tritt. You could stare at the walls for hours and not see them all. And these weren't just the photos you were accustomed to seeing... There was one of a young, clean-shaven Willie Nelson with short hair, wearing a suit and tie as he appeared in the fifties on the *Ernest Tubb Show*. There was also one of a clean-shaven Waylon Jennings sporting a flat top during his early days when he played bass with Buddy Holly and the *Crickets*, along with a picture of Hank Williams, Jr. with a short hair cut and no facial hair, also wearing a suit and tie.

Tootsie's was the unofficial Smithsonian of country music. It was more of a museum than a bar. And though the Grand Ole Opry had moved from the Ryman Auditorium to the new complex at Opryland twelve years earlier, *Tootsie's* was still the place where the real country music people gathered.

In the corner was a small stage where a guy with only a guitar entertained. Sitting in front of him was a big gallon size mayonnaise jar that had been scrubbed clean to collect tips. Playing for tips had been around for a long time, and Jack had done his share of it in the early days. He well remembered the days he had played all evening and went home dog-tired and reeking of cigarette smoke and spilled beer with less than ten bucks to show for his efforts... He never passed by one of these tip-singers now that he didn't drop in a twenty-dollar bill. It was his way of saying, "I know what it's like. I've been there."

Buddy ordered a Miller Lite and sat at the bar listening as the guitarist sang *Help Me Make It Through the Night*, but it was the pictures that captured Jack's attention. They seemed to transport him into another world and another time. Some were of the stars in their early days and you had to look twice to be sure it was who you thought. Others were photos of them in their prime. Some were old and yellow and bore the marks of having been there for years.

One of the first pictures that caught his eye was Kris Kristofferson. Jack had every album he had ever made, but his favorite was the *To The Bone* album. It was released shortly after his divorce from Rita Coolidge. Kristofferson spanned the emotions with this one. The lines of the songs spoke of Love and Hate... Anger and Resentment... Pleasant memories and Gut-Wrenching Despair... There was frustration and pain... Loneliness and Loss... And the stark reality of not giving a damn about anything.

Since Jessi's death, Jack had experienced all of these emotions, and at times it seemed he had lost everything, even the center of his very soul.

He couldn't understand why he had not been able to write these last couple of months. God knows he had tried, but the words just wouldn't come... His ability to write seemed to have died along with Jessi.

"Can I get you something to drink?" The waitress asked.

"Yeah, a Michelob, please." Jack answered, without moving his eyes from the pictures on the wall. If he looked away, he might miss one, and tonight he wanted to see them all.

Buddy had run into an old drummer friend from his rock and roll days, and they were sitting at the bar re-living the old times.

"Your friend's gonna get a stiff neck," Eddy said as he watched Jack slowly perusing the pictures from left to right and then from top to bottom, hesitating from time to time to dwell on a particular photo before moving on to another.

"He's going through a bad time right now. Just lost the lady he was going to marry a few weeks ago... You knew Jessi McCrae, didn't you?"

"Jessi McCrae?... What a voice that lady had! Died suddenly, didn't she?"

"Yeah, she died in his arms. I picked with both of them for a long time, and if there were ever two people who belonged together, it was those two... If he were a drinker, he'd be an alcoholic by now. Jack's a damn good songwriter, but since she died, the words won't come. It's been rough for him."

"Jack Roberts!" Eddy exclaimed as he realized who the tall man staring at the pictures was.

"I've never met him, but I sure have heard his music. The way that man handles a lyric is like no one else... When it comes to songwriting, he's the master."

Jack's tall, athletic frame seemed to sag from the strain of the past several months, and the lines on his face reflected the scars on his heart. Buddy wished it were within his power to lift the pain from the shoulders of his friend. Then he saw Jack reach out to a picture and even from a distance, Buddy knew who it was.

His fingers moved slowly and ever so softly over the image of her smiling eyes and her high cheekbones and down her face to her lips... The picture had been on the cover of her first album... Buddy remembered the three of them sitting around the kitchen table in Jess' apartment looking at the photographer's proofs, while Jessi tried to decide which one she liked best. They made funny jokes, and Jess finally said, "Okay, guys, get serious. Tell me which one you like best. If I'm lucky, I'll be in every *Kmart* in the country, and I want to look good."

The final decision would be up to her producer, but at least he had asked her to choose the one she liked best. She had wanted Jack and Buddy to help her decide, and strangely enough, the producer had also liked the one they had chosen. She had, indeed, been in every *Kmart* in the country and in every music store. This was the album that had lifted Jessi McCrae from a relative unknown to a household name.

Buddy saw Jack's fixed stare and watched him swallow, but he knew the lump in his throat was still there. Then with his fingers still softly caressing her picture, Jack spoke to the waitress who was delivering drinks to a nearby table.

"How about bringing me a bourbon - straight?"

"Thought your friend wasn't a drinker?" Eddy said as he glanced at Buddy, whose eyes were still fixed upon Jack. "That ain't no Shirley Temple he just ordered."

Three hours later Buddy still sat at the end of the bar keeping a watchful eye on his friend. He knew Jack had already had too much to drink. He had tried to get him to leave earlier, but Jack had refused.

All he had done for the past three hours was stare at the stupid pictures and drink. Buddy had never seen him drink like this. In fact, he had never seen Jack drink at all except for an occasional beer.

Why had he come here tonight?... And why was he so consumed with the pictures?... It was like the final reverie someone spends with the personal effects of a departed loved one, knowing that afterwards the mementos will be put away, always to be kept, but rarely, if ever, to be brought out again.

Buddy knew Jack had admired many of the people in the pictures, and a few of them had inspired his musical career, but Jessi was probably the only one with whom Jack had shared a close relationship... In many ways he had always been a loner. He was a Hell of a songwriter and was respected by most everyone in the business. Yet he had never been part of 'the establishment'.

Jack generally avoided the parties thrown by the big record companies, where 'everyone who was anyone' dressed in their finest formal attire and came to sip martinis and eat fancy hors d'oeuvres, and mingle with the 'powers that be' in the 'Big Business' of country music. He preferred to stay at home and work on his music or roam through the pastures of Curt's farm with Jessi's dog faithfully at his side or shoot baskets with the neighborhood kids. Consequently, he had never been a real part of the Nashville scene.

Once Buddy had heard him say, "I don't need all that nonsense. If I write good lyrics, they'll sell, and if I write junk, all the connections in the world won't help."

So, over the years Jack had quietly and persistently plied his trade in his own fashion, without feeling the need to be constantly exposed to the 'Business Hierarchy'. He had been very successful, but he had done it his way.

They had been to *Tootsie's* a lot of times, and Jack had glanced at a few of the pictures, but never like this. Usually he just listened to the music and reminisced with his friends, but tonight he was different.

The bartender interrupted Buddy's thoughts. "You need something to drink?"

"No, I'm fine."

Jerry had been tending bar at *Tootsie's* for a long time and felt certain Buddy was not about to stop at two beers. His drinking capacity went far beyond that.

But tonight Jerry was wrong. Buddy was watching his best friend 'drink himself under the table', and he had to stay sober to take care of him. Buddy wondered how many times Jack had watched him do the same thing and tried to get him out of there before he got into trouble, and then tried to sober him up enough to do the show the next night.

Buddy could almost hear his words, now... "Come on, damn it, drink this coffee and get some food in your stomach. You can play the guitar drunk or sober, but you gotta be able to walk out on stage."

Suddenly Buddy was aroused out of his reverie by a commotion in the back, and he saw a hefty bleached blonde patron escorting Jack out of the ladies room.

"Can't you read the sign, Buster?"

While it was obvious from her loud and brash manner that she had put away a few drinks herself, she could still tell the ladies room from the men's, which apparently Jack could not.

Buddy couldn't help but grin, as he made his way back to where Jack stood staring at the audacious woman who had just thrown him out of the ladies room.

Jack innocently tried to apologize. "Sorry, lady. I just had to go to the bathroom."

"Did you get the job done?" Buddy quietly asked.

"Hell no! She threw me out." Then he hesitated. "Buddy, I got to go... bad. I'm about to bust."

"Come on." Buddy took Jack by the arm and headed him in the right direction and wondered why they had to put the damn bathrooms so close together.

"Thanks," Jack said.

And as they passed the table where the rather large lady sat staring at him in disgust, Jack said, "You didn't have anything to worry about, lady. I just had to pee... You're not my type anyway."

Buddy would apologize to her later, but right now he had to get his friend to the bathroom.

After getting Jack to the bathroom, the correct one this time, once again Buddy tried to get him to leave, but to no avail.

"No Buddy, we can't go yet. I haven't finished looking at the pictures."

"I think you've seen enough, Jack. Come on. Let's go home."

"Just let me have one more drink. Then we'll go."

"You've had enough. Let's just get out of here."

"But I haven't heard the man sing."

"He's been singing all night." Buddy said in disgust.

"Well, I've been too busy to listen. But I'm gonna sit down right here and listen."

Buddy couldn't help but grin.

Jack slid onto a chair, almost turning it over, and then hollered to the waitress. "Hey, lady, bring me a drink."

Buddy looked at her and shook his head, and she nodded in response.

They listened as the singer did a couple of songs. Then came the intro that both Buddy and Jack knew so well.

When Jessi had first heard the song, tears welled up in her eyes.

"I want to believe you wrote that one specially for me."

And Jack had answered, "Who else do I write love songs for?"

She recorded the song and it became her biggest hit.

As the performer sang the first verse, Buddy watched the fixed stare on Jack's face. Then Jack stumbled from his seat and headed toward the man with the guitar. Buddy could see Jack was mad, and he hurried after him, not knowing what was about to take place.

"Give me that damn guitar!" Jack demanded. "You don't know how to sing it."

"Cool it, mister. And get your hands off my guitar! You're drunk, and you're way out of line."

"Why don't you take him home?" The singer said to Buddy.

"I'm trying! I'm trying!" Buddy answered in frustration.

Jack was still reaching for the guitar and demanding, "Let me have it. You're not singing it right. I'll show you."

"You don't have to show me anything. I know how to sing. What makes you think you know so much about it anyway?"

"Hey man! I'll tell you what I know. I wrote the song. And you can't sing it worth a damn!"

"Yeah, yeah, I'm sure you did... And you probably built Yankee Stadium and swam the English Channel."

Buddy turned to the singer, anger showing in his eyes.

"Fellow, you're the one that's out of line. At least he's got an excuse... He's drunk. Why don't you just shut up and quit making matters worse?... And let me tell you something else. He did write the song! His name is Jack Roberts... And he's right... You can't sing that song worth a damn. There was only one person who could. And she's dead! And that's why he's drunk tonight. He was going to marry her." Buddy paused, and then added. "I've known him a long time and I've never seen him drunk before, and I've never heard him put another singer down. He's not that kind. And if you look through that tip jar of yours, you'll find a twenty-dollar bill. It's probably the biggest tip you'll get tonight. He put it in there when he came in the door, not because he thought you could sing. He hadn't even heard you. He did it because he's been where you are, and he knows how hard it is to play all night for a hand full of change. He did it because he hasn't forgotten how it is, and because he still gives a damn... even if nobody else does."

Buddy was angry, not just with Jack, but with the whole crowd who showed so little compassion.

For a moment all was quiet, as Jack and the singer both stared at the floor, neither knowing quite what to say. Everyone knew it was Jessi McCrae of whom Buddy spoke. They had heard the story of how she had died in the arms of the man to whom she was to be married.

Finally, Jack muttered, "Sorry man, I was..."

The musician quietly interrupted. "Don't worry about it. It's okay."

Buddy steered Jack toward the door. "Let's get out of here."

Suddenly Jack's weight shifted, and he slumped against Buddy.

"I can't make it, Bud... I gotta sit down... I think I'm going to be sick."

The bartender, who had been holding the door open for their exit, helped ease Jack back into a chair. The whiskey had taken over, and he was as white as a sheet. The waitress handed Buddy a wet towel, and as he pressed it against Jack's forehead, he felt a sudden surge of air, and turned to see the big blonde who had escorted Jack from the ladies room fanning him with a menu.

"Where are you parked?" She asked.

"A couple of blocks up the hill."

"Go get the car. I don't think he's going to pass out just now. I'll stay with him until you get back, and then we'll get him in the car. If you keep the windows open and give him plenty of fresh air, I think you'll be able to get him home and in bed. Then if he passes out, it won't matter."

Buddy looked at the lady and smiled. "Thanks... Thanks a lot."

And as he hurried up the hill to the parking lot, he thought about the big blonde who 'hadn't been Jack's type', but who now sat beside him taking care of him, and he remembered what his grandfather used to tell him when he was just a kid.

"Just remember, son. There are more good people in the world than bad. Sometimes it just takes seeing somebody in need to bring the goodness out."

Buddy now realized how right his Grandpa had been.

CHAPTER 40

Over a year had passed since Jessi's death, and although he had not gotten over the loss, he had somehow learned to live around it. And, unlike the summer at Hendersonville, life was no longer void of meaning... But something was gone, and he was not sure if it would ever come back... He had lost his enthusiasm for music.

He had written a couple of songs that made it into the top forty, but for Jack, music was no longer the same. There were too many memories. Everywhere he went there were things to remind him of her... old friends, places they had played together, songs.

Finally, he had taken an old friend up on an offer that was made almost as a joke.

It was another one of those damn award shows, a black tie affair featuring the hottest performers in country music. Country music was at its pinnacle, and the show was being televised live all over the world.

Almost every female eye in the auditorium was fixed on him, as he walked down the aisle to his seat. He was wearing a black tuxedo and bow tie, and as usual was alone. They had heard the story of how Jessi had died in his arms, and it was reported he had not dated anyone since. Most women found him ruggedly handsome, though somewhat remote, and the combination made him particularly alluring.

As he waited for the show to begin, his thoughts turned to other awards shows. There was the one three years before, when like tonight, Jessi wasn't there. Instead, she was with her grandmother. It had been their night to receive the awards. They had been labeled the stars of the future, but the future had been so short-lived.

Suddenly the lights dimmed and the chitchat ceased as everyone waited for the show to begin. From high in the rafters, two huge spotlights pointed their beams toward the stage and then crisscrossed back and forth throughout the crowded auditorium, seemingly in search of one special star to shine upon. Finally, the two white lights merged and found that single figure who had been obscured by the darkness, standing alone on the big stage. And suddenly, out of the stillness, the host of this year's gala began to sing *Sweet Dreams*. It was Patsy Cline's great classic, but it was not Patsy Cline or this year's performer that Jack saw or heard... It was Jessi... She loved that song and often closed her show with it.

Being here was hard for Jack. The memories of last year's awards were still too fresh. Jessi had posthumously won every award for which she had been nominated. She deserved them, but that wasn't the reason she had won. She had won because she was dead, and because she died so tragically at the height of her career.

It wasn't fair to Jessi, and it wasn't fair to the other performers who had been nominated, but that's the way it's done. If you're a star and you die, they immortalize you. They did it with Hank Williams and Elvis, and with Marilyn Monroe and James Dean.

Everyone wanted a piece of Jessi. They didn't care about her, just the hype and the money they could make by commercializing her death.

He had not attended last year's awards, but instead, had watched them on television, at least as much as he could handle. When he could stand no more, he had cut off the t.v. and stared at the blank screen. It had seemed so strange. Jessi was gone, and the country music people were honoring her with all these awards, and he couldn't bear to watch. Buddy had been there to accept for her and to say all the proper things.

In fact, were it not for Buddy, Jack wouldn't be here tonight. Buddy had been nominated for *Instrumentalist of the Year*. He deserved to win, but whether he would remained to be seen. Buddy did not have the glitz and glamour that for some reason was so all-fired important. He just had the talent.

As Jack's mind drifted aimlessly from one thing to another, he completely missed the announcing of one of the winners. Then suddenly he was aroused from his daydreaming by the applause of the crowd, and he saw Buddy mounting the stage to the podium.

"Oh, God! Buddy had won!" And for the first time tonight a broad smile crossed Jack's face as he rose to his feet, joining in the applause. The little guy with the John Prine grin, who Jack had always said was the best guitar picker around, had finally gotten the recognition he deserved.

Buddy acknowledged several people who had helped him... the people at RCA, his manager, the fans. Then he paused. "But, most of all, I want to thank Jack Roberts, my long time friend. He's the best songwriter God ever put on this earth... you all know that. But he's more than that to me. He's the reason I'm here tonight and not lying in an alley somewhere half-stoned. If it wasn't for him..." Buddy hesitated and wiped a tear from his eye before he continued. "If it wasn't for him... and Jessi McCrae... I would probably be dead by now. They believed in me and helped me believe in myself." Then with a smile on his face he lifted the crystal accolade into the air and added, "This one's for them."

There was a hush over the huge auditorium as the audience listened to the Instrumentalist of the Year acknowledge his problem with the bottle, and express his appreciation for the help of his two good friends.

Once more Buddy leaned toward the mike while the audience waited.

"Amy, I haven't been the best Daddy in the world, but I've always loved you... and I still do," and he blew her a kiss.

Jack hoped Amy was watching. At last she had just cause to be proud of her Daddy.

Many thoughts ran through Jack's head. He remembered the day he fired Buddy, and the cold Christmas Eve he and Jessi had gone to Rome to get him... He thought of how Buddy had stood by him when Jess died, and how he had helped lift him from his despair at Hendersonville... It had been a struggle for Buddy, a struggle which only those who have coped with alcohol addiction can understand, and Jack was sure there was a lot he would never know about the really bad times. But tonight was the 'good times'. It was the mountaintop, not the valley... And Jess would be so proud of him.

* * * * *

After the show, there was a big bash at the Opryland Hotel. The lavish buffet was laden with every delicacy imaginable, and the bartenders were ready to quench the thirst of all who came to drink.

Although Jack had not come in a party mood, he found he was having a good time. It was nice to mix and mingle with some old friends, and he was especially glad to see Marge Scott. When he first came to Nashville, Marge had taken a personal interest in him and had helped open some important doors for him and the band.

"This town can be terribly intimidating to the new kid on the block." Marge had told him. "Just remember, you're good. Tell yourself that every day... because you are... and nothing's gonna stop you. Just tell the industry snobs to 'Kiss your butt'."

Marge never changed. She was warm and real, and, if she liked you, a true friend. They visited for awhile and shared a glass of champagne, and Jack promised to call her one day for lunch.

Finally, the combination of cigarette smoke, coupled with *Georgio*, *Chanel No. 5*, and all the other exotic fragrances wafting through the large ballroom became too much, and Jack walked out into the corridor for some fresh air.

As he stood staring out the window at the sparkling Nashville skyline, he heard a strange, yet familiar voice.

"Jack Roberts!"

It was Glenn Daniel, a teammate from his minor league days. Glenn had been traded to the *Blue Jays* during his rookie season in '75, and had gone on to enjoy a pretty good major league career.

It was nice to see someone from happier times... someone who didn't feel the need to extend their sympathy in the loss of Jessi or to eulogize everything she had ever done. Their intentions were good, but the constant reminder only made the healing process harder.

Glenn didn't mention Jessi. He talked baseball. After his playing days were over, he had coached for awhile, and was now Director of Player Development for the new expansion *Kentucky Stallions*. He was in charge of the entire minor league system, including scouting and signing young free agents, and it was obvious he loved his job.

They talked about the old days, and Glenn filled him in on what had happened to a lot of the guys they had played with. They laughed about some of the clubhouse pranks they had been involved in, and Jack conveniently forgot there was a party going on down the hall.

Finally, Glenn looked at his watch.

"Jack, I could talk all night, but I've got a plane to catch. I'm flying up to Michigan to look at this Avery kid... seventeen years old, and they say he's gonna be the next Nolan Ryan... only better... This kid's a lefty."

They shook hands, and Glenn had the feeling the smile that now lighted Jack's face wasn't there too often these days. He, too, had read the story.

As he started to walk away, he turned and smiled. "Hey, whenever you decide to give up this music stuff, you know you've always got a job with me."

CHAPTER 41

CHRISTMAS EVE

Jack and his mother had finished supper and were enjoying a cup of eggnog by the Christmas tree when he broke the news.

"Mom, what would you say if I told you I was going back into baseball?"

Virginia set her cup down and looked at him as if she wasn't sure she had heard correctly.

"I'm too much in shock to say anything, but I'm sure there's more to the story."

She listened intently as he told her of the chance meeting with Glenn Daniel and the more recent developments. "Their AA team needs a pitching coach, and they've offered me the job."

"I suppose you said 'Yes'." Her response was more of a statement than a question.

"Yeah, I'm gonna give it a try... I need a change, and I think I know enough about pitching to earn my salary. Besides, it might be kind of nice to put on a uniform again."

Virginia smiled as Jack continued to talk about his new career. She was one of the few people in the world, maybe the only one, who knew that baseball, not music, was Jack's first love.

Music was something that he did. He had chosen it and done well with it. He had loved it and, in turn, it had loved him back.

Baseball, on the other hand, had not loved him back. But even with all the pain it had brought him, he had never stopped loving it.

Music was in his heart, but baseball was in his soul... And she was happy he was going back.

CHAPTER 42

Jack sat alone in the corner of the clubhouse cleaning out his locker. Most of the players had already left for the bus station or airport. It had been a long season, and they were anxious to get home to their families and girlfriends.

He was glad he had returned to baseball. It hadn't been the same as when he played, but he had not expected it to be. The cliche 'You can't go back' was true, and he had known that long before he accepted Glenn's offer, but it had been a good year.

He had been assigned to the Stallions' AA minor league affiliate in Paducah as their pitching coach.

The *Paducah Palominos* won their division by six games over their nearest rival, but were eliminated in the first round of the play-offs.

It had felt good to put on a uniform again and be part of the game he loved so much. He had almost forgotten the smell of the ballpark... the distinctive aroma of popcorn, beer and cotton candy, seasoned with the lingering smell of cheap cigars.

The talent of the Palomino pitching staff was mediocre at best, but they were willing to learn. Jack worked with each pitcher individually, teaching proper pitching mechanics and demonstrating how adjusting a seemingly insignificant part of their delivery could make all the difference in the world in their performance. The players were receptive of Jack's instruction, and the results of his efforts were soon evident. By the end of the season the pitching staff had improved, with three of his starters being promoted to the AAA club, and one of them advancing on to the major league team.

The 1990 season had been a transitional period for Jack. Not only was he putting music behind him, but in a strange way, he was also putting Jessi behind him. He would never forget her, or stop loving her, but he had to move on with his life, and removing himself from the music business had enabled him to do that.

Two weeks earlier Glenn had dropped by the ball park on a scouting trip. He wanted to talk with Jack, so they went out for a burger after the game.

"Jack, Dusty Malone won't be back next year. He's got an offer from the Twins to manage and, as much as we hate to lose him, we won't stand in his way."

Glenn took another sip of his beer, lit a cigarette, and without warning asked, "Are you interested in the job?"

It was the last thing in the world he had expected. He had returned to baseball almost by accident with no real plans of making it a lasting career. More than anything else, it had been something constructive to do while time healed the wounds of losing Jessi.

Now he was being offered the job of major league pitching coach for one of the best young teams in the league, a team that was in first place as they spoke. He couldn't believe it.

"Whew!" Jack breathed a deep sigh of surprise and slowly shook his head in disbelief. "You've really caught me off guard."

"It's the chance of a lifetime. You've done a great job in Paducah, and everyone in the organization is behind you."

Jack took a long gulp of his Michelob and once more shook his head.

"Can you give me a few days?... I know it's a great opportunity... I just had no idea."

"Sure. I realize I've dropped a bombshell on you. We won't make an announcement about Dusty until after the World Series, so just let us know as soon as you can... And Jack, I hope you'll take it. This team is going places and with you in charge of the pitching staff, we'll go further."

*   *   *   *   *

The conversation haunted Jack, even more than the one with Glenn last fall. He lay awake at night trying to decide what to do. Glenn was right. It wasn't often a man with one year's coaching experience got a shot at the majors, especially with a team the caliber of the *Stallions*, but he wasn't sure if the move was right for him.

One of the drawbacks of life in professional baseball is having a lot of time on your hands, the long plane trips and the hours upon hours in a strange city waiting between the end of one game and the beginning of another. It had been during a two-week road trip last June with consecutive rainouts that he had pulled out his guitar and began to play. He had almost forgotten how much pleasure and contentment the instrument could give him. As the summer lingered on, he continued to play. Eventually lines came to him, and he couldn't wait to get them down on paper and weave them into songs. And before he knew it he was writing again, only now it was because he wanted to, not because he felt he had to.

The lyrics came free and easy, and while some were trivial tunes, others were quite good, and the weight, which had hung heavily upon him for so long, was now lifted.

The offer from the *Stallions* was a once-in-a-lifetime opportunity. It would not come again. However, if he took it, he would be saying goodbye to music. He couldn't do both. It was a choice he had to make, and it was not an easy one.

The previous night he sat alone with the spiral notebook which held the songs he had written during the summer. He read and re-read the lyrics until almost dawn. Maybe they weren't all that good after all. Perhaps he was kidding himself... But they were good. They were damn good! He could write again... Somewhere... somehow... the gift had returned.

And as Jack closed the locker and packed his last pair of cleats into a suitcase, he knew what he had to do.

CHAPTER 43

A feeling of pride came over him as he signed the contract.
"I think you'll be happy with your decision," the agent said, as they both rose to their feet.
"I already am."
Jack reached across the desk to shake hands, and then quickly left the office suite.
Down the hall the lady in the turquoise suit pressed the elevator button and glanced impatiently at her watch. Just as the elevator opened, she turned and started back up the hall. Apparently she had forgotten something.
He smiled as he observed her. She was indicative of the changing times. The stereotype myth about a 'man's job' or a 'woman's place' had been overcome, and women were an integral part of the business world. They were everywhere, in their neat business suits, brief case in hand, and always in a hurry.
She was obviously absorbed in her own thoughts and unaware anyone else was in the hallway until suddenly she looked up and their eyes met. For a moment neither spoke. Finally it was she who broke the silence.
"Jack! What are you doing in Chattanooga? I thought you were living in Nashville."
The look of surprise left her face as quickly as it had come and she extended her hand as if greeting a client or business associate.
"Actually, I was, but that's about to change. I just signed a contract on some property in the Cove."
"Oh, I envy you! It's beautiful down there."
"And what are you doing here? I thought you were still in Atlanta."
"Believe it or not," she smiled, "I'm practicing law. I came back to Chattanooga a couple of years ago."
Once more she glanced at her watch.
"I've got to be in court in LaFayette at one o'clock, but I've got a few minutes to spare. If you have time, I'll buy you a cup of coffee."
"Sounds good."
"Give me a minute to get a book I need."
The gold leaf lettering on the door read:

It was obvious she was not the same person who had stared out the window at him as he drove out of her driveway and out of her life fourteen years ago.

She had changed... but so had he. Time has a way of doing that. But one thing had not changed... She was still a very pretty lady.

The coffee shop was crowded with neatly dressed men and women carrying attaché cases, and easily identifiable as professionals. Several of them greeted Mary as she and Jack made their way to a corner table.

While they were glad to see each other, it was not easy to bridge the gap between two people whose lives had taken totally different directions, and at first, small talk was all they could manage.

Finally with the typical directness of a lawyer, she asked, "Are you married?"

"No, I'm not."

He felt no need to say more. Surely she knew about Jessi. The papers and t.v. had seen to it that the whole world knew their story.

Mary saw a hint of sadness in his eyes, and it was apparent he had yet to feel for anyone else the love he had felt for Jessi McCrae. Perhaps he never would. Sometimes you come so close to real love... then you lose it, and you never find it again.

"How about you?" He had noticed she was not wearing a wedding ring.

"No. Garrett and I were divorced in '83." She stopped, and Jack saw she didn't care to elaborate.

"And since?"

"Well...." her voice trailed off as if considering whether he was really interested or merely asking out of politeness. Then she continued. "I worked for a lawyer in Atlanta and went to law school at night. It was he who encouraged me to go to law school, and it's because of him that I'm where I am today. Unfortunately, he died just days before I passed the bar."

Again her voice trailed off as she thought of Bill.

"I practiced in Atlanta for awhile, and then got a chance to come back to Chattanooga. The children had always liked it here, and Mom wasn't in the best of health, so it seemed the right thing to do."

"I can't believe you've done so much, but apparently it's been good for you. You look great... Mary Howard, Lady Lawyer... Who would have thought it?"

"Probably no one, least of all me. But then, who would have thought Jack Roberts would one day be a famous musician? Entertainer of the Year, Song of the Year, Album of the Year... You've won them all."

"I've been lucky." He answered modestly.

"My daughter, Katie, loves country music, and you're her favorite."

Jack smiled.

"How old is she?"

"She's thirteen." Mary paused. "Jody's eighteen and will be going to college in the fall... I've got a couple of good kids, Jack. They're my greatest claim to fame." And then with a mischievous grin she added, "Although I'm a pretty good lawyer, too."

"I'll bet you are."

Again she looked at her watch.

"Jack, I'm sorry to have to run, but Judge Parrish doesn't have a lot of patience with tardy lawyers. In fact Judge Parrish doesn't have a lot of patience with anything. It's really good to see you."

"It was nice to see you too, Mary."

"Give me a call sometime."

As they parted ways, he thought how much had changed. They were no longer the same two people. There had been too many years, and too many tears, and too many forks in the road. Still, as painful as it had been in the end, there was a time when they cared deeply for each other.

* * * * *

The morning rain, which was supposed to clear out by midday, had paid no heed to the weatherman's forecast and apparently had set in for the day. As Mary contemplated the gloomy weather, she dialed the phone.

"Harry, I'm sorry to disturb you at home."

"That's all right. Peg has gone shopping and the Braves are having a rain delay, so I'm spending the afternoon with the cat and the Sunday paper... Are you at the office?"

Harry Killian had been Mary's partner for four years and he had never known her to go to the office on Sunday. She reserved Sundays for her children. Yet, somehow he knew that's where she was.

"Yeah, I'm afraid so. Jody and Katie are cramming for finals, so I thought I'd go over the evidence in the Perkins case one more time. I wish we were trying it in Chattanooga. We could win it here, but over there she's on home turf, and that could make a difference. I really want to win this one, Harry."

"I know you do, and so do I. You're well prepared and you'll do your usual fine job in presenting the case. That's all you can do. The rest is up to the jury."

"Yeah, I know."

Harry heard her worried sigh and remembered how many times he had felt the same frustration about a case. "Don't worry about it. Old Walt played the fool getting himself involved with that young gold digger. It's a shame, but there's not a damn thing you can do to protect people from themselves and their lack of good judgment. Now, go home to your kids and don't worry about it."

"I'm on my way. I just wanted to clear something with you. I'd like to take Jody and Katie to the beach the first week in June. I checked the court calendar, and we don't have anything coming up. Think you can manage without me for a few days?"

"Sure. If I can't, I'll hang out the CLOSED sign and go fishing. Like I told you before, there's only one month that's sacred to me."

Harry and Peg went to the mountains in August. They had a place near Asheville, and for years they had left the first of the month and stayed until they were ready to come home. They had been happily married for thirty years, and the time in the mountains was their gift to each other. Peg haunted the art galleries and gift shops, and Harry hiked in the mountains and fished for trout. After supper, they sat on the deck and in Harry's words, "sipped wine and acted like a couple of teenagers."

"Sure, take your kids to the beach. Kelly and I will get along fine. She runs the office anyway. And take more than a week. You've earned it. Now, go home and quit worrying about Perkins!"

Mary smiled as she closed her brief case and started toward the door. Harry Killian was a good business partner, as well as a fine lawyer.

As she walked past the darkened coffee shop, she thought of Jack. It had been almost a month since they had run into each other. He said he would call, but she had not heard from him. Like her, he probably led a very busy life. Maybe she would give him a call when she got back from Nashville. After all, it was the nineties, and it was no longer considered improper for a woman to call a man... and it had been nice to see him again.

*   *   *   *   *

"The court will recess until two o'clock, at which time we will hear closing arguments. In the meantime the members of the jury are instructed not to discuss this case with each other or with anyone else."

Judge Davidson sounded the gavel and quickly vacated the bench.

She could read the question on her client's face before he spoke.

"How do you think it's going?"

"Well, you never know for sure, but I feel pretty good. Her other marriages and the substantial settlements she received make her look less than honorable. I think we've dealt the heaviest blows so far, and I don't intend to let up in my closing argument. For the most part, the members of the jury seem to be intelligent, discerning men and women."

In spite of her optimism, worry still showed in her client's eyes.

"We'll give it all we've got and see what happens... Why don't you get some lunch, and I'll meet you back here at 2:00."

Mary watched Walter Perkins leave the courtroom accompanied by his son and daughter. She would do everything in her power for him. She just hoped it would be enough.

She quickly left the courtroom and hurried down the street to *The Slab Shack*. It was the closest restaurant and probably the most crowded. She thought of skipping lunch, but the coffee and juice she had for breakfast were long gone.

Her suspicions were quickly confirmed. Every table in the small restaurant was taken. She glanced nervously at her watch. There wasn't time to go anywhere else. She would have to wait.

"Hey Lady, if you'll buy my lunch, you can share my table."

Someone was obviously trying to be cute, and she wasn't in the mood for cute. Then as she turned and saw the man motion to her, a smile broke across her face.

"You're a lifesaver. I'm practically starved," she said as she approached his table.

"What are you doing here?" He asked, as he stood and pulled out a chair.

It was the same question she had asked him when they had met in Chattanooga.

"I'm trying a case. You remember Walter Perkins, don't you?"

"The hardware man?"

"Yeah, that's the one. His wife died a few years ago, and he married again. His new wife is twenty years younger and has a reputation for marrying older men, then divorcing them, and taking them for all they're worth. She even talked him into buying a house in Belle Meade."

"Walter Perkins?"

He found this hard to believe. Belle Meade was not Mr. Perkins's style. Belle Meade was where the millionaires lived. Jack knew Mr. Perkins and his first wife had worked side by side in the hardware store for years. They had scrimped and saved for their retirement, and had rarely even taken a vacation. They were honest, simple people who were well respected in the community, and they had never been known to indulge themselves in luxurious living.

"Yes. He and Priscilla were married for only a year and a half, and now she's trying to take everything he's got."

"That's a shame. I can't imagine Walter Perkins falling into that kind of a trap. He was always a good businessman."

"I know, but he was lonely and vulnerable, and that's the kind she goes for."

Mary paused to catch her breath.

"I'm sorry. I didn't mean to bore you with all this. How have you been?"

"Busy. I've been here in Nashville for the last few weeks. We finished the recording session this morning, so I'm going home tomorrow. Have you eaten here before?"

"No, I haven't, but I've heard it's good."

"They've got the best barbecue in Nashville. You'll like it. So, how's your case going?"

"We've finished presenting the evidence and have to be back at 2:00 for closing arguments. I feel pretty good, but I learned a long time ago not to second guess a jury. They will no doubt give her something, but I hope it's a lot less than what she's asking."

They talked openly over lunch, and unlike their earlier meeting, the conversation flowed free and easy.

From time to time, she nervously looked at her watch. It would be nice to talk to him... really talk... without having to cut it short to be somewhere else. Finally, she knew she must go. She needed to touch up her makeup and glance over her notes.

"Thanks for sharing the table. Maybe one of these days we'll meet and I won't have to rush off some place else."

She reached for the check, but Jack quickly picked it up, and for a brief moment their hands touched.

"You don't think I'm gonna let you buy my lunch, do you?"

"That was the deal." Mary answered with a smile.

She was enjoying the attention he was paying her, and for a moment the Perkins case slipped from her mind.

"You can get it next time," his smile met hers, "but today it's on me. It's not every day I get to have lunch with a pretty lady lawyer."

Mary smiled warmly. Today she saw a glimpse of the man she used to know.

"Would you like to hear my closing argument?... If you don't have other plans."

"Yes, I would."

As they entered the courtroom, she turned to Jack and with the slightest look of apprehension, said simply, "Wish me well."

There was a solemn look on his face as he answered.

"I always have."

She would have to think about that statement later. Right now the Perkins case demanded her full attention.

* * * * *

"Ladies and gentlemen of the jury, let me thank you for your attentive consideration of the issues involved in this case. I will try to be brief in my summation. Quite frankly, there is little I can add to what the evidence has already shown. The facts speak for themselves."

"My client, Walter Perkins, is the defendant in this case. He is a man of integrity and fairness. When it became evident that he and the plaintiff had irreconcilable differences and Mrs. Perkins asked for a divorce, he not only consented to the divorce, but, as he testified earlier... and the plaintiff did not refute... he offered her a substantial financial settlement. It was his hope that they could arrive at a reasonable settlement and avoid the trauma of a court trial. However, the plaintiff refused to even consider his offer, and instead filed this lawsuit, asking for half of his financial assets... Half of what this man has accumulated over a lifetime for a marriage that lasted less than two years. I don't know about you, but I would say the lady is a little greedy... no, let me re-phrase... I would say she is totally greedy and self-serving, and she has little regard for what happens to this man in his later years when what little she has left him is exhausted."

"Walter Perkins and his first wife, Sara, operated a hardware store in Chattanooga for over forty years, and raised and educated two fine children. In addition to being wife and mother, Sara Perkins worked with her husband in the operation of the family business. When the children were old enough, they, too, worked in the store with their parents. Through simple living and taking care of what they worked for, Walter and Sara were able to educate their children and put away a little money for their later years. They were proud people who made their own way in life, and who did not want to become dependent upon their children or society when their working days were over."

"Five years ago Sara Perkins died. A few years later Walter Perkins met Priscilla Maxwell, the plaintiff in this case, and after a short courtship they were married."

"Now, less than two years later, the plaintiff is desirous of dissolving the union, and somehow she feels she is entitled to half of what Walter Perkins and his first wife worked a lifetime to achieve. Priscilla Perkins' lawyer would have you believe that his client is physically unable to earn a living for herself. Now you know that is not true. The pictures which were introduced in evidence earlier, and which you will have with you in the jury room, show the plaintiff on the ski slopes of Aspen, Colorado. These pictures certainly are not indicative of a person unable to participate in physical activities."

"In addition to skiing, the plaintiff regularly plays tennis and swims, both highly physical activities. She also travels extensively, which can be physically taxing to an unwell person. In fact, Mrs. Perkins appears to be able to do just about anything physical except hold down a job. The evidence shows that Priscilla Perkins has never in her life held a real job... but then she hasn't had to. She has lived off the men in her life. The evidence has shown that each time her marriage relationship was dissolved, Priscilla Perkins has walked away with a substantial cash settlement. And this is what she is asking you to award her today... another substantial cash settlement, in fact half of everything this man and his wife of forty years managed to accumulate over a lifetime of hard work."

"I say to you... Priscilla Perkins does not need to further 'feather her nest'. She already has more than the defendant... and she never worked for a penny of it. I ask you, is this fair? Is it fair that she should literally 'put Walter Perkins in the poor house', so she can have more? How conniving!... How heartless!... How uncaring!"

"But then caring is not a part of Priscilla Perkins' nature. When her husband was in the hospital last winter, gravely ill with pneumonia, was she at his side like a normal caring wife? Did she even come to the hospital to see him? No, she did not! Rather, she admitted him on Sunday evening, and on Monday morning, with her husband critically ill, she left him and flew to Vail for another skiing trip. It was his children... not his wife... who left their jobs and came to Nashville to care for their father. I'm not making this up, folks. You heard the testimony."

"Priscilla Perkins was never a caring wife. She came into this marriage with one thought in mind... and one thought only... and that was to take this man... this good man... for all he was worth. Yet in spite of all this, Walter Perkins was still willing to offer, and did in fact offer the plaintiff a reasonable settlement. But she is not a reasonable person. She is a parasite who marries men, usually older men, treats them so disdainfully that the marriage soon crumbles... which is what she wants... and then goes after everything they've got."

"You are intelligent men and women. I ask you to put an end to this too often played scenario. The financial settlements she has received from the three other men who fell victim to her charm and her scheming should adequately provide her with the means to keep up the lifestyle to which she has become accustomed. And if, pray tell, that is not enough, then what, I ask of you, is so terribly wrong with the plaintive going to work and making her own living for a change? That's what the rest of us have to do."

"Walter Perkins is sixty-nine years old. He has never taken a penny that he did not earn. He is not a rich man, but through scrimping and modest living, he has accumulated enough money to provide for his needs as long as he lives... But not if he is required to give this woman half of his assets... This woman who, by her own actions, has proven that she cared nothing for Walter Perkins."

"As I recall, most of you are married. Let me ask you a question. How would you feel if you were lying in a hospital, gravely ill, and your spouse totally abandoned you to pursue his or her own personal pleasure?"

"I say to you, this woman showed not one iota of caring or compassion for this man. It didn't matter to her if he died in that hospital. She wanted to go skiing, and she wasn't about to let a little thing like her husband's illness interfere with her pleasure. All she cared about was his money... I think that is pretty obvious."

"I ask only that you be fair to Walter Perkins. He has already been hurt enough. Don't hurt him more by stripping him of his means to a meaningful existence in his older days. He is a good man. He deserves better than this. He certainly doesn't deserve to spend the remainder of his life in poverty, just so this lady, who has never worked a day in her life, can take her frequent jaunts to Aspen, Vail, Hawaii or wherever else suits her fancy."

"It will be your responsibility to make this decision. I am sure you will be fair, and that is all my client asks of you... to be fair."

* * * * *

The hardest part of any trial is waiting for the jury to return. She had been through it many times before, but it never got any easier.

Jack observed her as she talked with her client. Outwardly she appeared calm and confident, but he knew she could not help but be anxious. After all, people don't hire lawyers to lose. They expect them to win, no matter how high the cards are stacked against them.

He had been amazed by her performance. She was not overly dramatic like the t.v. lawyers. Instead, she spoke directly to the jurors with an air of sincerity, as she challenged them to be fair in their deliberations. She seemed to have their undivided attention, and every eye in the courtroom was fixed on her as she related the story of Walter Perkins' life, both before and after Priscilla.

There was an element of toughness in her that had not been there in the earlier years. He assumed this came, at least in part, from the necessity to take care of herself and her children as a single parent.

Whatever the case, she was a formidable adversary in the courtroom, and he was impressed with what she had done with her life.

In just over an hour the jury returned. The brief deliberation indicated the verdict had not been a difficult one to reach.

The judge sounded his gavel and addressed the jury, as the people in the courtroom waited in hushed silence.

"Have you reached a decision, Mr. Foreman?"

"We have, Your Honor."

"Please read it."

The courtroom was hushed as the foreman read the verdict.

"The jury finds in favor of the defendant. In view of the brevity of this marriage and the fact that the plaintiff is in no wise dependent upon the defendant for support, he shall not be required to pay the plaintiff any sum whatsoever in settlement of their divorce. Each party shall take with them what they brought into this marriage, and nothing more.

"The jury further awards the house located in the Belle Meade section of Nashville to the defendant, inasmuch as the same was purchased wholly with his funds."

Mary could not believe it. Not only had they won, but they had won big. The jury had not given Priscilla Perkins anything... not one red cent.

For the first time in days Mr. Perkins' eyes were bright as he arose from his seat and extended his hand to Mary. "There is no way I can ever thank you, Mrs. Davenport. It was your closing argument that did it."

"We just told the truth, Mr. Perkins, and they believed us. Sometimes truth is the best defense."

Mr. Perkins, normally a very solemn man, suddenly grinned.

"I don't suppose she's laughing at our settlement offer now." Then he added, "By the way, Mrs. Davenport, would you like to buy a house in Belle Meade?"

Jack was pleased for her. He knew she hadn't expected to win so overwhelmingly. She had felt the jury would give Priscilla Perkins something.

Once she smiled at him from the counsel's table, and the smile told him how delighted she was. He realized she had a number of details to take care of and would be tied up for awhile, so he quickly scribbled a note on the back of a business card and asked the bailiff to hand it to her.

There was a lot going on around the counsel table, and he wasn't sure if she would have time to read the note. But she did.

"Congratulations! You were great! Give me a call after you get through. I'll be at the hotel."

She nodded to him and silently formed the word, "Okay" with her lips.

As he left the courtroom, he was glad he had decided to drive across town to the *Slab Shack* for lunch instead of heading back to Chattanooga as he had earlier planned.

*   *   *   *   *

Jack was pleased with the album they had completed earlier in the day. He had recorded only once since Jessi's death, and the studio still seemed strange without her.

Recording and performing were a part of his career that had been good in its time, but his real love was writing. He hated the traveling and living out of a suitcase that comes with performing... Being in one city one night and half way across the country the next, doing show after show to nameless faces; and singing the same songs over and over until you think you'll go crazy if you have to sing them one more time. Shaking hands and signing autographs for hours at a time, and doing radio and t.v. interviews had long since lost their appeal. It was like a never ending merry-go-round.

That's the way it is in the entertainment industry... He realized that. But now he had control of his life, and the glow of the footlights and the roar of the crowd no longer mattered. He had enjoyed his 'day in the sun' and was perfectly content to leave the performing to others.

The quality of his writing had returned, and singers and publishing companies were eager for his new material. Some of the big name performers had recorded his songs, and several had quickly escalated to the top of the charts.

The only reason he had agreed to collaborate on this album was to help a new artist get her career off ground. RCA had just signed Carly Russell on a trial basis. He and Jessi had met Carly several years ago at a state fair in Virginia, and Jessi had been very impressed with her. Jessi always had a warm spot in her heart for struggling musicians.

"She's good! And she's such a sweet girl." Jessi had remarked. "I just hope someone gives her a break. All she needs is a chance."

When the record producer called and asked if he would consider singing on the album with Carly, Jack knew he had to do it... maybe more for Jessi than for Carly, but either way, he had to do it.

The chance meeting with Mary at the restaurant and the opportunity to hear her closing argument had made a good day even better.

A comfortable quietness permeated the car as they drove back to the hotel, each lost in their own thoughts. It had been quite a day for both of them. She was glad Jack had stayed over to have dinner with her. She was both elated and surprised at the outcome of the Perkins case, but most of all, she was just plain tired. It had been a grueling week.

Finally she spoke. "Mind if I kick off my shoes?"

"Of course not. Make yourself comfortable."

Mary leaned back against the headrest and dozed, opening her eyes only as the car stopped. When Jack returned to the car he was carrying a paper bag, which he handed to her.

"What's this?" She asked, obviously surprised, as she slid the bottle of wine out of the bag.

"I thought we should drink a toast to your victory."

She smiled, but did not answer. However, when they reached the hotel she carried the bottle upstairs.

"Come on in. I think a glass of wine would be nice."

"Are you sure?" Jack was hesitant. It had been a long day, and he could tell she was tired. Perhaps the wine had not been such a good idea.

"I'm sure."

She slipped out of her shoes once more and went to get a couple of glasses.

"I'm sorry I don't have goblets. Think these will do?" And she offered him two plastic cups of the hotel variety.

He poured the wine and then touched his cup to hers.

"To old friends."

She looked at him with a mischievous grin. "How are we supposed to make them clink?"

He smiled and looked warmly into her soft brown eyes.

"Sometimes you just have to make believe."

For a long time they sat in silence and sipped the sparkling wine. They had shared a lot over the years, but that was long ago. They were not the same anymore... They never would be. They had lived in two different worlds, and those worlds had been so far apart.

For Mary there had been Garrett and the children, then the divorce and the ensuing years of trying to make it on her own in a career still largely dominated by men. Life had not been easy.

For Jack there had been the years of striving to make it in baseball, then finally making it and so quickly losing it all. Then the years of struggle in the music field, cheap gigs that did well to pay the board and keep tires on the van... then Jessi... and happiness he never thought possible... God, how he had loved Jessi!... Then she was gone.

He and Mary were old friends, but they both realized that was all it would ever be. So much had happened in each of their lives that the other knew nothing about, things you would have to live through to understand.

The silence between them continued, as though neither knew what to say.

Finally, Jack got up to leave.

"You were magnificent today." He paused as he fumbled for the proper words. "I don't know quite how to say this, but I'm proud of you. I know you've worked hard to become the fine lawyer I witnessed today."

The words were trite, but they were genuine.

"Thanks. I'm glad you were there. I have worked hard, and it hasn't always been easy, but I'm sure it hasn't always been easy for you either. I guess we've both done all right for a couple of kids who weren't exactly born with a silver spoon in their mouth. I don't remember either of us being elected *Most Likely to Succeed.* Sort of shows what a bunch of dumb high school kids know."

The conversation was somewhat strained, but they had each managed to convey the message that, even though their present worlds were miles apart, they still cared about each other.

Jack placed both hands around her waist and without drawing her to him reached out and kissed her on the forehead.

"Goodnight counselor. Get yourself some sleep."

She smiled weakly. She had been up late the night before preparing her summation, and the day had taken its toll.

"I think I could use some," she yawned.

As he turned to leave, she asked, "Jack, would you like to come to dinner sometime?... I'd like for you to meet Jody and Katie... and I make a pretty decent pot roast."

"Sure. I'd like that. Just give me a call."

CHAPTER 44

The smell of new mown hay wafted through the valley. The abundant spring rain followed by warm sunny days had made for an early first cutting. The bright red Massey Ferguson tractors and hay balers were a common sight throughout the Cove as farmers harvested their hay for the winter. Jack's forty-acre tract was small in comparison to the large farms that made up the area. Most of the farmers raised either Hereford or Holstein purebred cattle, and they didn't do it for fun. It was big business.

Jack was not a farmer, and he had no intention of becoming one. He had bought the place in the Cove as the fulfillment of a lifelong dream. He had always loved the area. When he was just a kid, he had come with his dad to fish on this very site, never imagining that one day he would own the property.

He stood on the front porch of the stately farmhouse, his right foot propped on the banister, and surveyed the panorama that stretched before him. It was far removed from the hustle and bustle of the modern day world, and each day as he looked out at the surrounding mountains and rolling green hills, it was as if he were seeing it for the first time.

He could hardly wait to get started each morning on the projects he had planned the night before, and at the close of the day, sleep came easy. The tension was gone from his body, and he felt a peace he had not known in a long while. There was a lot he wanted to do, but there was no hurry. It would get done in time.

He cleaned the lake and stocked it with catfish and did some fencing. He had bought a couple of horses from the previous owner and had inherited a dog.

The Nelson's had bought a smaller place a mile up the road, but the big collie would not stay at the new place. He had been raised on the farm and apparently had no intention of living anywhere else. After several attempts at retrieving the dog and returning him to his new home, Mr. Nelson finally gave up.

"Looks like you've got yourself a dog, Jack. I don't know what to do to make him stay at home."

"Why don't you just let him stay? I can use a dog, and Jake and I have become pretty good buddies."

Mr. Nelson observed the look of awe in Jack's eyes as he looked out over his property, and remembered a similar feeling he had when he first moved to the Cove.

"You really like this place, don't you?"

"Yeah, I do," and the look of contentment on his face confirmed the simple reply.

They chatted awhile, and when Mr. Nelson started to leave Jake ran to the truck and licked his hand and whined, then quickly returned to Jack's side. It wasn't an easy choice, but Jake just couldn't leave this place. Jack could understand why. He hadn't lived here as long as Jake, but neither could he imagine ever leaving.

"I'll bring his doghouse back. He probably wouldn't take to a new doghouse any better than he did to a new home."

From the beginning there had been a special bond between the two of them, and the beautiful collie was rarely far from Jack's side.

Deer and wild turkey frequented the meadow, and squirrels were everywhere, feeding on the acorns and hickory nuts that abounded there.

Someone had abandoned a cat along the roadside, and by the time she reached Jack's place, she was half-starved and almost too weak to cry.

He offered her a bowl of milk, wondering if she would have the strength or the will to eat, but she began to lap the milk, stopping frequently to rest and emit a soft purr of gratitude. She responded well to food and kind treatment, and after a few weeks, she no longer looked like the same animal.

Neither Jake nor Miss Kitty had been part of the plan, but they fit in rather nicely, and late in the evening when Jack got out his guitar to sing or work on new lyrics, they comprised his audience.

Music was Jack's life, but it was not his livelihood, not anymore. If good lyrics came, he wrote them down, but he no longer felt a compelling need to create. In time perhaps he would, but right now there were other things that seemed more important.

The summer at Hendersonville had not done it. The return to baseball had not done it. But time, in its own way, had gradually begun to weave its magic thread of healing.

He often thought of Jessi, particularly toward the close of he day when the sun sank low behind the mountain. She would have loved this place.

In June, he drove to Fort Payne and took an arrangement of summer flowers for her grave. They were her favorites... daisies, lilies and wild flowers... like those in her grandmother's yard.

Each time it was harder to go back and he wondered if she would even want him to. When he walked away, it was as though he were leaving a part of himself behind.

He left the cemetery and drove out to the old homeplace where Jess had grown up. As he approached the house, he could almost smell the aroma of freshly baked bread.

Mrs. Hughes' niece, Marian, had bought the homeplace, mainly to keep it in the family, and had left the house undisturbed. The lace curtains still hung from the windows, and Mrs. Hughes' geraniums were in full bloom.

He wished he had brought his lawnmower. Marian lived in Kentucky and the young man she had hired to care for the yard obviously wasn't doing his job. Mrs. Hughes would have a fit if she knew the grass was so high.

Coming back was a bittersweet experience. The house was a reminder of happier times, but with Jess and her grandmother both gone, it seemed empty and forsaken, and he went away feeling much the same.

In August Curt and Lisa came for a visit and wound up spending a week. They loved Jack's place and promised to come back often.

"Don't forget! You always have a spare room at our place," Lisa reminded him, "and you know where to find the key if we're not there."

They were trying to adopt a child, a seven-year old. "We're too old for babies," Curt quipped.

Jack hoped things worked out for them. Curt and Lisa were good folks and would make wonderful parents, and the farm at Hendersonville would be the perfect place to raise a little boy.

*   *   *   *   *

The warm, balmy weather made it feel as if summer were just beginning, rather than coming to a close, but Labor Day signaled summer's final adieu.

They enjoyed barbecue, baked beans and slaw for lunch, and later in the afternoon Jody and Katie turned a freezer of homemade ice cream.

After lunch Mary and Jack relaxed by the lake while Jody and Katie rode bikes over the farm. It was plain to see Katie wasn't anxious to see Jody go away to school.

"She's going to miss him. They're extremely close." She hesitated. "And so will I. It's hard to imagine not having him home every night."

"He won't be that far away," Jack reassured her, "and I have a feeling he'll be home most weekends."

"I know... It's just going to be different."

While Jack wasn't a parent, he knew how hard it was to let go of the ones you love.

Jody had changed little over the years. He had simply grown up. He still had the thick shock of blonde hair and the ready smile that Jack remembered, and while he looked more like his father, he had his mother's ways. He was quite mature for an eighteen-year old, and Jack felt certain Jody would do well in life.

More than anything else, Jack noticed how caring and protective he was of his mother and sister. He had become the 'man of the house' early in life and had shouldered the responsibility well.

Katie was dark with auburn hair and brown eyes, and like Jody, she too was slender. They were both warm and personable, but there was a hint of sadness that seemed to linger in Katie's eyes, even when she smiled. He wondered if perhaps her parents' divorce had affected her more than it had Jody.

He remembered the pride in Mary's voice when she had first mentioned her children.

"They're good kids, Jack," she had said.

Indeed they were, and though they were raised without a father's influence, she had done a good job on her own, and she had every right to be proud of them.

He waved good-bye to Mary and Katie as they turned the car around and headed home. Jody had left earlier to pack. He would leave for college in the morning.

The phone was ringing when he entered the house, and he heard the answering machine kick in.

"Jack, this is Glenn Daniel. I'll be in Chattanooga on Tuesday to check out a pitcher. If you're going to be around, why don't we get together for dinner? Give me a call at..."

Jack interrupted the recorded message.

"Hey Glenn, I was just coming in the house when I heard your message. It's good to hear from you. How's everything going?"

It would be nice to see Glenn and talk baseball. Jack had said goodbye to baseball as a career, but he still loved the game.

After he hung up the phone, his thoughts returned to Mary. He wondered why they never talked about their past... Perhaps there was no point. They had twice had a chance at happiness and for whatever reason, it had not happened. But for a moment he wondered... "What if?"

* * * * *

The fall months were warm and pleasant and as Christmas approached, Jack felt a peacefulness he had not known in sometime. At least once a week he went to Chattanooga to see his mother and do errands. Sometimes he stayed overnight and awoke to the smell of freshly perked coffee and ham and eggs. If the weather was accommodating, Virginia set a table on the deck, and they enjoyed breakfast outdoors.

She enjoyed coming to the farm from time to time. She planted flowers and shrubbery in the yard, and helped select new draperies and carpet for the house. She loved the serenity of the place in the Cove, but more than anything, she loved seeing Jack happy again.

It was fun fixing the place up, and Jack was tackling things he had never done before. He painted the house and built a gazebo down by the lake, and kept the yard neatly mowed and trimmed.

On Sundays he often went to Mary's for supper. She was an excellent cook, and he looked forward to these invitations.

He had wondered if she was 'seeing' anyone, but he had not asked, and she had not said, although he was sure she had ample opportunity.

One Sunday evening as she was taking the roast from the oven, the phone rang.

"Would you get it please, Jack? I'm expecting a call from Harry about a deposition we have scheduled for tomorrow."

But it was not Harry, and Jack gathered from the conversation that the caller was more than a business colleague.

When she hung up the phone and returned to the kitchen she saw a sly grin on Jack's face.

"Who's Reece?"

"He's just a friend. We go out occasionally."

"Maybe I shouldn't have answered the phone."

"That's no problem. Reece works for J. C. Bradford. Their offices are in the same building as ours."

She placed the roast on the table and then looked up to see what, if any, his reaction was. But there was none. Only the sly grin remained on his face as he waited for her to continue.

"Reece's marriage ended in divorce a few years ago, and he's no more interested in a permanent relationship than I am, so it works out okay... It's nothing serious."

Jack understood. At this point in her life her children and her career were her priorities, and that was as it should be.

There was a lapse in the conversation, as if she had run out of words. Finally, she sighed, and somehow before she spoke, Jack knew what she was about to say.

"How about you? Have you had a serious relationship since Jessi?"

"No, I haven't."

She waited for him to continue, but he did not. Obviously it was hard for him to talk about Jessi, and she could tell he had not gotten over her.

On the way home that night, he thought about the telephone call.

"Damn! Another stock broker," he said out loud.

Then he realized he was being unfair. The man's profession did not make him another Garrett Davenport. Reece was probably a nice guy. And Mary was a mature business lady now, and not the same naive young girl Garrett Davenport had wooed and won twenty years ago. She would not make the same mistake again... Besides, it was none of his business who she dated.

Later that night as Mary dressed for bed, many thoughts ran through her mind.

How strange life is, she thought. In one way or another, we are all victims of our past. We hold on to it with a passion, whether it was good or whether it was bad, and in refusing to let go of yesterday, we let it rob us of tomorrow.

*   *   *   *   *

LATE CHRISTMAS NIGHT

Jack closed the book and automatically reached for his cigarettes, but they were not there. He had not smoked a cigarette in a couple of weeks, but the compulsion to reach for one was still present.

Jessi had not smoked, and he had quit after he met her. But after her death and during the lonely summer at Hendersonville, he had picked up the habit again.

It was the hardest time of his life... harder than giving up baseball... harder than anything he had ever endured... and the cigarettes were his crutch. They provided something to do to pass the endless hours of misery.

There were still times when it all came back so vividly... the feeling of despair, of being alone in that house with the rain pouring down... the feeling of being trapped in his anguish, and waking each day to face his loss all over again.

But time is indeed the great healer, and eventually the healing had begun, and while his grief was not completely gone, it was no longer his constant companion.

He still missed Jessi, and he would always love her, but life finally had meaning again, and he was able to find joy in the simple things. He had lost a lot, but he had not lost everything.

Jessi would not want him to grieve endlessly, but she would want him to remember, and that he would always do. She occupied a special place deep in his heart, and no one could take that from him.

The book he was reading was a special gift from his mother. She had discovered it in the attic while getting out the Christmas decorations, and had sat at the top of the stairway and stared at the book and thought of the year it first appeared under their tree.

It was the last gift she had taken from under the tree, and Jack knew the last gift was always the most special. When he and Jenny were little, they had raced through the packages hurrying to get to the last one, knowing it would be the best of all.

He could tell from the feel of the package that it was a book, and as he removed the last layer of paper, his eyes misted over...

TRAIL OF THE LONESOME PINE
by John Fox, Jr.

It was one of his dad's favorite novels, and he had given it to Jack many years ago.

Jack opened the book and saw inscribed in his father's distinctive handwriting:

Jack,

May you find your own Special Trail in life... and may it be a Happy One.

Love,
Dad

Christmas 1963

Jack hugged his mother tightly, as they each remembered the Christmas in this same room thirty years earlier when John first gave the book to Jack. The lights from the tree illuminated the room, and they felt very close to the one who had inscribed that message so many years ago.

* * * * *

Jack poured another cup of coffee and put the CD Buddy had given him on the stereo. It was an old Allman Brothers recording and contained several of the songs the two of them played years ago.

It was a time when everybody who could strum a guitar or beat drums thought they had the potential to become big rock stars, and amateur rock bands were the order of the day. They had all looked at life through rose colored glasses with little thought of the disappointments along the way.

His thoughts drifted, and for awhile he lost himself in that period of his life. For him, music had been only a diversion. He had other ambitions. He had a great curve ball and could throw his fastball almost ninety miles an hour. Someday he would be a big baseball star... the Dodgers... the Yankees... it didn't matter.

But dreams are only dreams. Sometimes they come true... most often they don't.

Then he thought of the inscription his dad had written in the book.

"May you find your own special trail in life, and may it be a happy one."

There had been a lot of trails in Jack's life, some of them happy, and some of them extremely lonely, filled with potholes and roadblocks, with no end in sight.

But things were different now. Life was good once more, and the holiday season had been the best he could remember since Jessi died.

The get-together at Curt and Lisa's was nice. The house that once had seemed cloaked in sorrow was filled with pleasant camaraderie among good friends, and he was glad he had gone. On his way home he stopped at his mom's. There was a familiar car parked in the driveway, and when he entered the kitchen it was as though he had stepped back in time. Virginia was busy preparing supper and Buddy was helping.

"I see nothing's changed around here." Jack joked as he reached for Buddy's hand. "How you doing, Bud? Still hanging out with my mom, I see."

"Best place in town to get a good meal." Buddy grinned.

The three of them sat down to a dinner of country-fried steak, mashed potatoes and gravy, and biscuits, and Virginia could not have been happier. She loved having them there together. Buddy had always been a part of the family, and she was so proud of the way he had turned his life around.

Buddy had not seen Jack's place, but the grin that crossed his face when he first saw it indicated his approval. Jake met them at the driveway, barking a friendly welcome, and Miss Kitty wound herself in and out of Buddy's legs as they walked up the steps.

"They're my family, Bud," Jack grinned as he reached down and patted them both.

The next morning Jack and Buddy saddled horses and spent the day riding over the place and enjoying the peace and quiet of life in the country.

After supper they sat in front of the fireplace in quiet contemplation and watched the embers burn low.

"Man, this is the life! You've got yourself a nice place here, Jack, and I don't know anyone who deserves it more."

"Thanks, Buddy. I like it here. Just remember you're welcome anytime. If I'm not here, Mom's got a key. Just make yourself at home. The fishing gear is in the basement. I don't get much farther away than Nashville these days, and I try not to do that too often. Mom thinks I should take a vacation, but I can't stay away from this place long. I've spent a lifetime on the road, and it's nice to plant my feet on solid ground."

Buddy nodded in agreement, and for awhile they sat in silence, each lost in their own thoughts of days gone by.

Finally Buddy broke the silence.

"You're doing okay, aren't you?"

It was more of a statement than a question, and Jack knew from the tone of Buddy's voice what he meant. He was talking about Jessi.

"Yeah, I'm doing okay. I still think about her... a lot... and I don't suppose I'll ever stop missing her. But I've found a certain contentment, and life does have meaning again." He paused as if he had said all he should. Then he continued. "There was a long time it didn't. I just went through the motions, day in and day out."

Again he paused.

"They say you eventually get over it and learn to live around your loss, but it takes time, Buddy. Man, it takes time... and it's hard." He had just confided more of his feelings about Jessi than he had to anyone. Perhaps it was what he needed. There was no one who understood better how hard it was for him to let go of Jessi than Buddy, and Jack knew the simple statement of concern came straight from the heart.

Later they got out their guitars and picked for awhile. It was good to have Buddy around. They had been together through 'thick and thin', and 'friends' seemed an inadequate description of their relationship.

"I never hocked it again, Jack," Buddy said as he gently stroked the timeworn guitar. It was the same one Jack had bought back from the pawnshop.

Buddy was doing well in the music business. Jack always knew he could, but there were times he wondered if he ever would. He could not stay off the booze. Jack had seen him hit bottom... rock bottom... but he had pulled himself up and turned his life around.

He was going on to Marietta to spend a few days with Amy. He had to be back in Nashville for a recording session right after Christmas. Kathy Williams, the hottest new singer around, was cutting a new album, and Buddy was playing lead guitar for her.

Virginia insisted he come by and eat Christmas dinner with them. "You have to come this way anyway. It won't be out of your way."

Amy and her mother would be going to her grandparents Christmas day, and Virginia knew Buddy would be alone for Christmas. Amy was all Buddy had left now. His mother had died a couple of years ago. Virginia and Jack were all that remained of their family, and it would seem like old times to have Buddy join them for Christmas.

Jack smiled as he remembered the day he fired Buddy... Then he remembered the cold Christmas Eve he and Jessi had gone to Rome to get him, down on his luck, broke as a bum, playing Santa Claus at the mall just to pay the rent on that one-room dump.

Then he thought of the summer Buddy had come to see him at Hendersonville, when he was about as low as a human being could get, and how Buddy had taken care of him the night he made a fool of himself at Tootsie's.

The two of them had traveled a lot of trails together, some rather rough and rocky, but through the years they had remained friends. And they always would. Life might take them in different directions, but when they did see each other again, nothing would have changed.

Jack's mind moved from one thing to another as he thought how pleasant the month had been.

The Sunday before Christmas he attended church with his mother at the Methodist church where they had gone when he and Jenny were children. The place was filled with memories.

While there were many new faces, quite a few of the folks were people Jack had known all his life, and it gave him a feeling of belonging as he sat in the pew beside his mother.

When Susan Warren was announced as the guest soloist, he was especially glad he had come. It was always good to see Susan, and as she sang the familiar lines of *What Child is This*, he remembered their summer of '74... It had been a difficult time for both of them, but together they had made it, each supported by the other.

He had not seen Susan since Jessi's funeral, and at the close of the service, he hurried to greet her. Her husband stepped aside and smiled as the two old friends embraced.

Phil knew that Susan and Jack shared a special friendship, and he didn't feel threatened by their open display of affection. He and Susan had a good marriage, and he knew she loved him. There was no question of that. But she and Jack had shared a special time together... a time that had helped both of them move forward with their lives. Phil also knew that Susan had needed to put some things behind her if the two of them were ever to have a chance, and it was Jack who had helped her do that.

Jack did not see Mary when she came in, and it was not until the service was over and he stood talking to Susan and Phil that he first noticed her. He was surprised to see her there. She and the children normally attended the Methodist Church in Brainerd. But Christmas has a way of bringing people home, and like many of the others, she had returned to the church of her childhood on this Sunday before Christmas.

They chatted briefly, and then she explained that she had to pick up Jody and Katie at the airport. They had been visiting their grandparents in St. Louis and were due in on a 1:15 flight.

He had not seen much of her lately. They had both been busy. She had a heavy caseload during the entire month of December, and he had made a couple of trips to Nashville, in addition to the party at Curt and Lisa's.

On Christmas Day he stopped by her house and carried her a bottle of her favorite perfume, and they visited for a couple of hours. He could tell she was tired. She had been in court until three days before Christmas and had overextended herself trying to make Christmas special for the children.

Usually the strain didn't show, but this time it did. It almost seemed she was ready for Christmas to be over. She asked Jack to stay for supper, but there was no way he could eat another bite after the huge dinner he had eaten at his mother's, and he could tell that tonight Mary needed rest more than she needed company.

Jack had been lost in his reverie, and it was eleven o'clock when he cut off the stereo and put his coffee cup in the dishwasher. The thermometer outside the kitchen window showed 12 degrees, and he was glad he had brought Jake and Miss Kitty inside.

He got ready for bed, intending to read some more, but he could barely keep his eyes open. Finally, he cut off the light and pulled the cover snugly around him. Outside the wind made a howling sound, but he did not hear it. He was immersed in blissful sleep. It had been a Good Christmas... a Very Good Christmas.

CHAPTER 45

The last two days had been a drag. Anti-trust cases were dull at best, and to make bad matters worse, Judge McClatchy was the trial judge. As usual, he had taken the case under advisement and would render his decision at a later date.

It was dusky dark as Mary drove back from Nashville. Katie was spending the weekend with Allison, and Jody was working on a term paper and wouldn't be home this weekend. They were seldom away at the same time, and the thought of coming home to an empty house was depressing.

Sometimes she felt her life was raging out of control. Her career was so demanding. The holiday season had come and gone, and it hadn't even seemed like Christmas. She had spent most of the month in court, and when she finally finished on the 22nd, there were only two days left to shop and make Christmas for the children.

She loved practicing law, but lately the frantic pace had almost overwhelmed her. There was so little time for her children or herself. She could understand why so many professional people wound up in the divorce courts. Either you neglect your job and do right by your family, or do your job justice and neglect your family. There seemed to be no middle ground.

She wished she could practice law the way Bill Johnson had. He took time to enjoy his work, chatting with friends who dropped by the office, and taking at least one day a week to go fishing or play golf. He worked hard and made good money, but he also found time to live, and lately she had not done much of that.

Jody was already in college, and Katie was growing up fast, and the last six months had afforded her so little time with them. That was the part she resented most of all.

It was not that Harry was derelict in handling his share of the work. He was working just as hard as she was. Their practice had simply outgrown them. They had hired a new lawyer, who would start on Monday. Hopefully, he wouldn't 'have an attitude', like so many of the young attorneys do, and would be more of an asset than a liability.

The house seemed deathly quiet when she unlocked the door and turned on the light. Everything was in perfect order. Katie had seen to that. The children had learned early on to look after themselves. They knew she worked hard, and they did their share at home. Katie could do the laundry and take care of the house better than a lot of adults, and Jody kept the yard in great shape. They were good kids, and whatever else her life lacked, Jody and Katie more than made up for it.

The flashing light on the answering machine told her there were calls, but there always were. That, too, was part of the life she had chosen.

She checked her messages. Maybe there was a call from Jody or Katie.

Hearing their voices made her feel better.

"Hi, Mom. It's 6:30 Friday evening. Thought you might get home early, but I guess not. I'll call tomorrow... around noon. Love you!"

The next call was from Reece. He wanted her to go to a concert tomorrow night.

Katie also had called. Mrs. Lewis was taking her and Allison to Six Flags tomorrow. Six Flags was hosting a special preseason 'sneak preview' weekend, and Katie was spending the night, so they could get an early start.

"Mom, I made spaghetti. There's plenty in the fridge if you want some. We've got two-day tickets, so it will be late Sunday evening when we get home. Mrs. Lewis said you're not to worry, she'll take good care of us. I did my homework as soon as I got in from school. It's all finished. Oh yeah, Jack called. He said he would call you later. Hope you won your case. See you Sunday. Love you, Mom!"

There was a call from the office and one from Blood Assurance. They were in need of Type B donations. She sighed. Right now she felt as if she didn't have a drop of blood to spare, but she would try to go by next week.

The last call was from Jack.

"Just wanted to invite you to supper Saturday night... if you don't have a better offer. Give me a call. Talk to you later."

Later as she lay in her bed, she thought of the past few months with Jack. They had become good friends, similar in some ways to the friendship they had shared when they were young, before they had fallen in love.

It had been almost a year since their chance meeting, and strangely neither of them had made any mention of the time they had spent together in Atlanta. It was as if it had not happened... But it had happened! And it was not a cheap, easily, forgotten affair. It was more than that, much more than that, at least for her it was.

She realized they had been forced to move past that time in their lives. Jody's accident had left them no choice. But to ignore it now as if it had never happened seemed unreal and wrong. And that's exactly what they were doing.

When Jack had fallen in love with Jessi, he apparently blotted from his memory the love he and Mary had shared as effectively as if it had never been.

She knew he had loved Jessi deeply. There was no denying that. She also knew that losing Jessi had all but destroyed him. But Jessi was gone!

There would come a time when they would have to talk about the past... particularly the time in Atlanta. The matter could not be skirted forever... or could it?... she wondered... So far they had done a pretty good job of avoiding it altogether.

She wondered if he would some day marry. If he did, it would likely be someone from his own world. He went to Nashville frequently. Perhaps he was seeing someone there. He had mentioned a Christmas party at Hendersonville, and there were probably other things he had not mentioned.

She had gone to the office Christmas party at Harry and Peg's and to a Holiday get together that some of Reece's colleagues had arranged at the Golf and Country Club. She hated country clubs. They reminded her of a period in her life she would just as soon forget.

Jack had come by on Christmas Day and a couple of times in January. He was working on some lyrics for a new performer and he hoped to go to Florida in February to see some spring training games.

Sometimes days, even weeks, went by with no contact between them, but it was nice when he did call or come by. The relationship they shared was pleasant, though unusual. The children were fond of him and seemed glad to have him around. He and Katie had even played tennis a couple of times.

It was rather unique, after all that had happened between them, that she and Jack still remained friends. And they were friends. She was confident of that. If she ever needed him, she knew she had only to call and he would be there... and perhaps friendship is the best thing two people can share... perhaps even better than love.

Eventually drowsiness overtook her rambling thoughts, and she pulled the soft blue comforter around her, prayed for the safekeeping of her children, and finally slept.

*   *   *   *   *

"This is Jack Roberts. Sorry I missed your call. Please leave your name and number at the sound of the tone, and I'll get back to you as soon as possible. Thanks."

She had expected to get the answering machine. The day was too nice for him to be in the house. It was eleven o'clock as she poured herself another cup of coffee and went out on the deck to sort through the mail that had accumulated while she was away.

The unseasonably warm weather seemed more like May than March, and it was delightful to be outside. What a wonderful day Katie and Allison were having for their trip to Six Flags!

She was tempted to put on her bathing suit and lie in the sun, but she needed to go to the grocery store and drop some things off at the cleaners. Jody had said he would call around noon, and as soon she talked to him, she would do her errands.

At 11:45 the phone rang. It was Jody, and they chatted for a half-hour or so. They were very close. Occasionally she wondered if there would be a time when this would not be the case, but she didn't think so. She believed that neither time nor anything else would ever undo the bond between her and her children. A lot of parents did not have this kind of relationship with their children. She was very lucky.

As soon as she hung up, the phone rang again. This time it was Jack. They talked for awhile. He, too, was outside enjoying the warm sunshine.

"Well, how about it? Do I get to take you to dinner or did Reece beat me to the draw?" He kidded.

"You wouldn't expect me to cancel my plans for the concert, would you?"

"Sure, I would! I'm selfish."

"Well, let's see..." she mused. "I suppose I could draw straws... It's a hard decision." She was putting him on, but it was fun. They were not always able to be this laid back with each other.

"Look, the guy is only offering you entertainment. I'm offering you food. For you that shouldn't be such a tough choice."

"It's not. I would love to have dinner with you."

"Good! Where would you like to go?"

"There's a place at Mentone that has the most wonderful marinated ribeyes. We'll have to have reservations, but you'll like it."

"Sounds good to me. You got a number? I'll see if I can get a table."

In a few minutes, he called back. He had reservations for seven o'clock.

"What time should I pick you up?"

"Why don't I meet you at your place. The restaurant is closer to you than to me."

Mentone was twenty-five miles south of the farm, and there was no sense in him driving all the way to Chattanooga and then back tracking.

"You'll like it, I promise you. I only go occasionally. It's quite a drive from here and normally I don't take the time, but the steaks are delicious, and they have the most wonderful home-made ice cream."

She was fairly drooling as she talked about the ice cream. As a teenager, cherry was her favorite... Jack wondered if it still was.

*　　*　　*　　*　　*

The gentle breeze they had felt earlier was now a gusty wind, and the fragrance of cedar saturated the air as the wind had its way with the trees. The night had an eerie feel, and as Jack escorted Mary to her car, he thought he heard the sound of distant thunder. Maybe he should suggest she wait, but the thunder seemed far off, and if there was a storm brewing, it was still miles away.

Suddenly, there was a robust clap of thunder, which almost shook the ground under their feet, followed by a display of lightning that lit up the valley. The storm was much closer than he had suspected.

"Let's get back in the house."

Her hand trembled in his as they ran toward the house. It had come up so quickly. The lightning danced like lasers all around them, while the thunder rolled and the wind grew stronger.

If she had not lingered at the door, she would have been on her way home, but she was glad she had waited. She felt safe here with Jack, and she would not want to be alone on the road in the midst of this storm.

As they reached the porch, the rain came. It beat upon the tin roof with a fury as the thunder and lightening continued.

He tried to close the door behind them, but the wind held it in an unrelenting grasp. Finally, it released its hold for a moment, and he was able to close the door, but not before another streak of lightning flashed, and they heard a gigantic crash, followed by the splintering of wood. It had hit a tree in the meadow.

A look of sheer panic was etched upon her face, as she clung tightly to Jack's hand.

"It's okay. We're safe now." He assured her.

But she wasn't sure. The sound of the thunder and the constant flash of the lightning made goose bumps on her arms, and her legs felt weak beneath her. She had never seen a storm strike with such vengeance.

They sat close together on the couch, Mary still clinging to Jack's hand. Once he noticed a quiver in her voice as she tried to speak, and he put his arm protectively around her and pulled her closer.

"Are you okay?" His voice was soft and caring.

"I think so. It was so sudden, so intense, as though we had no control of what was happening."

"You never do... In times like these, all you can do is wait, and eventually the storm passes over."

They were both very quiet, as they each pondered the reality of the statement.

The storm continued to rage on with no hint of ceasing. Once the lights flickered, and the digital clock on the stereo flashed. They had momentarily lost power, but it quickly returned.

"It was probably just a limb against a line," Jack explained.

For a moment all was still. Maybe it was about to be over. Then there was another loud boom, and the room was suddenly dark except for the sporadic brilliance of the lightning that at times seemed to engulf them.

She moved closer to Jack, and sensing her fear, he wrapped his arms tighter around her. He would light a lamp in a few minutes, but right now she needed him there beside her more than they needed light. The indomitable lady lawyer seemed fragile and afraid, and he observed something he had never expected to see in her again... She was not invincible... She needed someone.

Gradually the storm began to subside. They could still hear the distant sound of thunder and see an occasional streak of lightning, but the storm had passed, and the soft sound of rainfall on the tin roof and the warm glow of the kerosene lamp were quietly comforting.

Mary could not remember when she had been so frightened. She was strong and combative in the courtroom, and throughout her personal struggles she had exhibited strength and courage, but tonight she had acted like a frightened kitten.

"I'm sorry," she said apologetically.

"Don't be. It was rough out there. It would be stupid not to be afraid. I'm just glad you were here rather than somewhere out there on the road."

Jack poured a couple of glasses of wine and instead of joining her on the couch, pulled a chair up directly in front of her and touched his glass to hers.

"To the passing of the storm."

Unlike the night in Mary's hotel room in Nashville, tonight the glasses clinked, and they both smiled.

Then Jack sat back in his chair, his eyes fixed on her and without forewarning said simply, "Tell me what happened after I left Atlanta."

She was stunned. They had so carefully avoided the subject in the past, and now she wished they could continue avoiding it.

She had known they would one day have to talk about it, but now she wondered if it would not be better to leave well enough alone.

His eyes searched hers for answers to questions he had not dared to ask before. It was as if he were saying, "Tell me all there is to know."

She was not sure where to begin, or even if she wanted to.

"There's a whole chapter in your life that I know nothing about."

She still said nothing, and he wasn't sure if she intended to... but he had to try. He had to know.

"Once upon a time there were the two of us, but we lost each other. Then we found each other again, but our time together was so brief. It was good and right, and we made plans for the future, but those plans got changed by circumstances beyond our control." He hesitated. "I just want to know what happened after I left... Did you think of me from time to time? Did you ever wonder 'What if?' Did you care?"

"I know how I felt... What I thought... But I don't know how you felt or what you thought. I don't have any idea how you got from there to where you are today... Sooner or later we have to talk about this, Mary. We can't ignore it forever."

They were the same questions she had wrestled with herself. She knew they had to talk about it, but she didn't know where or how to start. But slowly and painfully she began.

She talked of the days that followed his leaving... of her despair and loneliness, mixed with her worry for Jody... of the endless days of therapy, and the haunting thought that God was somehow punishing him for her wrongdoing... all coupled with the contradictory feeling that she had done nothing wrong... she had loved Jack... and he had loved her... but still she was a married woman.

Jack hung on every word, never taking his eyes off her.

She told him of Katie's birth and how, as with Jody, Garrett had not been there. She spoke of Garrett's apathetic attempt to mend his ways, and then his quick return to his former lifestyle.

Jack had asked for it... He wanted to know it all, and "all" included the whole sordid story of the demise of her marriage.

She told him of the divorce and of Katie's childlike misconception that she, too, was being divorced by her parents.

She paused.

"Do you want me to go on, or have you heard enough?"

"I want to know... if it isn't too hard for you." He realized this was very painful for her, and that much of it had been carefully put to rest a long time ago, and now he was asking her to resurrect it. "I didn't realize what I was asking of you. If you'd rather not, it's okay. I understand."

There was a little wine left in the bottle, and he refilled her glass. She needed it worse than he did. It took a lot of courage to relive your past.

She took a sip of the wine and continued. She told him about Bill Johnson, how he hired her, cared about her, and encouraged her to go to law school. He knew she needed more than a secretary's pay to provide for herself and her children, and he believed she had an aptitude for practicing law. She told him of his unsuccessful bout with cancer, his determination to see her graduate law school, and how, even though he was too sick to be on his feet the day of her graduation, he had been there, and how he had died just a few days before she passed the bar.

Jack listened intently, and he sensed the depth of her feelings for this man. He wished he could have known the man. He was twenty years her senior, but that doesn't mean anything when two people care about each other.

Then he heard her last comment about Bill Johnson... "He probably cared more deeply for me than anyone ever has."

Jack knew he had no right to ask... but he had to know... at least he had to ask.

"Were you and Bill Johnson lovers?"

Her eyes had been a little downcast as she talked about this man who had befriended her and whom she had cared for so deeply, but now she raised her eyes and answered candidly.

"No, we were not. It was not a relationship that seemed to require that. We just came to care about each other in a special way, but there was a time near the end when the subject came up."

She smiled as she remembered the day in the hospital.

"We talked about the fact we had not been intimate... Actually we laughed about it and vowed to do something about it when he got out of the hospital... but we both knew he never would."

She paused, unable to go on, and Jack reached over and gently held her hand. He was glad Bill Johnson had been there for her, but it hurt to hear her describe this man's feelings for her... "He probably cared more deeply for me than anyone I've ever known."

"And no, there have not been a lot of men in my life. I've been too busy. I've dated occasionally, but on a more or less platonic level."

"And yes, I did think of you. And yes, I did wonder 'What if'... And yes, I did care." Then she was suddenly quiet.

He sat across from her, still holding her hand, wondering what he could possibly say. She had been so brave and so strong. When life had treated him unkindly, he had only been responsible for himself, but she had to fend for herself and her children, and he was sure she had always put their needs ahead of her own.

"Thanks for telling me. I didn't mean to cause you pain in remembering." He paused as he tried to imagine this time in her life. "I think you're probably the bravest person I know, and that Jody and Katie are the luckiest kids in the world to have you for a mother."

He took a final sip of his wine and got to his feet.

"Now I think we should go to bed. It's almost three o'clock."

"Jack, I'm not spending the night."

"Yes, you are! It's late, and there are probably trees and downed power lines across the road, and besides, you've been drinking."

Mary grinned. She had consumed only one small glass of wine. But he was probably right about the roads. No doubt there were trees down all over the place and she would be better off to wait until morning... Yet she couldn't spend the night with him in his house. There had been too much between them over the years.

He guessed what was going through her mind.

"I'm not asking you to share my bed. There are three extra bedrooms, and Mom keeps a gown in the closet."

She knew he was right, and realizing his intentions were honorable, she smiled and nodded okay.

He slipped an arm around her shoulder, and with the kerosene lamp, guided her down the hallway, stopping to get a couple of flashlights out of the hall closet. He held the light for her while she looked for the gown. Then he set the lamp on the dresser and turned the cover down while she got ready for bed.

"Are you okay?" He asked as he laid the flashlight on the nightstand.

"I think so."

"I'll be just down the hall if you need anything... You're not afraid?"

"Not anymore."

He bent over her bed, pulled the cover up, and tucked it gently around her. Then he kissed her softly.

"Goodnight... and thanks for telling me."

She felt like a little girl. It had been a long time since anyone had tucked her in.

When he reached the door, he turned and once more said goodnight. For a moment she wished he would stay with her... just sit on the side of her bed and talk for awhile... but he was right down the hall if she needed him.

She nestled her head in the pillow, breathed a sigh of relief that the storm was past, and soon slept peacefully.

* * * * *

The sunlight filtering through the partially open blinds told her it was morning, but it took a few moments to realize where she was.

The house was quiet, and she assumed Jack was still asleep. She pulled the quilt closer around her and snuggled in. For a moment she was tempted to remain in bed, as the chill of the room reminded her there was still no power in the house, but she resisted the temptation and fumbled through the closet for a robe. She needed to get home. Staying the night had not been part of the plan.

She crept quietly down the hall, trying not to disturb Jack, but as she passed his room she saw that his bed was empty. He had probably awakened earlier and gone outside to survey the storm's damage. But when she reached the living room, he was bending over the fireplace laying a fire. He had not heard her, and for a moment she simply stood and looked at him. He was ruggedly handsome in faded jeans and a flannel shirt.

Sensing her presence, he looked up and smiled.

"I was hoping to get things warm before you got up. It's like a barn in here. The electric company is working somewhere up the road. I heard the saws when I got up. They should have the power back on before long. In the meantime, I thought I'd get a fire going... Why don't you go back to bed until the place gets warm?"

"I'm fine."

Jack detected a quiver in her voice and knew she was cold. The storm had cooled the atmosphere, and unlike yesterday, the feel of winter was in the air. There had been no heat in the house all night, and the light gown and robe were not enough to keep her warm.

"If you're going to stay up, at least let me get you something warmer. You'll freeze in that outfit."

She did not argue, but followed him down the hall to his bedroom, glad to get the warm sweat pants and shirt he offered.

She washed her face in the icy tap water, ran a brush through her tousled hair and donned Jack's sweats. She laughed at her appearance in the mirror. She looked like a clown in the baggy blue sweat pants, but they felt wonderful.

He was sitting on a rug in front of the fireplace when she returned, and while the fire looked warm and cozy, it had done little to warm the living room, much less the rest of the house. He smiled at the sight of her in the oversized sweats.

"How do you think they fit?" She stood poised as though waiting for someone to snap her picture and grinned mischievously down at him.

"I'd say they were just about perfect."

"I'm glad you like them. I had them specially designed by my personal dressmaker for this auspicious occasion."

He was unaccustomed to seeing her quite so loose.

"You're crazy!" He laughed as she came to sit beside him in front of the fire.

He suddenly remembered that the gas grill had a separate eye for heating. They could at least have coffee, and there was some cheese Danish in the fridge.

It was a breakfast fit for a king, as far as Mary was concerned. She was not an eggs and bacon person, at least not in the morning, and she loved Danish.

"Now we know what primitive life was all about," she remarked.

"Yeah, but I kind of like it. You wouldn't have stayed the night if the storm hadn't come... Would you?"

"No, I wouldn't."

"And we'd both be eating breakfast alone."

"I suppose so."

For awhile they sat in silence, lost in their separate thoughts.

A log shifted in the fireplace, breaking the silence.

Then Jack spoke.

"Are you sorry?"

"About what?" She was lost in her own private reverie.

"That you spent the night?"

"No... It was nice. It's just that..." She stopped and then started over. "I'm just not accustomed to spending the night with a male friend."

"I'd like to think I'm more than just a friend."

She did not know how to respond. Of course, he was more than a friend, but she had been unsure if he cared to be more than that, at least lately. There had been a time, but that was before Jessi.

Not knowing what to say, she said nothing... She wanted to... She wanted to bare her heart and soul, but she couldn't. She had to maintain some degree of dignity. She could not beg for his devotion. Neither could she live in the shadow of another woman.

In the silence that followed, Jack sensed that she was sorting out her thoughts. Maybe she would speak them... most likely she would not. He knew her well. He, too, had been hurt, and with each hurt you tend to build your walls a little higher and maintain your defenses a little longer.

They sat on the bearskin rug in front of the fireplace, Mary staring into the fire and contemplating her feelings, while Jack watched her and wondered what those feelings were.

Finally, he moved closer and whispered, "Come here."

It was an invitation, not a command, and he reached out and pulled her gently to him.

She did not resist him when he eased her small back against the hollow of his chest and buried his chin in her hair, as his arms locked around her.

She felt small and pliable in his arms and he thought, as he had long ago, that he wanted to protect her always.

Once he felt her tremble as he slipped his hand under the thick sweatshirt and touched the soft flesh of her midriff.

For a moment she said nothing, then she turned to him.

"Jack, I'm not ready for this."

"For what?"

She looked so vulnerable. Then she smiled innocently and at the same time almost coyly.

"For whatever."

"All I want to do is hold you close and kiss you. Is that so wrong?"

"No, no, it isn't."

She turned to face him and let him pull her into his arms. She looked deep into his eyes, then tilted her chin and slightly parted her lips, and waited to be kissed by this man who she had loved for so long. It no longer mattered that he still loved someone else. She just wanted him to hold her and kiss her... She would take whatever she could get.

For a long time he held her and kissed her, and felt his body grow weak from her nearness. He wondered if she felt the same... He sensed that she did.

Finally, their lips parted and he looked into her eyes. He saw the trace of a tear on her cheek, and he wiped it away and softly kissed the place where it had been.

All of a sudden the lights flashed and he heard the heat pump come on. The power had been restored.

The fire had warmed the room and they no longer needed to sit so close to it. He lifted Mary to her feet. Once more he reached out to her, and once more she slipped eagerly into his arms, this time reaching up to kiss him. Finally, she separated herself from the embrace and smiled up into his eyes. The look he saw was both happy and pained... happy that they had shared this time together... pained that it was about to end.

"I really must go... This could become habit forming."

"I hope it does."

He could not take his eyes off her. He wanted to fix her image indelibly on his mind. It had been a long time since he had felt like this.

There was a nervousness in her eyes, as if she wasn't sure how to respond.

Finally she spoke.

"I've got to go, Jack."

"Don't run away, Mary. I need you."

"Jack, I'm not running away. You know how to reach me. Just promise me you will. I can't live like this, not knowing when or if I'll hear from you."

"You'll hear. I promise you will."

And this time she knew she would.

She quickly changed clothes and got ready to leave.

Jack wanted to follow her to the bedroom, to watch her undress, to hold her once again and cover her with kisses, but he would not. The 'whatever' that she wasn't yet ready for would be 'whenever' she was ready, and not before.

He stood staring into the fire, reliving the last twenty-four hours. They had spent the night in a cold house without heat or lights, but they had managed quite well, and in the midst of the storm, they had found something they had lost so long ago.

* * * * *

As Mary opened the door, the phone was ringing. What if it was Katie or Jody? What if one of them had needed her and hadn't been able to reach her? It was almost noon. She should have left Jack's earlier.

Almost in panic, she reached for the kitchen phone, but it was neither Katie nor Jody... It was Jack.

"I just wanted to tell you something." His voice was soft and tender, and she waited for him to continue. "I love you... God, how I love you."

She hesitated before she answered.

"Jack, please don't say it if you don't mean it."

"I mean it, Mary. With all my heart I mean it."

Once more she hesitated, but only for a moment. "I love you too... I always have."

Then all was silent. There was no need to say more. It had all been said.

"I have to go to Nashville tomorrow, but I'll be home Wednesday. Can I see you Wednesday night?"

"I'd like that very much. Give me a call when you get back."

As she hung up the phone, she felt the same feeling of weakness in the pit of her stomach she had felt when she left him at the farm. The yearning and the longing for him stripped her body of strength. It had been a long time, a very long time, since she had felt like this... And it gave her a sense of belonging... belonging to someone very special.

* * * * *

He hung up the phone and walked outside. The cold air stung his face, but inside he felt warm and alive. No longer were they 'just friends'. It had changed overnight. And he, too, felt a weakness that started in the pit of his stomach and permeated his whole body.

They had felt love... and they had spoken their love... and one day they would consummate their love. Until that time he could wait... He could wait forever if it took it... but he would not have to. This time there was nothing to stand in their way.

CHAPTER 46

The warm sunny days of April confirmed that winter was past and spring had arrived in all her glory. Jonquils and forsythia were in full bloom, and the dogwood trees were filled with buds. Pink thrift blanketed the slope along the driveway, and lilacs shed their fragrance on the spring air. Beauty was everywhere.

Each morning Jack awakened with a renewed sense of excitement. He spent most of the daylight hours working outside, and at night he wrote or simply relaxed and spent his time in quiet contemplation.

The feelings he had for Mary had been carefully put away when he left Atlanta, not all at once, but gradually. And little by little, they had been relegated to the distant past, not by choice, but of necessity.

Their chance meeting last spring had been a surprise. He had no idea she was practicing law. He had heard she was divorced, but thought perhaps she had remarried and was still living in Atlanta.

It was easy and comfortable being with her when they occasionally saw each other, although they were totally different people than before. Not only were their lifestyles different, but their careers were about as far apart as you can get.

He had difficulty thinking of her as a lawyer. A legal secretary? Sure! But he wasn't prepared for the rest, not until he saw her in court. Then he realized any delusions he had to the contrary were wrong. She was strong, and tough, and totally capable.

He had been a little overwhelmed by her success. She had come a long way since the early days in Chattanooga and their time together in Atlanta. The strength and confidence she showed were admirable qualities, but they were a part of her he had not seen before. She had changed, but so had he.

Friends they could be... More than that, he wasn't sure. He couldn't fall in love with anyone. He had had the one great love of his life, and he would never again feel that way toward anyone else.

However, once, a long time ago, he had felt that way toward Mary.

For the past year he had accepted her friendship, and she his, and they had believed this was all it would ever be... all they wanted it to be. They cared about each other, but they would never fall in love.

Yet, in the course of one stormy night they had dared to face their past, and in the facing, they had discovered something warm and real...

something that had laid dormant for a long time, but once awakened was as special and beautiful as before. He hadn't believed it could happen, but the spark was still there, and once kindled, it burned brightly.

He didn't know what the future held for them. But there was one thing he did know... he loved her... and she loved him... And right now that was enough.

* * * * *

Throughout the spring they spent every available minute together. They were gloriously happy times, as they rediscovered each other. The remembering no longer hurt as much as it had at other times, but rather it was part of bridging the distance between the past and the present. They could talk about the feelings they once had been forced to put aside, and this sharing brought them closer than ever.

They were free to be who they were, to share their deepest thoughts and emotions, and to drink freely from the fountain of love that twice had been denied them.

The addition of the new lawyer made quite a difference in Mary's workload. Rarely did she have to work late, and lately her cases had all been tried in local courts. She had been away overnight only once since March, and her job no longer dominated her personal life.

He usually joined Mary and Katie for supper on Wednesday nights. Sometimes he came early to play tennis with Katie. The two of them had become very good friends, and Katie did not seem bothered by her mother's closer relationship with Jack, although he knew Katie was aware things had changed.

One afternoon she spoke of it. They had finished their set and were taking a Coke break.

"You and Mom kind of like each other, don't you?"

Jack smiled. "Uh huh."

"I mean... *really* like each other?" She grinned as she looked at him, a little embarrassed to be inquiring, but at the same time determined to go forward with her questioning. "Like in 'love' maybe?"

Her eyes were fixed on him as she waited for his response.

"Maybe." Again he smiled.

It was obvious Katie intended to get to the crux of the matter. He was not sure if Mary had talked to her, or if Katie had just watched the relationship grow and knew things were different.

"Are you like... maybe gonna get married?" She grinned as she continued her interrogation.

"What does your mom say?"

"She doesn't, but I know she likes you... a lot. I mean..." She hesitated. "It's different from what it was before, isn't it? I mean... she's always liked you, but it's... just different."

"Katie, what would you think if we did get married?"

"I think it would be nice."

It had been said without hesitation, and Jack waited to see if she had finished. She had not.

"I'd be part of the deal, too, you know. You don't just get Mom. You get me... and Jody. Maybe you wouldn't care for that."

Why would she say a thing like that? Jack wondered.

"Katie, your Mom and I are not sure about marriage... There are things we have to work out, but they have nothing to do with you or with Jody... Mainly it's our jobs... I know you and Jody are, as you put it, part of the deal, and as far as I am concerned, you're just an extra bonus that comes with your mom." He returned her smile and continued. "I would be proud to have you and Jody. But remember, you guys are family. I'm the outsider. You and Jody are the most important part of your mom's life, and you always will be. The question is, 'Could you let me be a part of your family?'"

Katie wrinkled her nose as if seriously contemplating the question, and then smiled at Jack. "I like you... and Jody likes you... and I think Mom loves you... so I guess we'd let you join our club."

"Thanks, Katie."

Like a typical teenager, she was trying to be light about it, but Jack knew the conversation was tremendously important to Katie, and he hoped his answers had satisfied her. Sometimes it's difficult to explain to someone so young how two people can love each other and still have trouble with the idea of marriage.

It would be nice to be married to Mary... very nice. But they both had careers... very separate and very different careers... and there was a lot to consider. It would be simpler if it were like it was before, but it was not.

In time, they would work it out. They loved each other too much not to.

* * * * *

Helping Katie pack for camp brought back fond memories for Mary. She could almost feel the icy water of the natural swimming pool and taste the hot dogs and marshmallows they had roasted over the campfire. And at the close of the day, they would join hands and sing.

"Day is Done, Gone the Sun,

*From the Hills, From the Sky.
All is Well... Safely Rest,
God is Near."*

Camp Glisson was nestled in the mountains of Northeast Georgia and seemed far removed from the rest of the world. Mary had enjoyed it many summers herself, and she knew Katie would have a good time.

Jody was also packed and ready to go. He had taken a six weeks work assignment at school, after which he would be home for the rest of the summer.

They would soon be on their own, and she dreaded to see this happen, but time doesn't stand still. She had been so blessed to have them. Hopefully, they would want to go to the beach in August for their usual family vacation. There would come a time when this, too, would end, but right now they all looked forward to the time together away from the hustle and bustle of daily living.

Having gotten her children on their way to their respective destinations, Mary strolled about the yard and thought of past times and events in their lives. It hadn't been easy rearing them alone, but apparently she had done a few things right. Jody and Katie were kids any mother would be proud to call her own.

She thought of how much Garrett had missed. The opportunity was gone... The children were practically grown. One day he would realize this. Perhaps he already had. And for a moment she felt sorry for him.

The phone was ringing when she went inside.

"Did you get everybody on their way?"

"Yes, they left shortly after lunch. The house seems terribly quiet after they leave... How's everything with you?"

"I'm lonely. Can I come see you?"

He was flirting with her, using the 'lonely little boy' approach... and he knew it would work.

"I was hoping you would. I'm lonely too."

They didn't need reasons. They just wanted to be together, but it was fun to kid around.

It was wonderful for both of them... the loving... and being loved. All the barriers had been torn down, and they could be open and uninhibited with each other.

She checked the refrigerator. There was plenty of food left from lunch if they got hungry.

As she brushed her hair, she looked at herself in the mirror. She was wearing yellow knit shorts and a matching tee shirt with a scooped neckline and white sandals. Not bad, she thought. Hopefully he would find her as attractive as she felt. It was strange, she thought, how having someone love you enhances your self-image.

She could not wait to see him, to hold him and kiss him, to feel the warmth of his smile as he kissed her back, and see the yearning in his eyes. She had often dreamed of this, but she had not allowed herself to believe it could happen again. They had already had their chance. But it had happened... And in a marvelous crazy way, it had turned her world upside down. She was in love with Jack. And that was all that mattered. Time would take care of the rest.

CHAPTER 47

Mary was looking over her calendar and making notes on a yellow legal pad when Calvin arrived. Harry had a hearing in Chancery Court and wouldn't be in until later.

"Calvin, may I see you for a minute?"

She had hardly given him a chance to set his attaché case down, much less pour himself a cup of coffee. What a way to start a Monday! Why was she here so damn early anyway? It was only five minutes 'til eight, and she was already busy at her desk.

"Yes, mam."

She knew he was simply being polite, but she hated it when he said that.

"Calvin, you don't have to be so darned courteous. That 'mam' business makes me feel a hundred years old."

And this morning she did not feel old. She felt as young as the breeze.

"Yes, mam."

He had done it again, and they both started to laugh.

Calvin had proved to be a real asset to the firm. He was eager to work and willing to hit the books when he didn't know the answers, unlike so many young lawyers, who thought once they passed the bar, they knew it all, and never had to open a law book again. He was also personable and pleasant and had a good rapport with the clients, especially the older ones.

"How's your schedule this week?" She asked, as he took his seat.

"Not too bad... What do you need?"

"I need you to handle a couple of final decrees for me. They're set for Thursday morning. There's nothing to do but appear before the judge and get the decrees signed. They're already prepared and in the file."

"Sure, I'll be glad to. Which court?"

"They're both in Walker Superior Court at 9:00 o'clock before Judge Abney. It's the Johnson and Huddleston cases."

"Phoebe Johnson? The whiner?"

"That's the one. I'm sorry, Calvin. I'm not purposely unloading her on you. I just need to take a couple of days off... Besides, she thinks you're cute."

"Oh, Lord!" Calvin sighed and shook his head.

"Sure, I'll do it. Anything else you want me to take care of?"

"Not that I can think of. Just be careful. Barbara Huddleston will try to seduce you."

"I'll try to be strong." Calvin thought for a moment. "I don't remember her. Is she good-looking?"

"Yeah, she is, but she's also a gold digger."

"She'd be wasting her time with me," he shrugged.

They had a good working relationship, and she was glad to have him in the firm. He gave a hundred percent every day and was always willing to do whatever was asked of him.

"I have a feeling you're going to owe me for taking care of these two ladies, " he kidded as Mary handed him the files.

"Anything you ask, dear heart, anything you ask."

There was a certain glow on her face, and Calvin knew it was not a business trip that was taking her away from the office.

*　　*　　*　　*　　*

Jack bent over the bed and gently kissed her forehead, trying not to wake her. Then he quickly scribbled a note on the hotel stationery, placed it on the nightstand, and quietly slipped out the door.

It was ten o'clock when she awoke and read the note.

"See you later. I shouldn't be too long. I love you.
Jack."

He would not be back for several hours, so there was no need to get up. She almost never got a chance to sleep in, and it was wonderful to indulge herself.

The room felt cool, and she pulled the coverlet close, nestled her head into the soft pillow, and thought how nice it was to have this time alone with Jack. She was glad he had asked her to come with him.

A few months ago she could not have done it. She and Harry were literally breaking their backs trying to keep abreast of things at the office, and neither of them would have dared take a day off. Calvin had made a big difference, and they were no longer having to work day and night. Life was good! Never in her wildest imagination had she dared to believe that she and Jack would one day find the love they had lost... and that it would be even more wonderful than before.

She felt young and passionate and free. She loved him and he loved her, and nothing else mattered. They deserved this measure of happiness. Lord knows it had been a long time coming, for both of them.

The trip was a gift she was giving herself. Maybe it wasn't proper as she had been raised to believe "proper" to be, but she was happy, and she had not known a lot of happiness in her adult life, except for the joy her children had brought.

She placed her hand on the bed where he had slept last night and wished he were here with her. And a slight shiver caressed her body as she whispered, "I love you."

He was not there to hear it, but that did not matter. She had uttered the words many times before when he had not been there to hear them, but that didn't make them any less true.

It was almost eleven when she got up, showered and dressed. She would get a cup of coffee in the coffee shop and relax by the pool with a book until Jack came back from the studio.

It was almost four when he returned.

"I didn't expect to be so long. And it was so pointless. We didn't change a thing. Russ is a good producer. He just has this thing about wanting the writer to hear the song as its being recorded."

Then he reached out his arms to her and spoke the familiar words, "Come here," and as he lovingly drew her to him, she felt herself go weak in his embrace.

"I've missed you," she whispered as his mouth closed hungrily on hers.

"I've missed you, too, babe, but the rest of the week is ours to spend as we please."

It was still so unreal to both of them... their new found love that seemed to grow with each passing day.

"God, how I love you."

His eyes adored her in a way that words could not express, but she knew... He did not have to say anything.... She knew... Beyond any shadow of a doubt, she knew.

Gently he laid her back on the bed, waiting for some expression that she wanted him as much as he wanted her.

Immediately her arms encircled his broad shoulders, and she pulled him to her, as she arched her back and pressed her body against his.

As she pulled him closer, he sensed her passionate need for him, and knew it was every bit as strong as his for her.

They were so lucky, so unbelievably lucky, to get another chance, and nothing... nothing at all... would ever come between them again. This was forever. They belonged together. And this time it was for keeps.

Long after their passion was satiated, they lay in each other's arms, pledging their love, reluctant to break the spell of their lovemaking, yet knowing this was only the beginning. And Mary remembered a line she had once read.

"Tis a shame that love is wasted on the young."

They were not exactly young, but neither were they old.... Yet they were old enough to appreciate what they had. She had never known love could be so good, so right, so utterly trusting.

* * * * *

Their long weekend ended as it began, on a wonderful note.

The weather had cooperated fully, and it only rained one morning. It was the day after they had gone to Opryland, and it was nice to sleep late and spend the afternoon around the indoor pool.

Neither of them was hungry, as they had eaten lots of junk food the day before, and they didn't even leave the hotel until time for dinner.

"Where would you like to go?" Jack asked.

"You choose. This is your territory."

"Okay, let's go to the Mexican place where we ate the night after you vindicated Mr. Perkins."

Mary laughed. That was a strange way to put it, but in a way, she had.

"Oh yes, I loved that place."

He waited for her to finish dressing, and when she came out of the bedroom, he could only exclaim, "Wow." She was gorgeous. The pale blue linen dress with the multi-colored sash in shades of blue, green and melon showed off her summer tan, and the fragrance she was wearing was his favorite.

"*Beautiful,* isn't it?"

"Me... or the perfume?" She continued to be playful.

"Both."

He was not sure if khakis and a polo shirt were proper attire to accompany such a well-dressed lady, but she quickly allayed his concern.

"You look great. Give me a kiss and tell me you love me, and let's go pig out on enchiladas and sanchos."

He marveled at how she was all business and hard as nails in the courtroom, and yet how carefree and crazy she could be when the two of them were alone.

She had been a nut yesterday, teasing him unmercifully because he refused to ride the roller coaster.

He smiled as he thought of her taunting.

"You're a big macho athlete. Surely you're not going to let a little thing like a roller coaster intimidate you. Come on. I want to ride the *Cannon Ball*!"

"Mary, I told you, I don't ride roller coasters!"

"Come on. I'll hold your hand so you won't be afraid. Come on, please!"

"There's no way I'm going to ride that thing. And you shouldn't."

Just across the way they heard a similar conversation taking place between a little freckled face redheaded boy and his mother.

"Come on, Timmy, we'll ride the carousel again." The mother pleaded trying to lure him away from the giant steel monster. She was not about to go on that thing, and she didn't want him to ride by himself. But it was to no avail. He didn't want to ride the carousel. He wanted to ride the *Cannon Ball*.

Jack laughed as he listened to the exchange.

"Why don't you go ride with him? Sounds like he needs a partner as crazy as you."

Mary had come to have fun, and the Cannon Ball was part of it, and without hesitation she walked over to the little boy and his mother.

"Would you mind if he rode with me? My partner is a scaredy-cat." Mischievously, she cast her eyes in Jack's direction.

Jack nodded to the child's mother. "She'll take care of him."

And Timmy and Mary rode the Cannon Ball, screaming and laughing all the way, as Jack and Timmy's mom looked on in horror.

"I wouldn't get on that thing if they paid me." Jack remarked.

"Neither would I."

"You wouldn't believe it, but she's a lawyer... a very good one."

"Really?"

"I guess she gets a little tired of being businesslike all the time, and needs to let her hair down now and then. Me... I can think of better ways to relax."

Timmy's mom nodded in agreement, and about that time the huge, fiendish steel monster went into its double flip, and Jack turned away.

"I don't even want to look. You gotta be a little crazy to ride that thing."

"I wish I hadn't let Timmy ride. It's too rough."

Jack saw the apprehension in her face.

"They'll be fine. She has two kids, and she's a very good mother. She'll know what to say if he gets frightened."

* * * * *

"You were horrible to me yesterday," he grinned. "I really should make you go to bed without your supper."

She smiled up at him and her eyes grew a little moist as he closed the door behind them. She had given him a pretty hard time, but it was all in fun. She loved him so much, and they were having such a wonderful time together.

When they got on the elevator, he took her hand and smiled at her.... A smile that seemed to say, "I forgive you for being so mean to me."

He could melt her heart with a glance... He always could.

"I love you, Darling." She squeezed his hand.

"Me, too."

And he gave her a quick kiss as the elevator door opened.

Everything about their week had been wonderful. The little things... the stolen glances... the touch of their hands under the table... the private times they spent in each other's arms with the world so far away.

As she got out of the car at her house, she wondered if it ever would, ever could, be this good again. But of course it would. True love doesn't begin and end with a single event. It is ongoing, stretching from here to eternity. She would love Jack for the rest of her life, and she knew he would always love her. This was what life was about. It wasn't money or fame or fortune. It was loving and being loved.

CHAPTER 48

Darkness slowly enveloped the city, and daylight was replaced by millions of lights outlining the skyline of the vast city. The view from the skydeck of the Sears Tower was magnificent. Jack loved Chicago. It not only offered the excitement and glamour of big city life, but it had a certain warmth and hospitality seldom found in large cities.

Glenn had a ten o'clock meeting, so Jack spent the morning browsing through the Michigan Avenue shoppes for gifts for Mary and his Mom. Afterwards they went to Wrigley Field to watch the Cubs.

There was no place in baseball like Wrigley Field with its ivy-covered walls and rooftop spectators. It was an old stadium, but it had personality. It was baseball the way it should be. And the fans were incredible, never giving up on the Cubs, always hoping that this would be the year, even though their team hadn't won a championship since 1908.

Jack was glad he had come. Mary and the kids were in Florida for the week, and although they had invited him to join them, he had declined. It was their special time together, and he knew that with each passing year it would become harder for them to get together. Jody was already in college, and in a few years Katie would be too, and their lives would take them in different directions. He knew Mary cherished this time with her children, and it should be their time exclusively.

With Mary away, it had been easier to accept Glenn's offer.

"I'm gonna be in Chicago for a few days next week. Why don't you fly up and meet me? We can see a couple of games and do the town. I know how you used to love to play in Wrigley."

Jack and Glenn had a pleasant relationship, and since they were both 'unattached' and neither had a nine-to-five work schedule, they were able to take off whenever they chose and could pretty well call their own shots.

For the past couple of years they had enjoyed getting together from time to time. Usually the things they did centered around baseball. In March they spent a couple of weeks in Florida making the rounds of spring training. Glenn knew just about everybody in baseball, and Jack enjoyed the time they spent together.

Chicago was full of things to see and do. On Wednesday they saw the White Sox play and went to *Harry Caray's Restaurant* for dinner. Later they went to Grant Park and watched the lasers light up Buckingham Fountain.

In the background the moon cast its warm glow on the peaceful surface of Lake Michigan, and to the north the Chicago skyline illuminated the city. It was a spectacular sight.

For a moment Jack's thoughts drifted far away from Chicago. He wondered about Mary... what she was doing at this very moment... and if perhaps she might be thinking of him... and the miles between them suddenly seemed far too many.

"How about a nightcap?" Glenn asked when they reached the hotel lobby.

It was their last night in Chicago. Tomorrow Glenn would be going to Milwaukee to spend a few weeks at home, and Jack would catch a flight back to Chattanooga.

Glenn ordered a Manhattan, and Jack settled for a Michelob, and they listened to the singer in the hotel bar.

"She's pretty good," Glenn commented.

"Yeah, she is."

The conversation lagged. It had been a busy couple of days. Chicago was not a place to relax. There was so much to see and do.

Jack thought about Glenn. Ann had been gone almost three years, and they had not had children, so he was pretty much alone in the world. He understood why Glenn could not retire. He had nothing to retire to.

Theirs was one of the good baseball marriages. Glenn had adored Ann, and when she developed cancer, it almost destroyed him.

And then, as if sensing Jack's thoughts, Glenn spoke of her. He usually hid his feelings well and appeared the proverbial happy guy. But what a multitude of sadness a smile can often cover.

"It gets kind of lonely sometimes, doesn't it?... You know Ann and I married right out of high school and had been together half of our lives... God, I miss her so much."

"You had one of the best, Glenn. Ann was a special lady."

"Yeah, I did. People try to fix me up all the time. They think I ought to go out... get married... have a relationship... whatever they do these days. I don't say it will never happen, but I doubt it. I don't need a relationship. Hell, I'm still in love with Ann."

Jack knew exactly how Glenn felt. He had been there. Maybe someday Glenn would love again... Maybe he never would.

"How about you? You think you'll ever find anyone else like Jessi?"

Glenn had never once mentioned her name. Perhaps he knew how hard it was for Jack to talk about her. Perhaps he knew why Jack came back to baseball.

"Well, I'm seeing someone. She's pretty special. It took a long time, and I literally went through hell. Like you, I didn't want to get over Jessi. Her memory was all I had left, and I didn't want to give it up."

"We loved each other so much, so intensely, but, unlike you and Ann, so briefly."

It still wasn't easy to talk about her.

"I didn't want another relationship. I had had the best, and she was gone, and I knew I could never replace her."

Glenn's eyes rested on Jack's and urged him on.

"But it was different with Mary. I had loved her before I knew Jessi. We were high school sweethearts. She had wanted to get married while I was in the minors, but I told her we needed to wait."

Glenn nodded, remembering the strains put upon his and Ann's marriage as he struggled through the minor league ranks.

"I knew I had to devote myself completely to baseball if I was to have a chance at making it to the majors. And in the process I lost her."

"She married someone else... a damn woman-chasing stockbroker. He worked out of town most of the time, leaving her alone for weeks at a time. She could have gone with him, but he said she needed to stay in Atlanta and look after their home. Truth of the matter was he wanted to play his games, and he couldn't do that if she were with him."

"We ran into each other once when I was playing in Atlanta. It was the early days of my music, long before I met Jessi. My career was going nowhere. She was lonely and so was I, and we had a couple of days together. I know it was probably wrong. She had already seen a lawyer about a divorce, and we thought maybe we would have a second chance. I had a two-week gig in Charlotte, and while I was gone, she would see the lawyer and pursue the divorce. The next week her son was struck by a motorcycle. He was in a coma for days, and when he did come out of it, he was crippled up pretty bad. There was going to be months and months of therapy to try to rehab him. Her husband had good insurance and Jody would get the best care available if they stayed together. There was no way I could provide what Jody needed, so there was nothing for me to do but get out of her life and give them a chance to put their marriage back together."

"He hung around playing the dutiful husband and father role long enough to get Jody on the way to recovery and get her pregnant again, and then he was back to his old ways."

"I stayed around until Jody was out of danger. When I left Atlanta, I knew I couldn't look back. It was hell, pure hell, for the longest time, but there was nothing I could do. I had no claim to her, and I was barely making enough money to keep body and soul together myself. As much as I wanted to, I knew I couldn't take care of her and Jody."

As Jack paused, Glenn realized he didn't tell this story often.

"Last spring I ran into her in Chattanooga after all those years. She was divorced and had gone to law school and was practicing law. It was good to see her, but that was all that it was. I was still in love with Jessi. Whatever Mary and I had had was a long time ago. We were different people with different lifestyles, and she was no more interested in a serious relationship than I was. We were just friends. And for a long time, that's all that it was. It was nice and comfortable, and neither of us wanted it to be anything more."

"But one day I looked at her, and I saw someone I had come to love. We were still friends, but suddenly we were more than that."

"She didn't take Jessi's place... no one ever could. They each have their own place. It probably doesn't make a whole lot of sense to you. But you had one great love in your life, and you had her for almost twenty years. There were two wonderful women in my life, Glenn... I just never got to keep either of them..."

"Are you going to marry her?" The expression on Glenn's face was solemn.

"I don't know... I hope so... I get along well with her kids... There's no problem there. Trouble is I think we're both a little afraid to rock the boat. Everything is so good right now. If we dare to make it permanent, maybe what we have will be taken away."

Glenn sipped his drink and waited for Jack to go on.

"I'm sorry, Glenn. I didn't mean to rave on."

"Don't be. I'm glad you told me. Don't let what I said about my feelings for Ann deter you. You're young. You've never had a lasting love. Don't be afraid to take another chance. Don't let true love slip through your fingers. It's too rare to risk losing."

Glenn wished Jack well. They had been friends a long time, yet he had never known about the girl called Mary. But Jack was not a sharer, and neither was he. They both tended to keep their problems to themselves.

"When do I get to meet her?"

"How about Labor Day? Can you get away for a few days?"

"Sure. I'll look forward to it."

When Jack awakened the next morning, Glenn had already left for Milwaukee, but on the nightstand was a note.

"See you Labor Day weekend. I'll give you a call. Take care."

Jack packed his bags and reached for the first baseman's mitt he had bought from a street person in Grant Park, and smiled as he remembered the conversation.

"Hey Mister. Let me sell you a baseball glove. You look like a baseball player."

"Used to be."

"For real?"

"For real."

Jack took the glove and tried it on. There was nothing like the feel of a baseball glove... nothing!

"How much?"

"I take ten bucks."

"I only got a twenty. You got change?" Jack didn't figure he had.

"Nawsir. I ain't got nothing."

"Well, maybe it might be worth twenty."

"Yassir... yassir... it oughta be worth twenty."

Jack smiled as he checked to make sure he had packed everything, and once more he slipped the twenty-dollar glove on his hand, and there in bold script was the freshly signed autograph:

"GLENN DANIEL"
CHICAGO – JULY 1994

CHAPTER 49

With summer past, Jack thought perhaps he could get some writing done. He had an idea or two, but had not had time to develop them. He and Mary had spent every moment together they could these past few months, and his thoughts were centered more on her than on writing songs. Every night he thanked God for her and for bringing them together.

In the morning when he awoke his first thoughts were of her. A tremor would pass over his body as he thought how wonderful it was to hold her close and feel her body so soft and warm, and to know she loved him as much as he loved her.

They both realized how lucky they were to have another chance. While they shared a special physical attraction to each other, they shared something much deeper than that. They had known each other since they were kids, and their roots ran deep in the community where they had lived and grown up together.

They had gone to the same school and the same church, and she was the first girl he had ever kissed. They were only twelve at the time, and Mary was sure she had committed some terrible wrong.

"We mustn't ever do it again," she had said. "We're too young." But they had, and as time went by they had become more than friends.

He had dated other girls occasionally, mainly because you're supposed to. Mary also had dated others, but they had always come back to each other. And in the eleventh grade they had fallen in love, and they had known it was for real. But things had not gone as they planned, and for what they thought were all the right reasons, they had allowed love to slip through their fingers.

Now they had found each other again, and he would never let her go. Sometimes he awakened in the middle of the night and longed to call her just to hear her voice and know she was there.

One night he had called. It was three o'clock in the morning, but he knew she didn't have to work the next day, so it wouldn't hurt to wake her.

"Jack, I love you, too, but why don't we go to sleep now and talk about it tomorrow?" He could hear her yawn before she continued. "But I'm glad you called... You made my night."

For a moment there was silence between them. Then she spoke. "Jack, I wish you were here."

"Me too."

They did not speak of marriage. One day it would happen, but there was no hurry. No legal document or repeating of vows could make them any more one than they already were.

Glenn had come down for Labor Day, and they had all gotten together at the farm. Mary and the children were there, along with Jody's girlfriend. It was still warm enough to swim, and everyone was on his own to do whatever he chose. Jody and Gina rode horses and the rest of them pitched horseshoes and played badminton, and ate like food was going out of style.

It was obvious that Glenn liked Mary, and as he and Jack sat on the porch Monday evening after everybody else had left, he spoke of her.

"You're damn lucky, Jack. Don't blow it. Life doesn't give us a lot of chances at happiness. There are some sweet girls out there, but they're not pretty, and there are some pretty girls out there that aren't exactly sweet. Mary's both and if you don't marry her, maybe I will."

Glenn grinned.

"Like the devil, you will!"

"I just wanted to make sure you knew what you had, and that you didn't fool around and lose her."

Jack nodded in agreement. "I won't."

They sat for awhile in quiet contemplation as the sounds of the night drifted through the valley.

Finally, Glenn spoke. "I ran into Sandy Davis when I was in Milwaukee. We had dinner together. It was kind of nice to sit across the table from a woman and just talk, although about all we talked about was Ann and Rick. She invited me to come to dinner sometime."

Jack and Glenn and Rick had played baseball together in the early years, and Glenn and Rick had enjoyed a long career together. They had played on the same team and on opposing teams, but they had remained close personal friends. Rick had suffered a massive heart attack a couple of years ago and never regained consciousness.

He could tell Glenn's mind was suddenly far away and sensed he was remembering Ann... and Rick.

"You gonna go?" Jack asked

His words brought Glenn back to the present. "What did you say?"

"Are you gonna go see Sandy?"

"I might. She's a nice lady."

Glenn Daniel was one of the good guys, and Jack hoped that one day he would find real happiness again. He had a way to go, but hopefully he was beginning to move beyond his grief. He could not resurrect Ann anymore than Jack had been able to resurrect Jessi. It just takes time.

CHAPTER 50

Her teeth chattered as she pulled the thin hospital blanket around her. Her temperature was almost 104, yet she insisted she was freezing. The white shorts and blue tee top that earlier had looked so crisp and clean were now wrinkled and damp from perspiration. Fear showed in her eyes. She had no idea what was happening to her and neither did Jack.

He had not left her side since he brought her to the emergency room. The nurse had told him he would have to wait in the waiting room, but he had paid no heed. They would have to physically throw him out to make him leave her.

It had all happened so fast... Katie planned to go out for the school softball team in the spring, and Jack had been working with her. He knew firsthand there was no substitute for practice, and the harder you work, the better you get. First he would pitch to her and let her practice her hitting. Then he would hit her ground balls, and they would work on her fielding.

Her hitting was coming along, and her fielding was excellent. She had good range and seldom missed a ball, but today she wasn't herself. She had missed several easy grounders. It was as though she was just swiping at them, and Jack knew she was a much better fielder than this.

"I'm terrible!" She lamented. It was obvious she was frustrated with herself.

"Don't worry about it. We all have our days... You want to quit early?"

"No, I want to redeem myself."

The next ball was a soft grounder hit almost in her glove. It was a cinch, but she let it go through her legs. It was the ultimate goof-up, and she dropped her glove in disgust and for a moment he thought she was going to cry.

"Katie, are you all right?"

Her face was unusually red, and as he approached her, he could see she was wringing wet with perspiration.

"I'm just disgusted with myself. I can't do anything right today."

He knew something was wrong, but he wasn't sure what.

Then she asked, "Jack, are you cold? I'm about to freeze."

"Cold? Katie, it's 80 degrees out here. Are you sick?"

"I guess so... a little."

He felt her forehead. It was hot to the touch, and she was shaking like a leaf.

"Let's call it a day. Okay?" He knew he needed to get her home.

This time he got no argument from her, and he quickly gathered up the equipment and they headed for the car. He couldn't imagine what had made her so suddenly ill. She had been fine when he picked her up an hour ago.

"I wish I had brought a jacket."

"I've got one in the car."

He flung the equipment bag over his shoulder and put his other arm around her to keep her warm until they could get to the car.

"That feels good." She weakly smiled as he wrapped the jacket around her.

"We'll get you home and call your mom."

"Okay."

For a few minutes she was very quiet, and Jack glanced at her, thinking she might have dozed off.

"I'm sorry, Jack. I didn't mean to get sick on you."

"It's all right. Nobody gets sick on purpose. It's probably just some sort of bug you picked up."

When he unlocked the back door, Katie headed for the bathroom almost in a run. He started to the phone to call Mary, and then he heard Katie gag. When he got to her, she was sitting on the edge of the bathtub, bent over the commode, throwing up. He wet a washcloth and held it against her forehead.

Through pathetic eyes, she looked up at him. "I'm sorry. I don't mean to be so much trouble."

"It's okay. We all get sick sometime... You'll feel better now."

But he wasn't sure. She looked so wan and frail, and her face was an ashen color. He replaced the washcloth with a wet hand towel, and she wrapped it around her neck and slowly eased herself down the side of the bathtub and onto the floor.

"I need to stay here in case I get sick again... Did you get Mom?"

"No, I was about to call when I heard you getting sick. If you think you'll be okay, I'll call her now... Just don't try to get up 'til I get back."

"I won't."

She doubted she could stand on her feet anyway. Her legs felt like spaghetti. She sat on the cold tile, still wearing Jack's warm-up jacket. A little color had returned to her face, but she continued to shiver.

"Are you still cold?"

"Yeah," she murmured.

He got a blanket from Mary's bedroom and wrapped it snugly around her legs, and placed a pillow between her and the cold tub she was using for a prop. He hated to leave her, even for a minute, but he had to call Mary.

"I'll be right back. Just stay put while I call your mom. Okay?"

She nodded, and he was halfway down the hall when he heard her.

"Tell her, if she's not too busy, to please come home. I'm so sick."

"I know, sweetheart. I'll get her."

As he had feared, Mary was not in the office.

"I'm sorry, Mr. Roberts, she's out of the office. May I ask her to call you when she gets in?"

"Where is she, Kelly? I have to talk to her. It's Katie. She's sick, very sick."

"She's in Atlanta, but I can reach her... Where will you be?"

"I'll probably take her to the emergency room. She has a high fever and chills, and she's sick at her stomach. I don't know what's wrong, but she's a sick little girl. Tell Mary I'm taking her to Memorial. It's the closest."

"And, Kelly, please don't fool around. I don't know what's wrong with her, but she's very ill, and she needs her mother."

"I understand... Don't worry. I'll get her."

It was only ten minutes from Mary's house to the hospital, and Jack had expected Katie to be seen immediately, but that had not been the case. They had been waiting in the treatment room for what seemed like ages, and Katie still had not seen the doctor.

Jack was about to go see what was going on when a nurse poked her head in the door.

"Is she doing okay?"

"If she were doing okay, she wouldn't be here. I brought her here to get some help. When will a doctor be available? We've been here forty minutes, and no one has seen her yet."

"We'll get to her just as soon as possible. This is an emergency room, and we have to see the patients according to the urgency of their condition."

The well-rehearsed reply angered Jack even more. He didn't have to be told where he was. He knew it was an emergency room. That's why he had brought her.

"Well, I would say she's pretty urgent. She's a sick little girl, and no one has done a damn thing since we got here except make sure she has insurance."

He was angry. The emergency room had seemed like the proper place to bring her for immediate attention. Now he wondered if she might not have received quicker attention if he had taken her to her own doctor.

"The doctor was about to see her, but a drug overdose came in. Unfortunately, they get priority. I don't agree with it, but that's the way it works. They go out and try to kill themselves, and then we drop everything to save them. I don't mean to downplay the seriousness of your daughter's condition. When your temperature goes as high as hers, you're sick, but I don't think it's life-threatening. Try not to worry. The doctor will be with her in a few minutes."

He did not bother to tell her he was not Katie's father. All he wanted from these people was some attention for Katie. They could think whatever they pleased.

"Please don't leave me, Jack."

The last thing he had meant to do was upset Katie, which undoubtedly he had, but he was so frustrated. He knew she was frightened. He just wished her mother were here.

"I'm not going anywhere, Katie. Kelly just called from the office. Your mom's on her way. In the meantime, I'll be right here with you. Don't worry. You're gonna be fine."

Shortly another nurse with a clipboard came in. At least something seemed to be happening.

"I need to get some information... family history, etc. Are you Katie's father?"

"No, I'm not, but I'll tell you what I can, and her mother can supply the rest when she gets here."

He furnished all the basic information as it related to Katie and Mary. When she asked about family illnesses, he knew that Henry Howard had died suddenly of a stroke, and that Mary's mother had died of cancer.

"Does Katie's mother have any health problems?"

"Not that I'm aware of."

Then she turned to Katie.

"Katie, do you feel like answering a few questions?"

She nodded, and the nurse quickly went down the 'have you ever had?' list.

About the worst thing she had suffered from was chicken pox and an occasional cold.

"Any accidents?"

"No."

"Looks like you've been a pretty healthy young lady. What did you eat for lunch today?"

"Vegetable soup and a pimiento cheese sandwich... and chocolate chip cookies."

"That sounds harmless enough. I don't think it's what you ate... Just try to relax until the doctor gets here. It shouldn't be long now."

"Can you give me any information about her father?"

"Not a great deal. He and Katie's mother were divorced when Katie was quite young. I'm sorry I can't tell you more."

"That's fine. Thanks for your help."

Eventually the doctor entered the small examination room.

"Hello. I'm Dr. Stephenson. What happened to you, young lady?"

"I don't know. I was playing softball... I was trying to field ground balls when I began to feel weak and started chilling... Jack felt my forehead and said I was real hot, but I didn't feel hot. I felt like I was about to freeze. By the time we got home I was sick at my stomach, and I felt like I was about to pass out."

"Did you throw up?"

"Yes, sir."

"Had you been sick or feeling bad earlier in the week?"

"No, sir. It just happened all at once."

He checked her eyes, ears and throat, and then listened to her heart and lungs.

"Your fever's kind of high." Then he turned to Jack and continued talking to both of them. "I want to admit her and give her something to bring the fever down. That will make her feel better. We'll call her family physician, and he'll probably order a few tests, and we'll try to determine what we have here."

"The nurse will give you a shot, Katie. It should help cool your fever and stop the chills, but it will make you drowsy. You look as if you could use a good nap anyway."

"Can I wait until my mother gets here? I'd like to see her before I go to sleep?"

"How long will that be?"

Jack glanced at his watch.

"About thirty minutes. Her mother was in Atlanta, but she's on her way and should be here soon."

"Okay, I'll put it on her orders. As soon as she talks to her mother, ring for the nurse, and she'll give the injection. I'd like to give it now, but it will put her to sleep, and the assurance that her mother's here is also important, but we shouldn't wait more than an hour."

The doctor looked at his watch, and then back at the flushed face of his patient.

"If her mother's not here by six, we'll have to go ahead with it. Her fever doesn't need to go any higher."

"What do you think is wrong with her, doctor?"

"I don't know. It could be flu, but it's not really flu season... mono, maybe or strep. We'll get some tests started as soon as we get the fever down, and they should help us isolate the problem."

Jack followed him out into the hallway. It was the first time he had left Katie, even for a moment.

"You didn't mention the possibility of meningitis. My little sister was stricken when she was about Katie's age, and she died within forty-eight hours. Her symptoms were a lot like Katie's."

Dr. Stephenson saw the anxious concern on Jack's face, as he pleaded for assurance that Katie did not have meningitis.

"It's something we have to consider with these symptoms, but generally with meningitis they're a lot more lethargic than she is."

Katie had just gotten into a room when Mary arrived. A weak smile infiltrated Katie's flushed face as Mary bent over her bed and kissed her hot forehead.

"Mom, I'm glad you're here. I have to have a shot, and they say it will make me sleepy. I wanted to see you before I went to sleep."

"I got here as quick as I could, honey."

"I was afraid you might drive too fast and have a wreck."

Mary fought to keep back the tears. Katie always worried about her. It was almost a reversal of the usual parent-child relationship.

"Katie, I love you more than anything else in the world, and I'll be right here when you wake up."

"I love you, Mom."

Jack had stepped away from the bedside, so they could have their time together, but now he moved closer.

Katie looked up at him with grateful eyes. It had been a frightening experience, but he had been so good to her and had never left her.

"Thanks, Jack, for taking such good care of me." She hesitated for a moment, unsure of whether she should say it or not. Finally, she did. "I love you, Jack."

Mary looked from one to the other and smiled.

"I love you too, Katie." He could say no more. The last few hours had taken their toll on his emotions, and the tears were very close to the surface.

The nurse gently turned Katie on her side and gave the shot, as Mary bent over her bed and held her hand. Katie gradually relaxed as the shot began to take effect and finally she slept peacefully.

Mary looked at her watch. It had been only a couple of hours since she got the call from Kelley, but it seemed like an eternity. Nothing serious had ever happened to Katie before, and it had terrified her.

Jack motioned her to a chair and sat down in front of her, being careful not to block her view of Katie. She was wearing a beige linen suit with matching pumps, and her appearance was that of the well-dressed lady lawyer, but Jack did not see that. Instead, he saw what was written on her face... the anxious concern of a mother who loved her daughter, perhaps more than life itself.

Whatever lay ahead for him and Mary, he would never be jealous of her children. Because she loved them so much, she could also love him, and there would always be enough love to go around. Their eyes met, and he reached out and took her hand in his.

"I'm here... for whatever it's worth." His voice was soft and caring.

"It's worth a lot."

He was still wearing the white tee shirt and gray shorts he had worn to the ballfield, and his face showed the strain of the last few hours. Mary regretted she had not been there, but there was no one to whom she would rather have entrusted Katie's welfare. She knew Jack would take care of her.

Through eyes that quickly overflowed with tears, she looked at him and knew she could always count on him. He was a special person. He always had been.

"I love you," she whispered.

Only a few feet away Katie was breathing softly, and Jack told Mary step by step what had happened to Katie, trying to remember every detail.

After awhile the nurse came in and laid back the blanket that Katie had pulled so snugly around her.

"She seems to be cooling off some. I think the medication is doing its job. Mrs. Davenport, could you give us some information on Katie's father? We need to complete her medical history. You can come out to the desk or if you'd rather not leave her, I can bring the file in here."

"No, that's okay. I'll come to the desk. She'll probably sleep for awhile anyway."

"I'll stay with her." Jack offered. "I'm sorry. I was supposed to tell you they needed information about her father. I let it slip my mind."

"I understand. You've had a lot on your mind. I'll be back as soon as possible," Mary promised.

There was a troubled expression on her face. Jack assumed it was because she dreaded having to deal with Garrett, but if Katie was not better by morning, he knew she would call him. She had always tried to be fair with him, especially when it involved the children, and Jack knew she wouldn't keep Katie's illness from her father.

*   *   *   *   *

Just before dawn Jack awakened. All was quiet in the room. Mary had finally dozed off, and Katie was still asleep. He tiptoed across the room to her bedside and gently laid his hand on her forehead, trying not to wake her. It no longer felt hot, and he could tell her fever had broken.

As if sensing his presence, Katie slowly opened her eyes and smiled weakly. Then she closed her eyes once more, emitted a soft sigh, and was gone again.

"She's beginning to come out of it. Her temperature is almost normal."

He looked up to see a nurse standing by his side. He had not heard her come in. Apparently she was quite adept at slipping in and out of rooms in the still of the night without disturbing those who slept, whether it be the patient or the loved one keeping vigil.

"Is she doing okay?" Jack was anxious for some reassurance.

"I think so. The crisis appears to be past... She should be awake in a couple of hours."

Side by side they stood looking at Katie, each hoping for the best.

"She's a sweet girl. Is she your daughter?"

"No, I wish she were."

Somehow a little more explanation seemed to be in order. The nurse had been so good to Katie throughout the long night.

"I'm in love with her mother and in the course of things Katie and I have become very good friends."

The nurse smiled and straightened Katie's cover, and then quietly crept out of the room to check on her other patients.

He continued to look at Katie. While her skin was pale and she appeared exhausted from her ordeal, she was still beautiful. She had her mother's dark hair and complexion, and there was an almost angelic look about her.

For some strange reason he could not take his eyes off her. She looked so much like Jenny. Perhaps that was why he had been so worried about the meningitis. Finally he reached for his wallet and thumbed through it for the picture he had carried for so many years. He held it close to the night light, staring first at the picture and then at Katie.

He could not believe what he saw! They could pass for twins! They had the same coloring, the same dainty features, and even their expressions... half-serious, half-smiling... were the same.

Suddenly it hit him!... Katie was his daughter!

Very gently he placed his large hand over her small one, again trying not to disturb her. But he had to touch her... She was his... his very own flesh and blood. There was no denying it.

"I love you, Baby," he whispered as his eyes filled with tears.

Quickly he stepped away from her bedside, hoping he could make it to the door before his emotion completely overtook him. He did not want to wake Mary. They would have to talk later... but not now. Katie was still too sick. All that mattered now was making her well again.

Tears flowed openly from his eyes as he opened the door to the men's room. It wasn't fair! She hadn't just all of a sudden become his. She had been his daughter all these years, and he had not known. Why had Mary kept it from him? He had a right to know he had a daughter.

But maybe he was wrong... maybe she wasn't... but she was! He knew she was. Not only did she look like Jenny, she looked like him as well.

Then he thought of how sick she had been. What if something really bad was wrong with her? What if he should lose her just when he had found her?

But the nurse said she was better. They would run tests tomorrow. Then it dawned on him... Tomorrow was now today. They would find out what her problem was, and they would get the best doctors available, and she would be all right.

"Please God take care of her and make her well. Don't take her from me. I love her so much." Never before had he prayed a more fervent prayer, nor had more reason to hope.

Slowly he regained control. In time he and Mary would talk. Now he had to take care of Katie. He had not been there for her in the past, but he was here now.

His heart anguished for the lost years, the time he could never retrieve, but it also overflowed with joy. Katie was his daughter!... And he would always love and protect her.

*   *   *   *   *

The tests had confirmed it was mono, and Katie was home and doing well. She didn't have a lot of energy, but that was to be expected. The doctor said she needed rest and a good diet, and in a couple of weeks she could go back to school. In the meantime, Mary picked up her assignments so she would not fall behind with her schoolwork.

The worst part was the confinement. Katie would much rather be playing softball or tennis, but she didn't have the strength. Jack assured her that just as soon as she was ready, they would resume softball practice. In the meantime, he brought her books. Fortunately, she loved to read, and it kept her from getting too bored.

The day was warm, and Katie wanted to eat outdoors. Jack had called and said he was bringing a pizza. He also stopped at the bakery and picked up eclairs. They were Katie's favorite.

"You know you're going to be spoiled rotten when you get well, don't you?" Jack grinned.

"I suppose so. I guess that's the only pleasant thing about being sick. Everybody does nice things for you... When do you think I'll be ready to play softball again?"

"Let's wait and see how you feel... Maybe by the end of the month, if you feel up to it. I'll be ready when you are."

Mary smiled. It meant so much to Katie to make the team, but she knew it wouldn't be easy. The school had a good girls team, and only three of the girls were graduating this year. If Katie made the team, she would no doubt have to sit the bench the first year. She would hate that, but that's the way the system works. While Mary had not been an athlete, she knew the heartbreak of high school sports and the politics involved.

After supper Katie said she was going upstairs and read awhile... "That is, if you guys think you can stand some time to yourself?"

It was good to see her acting a little devilish. They had given her their undivided attention these last two weeks and taken no time for themselves.

"If we can't handle it, we'll let you know," Mary responded, with a mischievous grin.

Jack helped Mary clear the table and put the food away, and then they returned to the patio. They sipped iced tea and stared out at the still green trees in the yard. Before long they would begin to change colors and lose their leaves, and it would be fall, then winter. It was part of the plan, and it happened year after year, but Mary was never ready for summer to end.

Suddenly her thoughts were interrupted.

"When were you going to tell me?" His voice was quietly serious.

There was no prologue, no explanation of what he was talking about, just the forthright question... and though Mary had been lost in her thoughts, she knew instinctively what he was talking about.

She had known for a long time that some day they would have this conversation, but it still came as a shock. Without looking at him, she replied.

"I always knew there would come a time when you would know... Apparently that time is now."

Finally she looked at him, and the expression he saw on her face was a mixture of distress and relief. He waited for her to continue, and eventually she did.

"How long have you known?"

"Since that first night in the hospital."

She looked at him, and then glanced away.

"How did you know?"

"Just before daybreak I awoke and went to check on her. All of a sudden it hit me... Katie was my daughter... I don't know how I knew, but I knew."

He waited for her to respond, but she said nothing.

"It is true, isn't it?"

This time she answered.

"Yes, it's true."

His eyes were fixed on her, waiting for her to say more, but she could only repeat her previous answer.

"Yes, it's true."

"Mary, for God's sake, why didn't you tell me? I had a right to know. It took two of us to make her. Did you think she was yours exclusively... that I had no right to know my own daughter... to spend time with her... to watch her grow up? She's almost grown, and I've missed so much. I didn't get to see her take her first step, hear her call me 'Daddy', buy her a teddy bear. Nothing! I never even knew her until a year and a half ago. And then you didn't have the honesty to tell me she was my daughter."

Mary flinched as she listened to his cutting words. Then she saw the tears slowly begin to creep down his cheeks. Never before had she seen such pain etched on his face. She wanted to get up and go to him, to hold him and comfort him, to make the pain go away.

But he would not let her. She knew that. He was angry and hurt. And he had every right to be. He would reject any effort she made to console him. He would settle only for answers, and she wasn't sure they would be enough. And she had no answer to his most demanding question... "Why didn't you tell me?"

Sometimes there are no credible reasons why we do what we do. Sometimes we simply do the best we can, and hope that in so doing we don't hurt the people we love the most. Sometimes it works. Generally it does not. And with all our good intentions, the ones we love the most are the ones we wind up hurting in the end.

She had tried so hard to do what was right for Katie... and for Jack... and for everyone involved, but there was no way he would ever understand. He had not walked in her shoes. He did not know what it had been like for her.

Now they were both crying, and their eyes were no longer fixed on each other, but rather on some distant horizon, hoping, searching for answers which they both knew would not come easy.

Finally, Mary dried her tears and began to tell her story, hoping he would understand, at least in part.

"In the beginning I did not know... There was no way I could know. At times I thought she looked like you, but everyone said she was just like me. It was not until she was older that I began to suspect the truth.

One night I was looking through an old picture album and came across a picture of Jenny. It was amazing how much she and Katie looked alike. Then I began to see a lot of you in her, not just physical resemblance, but mannerisms, traits, things that were neither Garrett nor me, but which were very much you."

"She loved Garrett very much, and she was his favorite. We were trying to make it as a family, and I suppose I tried to make things work, at all costs. If Garrett had known or even guessed, he would have done everything in his power to have me declared an unfit mother and take the children away."

"After the divorce, I considered calling you or writing a note. I did not want, nor expect, money or anything else. I just felt like you should know. But you and Jessi were together."

Jack interrupted.

"That wouldn't have mattered. Jessi would have understood. Katie was my daughter. I had a right to see her, to have her with me."

"And what was I supposed to do?... Bring her to Nashville and say here's your daughter. She'd like to go on the road with you. She's still too young to be away from her mommy, so I'll have to come along too!"

He only stared at her. Her comments were hard, but they were nonetheless realistic. He couldn't have taken Katie with him.

"You're never going to believe this because in your mind you've already indicted me and found me guilty of all the things you want to believe I did wrong, but the truth is I tried... I tried to do the best I could to make a good life for Katie and raise her to be a good and decent person. I tried to be both mother and father to her. And I loved her... with all my heart I loved her... and whatever else I may have done wrong, I raised your daughter well."

"Maybe you found out about her late in life, but you've got a daughter you can be proud of, and if you want a relationship with her, you can still have it. She adores you. I can't change what is past, nor can either of us change what happened in Atlanta fifteen years ago, and the very thing that should mold us together will probably tear us apart."

"It's really sad, Jack. I love you. I'm not sure I ever loved anyone else. I thought I loved Garrett, but not the way I love you. But I'm not perfect. I realize now I should have done things differently, but I had Katie to think about, not just you. How would she deal with the fact that you and I 'fooled around' while I was married to the man she believed was her father?"

"Don't call it that. I hate that term... Fooled Around!" He repeated the words in disgust.

"Hell, Mary, I loved you. I didn't just 'fool around' with you. Give me credit. I've got a little more to me than that."

"Well, that's the way society looks upon it."

"I don't give a damn about society. That's not what it was. I refuse to believe that Katie is the result of 'fooling around'. I would like to believe she was conceived through an act of love between two people who cared very deeply for each other."

"She was."

Mary realized her earlier words had been poorly chosen, and they had offended, but, unlike her closing court arguments, she had not had the opportunity to prepare and edit her speech in advance.

"When I knew the truth about Katie, I could not come to you. I would have... believe me, I would have in a heartbeat. I would have humbled myself and fell at your feet, but you were in love with Jessi... I don't use her name lightly. From everything I've heard, she was a lovely human being. But there was not room in your life for both of us."

"So I got a job and went back to school and tried to prepare myself to take care of my children. I thought the best thing I could do for everyone concerned was stay out of your life."

"Your career was skyrocketing, and you and Jessi were in love. You had a right to be happy, and the least I could do was not get in the way."

"I read of your success and watched the awards shows, and once I saw one of your and Jessi's concerts. You were great, and she was lovely. But it hurt like hell to see the exchange of pure devotion between the two of you. I was glad I had gone, but when I walked out the door, I knew I would never go back. I just couldn't handle it."

Jack wasn't prepared for all he was hearing. For a moment he thought about the concert and wondered how he would have reacted had he known she was there. Obviously, she had cared a great deal or she wouldn't have exposed herself to that kind of hurt.

For a long while they sat in silence. They had come up against a stone wall, and it seemed insurmountable.

"It's hard, Mary, to deal with the fact that I never knew Katie, and she never knew me. Try to put yourself in my place."

"I'm sure it is... It has to be. But try to put yourself in my place. What would you have done?"

"I don't know... I really don't know."

He sat quietly, apparently having run out of words to express what he felt, but Mary knew the misery was still there. Maybe it would always be.

"There is so much of Katie's life I'll never know anything about. It's forever gone... And, selfishly, I wish she knew a little about me. I've had a few successes in life... I even won a few awards. It would be nice if Katie had known about them. Call it ego... whatever... I just wish she had known."

Once more he stared out at the horizon.

It was the first time she had ever heard him mention his success, and he did it almost apologetically.

"Jack, don't downplay your success. You were great. You and Jessi were household names. Everywhere I went I saw your picture and heard your songs. The love songs... I knew I wasn't the subject... but sometimes I pretended I was. Katie and I watched every award show. She was little, but she loved you."

"But she didn't know I was her daddy."

"No, she didn't. She was too young to handle that. But someday she would. I always knew that, and I kept everything I could."

Mary got up and went inside. When she returned she was carrying a large box, which she set in front of Jack.

"Go ahead. Open it." She urged.

It was filled with CDs, everyone Jack had ever made. He knew it hadn't been easy for her to buy those with Jessi's picture covering the entire front, but she had, and she had stored them away for Katie when she was older.

He continued to look through the box. There were videos of the award shows, all carefully labeled and dated. There was an expansion folder filled with various Music City publications and Top Forty Charts, and a glossy 8X10 photo of himself, which she had purchased at the concert. He had to give her credit. She had tried to preserve something to share with Katie when the time was right... something that said a little about who he was and what he had accomplished.

For the first time he smiled, as he closed the flaps of the box.

"Looks like Katie has a better collection than I do."

He had been so intent on looking at the contents of the box that he had not realized she was holding something else.

"These are for you."

She handed him two books: a photo album and a scrapbook, which she had carefully worked on over the years of Katie's growing up. He thumbed through them and occasionally smiled.

"Are these for me to keep?" He asked.

"Yes. I realized some day you would know about Katie, and I kept the album and the scrapbook for you."

"Thanks. I'd like to look at them better when I'm alone, if you don't mind."

"I thought you would. Just take care of them. I have only one copy of some of the things in the scrapbook, but I wanted you to have them."

"I don't know what to say except thank you."

"I'm sorry I've hurt you. I didn't mean to... I just did the best I could under the circumstances. I wasn't God. I couldn't make everything right.

But I did try, Jack, the very best I knew how. I wish it had been different. There are a lot of things I wish I could undo, but I can't."

"I'm sure you did what you had to. I guess we both did."

Again he hesitated, and simply looked at her. She had no idea what thoughts were going through his mind.

"I don't know where we go from here, but the one thing I do know is we both love Katie, and we love each other. We'll work it out. Just give me some time to deal with it."

She nodded.

"There's one other thing you should know. If something had happened to me, there's a safety deposit box separate from the one where I keep my legal documents. It has a letter to Katie from me, explaining, as best I could, the truth about her parents. And there's a scrapbook for her too. It contains a little about us. I wanted her to know who we were, where we came from, and that we did love each other, and were not just 'fooling around', as I so poorly put it. It contains some early photos of the two of us, a few valentines, even a love letter or two, which I would never share with anyone else. I wanted her to know that she should never have cause to be ashamed of the facts of her birth. I wanted her to know that her daddy was a good and honorable person, and I wanted her to love him as I had loved him."

"How was she to know about the safety deposit box? Suppose she never found it, and we never knew about each other?"

"Bill Johnson had a key, and he knew that if I died, there was something in the box for Katie, something very important. I knew he would see that she got it. Now Harry has the key, and he would have done the same if something had happened to me before you and Katie came to know each other. Neither of them knew what was in the box. They just knew it was important to me that Katie have the contents. I told Katie in the letter how to reach you."

He thought she was through, but she continued.

"There was also another letter in the box. It was addressed to you, and I asked Katie to give it to you."

The sun had gone down, and it was beginning to grow dark as Jack got up to leave. They had both had about all they could handle for one day.

"Would you like to see her before you go?"

He nodded and took Mary's hand, and together they climbed the steps to Katie's room. She was sleeping. Mary turned the night light on, and they stood and looked down at their daughter.

Jack's voice choked with emotion, as he bent over Katie's bed and gently brushed a wisp of hair back from her forehead.

"Goodnight, Sweetheart. I love you."

Mary knew Jack and Katie would be fine. They would survive all of this, but she was not sure if she and Jack would… only time would tell.

CHAPTER 51

What a wasted day! Jack thought, as he turned the key to his hotel room... The song was a good one. In fact Russ thought it was one of his best, but the recording session had been a complete flop. Kathy Williams had tried everything they suggested, and each time they listened to the tape, she only shook her head.

"It's just not right. There's something we're missing."

She looked first at Jack and then turned to Russ. "Think it might help if I tried speeding it up?"

Jack knew that wasn't the answer, but since nothing else had worked, they tried it. It was worse than before.

"I don't think it's the tempo." Kathy admitted.

Again and again they listened to the various versions and tried to find the problem. They were pros and usually one of them could figure out what a song needed, but today nothing seemed to work.

"Maybe the song's just not any good." Jack finally said in disgust.

But Russ and Kathy did not agree. They knew that Jack didn't kid himself about his lyrics. He knew whether they were good or not, and if they didn't pass his personal scrutiny, they wound up in the wastebasket, not in Nashville.

Finally Russ began to gather up the tapes.

"Let's call it a day. We're all tired... But I'll wager the farm this song won't go down the drain. It's gonna hit one of us 'smack dab' in the face what we need to do to get it right. Then we'll come back in here and record the damn thing, and watch it go gold."

Russ Ashby was one of the best in the business, and he and Jack had recorded together for many years. He knew a good song when he heard one, and Russ believed in this song.

Kathy had to catch a flight to Myrtle Beach, so she was the first to leave.

"You got a dinner date?" Russ asked.

Jack shook his head and finally managed a grin. "You asking me out?"

"Why not? Let's go to *The StockYard*. They've still got the best steaks in town."

They had a good dinner and tried to put the frustrations of the day behind them.

"Russ, when are you gonna come down and see my place?"

"Soon. I need to get away from this place for a few days. The rat race of the recording industry will drive you crazy." Russ paused. "You got any hoot owls down there?"

"Yeah, we got hoot owls," Jack grinned.

"Every summer I used to go to my granddad's in Alabama, and at night we'd sit on the front porch and listen to the hoot owls."

For a moment they were both quiet, each remembering simpler times.

"Sure enough, Jack, I'm gonna get down there one of these days."

But Jack doubted it. Russ loved the excitement and fanfare of the Nashville scene, and while he got frustrated when things went as they had today, he would rather be here than any place in the world. It was his life and sadly, Jack thought, his only life.

Later Jack looked about the empty hotel room and wished Mary was here. There was something about being alone in a hotel room that made him feel forlorn. It always had.

If he didn't have the appointment with Tom Jansen tomorrow, he would check out and head home. But he needed to get his will changed, and he had been fortunate to catch Tom in town.

He thought of Katie and called to check on her.

She was feeling much better, and the doctor had said she could go back to school Monday.

"I'm sure that made you real happy."

"Not really, but I am getting a little bored, and I miss everybody."

They chatted for a few minutes and then Jack asked to speak to Mary.

"Mom's in Atlanta. Harry was supposed to try the case, but his daughter was in a wreck. She was hurt really bad, and they're not sure if she's going to make it. He and his wife have gone to Tacoma to be with her."

"Katie, who's staying with you? You're not by yourself, are you?" He couldn't believe Mary would leave Katie after she had been so sick, not even for her job.

"Verna's here."

Verna Winkler was Mary's neighbor. She adored Katie and Jody and had looked after them before, and he knew Katie was in good hands with Verna. Nevertheless, Katie had been very sick, and although she was better now, it disturbed him that neither he nor her mother was there with her.

Katie sensed his apprehension.

"Don't worry, Jack. I'm fine, really I am. Mom wouldn't leave if I wasn't okay."

"I know she wouldn't, sweetheart. Where can I call her?"

"She's staying at the Marriott. I'll get you the number. You'll probably have to call her late. She uses the D.A.'s library in the evenings to get her case ready for the next day. It was 11:30 when she called last night, and she had just gotten back to the hotel."

"I'll give her a call. You take care of yourself, sport, and if you need me for anything, call me here at the hotel. Okay?"

Mary answered the phone on the first ring.

"Mary..."

"Hi, Jack. How are you?"

They talked for a moment, then she interrupted. "Jack, let me call you back. I just got to the hotel, and I need to call Katie and see if she's all right. She shouldn't be up this late, but she won't go to bed until she hears from me."

"She's fine. I just talked to her. She's worried about you though. She thinks you work too hard. Give her a call, and call me back when you get through."

About thirty minutes later Jack's phone rang. Mary was tired, but she seemed more relaxed now that she had talked to Katie.

"I hate being away from her. Harry tried to get a continuance, but Judge Teems wouldn't grant it. He's about as unyielding as a steel rod. He said 'I'm sorry about your daughter, Mrs. Davenport, but surely there are other members of your firm who are capable of trying this case. It's on the docket for 10:00 A.M., but I'll take some guilty pleas during the morning and postpone your case until 2:00 P.M. That should give you time to get someone to handle it. That's the best I can do... I've got a court to run.'"

"Can you imagine someone being so hard boiled? It was a horrible wreck, and they're not sure if Jill will make it." Mary sighed in disbelief that a judge would show so little consideration. "Harry knew I wouldn't want to be out of town with Katie still recovering, and he was willing to let Calvin tackle it, but Calvin's not ready, not for this case. I knew Verna would look after Katie, but Harry had to go to his daughter."

"Why didn't you call me? I would have taken care of Katie."

"You had a recording session."

"That could have been postponed."

"I know, Jack, but it wasn't necessary. Verna has stayed with the children before. She's almost like their grandmother, and besides that, she worked as a registered nurse for years. Katie couldn't have better care."

"My biggest problem right now is not Katie. She's fine. I simply haven't had a chance to prepare this case properly. Harry had prepared it completely, but he does a lot of stuff in his head, and when he does make notes, he scribbles, and I can't half-read his writing. So, for the most part, I'm having to wing it." Mary sighed. "A man's life is on the line, and I need to put up the best defense I can. I just wish I had a few more days to get ready."

"Do you think you'll finish the case this week?"

"I doubt it, but I'll be home for the weekend."

She suddenly realized she hadn't asked how the recording had gone. However, she sensed it had not gone well.

Jack confirmed her suspicions, but did not dwell on it. She had her own problems to deal with. They did not talk long. He knew she needed to get some rest. It was already past midnight, and she had to be back in court early in the morning.

"I'm glad you called, Jack. I needed to hear a friendly voice... Maybe you did, too?"

"Yeah, I did."

They said goodnight, and though they were two hundred fifty-miles apart, their thoughts were of each other.

* * * * *

Jack thought what a shame it was. She didn't have to work like this, but he knew it would be hard for her to give it up. She had paid too great a price to get where she was, and in addition to that, there was the excitement. He had heard it in her voice tonight. She was dead tired and worried about her daughter, but she was still exhilarated over the possibility of saving her client's life. Each case was a personal challenge, and she loved what she did.

There was one thing for certain... The guy couldn't have a better lawyer. She would give him her best. Jack knew that.

* * * * *

Mary thought about Jack's day. Usually the recording sessions went well, and it was only a matter of making a few minor changes and smoothing out the rough edges, but apparently that had not been the case today. She could tell he was disappointed, and so was she. The song was one of his best. It was about her, and them, and their long way back... And he hadn't been able to get it recorded. She felt a trace of jealousy. The songs he had written for Jessi always got recorded.

* * * * *

Tom Jansen's office was elegantly decorated in shades of burgundy, gray and kelly green, with huge peace lilies appropriately placed around the room. The massive desk was mahogany, and Tom's chair was a glossy burgundy leather. Everything in the room showed good taste, and it was obvious the interior designer had decorated the office with no regard to cost. Tom had expensive taste, but he could afford to. He represented some of Nashville's wealthiest, and the fees he charged were by no means modest.

"Good to see you, Jack. How's everything down in Georgia?"

For a few minutes they exchanged small talk, and then Jack explained the purpose of his visit.

Tom listened intently as Jack outlined the changes he wished to make in his will. Then he spoke candidly.

"I understand your wanting to take care of the child, but are you sure about the mother? After all, you're not even married to her. I'll do whatever you wish, but I suggest you not include her in your will... at least not at this point. Later if you still want to include her, we can do a codicil."

Tom's remarks annoyed him. He had not come for advice. He knew exactly what he wanted to do. All he wanted from Tom was to put it in proper legal form.

"Tom, Katie's not just 'the child'... She's my child. And there's no question in my mind about including Mary. I want her included now, not later. For fifteen years she has raised our daughter and done a very good job of it, and never once has she asked me for a dime. I've known her for a long time. She's completely honorable. Furthermore, she doesn't need the money. She's a lawyer, herself, a very good one. I don't have anyone except my mother, and now Katie and Mary, and I want her included." Jack paused briefly, and then continued. "And I am going to marry her... not just because she's the mother of my child, but because I love her."

Jack had made his point, loud and clear.

"I'm sorry, Jack. I didn't mean to be argumentative... I should have known better than to imagine you needed counseling. You knew what you wanted when you came in here. Now all I need to do is get your will drafted in accordance with your instructions."

Tom looked at his calendar before continuing. "I'm taking my wife to Tahoe next Friday for a couple of weeks. I'll try to complete it before I leave and give you a call."

"That's fine. I appreciate your seeing me."

They shook hands and Jack left the office, glad the appointment was over. Tom Jansen was a good lawyer, but he was also presumptuous, and at times a little condescending. Jack probably had just as much money as Tom. He just didn't feel the need to flaunt it.

* * * * *

"Hey, Marge... Jack Roberts. Are you up yet?"

Marge was the typical night person and held no claim to fame for rising early in the morning.

"Of course, I'm up. I just haven't decided to face the day yet. It's nice to hear from you, 'D-A-R-L-I-N-G'. Are you in town?"

"Yeah... and I thought I'd buy you lunch if you're not already taken."

"Oh, D-A-R-L-I-N-G, when you get my age, you're rarely taken. I would love to have lunch with you."

"Fine, tell me when to pick you up, and you choose the place."

"Give me thirty minutes to make myself beautiful... It really takes longer... but when a handsome young man asks me out, I don't give him time for second thoughts."

Jack smiled as he hung up the phone. He already felt better. Marge was like a ray of sunshine on a cloudy day, and one of his dearest friends in the music business.

She was a bit of a character, but she had taken him under her wing when he first came to Nashville. She introduced him to the right people and opened a lot of doors for him.

She was real, and forthright, and forceful when necessary, but she was gentle and caring, and a true friend.

Marge loved magnolias and martinis, and she loved to flirt and be flirted with. She had been married three times, and would quickly tell you that "One out of three ain't bad".

Unfortunately, her one good marriage had lasted only seven years before her husband's untimely death. Marge was a musician's agent before her marriage to Ron, and was well fixed financially. She had given up her career when they were married, and together they had traveled the world and, in her words, "lived and loved to the hilt".

After Ron's death, she came back to Nashville, worked when she chose, mixed and mingled with friends in the industry, and now and then picked out a struggling musician and tried to boost his career.

This was Marge Scott... different... flamboyant... completely uninhibited, but the truest friend a person could have. And just the thought of spending a little time with Marge made Jack feel better.

They went to a little Mexican Restaurant on the outskirts of town that she had suggested. The food was delicious, but he could not imagine anyone but Marge beginning the day eating fajitas. He laughed at her as she ladled on the hot sauce.

"Come on, Jack, get a little wild... Try the hot stuff. It's good for your blood."

"There's nothing wrong with my blood, Marge, but if I eat that stuff, they'll have to hose me down to put out the fire. I think I better stick with the mild sauce."

The food was wonderful, and it was good to laugh and be silly with someone. They chatted about themselves and mutual friends... and politics. Marge loved Bill Clinton and Albert Gore, although she was absolutely convinced that Hillary would have made a better president than Bill.

"Have you seen Curt and Lisa's little girl?" Jack asked. "You know they were dead set on a boy, but Angie was the first available, and they just had to have her. Curt told me the other day that they hope to have their little boy by spring."

"They're lucky kids to have Curt and Lisa for parents. Lisa invited me out for Sunday brunch right after they got the baby, and Curt wouldn't put her down, even when she went to sleep. He said she slept better when he held her."

"Do you go back often... to Hendersonville?" Marge continued.

She knew he had spent the summer there after Jessi died, isolated from the world. She had tried to call him, but he wouldn't answer the phone. Then one night about midnight he had called her and wept into the phone. And, sadly, she had known there was nothing she nor anyone else could do to help him... Only time would ease his pain.

"Yes, I've gone back several times. If I never went back, I would have to give up my friendship with Curt and Lisa, and I could never do that." He was very quiet for a moment. "It took a long time, but I'm okay now. I went back to baseball for a season to get away from the constant reminder. It was good for me, but it made me realize that music, not baseball, was where I belonged, and that I couldn't forever dwell in the past."

They lingered over lunch and then drove back to Marge's house in the suburbs.

"Can you come in for a few minutes? I'll fix you the best martini you've ever tasted."

"Sure, except I'll pour the liquor."

"Okay, big boy. You pour the liquor. You think I'm going to lure you into my den, ply you with booze and seduce you? And if I were thirty years younger, I'd try it. You can count on it."

"Marge, you're crazy."

Jack was laughing like he hadn't laughed all week.

"We'll even sit on the veranda if you think that's more proper," she grinned.

"Who cares about proper? Just make me a martini, and we'll sit wherever you wish, and who knows, maybe I'll seduce you."

388

They were both laughing like crazy at the totally nonsensical conversation they were having. Marge was indeed thirty years older than Jack, and neither of them had any intention of being indiscreet... They were just being silly.

He told her about the disastrous recording session with Russ and Kathy the day before.

"We tried everything we could think of. Nothing worked."

"Have you got your guitar?" Marge asked.

"It's in the car."

"Good! Go get it and let me hear the song. You want another drink?"

Jack shook his head, his mind obviously on the song.

"Maybe you can tell me what's wrong with it."

"Okay. I'm your captive audience. Let's hear it."

A soft fall breeze wafted across the porch as Jack sang his song. Marge sat motionless, captivated by the thought-provoking lyrics.

"I don't see anything wrong with it. I think it's perfectly beautiful, but Kathy Williams shouldn't be singing this song. It's not a woman's feelings the song expresses. The emotions are clearly those of a man, and it needs to be sung by a man. Why don't you play with the lyrics, change a few she's to he's, and record it yourself?"

"Marge, I haven't sung solo in a long time. I..."

She didn't let him continue.

"You just did."

For a moment they sat in silence... Marge still remembering the powerful lyrics, and Jack pondering her suggestion.

"I don't know if Russ would go for it."

"Russ will go for it if you sing it for him like you sang it for me. It's a beautiful song. You can pitch it to another male singer, if you want, and he'll probably do a good job and sell a lot of records, but he won't do it like you. It's your song... You feel it... and, in my opinion, the only trouble with the recording session was the wrong person was singing the song."

Jack sat speechless. It had never occurred to him to record it himself. He didn't know if he could. He had not tried to sing, except for the duet, since Jessi.

Marge sipped her drink and smiled ever so slowly at the handsome man who sat opposite her, and for whom she had long held a deep affection and respect.

Finally she spoke. "You're in love, aren't you? It's your feelings the song expresses."

He just looked at her without confirming or denying the fact... He didn't have to. Marge knew.

"Jack, it's no betrayal of Jessi to have these feelings for another woman."

He was still silent.

"What's her name?"

He picked up his glass and sipped slowly before he answered.

"Her name is Mary."

"Then this is Mary's song. Sing it for her Jack. That's all the song needs... to be sung by the right person. When you get ready to do it, I'd like to come to the studio. Just do it like you did it now, and you've got a hit... Believe me."

"Want to tell me about Mary?"

"How long have you got?"

"As long as it takes. I'm a hopeless romantic."

Jack had never known anyone with such an unselfish interest in his well being as Marge Scott.

"Thanks for sharing lunch, Marge, and for the martini... I Love You."

And he hugged her affectionately.

"I Love You, too, Jack. Now take an old fool's advice and don't let this lovely girl slip through your fingers."

Jack grinned. "I don't intend to."

"And don't forget! I want to sit in on the recording."

"Marge, I wouldn't do it without you."

* * * * *

As Mary dialed the number, she hoped for better results than she had had the last two nights, but on the third ring the answering machine kicked in.

"This is Jack Roberts. Sorry I missed your call. Please leave your name and number at the sound of the tone, and I'll get back to you as soon as possible. Thanks."

Where could he be? He always returned her calls, and usually he let her know if he was going out of town. She had called him Tuesday to see if he would like to come to Atlanta for dinner. She wasn't worried when he didn't return her call Tuesday night. There were a number of reasons why he might have been late getting home, but it was now the third day, and he still had not returned her call... Something was wrong.

She didn't bother to leave a third message. Instead she hung up and called Katie. After chatting for a few minutes and hearing about Katie's first week back in school, she asked if Katie had heard from Jack.

"Oh yeah, he called yesterday. He said he'd be back Friday."

"Be back? Where is he?"

"He's in Nashville."

"I thought they weren't recording until next week."

"Oh, he's not recording. He said he had some business to take care of."

Mary was puzzled. He hadn't mentioned he was going to Nashville, and for some reason she had the feeling the 'business' he was taking care of had nothing to do with music. It seemed he was spending a lot of time in Nashville lately.

"Maybe he's with Marge."

Mary didn't understand. It was obvious Katie knew more about his whereabouts than she did.

"Who's 'Marge'?"

"She's an old friend that he sees when he's in Nashville. He says she's real cool. She eats fajitas for breakfast and drinks martinis, and she's been married four or five times."

Mary couldn't believe what she was hearing.

"Katie, where did you hear this?"

"Jack told me. He and Marge have been friends for a long time, even before he knew Jessi."

Jack had never mentioned this 'Marge' person, and the mentioning of Jessi didn't help either. She had long ago come to terms with his relationship with Jessi, but it still hurt to be reminded of Jack with another woman, especially by her own daughter. And it appeared Jessi had not been the only other woman in Jack's life.

"Did he leave a message for me?" She asked, hoping for something positive from the conversation.

"No. He just said he'd be home Friday."

*   *   *   *   *

It had been a terrible day in court! Every time she attempted to make a critical point, the prosecution objected, and the judge sustained the objection and, for the first time in the trial, she began to question her ability to get an acquittal.

Friday afternoon traffic in Atlanta was always terrible, but today it was a nightmare. There was a bad wreck on the interstate where I-75 and the perimeter meet. Northbound traffic was backed up for miles, as emergency vehicles rushed to the scene. Even the Southbound side of I-75 had to be closed to allow Life Force helicopters to land and airlift the more severely injured to local hospitals. It had taken her four and half-hours to make the usual two-hour trip home.

As she unlocked the front door, the phone was ringing. She rushed to answer hoping it might be Jack, but by the time she picked up the receiver the caller had hung up. She unbuttoned her coat and heard a crash come from the hallway, and ran to see what it was. There in the floor lay several law books, along with countless pages of notes strewn across the carpet. She had set the stack of books on the hall table when she ran to answer the phone and apparently had placed them too close to the edge.

What a day!

After picking up the mess and finally getting the papers in some kind of order, she walked back to the phone to check her messages.

"Mary, this is Jack. I tried to call you this morning, but the desk clerk said you had already checked out... I was hoping we could get together this weekend. It seems like we hardly ever spend any time together... Give me a call... I miss you!"

The next message was from some man wanting to sell aluminum siding and offering a free energy efficiency inspection.... Just what she needed!

The final message was from Garrett's parents.

"Mary, this is Joe and Emily. We're on our way to St. Petersburg and would like to come by and see you and the children. Our plane will arrive in Chattanooga at 10:00 on Saturday morning. Let us know if this is not convenient."

So much for the quiet weekend with Jack!

*　　*　　*　　*　　*

MONDAY

"All rise!"

Mary and her client rose to their feet as the surly judge entered the courtroom. The jury had deliberated for almost four hours, which was neither a short deliberation nor an especially long one for a murder trial and, unlike the Perkins' case, the time they were out gave no indication of the verdict.

"Has the jury reached a verdict?"

"Yes, your honor, we have."

"Would the defendant please rise and face the jury."

Mary stood beside her client. He was twenty-three years old and was being tried for the rape and double murder of two Georgia Tech co-eds. It had happened at a party following the Georgia - Georgia Tech football game. Charles Parker admitted he was there and he admitted he had been drinking, as the Atlanta Police Department's blood test confirmed, but he denied raping or murdering the girls. DNA testing confirmed Parker had not been with either of the girls on the night of the murder. But every time Mary tried to introduce the DNA results in evidence, the prosecuting attorney objected and the judge sustained the objection. This was absurd. DNA testing was completely valid, and precedents for its use had been established in courtrooms throughout the land, but it was obvious this judge had no intention of allowing it in his court.

She felt good about her closing argument. It was the one time during the trial that she could speak to the jury without objection from the prosecution. She retold her case and attempted to show how her client could not possibly have committed this crime. She had done the best she knew how, and now it was up to the jury to do the rest.

"Mr. Foreman, would you read your verdict?"

"Yes sir... In the case of The People versus Charles Allen Parker, we find the defendant guilty of two counts of rape and two counts of murder in the first degree."

Her client's face was ashen as he listened in disbelief to the jury's verdict.

She placed a caring arm on his slumped shoulder and searched for words of comfort.

"Don't give up. We'll overturn this thing on appeal." She realized it was little comfort, but for now it was the best she had to offer Charles Parker.

It was the worst miscarriage of justice she had ever witnessed. She had never seen anyone like Judge Teems. He ruled with an iron hand and a closed mind. It was plain to see that he was caught up in his power and had allowed his own personal prejudice to rule, rather than the pursuit of truth. But to strip her client of his defense was a travesty of justice. Charles Parker was not guilty and she would do everything in her power to get the court's decision reversed and a new trial granted.

Her thoughts were interrupted by the judge's final words.

"Sentencing will be on November 18th at 10 A.M.... Court is adjourned."

*   *   *   *   *

As she walked out onto the steps of the Fulton County Courthouse, a hoard of reporters armed with microphones and note pads rushed toward her. Camera crews from the three networks and *CNN*, as well as numerous local stations, were there.

"Ms. Davenport... your reaction?"

"We were disappointed, to say the least. We felt the verdict was unfair, and that justice was not wrought."

"Then you plan to appeal?" Another reporter yelled over the crowd.

"Most definitely!"

"On what grounds?"

"Number One - change of venue. This case should not have been allowed to go to trial in Atlanta. My client had already been tried and convicted by the media before the case ever went to court."

"Number Two - The judge erred in refusing to allow admission of the DNA results. DNA is completely valid, and the precedent for its use as legal evidence has been well established."

"So you feel the judge's disallowance of DNA testing should get your client a new trial?"

"Absolutely! Judge Teems was clearly in error in his refusal to allow the DNA test results. They would have proved beyond a reasonable doubt that Charles Allen Parker was not guilty. It was a gross miscarriage of justice."

Maybe she should not have spoken so bluntly, but Judge Teems' handling of the case had been a complete travesty of the judicial process.

"What do you expect on appeal?"

"I expect the judgment of this court to be reversed, a new trial granted, and my client to be fully exonerated."

"Ms. Davenport, may I ask..."

"I'm sorry. It's been a long trial, and I can't answer any more questions. Thank you for understanding."

She forged her way through the crowd of reporters, who were still hurling questions at her, and into a waiting car.

It was 9:30 when she pulled into the *Marriott* parking lot. She had stopped at *Kentucky Fried Chicken* to get some dinner. Everyone in Atlanta seemed to recognize her from the much-publicized case, and tonight she simply wanted to relax and not have to talk to anyone.

The girl at the drive-thru window was interested only in the cute guy *KFC* had just hired and could have cared less who Mary was.

She got a *Coke* from the hotel vending machine and sat down to eat her dinner. The ten o'clock news was about to come on, and she was anxious to see how the media would present the court's verdict to the public.

It was the lead story, and the interview on the courthouse steps was shown in full. As she saw herself on t.v., she realized how exhausted she appeared. She knew she was tired, but she hadn't slowed down long enough to realize how utterly worn out she was. Now as she sat back against a couple of pillows propped up on the bed, she gave in to the tiredness.

She couldn't believe she had dozed off. She rubbed her eyes and looked at the digital clock on the nightstand... 3:35... It couldn't be three-thirty! She looked around the room. The television was still on, but the network had long since gone off the air. Snowy lines flickered across the screen and static buzzed in the background and on the nightstand sat her scarcely touched supper and the warm coke.

She had meant to call Katie and Jack after the news went off, but it was too late now. Jack would be leaving for Nashville in the morning to complete the recording and probably would be gone all weekend. Katie was going on a retreat with the church youth group, and also would be gone all weekend. The retreat had been planned for months, and the doctor said Katie should be fine and the outing would do her good.

The Parker case had lasted almost four weeks, most of which she had spent in Atlanta, and even when she was home on weekends, she spent much of her time preparing her case for the following week.

Now the trial was over, at least until the appeal process began, and there was no one to go home to. She had tried so hard to make everything work out, yet nothing had. She had lost the case, and although she was optimistic about the appeal, it would be a long, tedious process. Without it, her client would probably die in the electric chair. And she would do everything possible to see that that did not happen.

She was normally the ultimate professional and could handle whatever came along, but as she sat alone on the side of the hotel bed, tears filled her eyes and ran down her cheeks. She hadn't been there for Katie or for Jack. She had wanted to, but she couldn't... Her practice had to come first. A man's life was at stake. He needed her. But they needed her too... Where was she supposed to draw the line?

And to that question she had no answer.

CHAPTER 52

Kelley buzzed Mary and announced, "It's Jack on line two."

He rarely called her at work, and she knew it must be important.

"How about taking tomorrow off and let's go explore the Cove? The leaves are beginning to change, and it's beautiful. I'll even take you to the *Lookout* and buy you a steak."

He had missed her so much these last few weeks. Surely she could take a day off occasionally. After all, she was her own boss.

"Oh, Jack, don't tempt me! It sounds wonderful, and I'll probably hate myself if I say no, but I've gotten so far behind, I really need to work. Can I take a rain check?"

* * * * *

Saturday was her errand day, and it was pointless to suggest that for a daylong outing. But he wanted the occasion to be something special, so he made reservations for a dinner cruise aboard the *Southern Belle*.

Mary looked beautiful. She was wearing a dress of soft pink with a cummerbund of mixed fall shades and a matching jacket in case the evening air grew cool.

The prime rib was delicious, and Jack had to concede the fall colors along the Tennessee River were almost as pretty as those in the Cove.

Later he held her close as they danced to the music of the *Riverboat Ramblers*. And for awhile they were lost in the memories of a time when there were no cases to be tried, and no songs to be recorded, when they were young and carefree, and so in love.

Unfortunately, life was no longer so simple. But they were in love... and that was what mattered. The dreamy romanticism of youth somehow passes with the years, and in its place comes a richer, more, mature love. But tonight they allowed their thoughts to wander back to those wonderful days of youth when the only thing between them was the beat of two hearts.

When the boat docked, they walked hand in hand to the car, wishing the day would never end. Everything had been so perfect.

Ross' Landing held fond memories for them. It was here they had often come after a movie or ballgame, and kissed and embraced, and vowed to love each other forever.

When they reached the car, Jack didn't turn on the switch, but instead drew Mary into his arms. And his words were warm and tender. "Would you like to try it again... for old-times' sake?"

She yielded herself to his loving embrace and their lips met, and once again they were teenagers in love, dewy-eyed, and filled with deep longing for each other.

Finally, he reached for his keys and turned on the switch. "I guess we better go before the cops run us off."

Mary grinned. "It wouldn't be the first time."

"I know, but I'd feel a little foolish now... making love in a parked car under a street light."

"It didn't bother you then."

"Yeah, but then I was a stupid kid."

"We both were."

He looked at her and smiled. It was the same smile that had made her heart skip a beat so long ago... It still did... She could not remember a time when she had not loved Jack Roberts.

* * * * *

Later as they sat close together on the couch enjoying a glass of wine, Jack again brought up the subject of a day in the Cove.

"Save a day for me next week... Okay? You've got to see the Cove while the leaves are so pretty. You choose the day. It doesn't matter to me. I just want to spend some time with you... a whole day, just the two of us, tromping through the woods, sitting by the creek... whatever makes you happy. Lately we've had so little time together."

His arm tightened around her, and he resisted the urge to make love to her. The ring was in his pocket, and tonight he would ask her to marry him. He had waited for this moment so long.

"Right now I'll settle for a day, but I want more. I want to spend all my days with you... 'the rest of our natural lives', as you lawyers say. I love you, and I want to marr..."

"Jack," she interrupted, "I can't next week. I have to go to New York."

Apparently she hadn't even heard what he had started to say.

"New York? Why are you going to New York? You've just spent three weeks in Atlanta, and you said you were through with the out of town stuff, that Harry and Calvin could do whatever they chose, but you were through with it." It didn't make sense. Exasperation was reflected in his voice. "Don't I count for anything? Is there never going to be any time for us? I'm tired of the way we live our lives... one of us one place... the other some place else. It's no damn good!"

She said nothing. It appeared she had no answers to his questions.

"You don't really give a damn, do you? Not as long as you have your almighty career. I don't matter... Katie doesn't matter."

"Jack, that's not fair! I love Katie, and I'm a good mother! Don't ever accuse me of not caring about Katie! In fact, that's part of the reason I'm going to New York. If you'll give me time, I'll explain."

"When I was trying the Parker case, I came to the realization that things had to change. I was spending too much time away from Katie. She's at a crucial age, and I need to be a part of her life... certainly more than I've been lately. She'll be dating soon, and there will be problems... There always are... I want to be there to console her when someone breaks her heart, as surely they will... and I want to be there to share her joy when things are good."

"I don't like what my life has become. I don't have time for my family. I don't have time for you. And I certainly don't have time for myself. My life is a whirlwind that never seems to stop."

He still didn't understand what this had to do with New York.

"A few days ago I had a call from Chip Johnson. There's an opening in his firm, and he wants me to come up and talk to them. It's corporate law, and the pace is much slower. It's a large firm, and I'd work nine to five, four days a week. I realize it would be different, but I think I owe it to myself to check it out. They may not even offer me the position... who knows... but I told Chip I would come to New York and talk to them."

"What about Katie? What does she think about this?"

"I haven't told her yet. She has always loved Chattanooga... It would be an adjustment for her." Mary admitted.

"So, your solution to being overworked here is going to New York, and in time being overworked there?"

He shook his head in dismay. It wasn't rational.

"I don't believe you, Mary. You would take your child a thousand miles away to a place she has never been... away from her school, her friends... and say you're doing it for her. Hell, Mary, you're doing it for yourself! You're not doing it for Katie!"

"And what about me and Katie? I have a right to be with her, you know. She's my daughter too! I've already missed fourteen years of her life. You have no right to take her away from me now!"

What Mary saw on his face was a mixture of anger and sadness.

"And what about you and me?... I guess this does it for us."

Again he paused, and she waited for him to deliver the next blow. Jack didn't get angry often. But when he did, he didn't mince any words. And she knew he wasn't finished.

"Maybe there never was an 'us'. Maybe we were just pretending it was real... that this time nothing could come between us."

"Maybe that was what tonight was... pretending. Maybe the time we shared in the parking lot by the river meant nothing to you. Maybe you were just pretending. But I wasn't! I believed in 'us'. I believed we had a future... together... not a thousand miles apart. We've had enough of that! I love you. Damn it!... I've loved you for a long time. I was about to ask you to marry me, but you didn't even hear what I was saying."

She looked away. He was right. She had not heard him.

"Where in the Hell do I fit into the picture? Apparently, no place at all... If you can't find time for an occasional day with me, why should I imagine you'd want to spend the rest of your life with me?"

"You'll get the job... You're a good lawyer... Chip will recommend you... They'll offer you a fantastic salary, and you won't turn it down. I'd say it was a 'done deal'."

She didn't argue the point. He was right. The job was hers if she wanted it. Chip had practically said as much.

Finally, she spoke.

"Jack, I love you. You know that! I always have..."

In anger he interrupted her.

"Mary, that's crazy! You don't leave someone you love."

For a moment she said nothing. She was struggling with her response, knowing full well what Jack's reaction would be.

"I thought maybe... if it worked out... you might like to come to New York with us?"

"No, Mary, you didn't think that! You know me better than that! I'm not a big city person. I bought the place in the Cove to get away from the city... I don't even like Nashville... What makes you think I'd want to live in New York City?"

"Well, for someone who doesn't like Nashville, you've been spending a lot of time there lately? Is it Kathy Williams or Marge Scott that takes you away from the farm so often?"

"Mary, you're being ridiculous. My first trip was for the recording. I told you about it. The whole effort was a failure. We didn't get anywhere. The second time was a business trip. The third time we worked on the recording again."

He sighed, and then continued.

"You were in Atlanta. What difference would it have made? If I had been at the farm every day, we still couldn't have spent any time together."

The whole thing was stupid. She had never been jealous of his work or his associates before, but apparently she had a problem this time, and he tried to explain.

"Kathy Williams is twenty-three years old. She's a nice girl, but I don't want or need a twenty-three year old. I don't know where you got all this stuff. I've told you over and over I love you. I don't go to Nashville to fool around. It's business... that's all it is."

"And Marge Scott? Is she business too?"

"I don't know where you heard about Marge Scott, but I'll tell you about her, since you're so damn sure I've been going to Nashville for the sole purpose of 'fooling around'."

"Marge Scott is seventy years old, and she's probably the dearest friend I've got in that town. When I first went to Nashville, she did more to help me than anyone else... not because she was looking for a younger man to play around with, but because she believed in me... probably even more than I believed in myself. She knew practically everyone in the industry, and she saw to it that I met the right people and urged them to give me a chance."

"Whatever success I've had in the music business, I owe in part to Marge Scott. I've never forgotten that... I never will. She's my friend, and I'm sorry to disappoint you, but she's not my lover!"

Mary believed him. She had foolishly misread his repeated trips to Nashville. She had been separated from him and from Katie... worn out, frustrated, and fighting a court battle she didn't expect to win, even though her client was innocent. But most of all, she had been lonely. When she had tried to call he was always gone, and foolishly she had allowed herself to believe he was having an affair. For the last six months, they had vowed their love for each other, and they had made love, but not once had Jack mentioned marriage. Now that he knew about Katie, he suddenly wanted to get married. How noble of him! She didn't need his gallantry. She had done quite well on her own, and she would continue to.

He didn't need her... He never had... He had needed only Jessi.

It was sad, she thought, that he and Jessi never had a chance. The two of them would probably have made it. They shared common interests and a common career.

But she and Jack were different. Their lives had moved in different directions. Over the years they had spent apart they had each learned to 'do it my way' and made it work. Their respective success and the independence that success inevitably brings had made them both self-sufficient.

They had dared to believe they needed each other, and had tried to find their way back to what once had been, but it hadn't worked. They had been foolish to believe it could.

Similar thoughts raced through Jack's mind as he tried to sort things out.

Finally, he voiced his feelings. "I guess it's true what the Bible says... 'To everything there is a season.'... And it looks like the season for us is past... It's sad, but it's true... A part of me still wants to make it work, but it's too late."

He got up from the couch and made his way to the door. He was leaving, and there was nothing she could do to stop him, but she had to try.

"Jack, please don't go. We can work it out... if we try."

"I'm sorry, Mary. I've done all the compromising I can. Good luck to you... whatever you decide."

And the door closed softly behind him.

CHAPTER 53

Jack sat alone on the balcony of his motel room, his feet propped against the banisters, and watched a storm brewing at sea. The lightning danced on the distant horizon as the evening breeze blew in from the Gulf.

Three days ago he had hurriedly packed a few things, made arrangements with Mr. Nelson to feed the animals, and headed for Panama City. It was not a trip he had planned or even wanted to make. He just had to get away.

As he traveled down I-59 he almost took the Fort Payne exit. Then he realized his problems had nothing to do with Jessi, and visiting her grave would only add to the misery he already felt.

Over the last few days he had probably walked fifty miles up and down the beach, alone with his thoughts. He needed to work through some things, and there was no way he could do it at home with constant reminders of what might have been all around him.

The trip had not been without purpose. There were things he had to put to rest. Maybe then he could go home and get on with his life.

He would continue to see Katie, and when the time was right he would tell her. She deserved to know. He wanted her to know, in case something should happen to him, that he had made adequate provision for her future.

He tried to concentrate on other things, but his mind kept returning to Mary. Although he loved her very much, he could not settle for the few hours now and then that her busy schedule allotted him. He knew that when he walked out of her house Saturday night.

What he needed now was the courage to stay away from her until he felt he could live without her. And it wasn't easy. God, it wasn't easy.

On Monday morning when he got up, his arms ached to hold her. He almost picked up the phone to call her, to retract the harsh things he had said, but they were true. Everything he had said was true.

Her career meant more to her than he did, even as his baseball career had meant more to him than she had. But they were a couple of kids then. They didn't know what was important... and what was not.

They had lost each other then, and now they had done it again, each time for the same reason... Their careers came first.

He had wanted to play baseball more than he had wanted to be with her, and although he had wanted both, he had wanted baseball more.

Now she wanted to pursue her career more than she wanted him. It was as simple as that.

He loved her... and he wanted her... More than anything in the world, he wanted her. This time he had thought they had a chance. They were older, more mature, and they knew what was important. At least he thought they did.

Like a pendulum, his thoughts swung to and fro... Maybe he could make the necessary adjustments. He had lived alone most of his adult life anyway. Maybe it wasn't that important to have her home every night... But it was! He was tired of being alone. He was tired of being lonely. He couldn't settle for second place. And that's the way it would be... Her career would always come first.

He avoided people as much as possible. The smiles on their faces only intensified the emptiness he felt. He was so alone, and he wondered if it would always be like this.

But, of course it wouldn't. This, too, would pass. Life would go on, and he would survive. He always had... He would now. If life had taught him anything, it had taught him survival.

* * * * *

Again and again Mary dialed the number, and again and again she got the familiar recorded message. Either he was out of town or he had no interest in talking to her, and was relying on the answering machine to see that he didn't have to.

A week passed, and each day was the same. It was as if he had vanished from the face of the earth, and although they lived less than twenty miles apart, she wondered if she would ever see him again.

She had been a fool to even consider Chip's offer. She didn't know anyone in New York. Jody went to Vanderbilt and frequently came home on weekends. If she moved to New York, she would see him only on holidays and maybe a few times during the summer.

Katie's friends were all here, and what few friends Mary had also lived here. They were mostly business colleagues and a few people she had known years ago. Since she moved back to Chattanooga, her life had evolved mainly around her children and her job, and she had not taken the time to develop new friendships. She had, however, had Jack... Now she had lost him.

At night she cried, her head buried in the pillow, hoping Katie would not hear. She was a grown woman, mature in every respect of the word, toughened by years of making it on her own, and capable of coping with whatever hand life dealt her. But suddenly she was not coping very well. With the exception of losing one of her children, there was nothing that could hurt like losing Jack.

The soft closing of the door when he left told her that he was through trying. He had tried to get her attention, to assert his need to be with her, but she had been too busy to notice. Their relationship had suffered because of her job, and she had done nothing to prevent it.

He had not slammed the door in anger. He simply said "Good luck," and turned and walked away. She knew he would not be back. When Jack believed in something he committed himself completely, but when it was over he moved on. It had been like that with baseball. It had been like that when he left Atlanta after Jody's accident. Jody had needed her more than he did, and Jack quickly got out of her life, and she had not heard from him again until their chance meeting in Chattanooga.

What a fool she had been. He had loved her. There were times when she had her doubts, but in the end, she knew... beyond a shadow of a doubt she knew.

And she loved him. For so long she had loved him. She had had a chance at happiness, and she had let it slip through her fingers. He did not know... He would never know... how much she had wanted to spend that day in the Cove with him, but she had been 'too busy'.

When Chip called, she had just finished the Parker case, and she was disillusioned with the whole justice system. Maybe she needed a change. Maybe corporate law was the answer. She was bone weary from working day and night, and when she had tried to reach Jack, he was always in Nashville, doing who knows what with who knows who.

He appeared to have no intention of making a permanent commitment to her and seemed quite happy to leave things as they were. Maybe he loved her, but he didn't love her enough... Something had changed. Before, he only went to Nashville occasionally. Now he was there every week.

When Chip's call came, she was in the perfect frame of mind to be tempted by the offer. It was exciting and prestigious, and Jack had certainly not given her any reason to stay in Chattanooga.

Chip loved New York, and it was right for him, and he was obviously getting rich there, but it was not right for her. She was a small town girl. At times she had felt intimidated by Atlanta. She certainly would be swallowed up by New York City.

Katie wouldn't be happy there. And what Jack had said was true... It wasn't right to take Katie away from him. The fact that she had even given the offer a second thought seemed completely irrational now.

She threw herself into her work in an attempt to forget her problems, but it was no use. He was the first thing on her mind when she got up in the morning and the last thing on her mind when she finally fell asleep at night.

She wondered where he was and if he was okay. If she could just know that, it would help. She thought of calling his mother, but she had to maintain some dignity. If Jack wanted to get in touch, he would. If he did not, he wouldn't... It was that simple.

The second week began as the first, with no word. It was raining when she left for work Monday, which only added to her depression.

Katie was having trouble with algebra, and Mary had not been able to concentrate enough to help her. She would get herself together today, and tonight she would try to help her.

Later that night as Mary was getting ready for bed, Katie came into her mother's room and sat down on the bed.

"Mom, I'm sorry about you and Jack. I know you miss him... and so do I."

"Yes, honey, I do... but I'm sure he'll be in touch with you when he gets back in town... I really don't know if he's out of town, but I assume he is. He doesn't answer his phone... Just remember, it's Jack and I that have a problem, not you and Jack. I'm sure he'll call you soon."

"Why should he keep in touch with me if the two of you stop seeing each other? After all, I'm your daughter, not his. He doesn't have any reason to see me."

Katie's words stunned Mary, and for a moment she didn't know what to say.

"But I'm sure he will. He's very fond of you, Katie."

She had been so caught up in her own loneliness that she had not realized how much Katie missed Jack.

"Mom, is there something I'm supposed to know that nobody's telling me?"

Again she did not know what to say. She had hoped that she and Jack could tell Katie together. She was still somewhat young to handle this revelation, and having to admit to her own daughter that she had been promiscuous was not something she looked forward to.

"Katie, sweetheart, just give me some time. This is hard for me right now. I've lost someone I care a great deal about. I'm not myself... I'm sorry. Just try to bear with me."

"I understand. It'll be okay, Mom. You'll work it out."

As Katie said goodnight and started to leave, Mary hugged her tightly.

"I love you, sweetheart... Sleep good."

"I love you, too."

As she looked at Katie, Mary thought how much she looked like her daddy. She would not tarry long in answering Katie's question. If she was old enough to ask, she was old enough to know the answer.

* * * * *

As Jack walked across the hotel lobby toward the elevator, the desk clerk called to him.
"Mr. Roberts, there was a call for you... A Mrs. Virginia Roberts... She asked that you call home as soon as possible."
Jack didn't take time to go to his room, but asked if he could use the desk phone instead.

* * * * *

"Mom, what's wrong?"
His first thought was Mary or maybe Katie.
"Jack... Robert Bradshaw called this afternoon... It's Mr. Bradshaw. He's in the hospital in Palm Beach."
"How bad is it?"
Jack knew the answer before he asked. Robert wouldn't have called if it weren't serious.
"He didn't go into detail. I told him you were out of town, and he said not to bother you, but I knew you would want to know."
"Did he leave a number?"
Virginia gave Jack the hospital number and Robert's home number.
"I'll see what I can find out and call you as soon as I know something."

* * * * *

"Mom... It's congestive heart failure. Robert said he's not in much pain... He's just weakening away. He was asleep, so I didn't get to talk to him."
Jack tried to swallow the lump in his throat, but it wouldn't go down.
"I'm leaving tonight... I don't know how much time he's got and I want to..." He didn't finish the sentence. He couldn't bring himself to say, "I want to see him one last time."
"I'll call you after I get there."
Virginia knew he would go to Mr. Bradshaw. She had never met the man, but she had heard Jack speak of him often, and she knew he held a special place in Jack's heart.

"Jack, please be careful. I know you're not going to get any sleep tonight."

"Don't worry, Mom. I'll be okay... I probably wouldn't sleep if I waited 'til morning to leave."

"I know... I love you."

"I love you too, Mom... I guess I'd better get going... I'll call you when I know something."

He hurriedly packed his bags and checked out of the hotel. He would have to drive all night, but if he made good time, he would be in West Palm Beach by mid-morning. He only hoped that would be soon enough.

*   *   *   *   *

He stopped at the information desk to get Mr. Bradshaw's room number. As he walked down the hallway to the room, he saw a couple of little black children playing quietly outside the door. This made him smile. He had never known a time when Jacob Bradshaw wasn't surrounded by children, and now shouldn't be any different.

It had been twenty-two years since he first met Mr. Bradshaw, and eleven since the Christmas he and Jessi had stopped to see him. A lot had changed over the years... He was no longer a wide-eyed rookie baseball player or an unknown singer/songwriter... And Jessi was no more.

He had mixed emotions as he entered the room.

The old man was sitting up in the bed and looked a hundred years old, but he always had. Robert had told him on the phone that Mr. Bradshaw was ninety-four.

A broad smile broke across the old man's face when he saw Jack walk into the room.

"Jack Roberts! Well, I'll be."

The old man reached out a thin wrinkled hand, but Jack needed more than a handshake. As the two embraced, Robert excused himself to get some coffee, so they could have some time alone.

"I hear you're having a little trouble." Jack didn't know what to say.

"Yeah, my old ticker's 'bout to give out on me... I've had a good life though. The Good Lord's been mighty good to me. I've had a good family and good friends like you."

Jack struggled to hold back the tears. The old man knew he didn't have long, and there was no need to try to placate him.

"You know it's been thirty-two years since I seen Emma."

Emma was Mr. Bradshaw's wife, and over the years Jack had heard him speak of her often, and he knew he had never stopped loving her.

"I'm looking forward to seeing the old girl," he continued, "and Miss Jessi, too."

Jack couldn't help but smile.

"Yeah, I remember about you and Jessi... You told me once that if you were a little younger, you'd beat my time."

Mr. Bradshaw smiled.

"Son, they ain't nobody could beat your time with Jessi. She loved you more than anybody." And for a moment neither of them said anything.

Jack marveled at the way he was facing death... smiling and reliving the good times. It almost seemed an adventure for him... but that was what life had been for Jacob Bradshaw... an adventure. And it was obvious that his imminent death was merely a passage into a new and exciting place where he would reunite with loved ones who had gone on before, and where he would wait by the creek bank, fishing pole in hand, for those yet to come.

"Jack, you remember the first time we met and how you came home and stayed with me 'til the other ball players got there?"

"Yes sir, I do."

"You remember what I told you that first day at the ball park?"

A spontaneous grin broke across Jack's face.

"How could I forget?... You told me I was either a liar or a damn fool."

"Well son, I ain't been wrong about a whole lot of things in my life, but I was wrong about that."

"You remember the Christmas you brought Miss Jessi to see me?" The old man continued.

Again the tears returned to Jack's eyes and he could only nod his head.

"That was a good Christmas!"

Mr. Bradshaw paused as if he had just thought of something out of the long ago past.

"Jack, what ever happened to that little dog I gave Miss Jessi?"

Jack dropped his head and took a deep breath.

"About a month after Jessi died, he got sick. He wouldn't eat or run and play, and he didn't seem interested in anything. I took him to the vet, but he couldn't find anything physically wrong. He knew about Jessi, and he asked if she and Toby were close. When I told him they were inseparable, he nodded and said, 'The problem with this dog is a broken heart.'... A week later Toby died."

The old man wiped his eyes. With his own problems and knowing he didn't have long on this earth, only the story of Jessi's little broken hearted dog could bring tears to his eyes.

"They'll never be another Jessi."

Jack sighed. "No sir, there won't."

They visited for awhile, and laughed and talked about the time they went fishing and didn't catch anything.

"Rocky said we talked too much."

"He was probably right," Jack answered.

They talked about Robert and how well he had done. Mr. Bradshaw was proud of his grandson. He had gone on to pitch at Florida State and had done quite well. He had graduated with a degree in accounting and now had his own tax service.

The conversation flowed from one thing to another. It was natural and easy, and they were able to put the looming reality in the back of their minds and just enjoy being together.

CHAPTER 54

It was 7:30 and, although Virginia was already up and reading the morning paper, the ringing of the phone startled her.

"Mom... Mr. Bradshaw died last night."

"Jack, I'm so sorry."

"It's okay... I'm all right... I got to talk to him for a good while yesterday afternoon. We laughed and talked about the old days, and had a good visit... He slipped into a coma about 8:30 and died shortly after midnight."

"Jack, I wish there was something I could say."

She heard him sigh into the telephone.

"I think he was stronger than any of us... He knew he was dying, but it was okay... I'm just glad I got to see him before he died."

Virginia realized that, more than anything else, Jack needed a listening ear, and that much she could provide.

"I'm going to stay for the funeral, and then head home on Saturday."

It was one of those times when she would give anything to be able to ease his sorrow. No matter how old he was, he was still her son, and it hurt to see him in such pain.

Finally, she said simply, "Jack, I love you."

"I love you too, Mom. I'll see you Saturday."

CHAPTER 55

Jack said good-bye to Robert and Jamica Friday night. He would leave for home early Saturday morning. It was a long drive, and he had done all he could do in West Palm. Now it was time to clear out and let the Bradshaw family get back to normal.

Jamica had wanted to get up and make breakfast, but he insisted there was no need. "There are plenty of *Hardee's* up the road." But when he awakened he smelled coffee, and found she had set the coffee maker for four a.m.

There was a note on the kitchen table.

We'll call you when we're in Chattanooga in May... Thanks for being here... The coffee should be making, and there are sweet rolls in the refrigerator.
Love,
Jamica

Robert had done well. He had a successful business and a beautiful home, but his greatest accomplishment was his choice of a wife. Jamica was not only a very pretty Latin lady, but she was warm and caring.

Beside the note was a picture of Mr. Bradshaw and Jack. It had been taken the last day of spring training in '73. A yellow post-it note read, "Thought you might like to have this."

Jack smiled as he looked at the picture, and then carefully placed it in his billfold, and poured a cup of coffee. The picture, as well as Mr. Bradshaw's death, reminded him of a simpler time in his life when all he had to worry about was food in his stomach, a place to lay his head, and making the baseball team.

He found a Styrofoam cup and poured another cup of coffee, turned off the kitchen light, and was homeward bound.

* * * * *

It was late afternoon when he reached Cartersville. It would be out of his way, but he still could make it before dark. And he left I-75 and headed west toward Fort Payne.

The cemetery had been recently mowed, and he stooped to brush some dried grass from Jessi's marker. It was a simple stone, not what you would expect to mark the final resting place of a big star, but it was indicative of the life she had led.

Even with all her fame, Jessi was a simple, private person. She didn't get close to a lot of people, but to the ones she did, she was as good a friend as anyone could have.

He thought about how she had cared for her grandmother and for Buddy and, though she had known him only briefly, for Mr. Bradshaw.

"Jess, Mr. Bradshaw died... I guess you already know that though."

He paused and smiled. "If there are fishing holes in heaven, I suppose the two of you have already caught a mess of catfish."

He reached down and pulled some weeds from around the stone that the mower had missed.

"I miss you, honey... I try to go on. I know that's what you would want, but it's not easy."

Once more he stared at the simple inscription on the marker. It hadn't rained in weeks and the sandy soil was dry and powdery. He took his finger and slowly drew a heart in the bare spot next to Jessi's marker, and whispered, "I love you."

A few feet away was a smaller indentation, where Toby also 'rested in peace'.

Jack smiled as he remembered how he had slipped into the small country cemetery in the wee hours of the morning, carrying only a shovel and the little black dog wrapped carefully in a quilt. Most people wouldn't understand, but Jessi would... and Toby would... and God would.

* * * * *

When he reached Chattanooga, he had driven about as far as he could. He had been on the road since four a.m., and the light in his mother's living room was a welcoming sight.

"Hi, Mom."

"Jack, I'm so glad you're home. I was beginning to worry."

"It's been a long day." He sighed. "I guess I'd forgotten how far it was from West Palm Beach."

"I've got beef stew and cornbread. I hope you haven't had supper."

"No, I haven't. That sounds good, but let me get a shower first."

Virginia Roberts knew it had been a hard two weeks for Jack. It was written on his face. He had not told her, but she was sure there were problems between him and Mary... and then Mr. Bradshaw.

She turned the stew on to heat and asked, "You are staying the night, aren't you?"

"Yeah, I am. I've had about all the driving I can handle for one day."

When he came in the kitchen, he looked somewhat revived, but still very tired. Before he sat down to eat, he walked over to her and hugged her. "Mom, I love you. No matter what else goes wrong in my life, you're always there."

"I love you too, Jack. Now, eat your supper before it gets cold."

Jack grinned. He wondered how many times he had heard her say that when he was growing up. Tonight it was kind of nice to have someone fuss over him. Later, when he went to his bedroom, he found the bedcover already turned down.

It was good to be home.

* * * * *

He had gotten a good night's rest, and had enjoyed visiting with his mother after breakfast. Last night he had been too tired to talk.

It was almost noon when he got to the Cove. There was a stack of mail in his box, which he would wade through later, and an unstamped letter tucked in the front door. He recognized the writing.

Hey Jack,

Sorry I missed you. I'll see you at Christmas. I'm staying busy. This is a picture of Amy. She's a straight-A student. I reckon she got her brains from her mom and her good looks from her dad. Take care! Give me a call sometime.

Buddy

Jack grinned. It was probably the longest letter Buddy had ever written. Amy was a beautiful young lady, and there was no mistaking she was her daddy's pride and joy.

He unpacked his bags and put a load of clothes in the washer, and then checked the messages on the answering machine.

"Jack... This is Glenn. Just called to touch base. Hope all's well with you. Give me a call when you have the time and the inclination. Give my best to Mary... By the way, I'm going to Sandy's for Thanksgiving... See you soon."

* * *

"Jack... This is Russ... The record is in production and is scheduled for release in early December. It will be another gold record... Mark my word. Give me a call when you get in."

With all that had happened lately, he had almost forgotten the recording.

There were a lot of clicks... Apparently they weren't important or they would have left a message.

* * *

"Jack... John Harlan... I've got a damn stock that's about to take off. You need to buy the Hell out of it. I guarantee it'll make you some good money... Not that you need it... Call me if you're interested."

John Harlan cussed like a sailor, but he was a good stockbroker, and he usually knew what he was talking about.

* * *

Then there was a familiar female caller.

"Jack, this is Susan. We've got a little boy. He's 21 inches long... weighed only 6 ½ pounds... kinda' scrawny... but he's fine... just needs fattening up. We named him Phillip Jack... after the two favorite men in my life. Phil is fine... just excited about being a new daddy... Take care of yourself. We'll be home for the holidays. Hope to see you then."

A "little shortstop"! Jack smiled as he thought of Susan. She and Phil would be great parents.

"Phillip Jack," he repeated. No one had ever named a kid after him before... It was kind of nice.

He ordered flowers for Susan. He would get his mom to select something for the baby later. That was her department. When the kid was old enough to play ball, he wouldn't have any trouble with the gift stuff, but he didn't know a lot about babies.

He had wondered if there might be a message from Mary, but there was not.

CHAPTER 56

Since he returned from Florida, Jack had spent most of his time in the woods cutting firewood. The cool fall days were perfect for outdoor chores, and being alone in the woods with only the sound of the birds and the buzzing of the chain saw proved to be good therapy.

Today the mid-morning rain had driven him indoors, and he had spent the last couple of hours clearing his desk, returning phone calls and writing checks. The last check he had written was to the Macedonia Methodist Church in West Palm Beach. The small congregation had been trying for months to raise funds to replace their worn out air conditioning system, and the meager sum they had managed to accumulate was still far from enough to do the job. The check he had just written, in memory of Jacob Bradshaw, should be sufficient to take care of it.

He had called Glenn earlier in the day and left a message, and when the phone rang, he assumed it was Glenn.

"Jack?"... The sound of his voice took her by surprise as lately she had come to expect the usual recorded message.

"How are you?" It sounded trite, but it was all she could manage.

"Fine... and you?"

He was polite, but nothing more. And it was plain to see that nothing had changed.

"I'm fine." She hesitated for a moment. It would have been easier to leave a message on the machine.

"Jack, I'd like to talk to you for a few minutes."

For a moment there was no answer, and she rather expected him to say there was nothing to talk about.

"Do you want to talk on the phone?"

"I'd rather talk in person, if it's okay."

"When do you want to talk?"

"Whenever it's convenient with you."

"How about this evening... about 6:00?"

"That's fine."

"Where?"

Everything he said was brief and constrained.

"Would it be alright if I came to the farm?"

415

Again there was hesitation on his part, and she realized it had been a foolish suggestion. She simply thought it would offer more privacy to say the things she had to say.

"I can meet you some place else, if you prefer," she quickly countered.

"You're welcome to come here if you want."

At least he had consented to talk to her.

"Okay, I'll be there at six."

As she hung up the phone, she thought how quickly things had changed. He was so distant, so cold. She almost wished she hadn't bothered to call, but there were some things she had to say... some things he had to know... before he judged her so harshly.

*　　*　　*　　*　　*

At five minutes 'til six, the silver Lexus pulled into the driveway. He wasn't sure what she wanted to talk about and, actually, he would just as soon not see her.

It had been agonizing at first, but staying busy kept him from thinking of her as often as he had the first few days. Perhaps he would get over her in time, but the only way he could do it was by not seeing her.

He watched as she started up the walkway. She was wearing a soft gray skirt with an off-white blouse and a coral cardigan, and the sight of her produced mixed emotions. But mainly he felt sadness... sadness that two people who really cared for each other never seemed to make it to the finish line. Suddenly he wished she had not come. The last two weeks had been difficult enough, and he wasn't anxious to relive the pain.

They sat opposite each other in the room where they had often shared cozy intimacy, but today there was only formal courtesy. The day had been cool, and Jack had lit a fire in the fireplace, and while the room was warm, the reception Mary encountered was cool and almost indifferent.

She tried to break the ice.

"How have you been?"

It was the same question she had asked on the phone, and it produced the same response, and nothing more. He was not making it easy.

"Jack, I don't know quite how to begin, but there are some things you need to know. I don't expect them to change anything, but I can't just close the book on us without telling you."

The solemn look on his face did not change as he waited for her to continue. She could tell he was anxious to get the encounter over, and for the first time she wished she had not come. There was an aloofness about him she had not expected, and she felt like an intruder in his house.

"Jack, you really don't want me here, do you?" She picked up her purse and started to get up from the sofa.

"You said there were things I needed to know. I'd like to hear them."

She looked at him in exasperation. "Then don't treat me like an unwelcome guest!"

He could offer no rebuttal for that was exactly how he was treating her.

"I'm sorry... Can I get you something to drink? I just made a fresh pot of coffee, and there are cokes in the refrigerator."

"Coffee will be fine."

The tension between them seemed to ease ever so slightly, but communicating with him was still awkward. She sipped the hot coffee, took a deep breath and began. "When you walked out my door a few weeks ago, I knew you wouldn't be back. I knew exactly what you were feeling. You believed my career meant more to me than you did, even as I once believed baseball meant more to you than I did."

"The hardest part of it all was I knew you cared for me. But you were pursuing a dream... a dream I didn't fit into. Your first commitment was to your career, and at that point in your life there was no time nor place for me."

"I think you had the same feeling a couple of weeks ago... That I didn't have time for you... That my career came first... And I suppose you were right. I was chasing a dream too... The wrong dream... except I wasn't aware of it until you walked out the door, and I knew you were not coming back."

"Wherever you've been these last few weeks, I suspect you've been trying to put me out of your mind, and it appears you've done a pretty good job of it."

She paused and something in her eyes told him she was remembering, and the remembering was painful.

"In time it happens, slowly, gradually, and eventually days go by when you don't even think about it at all. But then something happens to remind you, and you wonder... 'What if we had tried a little harder?' But then it's too late. And once again you try to push it out of your mind, thinking it will go away, except it doesn't, not completely."

She sighed and then continued.

"You were right. I was committed to my career and the success that I believed was fulfilling all my needs. Then you came along and upset my nice little playhouse. I fell in love with you all over again. I tried not to, but it happened, and eventually you fell in love with me, although I'm sure you tried just as hard not to."

"I was obsessed with my career, and when you and my job collided, it was you who got put on hold. I realize that now, although I didn't at the time. It took the closing of a door to tell me how wrong I was."

"Whatever I say is not likely to change anything between us... You made your own assessment of the situation, and I suppose you were pretty close to being right... Then you walked away."

The words were hard for her to say and just as hard for him to hear... Admittedly, it hadn't been easy for either of them.

She continued. "But please give me my day in court." The legal innuendo had somehow slipped into her comments in spite of her efforts to avoid it.

Through still solemn eyes, the slightest grin crept across Jack's face. "I suppose you're entitled to that."

She glanced at her watch.

"How long have you got?"

"As long as it takes."

"The night of the storm I told you a little about my life after our time together in Atlanta, but not all. Forgive me if I repeat myself."

"It's okay." This time his voice was a little gentler. He settled back in his chair, unsure of what he was about to hear.

Finally she began.

Sometimes he dropped his head as she spoke, but mostly he looked at her, his expression rarely changing. At least he was listening, and that was all she asked.

"When Garrett and I were divorced, I did not ask for alimony, but only half the equity in our house. A friend of Garrett's bought the house, and I'm sure there was money passed under the table and the house brought more than I was told. However, that's over and done with, and the money I received was enough to rent a modest house close to my work."

"Bill Johnson gave me a job and a lot of good advice, and I was in need of both." Her voice quavered with emotion as she spoke of her former employer.

"After about six months, he called me into his office and told me he wanted to talk. I thought at first he was going to let me go. Katie had had the flu, and I had missed several days from work. Instead, he told me I ought to go to law school."

"'Mary, you're a good secretary, but you're never going anywhere in this job. I won't kid you. Law school's tough, but you've got the aptitude, and you can do it, and I know you need the money.'"

"I knew he was right. The secretarial job was all right for then, but it would never lead to anything else. So I took my grandmother's legacy, which I had sworn I would never touch unless I had to, and used it to pay my way through law school."

"I worked during the day and went to school three nights a week. The other nights I spent studying until I couldn't keep my eyes open any longer. I missed spending the time with the kids that I was accustomed to, but if I was ever to get ahead, I had to make sacrifices. I lived that way for three years, then just as I finally finished school, Bill died, and I no longer had the guidance and tutelage of the man who had steered me in that direction."

"After the funeral, I stood in the cemetery and clutched the check Chip had handed me. I was reluctant to take it, but Chip and Sandy insisted. I would put the money in the bank, and it would be my security blanket, just as my grandmother's money had before."

"I agreed to stay on and complete the cases Bill had been working on and collect the fees that were owing him."

"Chip suggested I keep the office. He said, 'You have to practice somewhere, and the rent is reasonable. Dad has a good law library, so you should have all the books you need right at your fingertips.'"

"I drew deeds and wills, and managed to pick up a few small cases. One insurance company out of the five Bill represented decided to stay with me. It was the smallest one, and they tended to settle their claims, rather than litigate, so it didn't generate much income."

"It was rough... Months went by when it was all I could do to pay the rent and buy groceries. I had expected it to be hard getting started, but not that hard. I tried not to have to resort to the money in the bank, and somehow I managed."

"One day I got a call from one of Bill's colleagues. He asked me to serve as co-counsel on a rape case. I knew nothing about criminal law, but I needed the money, and more than that, I needed a chance to prove myself, so I accepted. He pushed me to the forefront in the case."

"I'll never forget what he said... 'Let's see what you can do. This kid needs all the help he can get, and a defense lawyer who's not only a woman, but also a mother, may be just what it takes'."

"On the third day, when we adjourned for lunch, Ken said, 'You've got to stop letting them push you around. The damn D. A. is grinding you in the ground, and the judge is letting him get away with it. When we go back in there this afternoon, I want you to come out swinging. Object to that crap they're trying to introduce in evidence. Don't let them get away with it! You'll get some of your objections overruled, but you'll get some of them sustained. Get tough, Mary! If you don't, that kid hasn't got a chance'."

"That afternoon I changed my approach from that of a diplomatic lady lawyer to that of a mother lion fighting to protect her cubs. I looked at my client and pretended it was Jody sitting in that chair, and I fought with all my might for his acquittal, and we wound up getting a not guilty verdict."

"You did great when you got tough, Ken complimented me. Now don't let up. Camp out at the courthouse and take every court-appointed case you can get. They don't pay much, but they get you exposure."

"I don't really like criminal law, I answered."

"You can't afford the luxury of practicing the kind of law you like! Maybe later, but not now! Establish yourself as a good criminal lawyer, then you can do whatever you like. I guarantee you, they'll come to you."

"And that's what I did. I took every case they offered me. And most of them were scum, the worst sort of scum, but they were entitled to a defense, and I gave them the best I had, and now and then one of them thanked me."

"The fee I had earned on the rape case was enough to keep us going for awhile, and I used some of the money from the court appointments to buy some decent clothes. I knew it was important to look professional."

"And as Ken had said, my practice began to grow. I was gaining the reputation of being a tough lawyer and a formidable opponent in the courtroom. And now they were coming to me."

"Word got around, and one day Harry called and offered me an opportunity to work with him on a case. Apparently, he liked what he saw. He offered me a job, and six months later, a full partnership."

"I had found something I could do, something I was good at, and I was proud of myself. By nature, I was not a strong person... You know that. But I had learned that you have to be strong to survive. I was determined to make it on my own and never again have to be dependent on anyone. I was a good lawyer. I no longer had to worry about how I was going to make it... I had made it!"

"If I was faithful to my career, it would be faithful to me. My children would be well housed, well fed and well educated, and it didn't matter whether Garrett ever paid another dime's child support. I could take care of my children."

"We had a nice home with a fireplace and a swimming pool, and a decent car for a change. My services were in demand, and the money I was making was more than I ever dreamed. I was committed to my job, and I was good at what I was doing."

"It was a nice little formula... my children and my job. Nothing else mattered."

For the first time he interrupted her, and his eyes were hard and accusing.

"You let Garrett pay child support for Katie rather than call on me?"

"I had no choice. If Garrett had ever suspected Katie was not his child, he would have tried to take both of them away from me. I couldn't take the chance of losing my children. And I had to have some financial help to feed and clothe them until I could take care of them on my own."

She paused, and Jack waited for her to continue, his eyes fixed intently on her.

The tone of her voice grew softer, more solemn, as she posed the simple direct question.

"Would you have believed me if I had come to you and told you Katie was your daughter?"

Jack hesitated, and the expression on his face was no longer as intense.

"I'm not sure. I guess I would have wanted proof since you were living with your husband at the time we..." He did not finish the statement.

"Sometimes the facts don't come all tied up in nice, neat little packages, Jack. Sometimes we don't even know what the facts are."

Her voice trailed off, and so did his thoughts. For a moment he pictured her alone and unsure, facing some hard decisions with no one to help or to care.

Finally, she spoke, and her words interrupted his thoughts. "Whatever you may think, I did the best I knew how under the circumstances."

"I suppose I'm not in a position to think anything... but it hurts to know someone else was keeping up my child."

"I understand... A lot of things hurt, but somehow we find a way to get through them."

For awhile they sat in complete silence. Finally she continued her story.

"I got asked out some, but I rarely accepted. When I did, it was someone safe, someone like Reece who was looking for nothing more than an occasional concert date. I didn't need a social life. I had my work. It was exciting, challenging, and financially rewarding. And while it often required personal sacrifice, that was okay. I could handle that. The one thing I would not sacrifice was my commitment to my children. They were the most important things in my life... And even though I was a working mother, I was a good mother. I loved my children and cared for them, and they knew I was there for them."

As he looked at her, many things ran through his head. He had not realized how hard it had been for her, nor how much credit she deserved.

"Then you came along, and things changed. I had someone I enjoyed being with and, in time, someone I allowed myself to love. It didn't matter that you were still in love with Jessi. Maybe in time that too would change, but if it didn't, if you never loved me again, you had loved me once. At least I had had that."

"Over the years I had learned to give myself completely to my work. It was the only way I knew to do it. I had worked hard to succeed, and I couldn't let anything get in the way of my success. It was my security. If all else failed me, I had that."

"I didn't know how to 'ease up'... I didn't know how to make room in my life for you. So you got the 'leftovers', while the preferential treatment went to people who couldn't care less about me... except when they needed me."

"I don't know what you think about me, but I had to try to explain how I came to be the person I am."

He had dropped his chin in contemplation of all he had heard, but slowly he raised his head and looked at her.

"I told you once before that you're probably the strongest person I've ever known. I still believe that. I can't tell you how much I admire you, and how much I appreciate what you've done for Katie... I've wanted to tell you that I had my will redrawn a couple of weeks ago to take care of Katie... and you. I hope that, in some part, it will make amends for the past."

"Thanks. I appreciate your concern, but that's the least of my worries."

It was obvious that money was no longer that important to her. But there was a time when she had needed it, when it could have made life easier for her, if only he had known.

Once more her words interrupted his thoughts.

"One thing further I want to tell you. Harry and I discussed some things last week. We're making some changes in our practice. We've hired another lawyer, and as soon as Jill is better, she'll also join the firm. Her marriage was already in trouble, and the accident apparently finalized things, so she's moving back to Chattanooga. Two extra lawyers in the firm should relieve our workload tremendously, and Calvin is now ready for some heavy-duty court work. Both Harry and I intend to take more time off. We're going to start with four-day workweeks. One of us will take Monday off, and the other will take Friday, and we'll make other adjustments as time goes by."

She waited, hoping for a reaction, but there was none. He gave her credit for what she had accomplished... He admired her, but that was not enough. Two weeks ago he had loved her... He had wanted to marry her, but apparently he had succeeded in putting all that behind him.

She had felt it when she came in the door... the distance, the cool aloofness, but she had dared to hope that the love which had burned so brightly for the last year had not been completely extinguished... that maybe the flame could still be fanned. Just once she thought she had seen a glimmer of that love in his eyes. Apparently she was mistaken.

Finally, she reached for her purse. It was time to go. His eyes met hers, and for a brief moment she thought she saw the look again.

"Jack, just tell me you don't love me, and I'll walk out that door and never bother you again."

She was begging... And she was not accustomed to begging... But she had to try. If she walked out that door, she would not come back... It would be the end for them.

For what seemed like an eternity he stared straight ahead, without so much as shifting his eyes, but he said nothing.

She bent to pick up her sweater and when she looked up, his eyes were fixed on her. Finally he spoke.

"I can't tell you that." His words were slow and pained.

"Then why don't you give us a chance?" She pleaded.

"I've spent two weeks trying to get over you, Mary. I don't want to go through that again, ever."

"I've spent twenty years trying to get over you, Jack... Please don't send me away. Give it a chance... unless there's someone else."

"There's no one else."

"Then why are you writing us off without even trying?"

"I just don't want to be hurt anymore."

"Neither do I. I love you, Jack. I always have."

A lump formed in her throat, as tears slowly filled her eyes. In his eyes she saw tears also forming. Instinctively, she stepped toward him, and he met her halfway. His arms reached out for her, and he drew her to him, and they stood in the living room, clinging to each other.

"I love you, too."

As they kissed, they tasted the saltiness of their co-mingled tears, which flowed freely, wetting their faces with a healing moisture. Neither of them spoke. They didn't have to. Their tears said far more than words could say. For a long time they clung together and cried. It had grown dark, and only the glow of the fireplace illuminated the room. After awhile he looked down at her and brushed away her tears.

"Why is it so damn hard for us to love each other?" He asked.

Her answer was simple and direct. "Because we've always let other things come first."

"I love you so much I would take you anyway I could get you."

"No, you wouldn't, Jack... and you shouldn't. We have to be first with each other."

And as he nestled his chin in her hair, he knew she was right.

He held her close, then slowly guided her toward the bedroom. She didn't know what was happening, and it didn't matter. She just wanted him to hold her and never let her go.

When they entered his room, she saw their image in the mirror above Jack's dresser, and for the first time she smiled, and he smiled back at her, but the tears did not stop falling. They were not tears of sadness for what they had almost lost, but tears of joy for what they had found.

He eased open the dresser drawer and opened the blue velvet box. And as he placed the ring on her finger, he whispered, "Please marry me."

As she stared at the beautiful two-carat diamond ring, once again tears filled her eyes.

"Yes, yes, I will," and once more their lips found each other.

The ringing of the phone startled them, but they continued to hold each other... The machine would get it.

Then they heard the familiar voice, "Mom... It's Katie... Are you okay?"

He reached for the phone and pushed the speaker button.

"Yes, Sweetheart, I'm fine."

"Katie," Jack interrupted, "We're both fine... We love you."

"Mom, it's getting late. I'll worry about you driving home alone. Why don't you spend the night?"

"Thanks, Katie." Mary smiled.

And almost in harmony, they said, "Goodnight, Katie."

"Goodnight. I love you both."

Mary turned to Jack and wrapped her arms around him, and once more he drew her close and sought the warmth of her lips, as the full moon shone through the window.

Somehow, they had finally found their way back to each other, and they both realized that while Yesterday's Gone... tomorrow, with all its hope and promise, lay ahead... And this time nothing would stand in their way.

LAMAR FINE & MARY AGNES FINE

245 Garretts Chapel Rd.
Chickamauga, GA 30707
Tel. (706) 375-2062
E-mail: Lamarfine@aol.com

Thank you for purchasing *Yesterday's Gone*. We hope you enjoyed reading it as much as we enjoyed creating it. *Yesterday's Gone* is our first book, and we welcome your comments.

We are currently working on another novel, tentatively entitled, *What Might Have Been*. We also have some ideas for a sequel to *Yesterday's Gone*. Please let us know if you would like to read more.

Lamar & Mary Agnes

Remember "Yesterday's Gone" makes the perfect gift for Birthdays, Anniversaries, Christmas, or simply as an "I Love You" gift.

To Order Additional Copies

Of

Yesterday's Gone

Please Send Your:

Name: _____
Address: _____

Telephone: _____

Along with $12.91 (tax included)
plus $3.50 per book shipping and handling to :

Lamar & Mary Agnes Fine
245 Garretts Chapel Road
Chickamauga, GA. 30707

If you are ordering locally and would like to save the $3.50 shipping fee, please call Lamar or Mary Agnes Fine at (706) 375-2062 to arrange to pick up your copy of *Yesterday's Gone.*